AGAMEMNON

BOOK ONE

PALISADE

WRITTEN BY

L.B. DUKE

Publishing Coordinator – Sharon Kizziah-Holmes

Springfield, Missouri

ISBN -13: 978-1-970560-18-3

Dedication

To the men and women who are currently serving in any branch of our military, and to all those who have come before, sacrificing themselves for our country's freedom—I thank you for your service and professionalism on the job. I have not served, unlike my brother and father before him. I am writing this book with you in mind, but if I misplace a rank or its order, please forgive me. Research only goes so far without actually living and serving as you have.

I also dedicate this book to the generations of science fiction authors who led me down this road and inspired me. Robert Heinlein is first on my list because he was the first author of this genre I ever read.

Lastly, I give this book to my brother, without whom I wouldn't have strayed from the path the story was taking. "They wouldn't do that! Now write it again, but with..." That was pretty much how our collaboration went—ha! Good job, Russell!

L. B. Duke

ACKNOWLEDGMENTS

This book would not have been possible without the help of the military. My mother instilled a strong understanding of writing in her children while we were in high school. My brother was my consultant throughout this book and others; I could not have completed them without his invaluable help. My editor and beta readers also encouraged me to march on—thank you, guys!

Of course, none of this would have been possible without years of reading the fathers of science fiction—Asimov, Heinlein, Clarke, Saberhagen, Frank Herbert, Zelazny, and so many others.

Most importantly, I want to acknowledge the child of the man who read so many books in this genre that I finally found the courage to write one of my own.

L. B. Duke

1

The AGAMEMNON III returned to normal space just outside of the star system B-621. Though little could be seen except for the distant point of light at the system's center, the entire plate of the of the stellar mass was filled with gases spiraling away from the star filling the overall space. Quite beautiful and rare.

Commander Barnes looked to his screens and verified their location beyond the Oort cloud. "Take us in, Mr. Taylor."

"Aye, Commander." The navigator made adjustments to his station and the huge ship began to move.

This system had been discovered several years ago and had two M-type planets exactly right for Man. Both were one gravity spheres with suitable environments for colonization. The AGAMEMNON III did not have colonists on board, but it did have various experts at settling a new world along with terraformers. The colonists would come later when the planets had been fully surveyed. The entire system would have to be explored for the new residents' safety. Also, any unruly neighbors had to be examined should they prove a threat to this new colony. As far as the original survey had concluded, none were closer than seven lightyears. Of the three known alien races, only one had spaceflight but they were still within their own system, they had not achieved Faster than Light travel. The other two were preindustrial so hardly a threat. And none of the three were Man's ancestors.

So far, five new races with Man's genes were discovered. All lived on half-gravity worlds and were considerably shorter than their descendants.

In the distant past, Earth's past, a group of aliens known as 'Enki' kidnapped thousands of humans to stock other planets. These humans were mostly from Earth's bronze age, migratory and largely animal herders. The Enki captured these humans over a period of thousands of years. Entire villages disappeared with little if any record of them even existing. Why the aliens did this and to humans was unknown, the Enki had quietly vanished from the galactic playing field. Earth having discovered so many ancestors became furious at this unjust and brutal rape of their world. Fortunately, all five were star-faring, healthy and curious about the universe around them. They were not ready for their tall cousins they eventually met. And they were shocked to find that their descendants were used to a full gravity planet but that they had to adapt to half-gravity worlds that the Enki preferred...they could no longer live on a 1G planet like their home.

"Commander, we have passed the outer planets and we are approaching Beta Four," one of the midshipmen said. Commander Barnes nodded and looked around the spacious command deck deep within the starship. On view screens he could see the AGAMEMNON III passing through bands of gas as it raced into the system. Force shields brushed aside the folds of gas; molecules thick with occasional bits of ice intermixed with bright colors reflecting its sun.

"Steady on. Give my compliments to Lieutenant Commander Bayer and have her report to the bridge."

He marveled as the ropes of gas and other particles drifted by the huge ship only to reform in its wake. Even though he knew this system was approximately four billion years old, much like their home, B-621 acted like it was new, only in the final throws of creation. *What fun,* he thought!

About that moment, the gate near the elevators quietly 'pinged' and Lieutenant Commander Bayer stepped through the roiling light as if it was water. She approached the commander, "Very pretty, hmm?" She smiled up at him.

"I have to admit this is very interesting." He looked down at her and smiled. Lieutenant Denise Bayer was vertically challenged and somewhat stout but what she carried between her ears almost frightened the commander. The woman was incredibly smart.

"My crews are ready. We will drop off the first set as we

pass Beta Four and the rest when we get to Beta Three. The satellites will be dropped at the same time." The commander nodded knowing full well that Lieutenant Bayer had everything in hand.

She should have already received a commission, a ship of her own but Denise liked playing second fiddle to the commander. That way she could run a ship the way *she* wanted, regardless of the commander holding the keys to the ignition! Still, he thought it was time for her to move out of her comfort zone. The THOMAS MORE was about to be released from its trial runs. He pitied the person that became her Second in Command. Denise would be down in Engineering ripping everyone a new one while her second would be wandering the bridge not knowing what to do. He chuckled a bit at that.

Lieutenant Commander Bayer looked at him, "What?"

Commander Barnes waved her off, "I'm thinking about something my son said." Bayer narrowed her eyes; she knew B.S. when she heard it.

As the ship flew by Beta Four, several research ships slipped away along with a clutch of satellites. The world was white with orange and green highlights around the equator. It was a cold world but with a little productive acreage circling the planet, several million square miles of it was a good start.

Lt. Bayer walked over to a nearby station and checked on the status of the smaller ships. They would not land for a few days until a full orbital survey was completed then ground crews would land to begin an onsite review of the surface. They would be there for several weeks until every living microorganism up to and including animals were studied and determined to be safe.

Commander Barnes, though weary of such mundane chores of settlement protocols though he would take this opportunity to catch up on some reading, maintenance of the ship and fitness of its crew and basically to rest. Three recent battles with the Wolverines required a break. These were a bad-tempered six-legged species that resembled Wolverines, so the name stuck. They also thought they owned the universe. Their temper did not improve when they found out humans thought otherwise and proved it.

He was considering having some lunch with the lieutenant Commander as a form of company morale and to find out what the little scamp had been up to in his engine room when an ensign called for his attention. They were still a few hours from Beta Three when he called out, "Sir? I'm picking up a distress signal from the asteroid belt beyond Beta Five." The commander walked over and looked at the communication desk the man was sitting at.

"Are you sure it's not one of our satellites?" The man looked hard at his screens and answered, "No Commander, there is no IFF. It is alien in nature, but it does repeat like a call for help. It's very weak."

Commander Barnes thought, *this system is getting more interesting by the hour!* "Lieutenant Bayer, would you..."

"I'm already having a ship prepped. Two more riding shotgun just in case. Should I notify the Master Chief?"

Commander Barnes grinned. Nothing like having a tight ship! "Best speed Lieutenant. I want information back as soon as possible! Join me for lunch at thirteen hundred and we'll see what they have."

Specialist Bale Jackson breathed shallowly as the rescue vessel sped past Beta Five heading for the distant distress signal the pilot could lock on with her sensors. The high gees were causing his left shoulder to ache as it was still healing from a wound where a Wolverine had bitten him wanting to take his arm off...or tried to. Bale dispatched the female by ripping it in half, but he did bleed a little from the fight. The doctor said he was fixed up, but the shoulder still felt funny. Nanos could do amazing things, especially when he was augmented like now but that did not mean it didn't hurt a little.

"Baywolf, just suck it up! We're almost there," Nick grinned at him from an opposite seat. The ship vibrated all around them, each of the soldiers inside shaking with the speed now at approximately 0.04 of TL 1, just under the speed of light. That the pilot could fly at this speed within the system was a mystery all to itself. Plus she had to dodge the occasional asteroid; it made for a rough ride.

"Knock it off, Cage! Leave the kid alone," Master Sergeant Gantry grunted at the other Sergeant. Bale hated his nickname given to him during boot. He knew it was a play on his given name and the famous story about Beowulf. The other six in his squad chuckled and looked at Nick. "Ah Sarge, I was just boosting the kid. He looks a little green to me." The man laughed, others just shook their heads, the double entendre not missed by anyone even though Mr. Jackson had been with them two years now. They had all been there with Cage, and Bale being the newbie was the latest for the hazing. Only Sergeant Gantry could cause Cage to shut up! Gantry, the name fit, the man was huge!

The pilot called back, "I have it on my scope. Get ready to deploy." Fortunately, the ship was slowing down, there were a lot of rocks nearby. The men closed their helmets and pulled up their displays to look at the stranded ship.

It appeared pretty banged up, perhaps for being so close to the edge of the asteroid chain of rocks from a destroyed planet millions of years ago. Bale zoomed in on the image and found the ship was very small, only 100 meters or so long. **Ranger One going high.**- click. **Ranger Two, I've got your six.**- click. Bale could hear the gunships speaking to the pilot. Their rescue ship came to a stop several hundred meters from the wrecked vessel.

"Master Sergeant, I detect a slightly higher radiation count than background, mainly aft. No fuel nearby," the pilot said. Gantry grunted affirmative. "Datsun, you've got Dr. Tamore with you. Baywolf, you get the engineer...check the engine. Cage, you've got point."

Everyone said, "Copy."

Dr. Tamore was a systems specialist, especially with alien vehicles. The engineer was from the crew of the AGAMEMNON III. They were in the forward passenger compartment as they were not augmented. The soldiers were much larger and had to be transported in the cargo hold.

Air cleared from their ship and everyone but the pilot got out.

Bale was always entranced by open space. The vastness of it never bothered him and space walks were fun! Tracy Reynolds, the engineer caught up with Specialist Jackson and hooked her tether to Bale's belt. Cage spun ahead of everyone and flashed over to the alien ship; his gun was out. Bale looked over at the engineer and was intrigued by all the equipment she carried, most of it built into her suit. How she got around in that thing was amazing. It would all get in the way if she had to run. Though he could not see her face through the helmet's shield she appeared to look at him, "Don't worry about me, sir. I'll be all right."

Bale nodded, "Just do as I say and don't get upset if we have to move fast."

They could hear heavy breathing coming from Dr. Tamore. It appeared he was having a hard time in free fall. "Just take deep breaths and close your eyes if it will help. If you throw up in your suit, PHD or not, you get to clean it up!" Datsun could be so reassuring. Bale smiled at the thought of the Doctor gagging while cleaning his suit.

"Shut it Datsun! Cage, what have you got?" Sergeant Gantry asked.

"One busted up machine, Sarge. They actually have a windshield on this thing, and it's cracked, go figure." Everyone chuckled. "Come on over, you're covered."

Bale checked his line to the engineer and fired pulse rockets on his suit to move over to the 'busted up machine'.

Fortunately, the alien ship was oriented with the asteroid field, aligning with the magnetic field of the band of rocks circling the far-off star. It no longer tumbled but the ship's butt was facing forward. Bale headed for the engine compartment with his passenger in tow. Readings on his helmet confirmed the extra radiation coming from the ship but it was not dangerous to them in the suits, at least not for a few days.

Once meeting the ship, Tracy released four bright lights that floated around her and followed her head movements sweeping the engine from one end to the other. Bale found the movement of lights a little dizzying and decided to watch the perimeter and surrounding space. The engineer pulled out a complicated scanner and began walking all over the engine with her magnetic boots while pointing the device this way and that.

Dr. Tamore and Datsun landed near the windshield of the broken vessel. It was cracked in several places along with its frame being slightly bent; there would be no atmosphere inside. Dr. Tamore lost his fear of perpetually falling and studied the glass, or whatever it was. "Bring me a light please, Mr. Kono." Datsun rolled his eyes inside his helmet and lit up his suit, the skin of the suit bathed the entire front of the ship in a brilliant white. "Thank-you, that's much better."

Shadows danced through the glass and shaped chairs, consoles and other devices in a deep contrast with the light. Definition was difficult without an interior light, but it was clear, no one was home. The bridge of the small ship was empty.

"Um, Mr. Kono? Could you make a hole for me to put a camera through?" Datsun place his legs near the edge of windows frame. "Move over there, Doctor."

Datsun punched his fist through the glass and with one hand yanked the entire shield out of the frame to fly off into space.

"Er, um...yes, I guess that will do. Thank-you again." You could say that about Dr. Tamore, he was always polite.

Master Sergeant Gantry and the rest of his team floated around the small ship keeping an eye on the two civilians and their keepers. Cage floated way above them and circled the area with enhanced microwave, laser and radar capabilities. He was armored more than a tank helped too. No one or thing would get near them with Cage on point. On a private channel, Gantry contacted Spc. Bale, "How's she doing? Find anything interesting?"

Bale -clicked- back on the same channel. "Nothing so far Sarge but if I have to put my two cents on it this ship looks human. But the engine is huge! It makes up more than 70% of the entire structure. The crew compartment must be awfully small." Gantry did not mind lower ranked non-coms to voice their opinions, but it was not encouraged. Speak only when spoken to being the motto. But in Baywolf's case, he had always paid off in his observations. Gantry always listened and gave Baywolf a pass...but only to a point. "Keep an eye out, Over!"

Dr. Tamore was getting excited! This was a human ship!

He had managed to float into the hull of the abandoned ship, but he found the quarters of the bridge to be cramped. Though not tall himself, the ceiling was a bit low, and the walls and stations were too close. Plus he noticed the chairs were small, even for a man of his limited dimensions. It was then that he realized that the chairs looked the size like the ones for middle-school children, a reminder of his time with his then preadolescent daughter during a Parents night. The teacher required that the parents sit in the same chairs as their children. The kids fit all right, but everyone had a laugh at the adults trying to fit in the diminutive chairs.

Could it be? He looked further around the cabin and discovered some blinking lights. They were very dim but some still seemed to be working. The ship was not entirely dead but where was the crew? He spotted a narrow hall leading back into the crew's quarters. There was no way he would fit in that! Mr. Kono had to stay outside of the bridge as he was much too large for the cabin.

Dr. Tamore unleashed his camera and sent it back along the hall. On the display of his helmet, rows of storage lockers and some debris floated around the camera lens. It was very dark, so he turned on the camera lights. More debris brushed past the lens of the machine as it chuffed around the small space. Beds, again small, countertops a bit lower than usual and then the camera caught a glint coming off some kind of metal nearby. Dr. Tamore rotated the image and found three vertical slabs of...something. They were metallic but of what type, he had no idea. They appeared to be brushed gold in nature but were a little dim for gold.

As the camera panned up, he discovered more blinking lights on two of the cabinets. The third nearest him was dead. Then he saw small windows near the top of the boxes.

The camera moved up and Dr. Tamore looked into the windows...he gasped! He had found the crew!

2

Tracy watched as Specialist Jackson connected more cable to the hibernation tanks, more like coffins, she thought. And one in fact was, the occupant dead for no apparent reason but he had been dead a while, completely desiccated from years of hard vacuum.

Once the trio had been discovered by Dr. Tamore, she and Bale had been called back to the forward compartment to help in the matter. A power kernel had been attached to the ship to provide energy for the computers. Kernels were nothing new, but this type had been developed by Dr. Tamore to power up alien devices. Alien vehicles or machines did not come with instructions as to how they worked or where to plug in a battery. Dr. Tamore's kernels could use nanos to enter the machine and find the right routes to power it up, quite ingenious!

The computers were stripped of all information and the language of the aliens, or in this case early humans, their ancestors. The other soldiers cut out the hibernation capsules and linked them together with another small kernel to keep them working, except for the one. The man inside was as dead as his machine.

"What do you think, sir," Tracy asked Bale?

"Call me Bale, please...except in front of the others." He grunted as he attached the last power coupling and cables to the last capsule. Bale looked briefly in the window and saw a human woman. He saw curly blonde hair surrounding a heart-shaped face with a pert nose and full lips. She was pretty but she was also somewhat little, like a teenager.

"Hurry up, people! That arm of gas is approaching fast and I don't want my paint job ruined!" Everyone laughed but moved quicker to transport their gear and the alien astronauts back to the ship. The gas would not hurt them or their ship, but it could move some of the smaller rocks in the asteroid field about, some out of their eddies and possibly to them. The gas, though very thin moved at over 1800 kph. With the ice in it, sandblasting would feel like a backrub.

Two of the soldiers placed bubble nodes at either end of the alien ship. "Stand back everyone!" Everyone got away then Sergeant Gantry toggled a switch on the arm of his suit. Immediately, a silver ovoid surrounded the abandoned ship, a large stasis field that protected the contents indefinitely. They might need to come back for it one day to study the remains. One of the troops placed a small rocket on the silvery surface, turned it on and backed away. A few seconds later, the silver shape disappeared into the asteroid field. Its homing beacon would last several thousand years.

Bale shrugged inside his suit but only furthered the itch he could not reach on his left shoulder. "They are definitely human but that was a weird ship. Why only three crewmen with that monster of an engine on the end?" Bale looked ahead as their convoy approached the rescue ship. "If I had to guess, they were an advance exploration team. But where is the Carrier? I don't know, Mr. Reynolds."

'Mr.' was not a slight to the female engineer but it was an honorific for all genders while on duty. It saved time and did not balk at silly notions of who was in charge, even if the commander was a woman. It had nothing to do with their military culture being primarily patriarchal, it was just the Navy's way.

Bale looked back at Tracy to see that she was still in tow. She cruised easily, her back to him while she typed and moved images and information over a virtual screen in front of her. He could see several deep scans of the engine and then others of the crew compartment, the last being small but suitable for the crew. "What are you doing? Can't you wait until we get back to the ship?"

Tracy ignored the question but answered his first comment, "That ship could pull 2.3 TL, hence the big engine and you're right, it was a forward scouting crew...they got here quick! There is a colony ship out there somewhere heading this way!"

Commander Barnes and Lieutenant Commander Bayer were watching the feed from the rescue team as they drank coffee after a brief lunch.

"Looks human to me too," Denise commented. The commander nodded and said nothing. That it was Enki technology was not surprising, but it had certainly been modified; humans were good at that! It had been surmised that the Enki had captured other species over the millennia but when they discovered humans, it was thought that humans were more adaptable to populate a new planet...as slaves. What the Enki did not know was that humans hated slavers. *And we tend to kill our slave-masters. We tend to pick up technology quickly too!*

Another image of the hibernation tanks being transported back to the main rescue ship flowed across the screen. A rolling text scroll was at the bottom with a 'key' to siphon the material direct to his personal link. Commander Barnes ignored it, rather enjoying his crew at work on the images. The Master Chief would be pleased with their performance.

"Hold it...ah," Denise swiped the air in front of her. The scrolling text enlarged, ran for half a second then the icon for a siphon was blinking red. Commander Barnes looked over at his Second, *what's going on?*

"Oh my! Commander! We need to go to Red Alert immediately!" Lieutenant Bayer was flushed with excitement and not a little fear. The commander smiled at her and spoke to the bridge, "Belay that order. Maintain Yellow alert but inform the rescue team to make haste."

"Denise, what the hell!? Panic is not like you." He waited, baiting her.

"You haven't seen the last..."

"Yes, I saw the scroll before you stole it from me. Something about the ship being an exploratory or scout ship?"

Denise was beginning to feel like a fool. She had worked for this man for three years and he was always damnably calm, it irked her no end! "Somewhere, another ship is coming to this system. Maybe they are human but if so, there are no half-gravity worlds here! What will we do with them?"

Commander Barnes had already reached the same conclusion. That another race was desperate enough to leave their own world to colonize another spoke volumes; it was generally a one-way trip for any species. And when they got here, the other race would discover the horror of their mistake. The scout ship made sense but somehow was not able to get back to their mother ship. Hopefully, the information gathered from their computers would give much needed information as to the problem. It also might shed some light on the general demeanor of the new humans...some had proven to be difficult.

The lieutenant was still flustered so Commander Barnes gently guided her, "Please send out four ships with long-range sensors beyond the Oort cloud and see if we can find these colonists. We will continue to Beta Three. Have the two gunships escorting the rescue vessel stop off at Beta Four and orbit there until further notice. And Denise, calm down." He smiled at her. She blushed and rose to leave, "Yes Sir!"

3

Bale stepped out of the shower thankfully the smell of his suit was gone. Dr. Tracy Reynolds had invited him to lunch with her and her husband. He had begged off but she insisted. "Mess Hall Six, Dan only gets an hour for lunch and it's close to his department. 1215 and don't be late!" Tracy laughed as she walked away. Bale grumbled to himself; social interactions were not the norm for him but the woman was nice. Oh well.

He called ahead to inform the mess hall of his attendance. Though there were only two hundred active augmented Marines at any one time on board, the mess halls had to be warned of their meal requirements. Augmented men and women ate a lot of food, four times a day...they burned a lot of calories!

Bale just finished dressing when Cage poked his head into the locker room. "Baywolf, Master Chief wants you on the bounce!" He grinned at Bale's surprise, "You shouldn't have pinched that engineer's butt." He laughed and walked out of the room. Bale did not know what to say, *but I didn't do that!* And then he realized he was being hazed again by Nick. Damn that man! But now he had to meet with the Master Chief. What was going on?

A few minutes later, Bale knocked on the Master Chief 's door. "Come in!" He entered a unit larger than his own, but it was spare of any decoration except for the Trident and Sword of the Master Chief. Inside he found the Master Chief and the Master Sergeant. Gantry was huge as ever, only slightly taller than his boss. Bale saluted them both and waited. *Am I being dressed down? What did I do wrong?*

The Master Chief spoke to Gantry, "This is the young man you were talking about?" Gantry nodded without saying a word. Sweat was beginning to form on the back of Bale's neck. The Master Chief turned to his desk and picked up a folder that Bale could see had his name on it. The man leafed through a few documents and closed the folder. "I see that you were wounded during our last engagement with the Wolverines. Are you fit?"

"Yes Sir!" Bale remained at attention; he had not been given permission to stand 'at ease'.

"Are you sure about this one?" The Master Chief looked to Gantry. "Yeah, Mike. He's got the goods."

"He's a bit young but I'll go with your recommendation. He does have a good record." The Master Chief turned to Bale. "Mr. Jackson, you will unaugment by 1700 and have dinner with the commander and his staff by 1800. Tomorrow, depending on the commander's impression of you, you will gain a promotion to Third Lieutenant and Cadet officer's training will begin in one week." He smiled at Bale, "Don't let us down, son. Dismissed."

Gantry walked over and led the surprised young man out of the Master Chief's quarters. "Walk with me." Bale nodded and followed the huge man.

As they walked down the hall, men and women moved out of the way and stood against the walls while saluting Gantry as they walked by. Even Nick moved to a wall and saluted but he winked at Bale as they went by.

"As you know, only augmented can become officers. Civilians can reach the rank of third lieutenant, but they are as useless as tits on a snake. When you dine with the commander tonight, keep in mind that he has served for nine years as an augmented before becoming an officer. Though he is at normal height, he has advanced augmentation...he can rip you apart. I 'dance' with him in the gym for his exercise and I always walk away with bruises." Bale swallowed hard at that thought.

"Um, sir? Why am I being considered for officer training?" They had reached an elevator. Gantry turned to look back down the hall. No one was there.

"Your instincts, forethought and observation skills come to mind. Plus the death of your family on Orthos created in you a distinct pathology against the Wolverines. Many people committed suicide after that colony was destroyed...you did not. We have watched you since. You are a block and a very secure one for a team. Now we want you to be a team leader."

Gantry turned and placed his hand on Bale's shoulder, "Be the man that I know you can be and make us proud. I will be honored to salute you when you get your pips." Gantry pushed the button for the elevator. "I understand you have a lunch date, don't be late."

With that, he laughed, slapped Bale on his shoulder and walked away.

Bale entered the elevator and turned to salute the Master Sergeant one last time. The doors closed...*What am I going to do now?*

4

Specialist Bale Jackson arrived on time for lunch with Tracy and her husband, Dan. He gathered his plate from the lunch line. It was oversized and stacked with chicken, steak, eggs, multiple vegetables, fruit, cheeses, a large thermos of coffee and a half gallon of milk...all the necessary things for a growing boy.

He looked around the mess hall and spotted Tracy waving at him from across the room. Though the tables were spaced wide apart about the cafeteria, it was not for privacy but for the few Augmented enjoying lunch. Normal sized people could get hurt by accident in tight quarters with an augmented around. He nodded to two other soldiers already eating at their table. Bale walked through the lunch crowd with slow and deliberate steps, even then people gave him a wide berth. Seven and a half feet tall, fully 500 lbs. of raw muscle made anyone want to give him room.

He smiled shyly as he arrived at Tracy's table. She looked up to the tall young man in front of her. Brown-headed, a strong nose centered between bright green eyes and a shy smile. "Bale, have a seat. Here is my husband, Dan Reynolds." The portly man stood up and shook hands with Bale after he put his meal down on the table. "Glad to meet you, sir! And thank-you for watching out for my wife," he grinned. Then looking at Bale's tray, "Son? Where are you going to put all that?" He and Bale laughed together.

"Actually, this is a light lunch," Bale winked at Tracy. "And please sir, call me Bale."

Small talk proceeded as they ate. Bale discovered he liked Tracy's husband with his friendly humor, and he did not bother Bale with engineering small talk which would have gone right over his head. They were a good couple.

"I had to augment once for a couple of days a few years

ago. We had to realign the TL coils on the AGAMEMNON II. Machines did most of the heavy lifting, but those machines weigh a lot, so I was one of twelve given the job. I never want to do that again! I was sore for a week after I unaugmented."

Bale smiled, not everyone was cut out for the process. It took a special physique and attitude to handle long periods of augmentation. Soldiers were deeply scanned for their ability and could deal with the change to their bodies for weeks on end. Bale had been on duty for three weeks and until today, he thought he would be augmented for another two as was normal for a rotation. Five weeks on, two weeks off except for special situations, namely war. Now he was going to be normal for months as a cadet, that is if the commander approved of course. Bale preferred being augmented...this would take some getting used to.

Tracy watched and was fascinated as Bale ate his chicken, bones and all. Bale liked the cooked marrow as he crunched on it. He would have munched up the T-bone too but decided that might be a bit much for the Reynold's to witness. At his larger size and overall strength, he could bite through a number three rebar if necessary.

"Guess what a little bird told me?"

Dan started laughing, "He's not that little! A scant taller than this young buck." Tracy elbowed her husband and smiled back at Bale.

"I hear you're getting a promotion. Good for you!"

Bale blushed, "It's not finalized but yeah, it might happen. I'm supposed to have dinner with the commander tonight." Dan looked over at his wife in mock surprise.

"Bravo! Good for you son!" Dan leaned over the table and slapped the young man on the shoulder. Bale winched and rubbed his left shoulder. "Um sorry, did I hurt you?"

"No, no its just a wound that I got from a Wolverine. The doc says it is healed but it feels weird. I can't explain why but it itches all the time and aches some too."

"Um yep," she looked at her husband. "Just like your phantom leg. Have you got some of that stuff with you?"

"Yes ma'am, I do!" Dan reached into one of his many pockets and pulled out a small tube of ointment. He handed it over to Bale, "Some time ago, I lost the lower part of my right leg in an accident, damn caliper from a dehydrator, industrial sized. Sheared my leg right off! Well, they grew me a new leg, but the darn thing itched like mad! The doctor said I had 'phantom leg syndrome', that I was imagining it. Drove me crazy but Tracy found this cream that I can apply around the new part. It makes the itch go away. I don't use it much anymore, but you are welcome to what I have left." Dan started to give instructions to Bale when a short chime announced the end of lunch, ten minutes before returning to work.

Dan leaned over and kissed his wife on the cheek, she placed her hand on the side of his face and leaned into the kiss. "See you later, honey. Love you!" He stood and turned to Bale, "Thank you again for watching out for my wife. I always get scared when she goes outside. Later!" He walked out of the room.

Bale watched him go, "Nice guy, your husband. I like him!"

"He's a peach and he's good with the kids." Bale was startled; he hadn't realized that they had children.

"Now put a little dab of this on your shoulder and rub it in good. That should be all you'll need for six hours or so." She stood up, walked around the table and gave Bale a hug. "I've got to go too. Thanks for coming to lunch. And when you meet the commander, be just like you were here at lunch, funny and respectful. You will do great!" She hugged him again.

Bale felt funny but then realized he may have gotten a new family out of the deal, at least a new older sister.

Tracy walked down the hall back to her lab. She smiled as she thought about the young man, so shy and sweet. The ointment she had given her husband and now to Mr. Jackson was a placebo, it was worthless but if they thought it helped them get by, all the better!

Dr. Tamore with the help of his assistant Dr. Munson reviewed the data once more. They had to call in a linguist for the language was part Enki and French in nature, the written form was all Enki but a modernized version of cuneiform with many more symbols for communication, especially where it involved technology. "So far, few surprises. It resembles the Malari more closely than the other five languages we have discovered. I imagine they were taken about the same time as them, about 4200 years ago." Dr. Munson rubbed his forehead then looked up to Dr. Tamore who was standing behind him.

"Have we got a name for their race?" Dr. Munson scrolled through some pages of documents on the screen that had been ripped from the damaged ship. 'Teknoman' is the best I can determine but it references earth or dirt, I'm not sure why." Dr. Munson turned to the petite woman, the linguist waiting on them.

"Karen, have you gotten a handle on the spoken word yet? We'll need something when we wake her up." The woman nodded, "Yes, it is a variation of Malari but not so heavy on the consonants. I could be wrong, but I feel the word 'Teknoman' is 'Terran', meaning earth born. They might still remember Earth!"

Dr. Tamore was not going to put too much stock in that right now, but it was an interesting theory. Time would tell after the female Teknoman woke up.

He walked over to a glass wall separating them from the one hibernation tank alone in the room with a full medical staff. It had been discovered through the ship's records that she was the pilot. Her name was Sana de Verico Abbicon. Approximately 25 years old. They were not sure about the spelling as cuneiform with the modern mix and switched to English might be a stretch even for the interpreter computer.

She and her crew had been stranded there for approximately six years. Since their supplies were limited, they had wisely decided to return to hibernation until help arrived. The other survivor was a geologist, the third was the officer on board. His death had been caused by equipment failure, perhaps a rupture of his capsule when the ship got randomly hit by the occasional rock from the nearby asteroid field. They didn't know only that he died sometime after their first year back in hibernation. Fortunately, he had not felt a thing, the officer went from a deep sleep to one more permanent.

“Dr. Wilson,” Dr. Tamore spoke through the intercom. “You can begin now.”

The man inside, indistinguishable from the other aids and nurses in the room because of their hazmat suits nodded back and pointed to another woman. Dr. Tracy Reynolds, having read all the documents on the operation of the hibernation tank pushed a couple of icons on her tablet. The capsule began to hum.

5

Sana's dreams were coming back to her. Her brothers chasing her around their yard with the large orange sun blaring down on them during a warm summer's day. A shift and she was in Explorer two screaming at Ser Xengot who tried to take control of the ship during its rush to the asteroid field. Another blur and she was hugging her mother before Sana boarded the colony ship. '*Be safe, my daughter!*' The blur continued as she was hugging a man she could not remember but she could still hear her mother in the background...*Be safe...be safe!*

Then pain jumped on her chest and she heaved! A warm blast of air washed over her body. She opened her eyes in fear. The dream receded and consciousness took over. Lights within the capsule came on. A quiet voice let her know that she was awake and that the tank would open in two minutes. Outside temperature was a comfortable 23 degrees Celsius. She could feel gravity as she lay on the mattress. She was in the ship! They had come for her crew!

Tracy watched the various meters on her screen. The patient was waking up but it was a long process. The body had to be warmed, hibernation chemicals flushed from her system and nutrients added back in, plus some adrenaline. Brain activity started first and went on about three seconds before her heart was started. All of it automatic. This technology was amazing but still primitive to their own. Stasis was a better preserver of tissue than this machine, but she guessed this was the best they could do. It was after all an Enki invention.

Sana waited, enjoying the warm air and the pain leaving her chest. She could see out of the view screen but the room her capsule was in was dark. A faint light was in the distance, but she realized that was normal for the newly revived, their eyes not having been used in a while. Sana wondered how long she had been in hibernation. She would not know that until she got out of the glorified sleep box.

"Okay, it's about to open. Is the linguist...oh, hi! There you are. Be ready." Tracy looked at the petite woman and realized she was a good choice for this first contact. Shorter than even Tracy, the woman still had a couple of inches on the woman in the box. Karen smiled behind her mask, "I'm ready. I just hope she is. Sana, right?" Tracy nodded, "That's what they tell me."

The doctors and staff waited not knowing the condition of the patient. Blood would have to be drawn and analyzed, her general health determined as gently as possible and of course her mental aptitude. Hibernation tanks were not the best for a healthy brain.

Sana watched as the lid of the box opened. She was exposed to the air of the colony ship...but it smelled different. A tall young woman approached and gave her a smock she could pull over her naked body. Sana found the sleeves and put her arms through. The nurse helped her sit up then tied the back, she then gave her a pair of shorts that felt weird, comfortable but strange. She was helped out of the box and the nurse held onto her as Sana adjusted to being in gravity again, it had been a while. Though she was a little nauseous she turned to the nurse, "How long were we inside?"

The woman looked at her with blue eyes. Blue? Maybe they were contacts, Sana did not know. Then she noticed the woman had olive skin with slanted eyes.

"You have **** asleep for six *****."

Sana could barely understand her, the accent was so strange. She pushed away from the nurse and fell back against the hibernation box. She could hear other voices in the room, they sounded anxious. "******, calm yourself. You *** negative on your ***ship." The nurse was making no sense!

She wanted to run but could barely stand. What was going on? Sana was not on her ship?

Then another shape walked out of the darkness, and it was huge. Fear consumed her! It had the shape of a man, perhaps another nurse or doctor but he was a full head taller than the nurse! He pulled down his mask and smiled at her. He appeared human but he was so...tall! He said something to the nurse and stuck out his gloved hand to Sana.

Sana screamed!

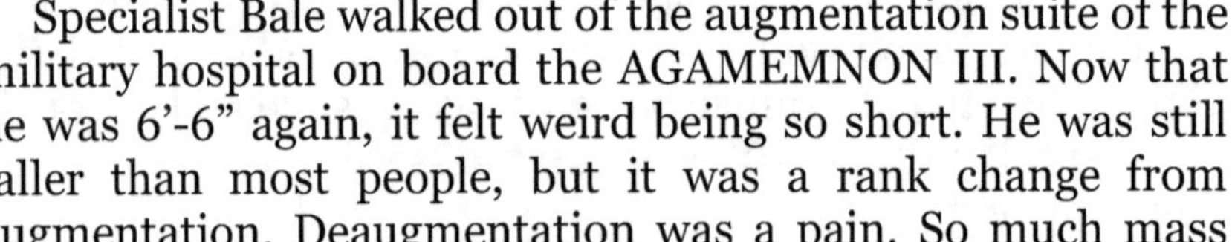

Specialist Bale walked out of the augmentation suite of the military hospital on board the AGAMEMNON III. Now that he was 6'-6" again, it felt weird being so short. He was still taller than most people, but it was a rank change from augmentation. Deaugmentation was a pain. So much mass had to be removed by the same nanos that made him Augmented, some 240 pounds of muscle, bone and special organs for a soldier. Plus, he was hungry. Yep, the food had to go too.

But the doctor surprised him, "Son, the commander has authorized me to proceed to advanced Augmentation according to your new rank...this will take a little longer than twenty minutes."

New rank? Oh, yeah, Bale remembered what the Master Chief had told him. He found out from a 1st Lieutenant that he was now an E7. "You can't eat with the commander and his staff without that," he laughed and pinned Sergeant Bale. The extra stripe along with the pay increase was nice but Advanced Augmentation?

The Doctor removed most of the mass, then proceeded with something very few get to experience. Steel-Ceramic joints...all of them including his jaw, extra tendons and ligaments, carbon fiber filaments in all his bones, extra ribs, his heart was replaced with a stronger version like for a horse, all his arteries and his veins were double-wrapped with carbon fiber, his vision was enhanced into the infrared and ultraviolet and Bale's implants were replaced with officer grade computers. His second stomach had to go but the resilience of his new body was extremely efficient, he would not need the extra fuel.

Nick Daniels was the only soldier with Advanced Augmentation that Bale knew personally, Point warriors got it as a matter of course. He had once watched Cage, his nickname, attack a vaulted wall that some Wolverines hid behind. Bale was a little busy defending their rear when a five-ton vault door slid through a nearby wall like it was butter. You do not screw with anyone with advanced anything! Cage went into the room which turned out later to be a mess hall for the Wolverines. After Cage was done, some sixty of the nasty species became wall paint.

That was the first time he saw Cage cry. The man may be a tank, but he cared for children...and the ones the wolves did not eat, they killed out of spite when they heard Cage coming through their wall.

And now Bale was an equal to Cage, even if shorter. He would have to have a long talk with Nick what it was like. At least this new evolution for Bale did not change a man's perspective...Cage was proof of that!

Bale struggled to walk with a normal gait, but he was still in some pain from the transformation. Mercifully, his shoulder did not hurt anymore...just his whole body! He only had ten minutes to change into his dress blues and arrive for dinner with the commander. The Doctor had given him some painkillers and told him to hurry.

That the painkillers were another placebo that made the doctor laugh. *Give the body something the brain thinks will help is enough.* Except for major wounds, he wondered if his profession was even necessary.

Reconnaissance ship four was drifting high above the system plane. It was at reduced power to enable a scope of deep space. Ensign Davies adjusted his station and scanned another sector. "This is so boring," he said!

"Davies, if you hate this job so much, I can put you back on a survey team." The lieutenant laughed. He knew the kid was bored, so was he but this was their job even if they were only eight hours into it.

"Sorry, lieu but my butt is killing me." He pushed another icon and waited. The other three ships surrounded the system and scanned space for the missing colony ship. Though the ships were originally fighters, they had been modified for reconnaissance work with extra gear and long-range sensors, small, very fast and if need be, they could fight.

Davies sat behind the lieutenant and ran the sensor array; the lieutenant was the pilot. Both were suited up in the cramped vehicle. Another hour passed while Davies decided he wanted a snack. As he was pulling a power bar from a leg pocket, his station pinged. "We may have something."

The lieutenant sat up straighter and tied his screen to what Davies was seeing. Davies immediately became a professional, all boredom gone. "Range, about two light years. Speed...hold on a minute." He moved a few icons around and another screen overlapped the original. He waved it over to his system's screen near his elbow. "TL 1.2 and it's a big mother! Heading right for us. We've got them!"

The lieutenant smiled in his helmet, "Good work, Davies. I'll notify group." He made the call, noted the location and speed for AGAMEMNON III. Another flyer waited off her bow and fired up. This was a heavily armed ship with four crew and a brace of soldiers. They would go out to meet the colony ship. The engines powered up the troop carrier and moved it away from its mother ship. Then it jumped to TL 8 and disappeared out of the system, racing for the colony ship, only an hour away.

The two men in the reconnaissance ship stayed on station watching the troop carrier leave normal space. "Ya know, lieu, if we had left that ship alone, it would still be over two years getting here."

The lieutenant nodded, "It might be for the best, at least until the commander decides what to do with them."

Then another call shouted out from Reconnaissance I, "Tally Ho! I got a possible bogey at 7 lights out. Moving at TL 3.4...Wolverines!"

6

Specialist E7 Bale Jackson arrived at the commander's Mess at the appointed hour, 1800 sharp! Since this was not a formal affair, he was only required to wear his dress blues without all the lettuce. His only insignia was his rank and a small gold hammer stating that he was an Advanced Augmented. This was required to inform all military and civilians alike that he was not to be messed with. He also had a small pair of playing cards attached to his jacket, a pair of threes. Cage had sent him a text telling Bale to contact him when free, preferably at the gym to discuss his new attributes. Bale groaned at that one, he did not want to 'dance' with Cage.

Guards near the entrance saluted him and opened the doors into the Dining hall. They did not have to salute him as he was of approximately equal rank as a noncom, but it was a privilege afforded to all that sat at the commander's Table.

Several officers were already present. They were standing around the large ornate room talking to each other, some looked over at him then ignored his presence. Bale swallowed and tried to remember what Tracy had told him...just be calm. A steward brought him a glass of sparkling water that tickled his nose but did a good job of settling his stomach. The two crackers he ate in his room barely made a dent inside his empty guts, his stomach now meeting his backbone, at least it didn't rumble.

A chime sounded and all the men and women approached the table and stood behind a chair waiting for the commander to enter the room. A door near the back opened and Lt. Commander Bayer and Commander Barnes walked in. Everyone immediately stood at attention!

A flag unrolled from the ceiling to the side of the room. It was the Terran Federation Flag. Lt. Commander Bayer shouted, "Port side, about face!" Everyone with their backs to the flag swiftly and precisely turned around. "Salute!" Everyone in the room saluted the Flag of the Terran Federation.

"Declare!" Everyone recited the oath of the Terran Federation. Bale felt his heart swell as he followed along. "To protect, to share and to guard..." Bale knew it by heart, everyone learned it as children, but it was sworn in when you joined the military. Your body belonged to the emperor along with your soul to Terra Firma.

"At ease, gentlemen and please be seated." The commander said this to all including the women, it was the Navy way. First Lt. Commander Bayer's chair was pulled out by a steward on the commander's right. She *was* his right arm! Then everyone sat as stewards pulled out each of their chairs. Bale was the only one standing in the room other than the stewards who just looked at him.

"Mr. Jackson," the commander said. "Would you come join me on my left?" Bale could not feel his legs but found himself standing next to the commander wondering how he got there. Another steward pulled out the chair next to him and indicated that the soldier should sit down. Bale stumbled into the chair and amused the others in the room. He was so nervous!

The commander grunted and silence settled over the hall.

The first course was brought in, a small bowl of minestrone soup, the menu being Italian tonight. Again, Bale did not know what to do as he had two spoons, three forks and a butter knife and a steak knife plus some silly little thing like a tiny fork for olives. He heard a small 'ting' and looked up to see Lt. Commander Bayer staring at him. In her hand was one of the spoons with a wider face. She winked at him and began to eat her soup. He found the appropriate spoon and joined in. Surprisingly, the soup was great!

He was so hungry Bale wanted to toss the spoon and grab the bowl and pour it down his throat! But he stuck to one spoonful at a time. The commander smiled at him and continued eating as well. Dishes were removed and a small salad was brought in, Caesar apparently and it was good too!

People began to talk amongst themselves, some complimenting the commander's Chef. The commander said, "Thank-you! I'll be sure to tell him."

Lt. Bayer finished her salad and looked up at Bale. "So, Mr. Jackson, you've been on board for two years?" Everyone stopped talking and waited for his answer. "Yes ma'am." Bale did not know what else to say.

"If memory serves, you've been in several engagements with the Wolverines. Anything interesting to report about those fights?" Again, Bale was not sure what the lieutenant wanted from him.

"They're not very good with guns and they hit hard!" He blushed as everyone around him laughed.

The commander smiled at the young man. "I understand you had a personal engagement, hand-in-hand with one of the enemies." Bale hated to remember that incident, not that he had killed the Wolverine but that his suit had to be dry-cleaned twice after that to get the smell out.

"Yes sir, I turned the six-legged beast into a pair of threes." It was a common phrase used among the Marines.

There was silence in the room, one of the female officers down the commander's Table turned white as a sheet. Bale was scared; did he say the wrong thing in front of the commander?

Commander Barnes narrowed his eyes at Bale, paused...then started laughing! Everyone in the room burst out laughing too except for the one officer who excused herself and left the Dining Hall. Lieutenant Commander Bayer was slapping the table with tears coming out of her eyes. She was laughing so hard she almost tipped her water glass over.

"Very good, Mr. Jackson! I don't mean to brag, but I once got a Full-House." The commander continued laughing along with everyone else. A full house meant you removed five of the six limbs from a Wolverine while it was still alive, it had to by hand, they did not live long after that.

Bale smiled sheepishly and finished his salad. That his commander could do that was enough for him. He would follow this man into any battle!

More courses arrived. Ground coffee and red wine marinated flank steak, braised mushrooms with calamari and noodles in a marinera sauce, slivers of lemon butter chicken on couscous, various vegetables and the finale', Tiramisu served with coffee.

While the stewards were clearing the table, everyone stood around the commander as he talked with young Mr. Jackson.

One of the officers asked Bale about his parents not realizing that they had died with the rest of his family on Orthos, the colony that the Wolverines had found and destroyed. His entire family and assorted Aunts and Uncles, cousins and of course his brother and sister died there. Bale had just joined the Navy and was not there to join them in death.

"Damnit Chuck!" Another took the officer by the arm and led him away while whispering in his ear. 'Chuck' turned around and stared at Bale and ducked his head in shame, he had not known the officer-elect was an orphan from Orthos.

Commander Barnes glared briefly at the offending officer then turned back to Bale. "Mr. Jackson, I understand you were the first to identify the alien explorer ship as to being human?"

Bale spent a little time reflecting on the question the other officer had asked him, about his parents. It was to be expected for officer training and Bale did have some experience dealing with the subject. But being yanked back to those first weeks after boot camp when he was finally told about Orthos was hard. The man did not mean anything by it, he just didn't know about his family.

"Yes sir, it just seemed human to me. I've studied the other fallen of the human race and their Enki machines...this looked the same."

Bale thought some more, "Sir, may I have a moment with that officer, with your permission?"

The commander thought a bit, nodded and said, "Don't hurt him, he's my best Astrogator."

Bale walked over to 'Chuck', his friend backing away. 'Chuck' eyes grew when he saw the golden hammer on Bale's collar. Bale had to give the man credit, he stood his ground, not a good thing to tick off an Advanced Augmented. All officers were augmented even in their normal form but Advanced were dangerous, even for them.

Bale stopped before 'Chuck' and waited. The officer knew this young man was an experienced Rifleman and was deadly!

Bale stuck out his hand, "I know you weren't aware that my family was on Orthos when it was destroyed. Please, in the future I would recommend that you study an officer-elect's history." The man nervously shook the young man's hand hoping he would not crush it.

Bale turned away relieved that he had not hit the man, the officer would have died, and the commander would have had no choice but to execute him.

Commander Barnes watched the whole display and approved the young man's manner. He would make a fine officer! Lieutenant Commander Bayer walked up to the commander, "Can I keep him?" She grinned at him.

"You get the engineering types and nerds. No, he's all mine!"

7

Sana woke up in a hospital bed. She knew it for one as there were side rails on the bed but like nothing she had ever seen before. They were up protecting her from falling off the bed. When she managed to sit up, the room swam a little but she felt better. The side rails were a good call even though over large for her, the floor was almost down as far as her shoulders to the mattress. Had she fallen off the bed, there might have been some damage.

She brushed her hair aside with her fingers and discovered a pair of plastic-like devices that immediately fell off her ears, another on her forehead that had slid off unto the sheets. Sana looked around in alarm, still a little groggy from the day before when she woke up. She reached for one of the rails and discovered that she was wearing a uniform, close-fitting but comfortable. There was another device clinging to the arm of the fabric, but it could not be removed, there were several gages and blinking lights that meant nothing to her.

Sana was feeling proud that she managed to slide off the mattress and stand on the floor. The gravity suggested a world but the smells did not. When she looked around, Sana noticed that the ceilings were more than twice her height. And the light coming through the windows was a bright white with a tint of yellow. This was not her sun or her world, much less the colony ship. Where was she?

Karen Ito braced herself for the meeting with Sana. She had worked all night and part of the next day on the language of the alien or 'fallen' humans. It was not as difficult as some of the fallen languages. The most difficult was the Qun'ten Clan as it was part Latin. That any of these races still had roots in the Terran languages was a gift and very strange for them to remember after thousands of years of captivity.

She walked past the nurse's station nodding to them. One of them was clearly upset as she held onto her patient tablet and the nearby countertop. Karen was a little nauseous herself. It was one thing to be in freefall but another to be in half gravity and this little section of the on-ship hospital was now adjusted for the alien patients, Sana and the Geologist; he was yet to be awakened. They needed to talk to the pilot first.

Karen knocked on the door and walked in. She saw the young woman standing by the bed looking at her. She was young and very pretty. Not quite 4'-11" tall with curly blonde hair and brilliant hazel eyes. Sana had a good figure for one so tiny but in her world, she was probably of normal height. She was human all right, the tests given to her, blood drawn proved that, but she was a scaled down version of a Terran human. Perfectly proportional just shorter.

Karen took a breath and hoped the learning program the girl had been listening to during her sleep had taken effect. "How are you feeling?"

Sana understood the woman now since she was speaking English. How was this possible? "I'm fine. Where are my shipmates?"

Karen didn't make any sudden moves, she wanted the woman calm, "Please speak in my language. You now know how to do that."

Sana trembled, she understood the woman again. She struggled to find the words in her mind and to form them on her lips. "I fine...where my crew?"

Karen smiled, "Very good, you will get better at it in time. Now we need to talk. Could we sit at that table over there?" Karen pointed. Sana nodded and walked over to the 'table' the woman indicated. It had two chairs, but one was a bit higher than the other. Karen took the shorter chair but still had to bend her toes to the floor to touch it, she was only 5'-1" tall. She pointed to the short bar stool, the only chair found to fit Sana and waited.

Sana found the chair comfortable, but she did have to climb into it. Her head was now on the same level as the nurse across from her, this made her feel a lot better like they were equals.

Karen held out her hand and said, “My name is Karen Ito. Pleased to meet you!” Sana looked at the outstretched hand and did not know what to do, but she got the idea. Men on her world could ‘shake’ hands with each other but not with a woman, it was a cultural taboo. Sana reached out and clasped the woman’s hand and discovered it was soft but strong!

This is going well, so far, Karen thought.

“If I speak too quickly then tell me and I will slow down. Also, if there are any terms you do not understand, then speak in your language and I’ll try to explain.”

“Our species is called Terran. We are from a planet called Earth.” Sana’s eyes widened and Karen noticed. “We discovered this system about twelve years ago. Our ship and crew are here to colonize two of the planets for our race.” Karen paused, “I’m sorry if this is hard to absorb but give it time.”

Sana was shocked! Were they Teknoman too? Not possible as they were so tall! Sana realized that they had chosen a short person to represent them, to make first contact with her species yet she and the woman looked so much alike, not coloring but shape and musculature. Was she human?

“What does ‘absorb’ mean,” she asked?

Karen thought for a minute. She spoke in Sana’s language, badly, “Think of a dry sponge placed on a pool of water and the water is pulled into the sponge. That means to ‘absorb’ in our language.

Sana considered it and agreed that was a good analogy for ‘absorbing’ information. And she was impressed that Karen went to the trouble to learn her language!

“What of my crew?” Sana was worried that the men were held in separate cells and being interrogated.

Karen frowned and looked at her lap. “The officer on your ship died a year after returning to hibernation. The ********* is alive but is still in hibernation."

Sana asked about the confusing word. Karen struggled to find equal terms in Sana's language, but she got the idea. 'Geologist'. Okay, that was a good strong word for him.

"How did Ser Xengot die?"

"We don't know only that his pod stopped working some years ago. We suspect that another rock from the asteroid field struck your ship and damaged some component."

They both worked hard to understand each other. Karen learned many new words and archived them in her database through her implants. Sana was becoming more familiar with the 'English' language though there were still some gaps to be overcome, mainly verbs and adjectives. English was turning out to be a rich and floral device for describing things Teknoman could not do, even if it was difficult to learn.

"When can I see Mr. Bisset?" Sana needed a friend to help her cope with their new situation.

"We can open him at any time but first we would like you to know our world. It will make it easier for him to understand if you understand us first." Karen thought that was a good answer, at least it was the best she could do for now.

Sana thought that was not a bad idea but still, she had to wonder why they were taking such care of her.

"Why do we look alike?" Sana blushed, "I mean not your hair..."

Karen smiled, "I know what you meant. We appear human but we are taller." She took her hand and raised it above her head. "Sana, this is going to be hard to believe so have a willing mind to consider what I am going to tell you."

Karen took a deep breath, here we go! Sana knew this would be good, but she hoped it would not be too upsetting.

"Thousands of years ago, many peoples of our world disappeared from several locations around the planet over a period of at least 4000 years. They were never heard from again. It was first thought they had migrated, but no evidence could be found of that. Maybe they died out. Again, we did not know. But once we Terrans entered intergalactic space we discovered five new human races, ones that were human like us! They had the same genes as we do, musculature, organs and even blood types. But ALL of them were short like you. We were excited but confused until we found out all the races were from category M 0.5 gravity worlds. You were short for a reason."

Karen watched Sana very carefully. She seemed to be 'absorbing' this information just fine, but Karen could tell she was getting excited. "Once we learned their languages it was clear they were from Earth...your home."

Sana was trembling more as the story unfolded.

"Sana," Karen said. "You are our ancestors!"

8

Lieutenant Rose Parks directed the pilot to get near the huge ship but only within a thousand meters. They found the colony ship pretty much where it was discovered by the reconnaissance group. It was still moving at TL 1.2, slow for light speed but then the craft was massive! Fully 1000 meters long, a cylinder over 200 meters in diameter. The crew quarters near the front rotated emulating gravity. Someone must be awake.

"Drop two ribbons Fore and Aft."

The navigator/communication officer punched a button. "They are away, Sir."

"Gate us to the AGAMEMNON III. Once data begins to come on board, send it to them. Sergeant Deeks, ready your men." She got a confirmation from the woman in charge of the boarding crew.

Now all they had to do was wait to see if the crew would notice them. Lt. Parks sipped her coffee and hoped for the best.

The young man walked casually along the hall leaning into the spin while holding his breakfast. He yawned and tried to wake up. He had been awakened for his two years shift a few days ago and he still was not fully acclimated. A spice drink would charge him up when he got to the bridge!

Two of the other 'night' crew acknowledged him. "C'mon Jeerish, you've been lagging for two days now!" The banter was meant in fun. "Yeah, and I remember you throwing up for several hours after decanting," Jeerish responded. He wolfed down some eggs and then looked for the drink spicket.

Once he found his seat with a fresh cup of hot spice,

Jeerish opened his screens to look over his Wards, his wife was one of them. He had a camera zoom in on her hibernation tank. All the lights were green and her face through the porthole was serene. Unity, how he missed her!

The camera pulled back and viewed the rest of the colonists. Row after row of people in their pods spiraling down the shaft of the sleep camber, more than thirty thousand of them. All of them his responsibility. He munched on a biscuit and then warmed up the rover in the next camber. It was his turn to take a tour of the colonists inside the ship.

After breakfast, he was about to put on his suit, the sleeper chamber being in vacuum required it, when one of the pilot's screens began to flash. **Proximity Alert!** **Proximity Alert!**

All three men jumped to their stations and pulled up radar and cameras. That an asteroid had gotten this close without notice was scary. Hopefully, it was a small one that their meteoroid canons could blast before it hit the ship. What they saw on the screens was not what they expected...another ship flying along with them.

Lieutenant Parks nodded to the communications officer, "Link us up." Another volley of cannon hit their shields to no effect, that needed to stop!

"Attention Explorer, we are a Terran Federation starship. We mean you no harm." She could see the crew in the forward compartment become startled as her voice came through their speakers. Rose could not understand the language, but the computer converted English to Teknoman easily. She could see them because the nanos had tied into their systems. If need be, she could run their ship for them.

Rose could hear them speaking to each other too. "What should we do? Terran? That's a myth, right?" The men were checking their boards and screens. That they just found out that they were not the only species flying the stars was disconcerting. "They must have some kind of shield; the cannons didn't bother them at all!" They could see the

Terran ship near them, an angular thing much smaller than the Explorer but it looked deadly.

One of the men cleared his throat and spoke, "What do you desire, Terran Federation ship?"

"You are speaking with Lieutenant Parks. The star system you are heading for is occupied by us. We found your survey craft with two survivors on board in hibernation. The third died of a malfunction in his pod several years ago. The other two are fine. We are speaking with the pilot now. Soon you will be in communication with her." Rose let them digest that for a bit.

The other two crewmembers looked to Jeerish as he was the lead officer on this rotation. They had all wondered what had happened to the survey crews, but Lieutenant Parks said they found only one ship and it was damaged somehow. "You said you found one of the survey craft, what of the other two?"

Parks did not know. "We were unaware there are others. This was the only one that sent out a distress signal. I'll inform our Commander and he will send out rescue teams to find them, if possible."

"Thank you for that, Officer Parks. You say you came from Palisade, the system ahead of us? When did you leave? We've been in route for 15 years with two more to go."

Here it comes, thought Lieutenant Parks. "We left there an hour ago."

There was a long pause, she could hear the men talking amongst themselves. "Impossible! One hour? They're lying, no technology exists that can leap that fast!" Jeerish motioned the men to be quiet. "Um, Lieutenant Parks, you'll have to pardon us, but it is our understanding that nothing can move faster than 5.2 Trans light and that's only in theory.

"Our technology is different than yours. We got to you at TL 8...we can go much faster if necessary." Parks shrugged a little, it was not really bragging, was it?

Jeerish didn't know what to say. TL 8 or above?

"Explorer, are you in need of any assistance?"

"Not at this time, Lieutenant Parks but we are low on fuel.

We will arrive in approximately two years with barely anything left," Jeerish paused for a bit. "Would it be possible to view an image of you?"

Parks nodded to the communications officer. Jeerish didn't know what to expect but to see another human on his screen was not it. He was thinking it was going to be an alien monster. The woman did seem a little odd as she was dark skinned, almost black with short wiry hair and blue eyes. Was she a mutant? Behind her he could see other men sitting at workstations different from his own and they ranged in all sizes and colors. The Terrans were a varied race!

"Lieutenant Parks, we had no idea you were human! We are human too...but then you already know that coming from our missing crew on the survey ship." He did not realize that Parks could see him from a camera the nanos had built in the control cabin. "Can we talk to the pilot and the other survivor? Can they be returned to us?" Jeerish could see the woman on the screen nod, "In time but there is a situation that requires our immediate attention. We are already planning to bring you to them, but we need to review your ship to ascertain how to go about that. Would it be possible for two of our engineers to come on board to look over your engine? We may be able to get you to...Palisade(?) as you call it with much less time on your arrival date. You will require modifications to your ship to increase its speed. The situation is we discovered another race nearby that is extremely aggressive and dangerous. We would like to have you in the Palisade system before they discover you."

Jeerish was alarmed! It would be a blessing to reach the new system ahead of schedule but to give access to their ship required a great deal of trust. The captain would have to be awakened to make that call. One of the crewmen went down an access tube to waken the man, still asleep on this rotation.

"Lieutenant Parks, we need to wake our Captain. I cannot make that decision without him. It shouldn't take more than an hour for him to respond to your request."

"Very well, Mr....?"

"Jeerish, Sub-Captain Martin Jeerish." He was embarrassed that he had not introduced himself before.

"Good, Sub-Captain Jeerish. You will see a few people flying around your ship. We will touch nothing, but we need to ascertain the modifications that will be necessary. With your permission, of course."

Jeerish could see no harm in that and what could he do to stop them? So far as he was concerned, they were a very advanced race of humans. And if the myth was true, they were from his home world, Earth.

9

Commander Barnes walked onto the Bridge and was immediately met by a midshipman with a message from Reconnaissance I. There was a Wolverine ship several light years away passing by. They might be too far out to spot the colony ship especially as it was 90 degrees clockwise from them in this sector of space.

"Mr. Taylor, what do we know about that ship? Is it alone or part of a convoy?"

"Unknown, sir. It is too far out for detailed information except speed and direction. It is heading away from us."

Barnes frowned, that was good fortune for the wolverines but where had it come from and where was it going? The Wolverines were incredibly aggressive and therefore war-like. Their technology was nowhere near human strength, but they had managed to destroy one of the human colonies, the same one Mr. Jackson came from. The Wolverines had gotten lucky in that the colony had not received any defense platforms as it was located far away from Wolverine space, or so they thought. That mistake cost the lives of over 18 million people on a pristine planet. All new colonies were now heavily armed, and the loss of lives would never happen again!

"Lt. Commander, I want a ship to verify that marauder and destroy it if necessary. Capture any information you can and let it go. Otherwise, if it contains any details about this system then kill it!"

"Yes Sir!" Denise began to fill out the crew on a stealth ship. She envied Commander Barnes' aplomb when dealing with an emergency. He was always soft-spoken when confronting a crisis and Wolverines were certainly that! She debated putting Mr. Jackson on that ship but he was still getting used to his new body. Sergeant Jackson would be formidable, but his coordination might still be off. Time for that kind of pay-back later. Team Charlie would be the go-to Marines to deal with the Wolverines.

Sana and Karen walked out of the hospital room; she had told Karen she was hungry. The Doctors had cleared Sana for interaction with the crew. Her inoculation was hardy enough to prevent her from getting polio, tetanus, measles, chicken pox and almost any virus the modern humans contained. All her viruses were too primitive to survive contact with her larger cousins.

Sana was shocked at how tall these humans were. Six feet or more, male and female though the females tended to be shorter. A shriek of laughter and Sana saw some children running down the hall towards them. Some were taller than her, but they were obviously kids. They ran past as Karen put her arms around Sana. "You'll have to be careful around us. We live on a full gravity world, so we are stronger than you. I hope that doesn't upset you."

Sana blinked, "Yes, I get it but children? You have children on a war ship?" She watched as the children receded, some jumping just to touch the ceiling three meters above them.

"They shouldn't be in this part of the ship, but someone must have lost them in the traffic," Karen laughed.

Sana could relate to the traffic, there were plenty of people around going this way and that. Some looked at her in startlement and others just ignored her. They were all very tall.

"You are not a nurse, are you," she asked Karen.

Karen smiled, "No, I'm a linguist. I specialize in languages. It was thought you might be more comfortable with someone short. And I am that, very short for our race. Here is a dining hall. Let's eat!"

Bale had been taking his meals in the lighter weight

cafeteria for a couple of days now. He had to visit the doctor in this sector for the Advanced Augmentation to see how he was coping with the changes. Cage had been a big part of that by beating the crap out of him in the gym. Mostly exercise but also to get used to dealing with greater strength. The lighter gravity was also a blessing on his sore muscles...Cage had not been gentle.

He just sat down with his meal when two short women walked into the restaurant. Karen Ito did not know Lieutenant Jackson but knew he was on the crew that had saved the survivors from the wrecked survey ship. They grabbed their trays and approached his table. “Mr. Jackson, may we join you?” Bale stood up and invited the two women to sit down, “Of course.”

Karen shook hands with the man and turned to Sana, “Here is Lieutenant Jackson, he was one of the crew that rescued you and Mr. Bisset. Mr. Jackson, Sana Abbicon from the Colony starship Explorer.” Bale smiled and reached across the table to shake her hand, “Pleased to meet you. By the way my rank is now 3rd Lieutenant Jackson.”

Sana just stared at his hand, should she shake it like he did with Karen? Though it was a taboo in her culture, apparently the Terrans had no such reservations. Her hand was swallowed by his hand like hers belonged to a child. “Thank you for saving us.”

They all sat down and began breakfast. Sana looked at her plate and immediately recognized the eggs, but the pink colored meat confused her. “What is this?”

Karen giggled, “It’s called ham. It is meat from a farm animal. Particularly good!” Sana took a tentative bite and realized it was delicious! The other cereals, bread and fruit, though different were good too.

Sana had a lot of questions, mainly about Terra but she decided to start small. “Everything on board your ship is... large. This ship must be huge! But since you are as you say a full gravity species, how do you have this section at one-half gravity? Are you rotating the entire ship slower just for my benefit?”

Karen’s eyes gleamed and Bale choked on his coffee.

"Ah no, we have artificial gravity. We can change any section to whatever level of gravity is necessary," Karen responded. Sana was stunned! How was that possible?

"So, Lieutenant Bale, I now understand congratulations are in order. You have been selected for officer training. Will you be rotated back to the academy on Earth?"

"Not now," as Bale wiped the rest of the coffee off his shirt. He had embarrassed himself in front of the colony woman...not much of an officer-elect he was going to make. "I'll rejoin the other cadets here on AGAMEMNON III to begin training in a week. I may go to Earth but that could be awhile."

Sana struggled to follow along, but she managed to get the drift of the conversation. She looked up at the large man across from her with his brown hair and beautiful green eyes. "I'm sorry I startled you, it's just that artificial gravity has been a dream of our people for some time, but the power consumption is too large to, um..." Sana whispered to Karen something in her language. "The word is 'conceive'."

Bale had forgotten that the woman was a pilot and quite possibly an officer in her world. She had experiences that he probably did not share, as yet. But what made him forget his shirt was her wonderful hazel eyes surrounded by the curly blonde hair. Damn but she was beautiful!

A chime sounded at the end of breakfast. The few others in the cafeteria rose to go to work. Bale stood, "I've got an appointment with the purser about my new suit. I got measured yesterday and it should be ready sometime this afternoon."

Karen had watched the brief interplay between Sana and Bale and smiled to herself as she finished her coffee. *Smitten already?* They were different from each other, different cultures not to mention size. The man was easily over six feet tall and poor Sana's head barely met the man's chest but there was an obvious attraction there.

"Lieutenant Jackson, you mentioned you have some time left before you start your officer training. Would it be possible for you to take Sana on a tour of the AGAMEMNON III? Perhaps outside as well?"

Bale barely heard her as he was falling into the young woman's eyes. What was it about her? "Um, yeah. I mean I would be glad to! Do you have a suit? Never mind, we'll get you a new one."

"You two run along, I have some data that needs to be loaded into the main computer. Have fun!"

Sana was nervous, this was only the second Terran she had met. The doctor did not count since she had fainted. And yet, somehow, she felt safe with Bale. "Don't forget the full gravity sections once you leave the hospital. Be sure to turn on her uniform or she might break something. Later!" And Karen walked out of the cafeteria.

Sana looked up at him, "My uniform?"

"Yeah, I mean yes, it has a field converter built into it so you can walk into the full gravity sections. Okay, let's go get our suits" Bale was excited that he got to spend some time with this woman. What was it about her? They walked down the hall and she saw a red line that wrapped the walls, floor and ceiling. Bale stopped and gently pulled her arm to him. She was startled at the familiarity of his touch but became fascinated by what he did next.

He touched a screen on the device of her arm, moved his finger about barely touching the screen until he got to a page he wanted. "Good, you've got power for the next three days. It will warn you several hours before the battery runs out. Okay, let's turn on the converter." Sana felt nothing but her suit did feel a bit warmer. "Okay, there's a gate right over here that will take us to the Purser's office. He will give you a suit and while you are there and he will probably assign you your quarters," He saw the confusion on her face. "Where you will live while onboard the AGAMEMNON III." *Oh!*

The lieutenant, her escort moved to a wall of vertical water. Sana could see ripples on the surface like raindrops falling on it. Bale touched the edge of the wall, "Purser's office, material." The wall rippled again and a voice said, "Enter".

Bale looked down at the beautiful creature standing next to him, "This will be a little strange, but you'll get used to it. Hold my hand then step with me as I go in."

Sana was getting scared. There was so much about this ship that frightened her and yet so much of it was familiar, like having breakfast with her two new friends. But walking into a rectangular water door was weird. She did not want to get wet!

Sana stepped with Lieutenant Jackson as they walked through the water.

She almost fainted again when she found they were in another corridor facing a door that said Purser's Office. One second, she was near the hospital, next Sana was in a carpeted and completely different part of the ship. How?!!

Bale held the door for her and they approached the Purser's desk. Sana could barely see above the desktop. The woman there checked on his order and said his suit would not be ready until tomorrow. "How about measuring Officer Abbicon for a new suit?" The woman looked at Sana and smiled, "Are you a size 7 or a Junior 8?" Sana had no idea what that meant other than it must be a size for a suit. "I...I don't know."

"I'm going to go with a size 7-8 but we'll have to let out the front a little." Bale blushed and both women thought it was cute. "Come on back and we'll get you fixed up." The two women went into another room. Bale checked his messages and discovered he had almost flunked his math. At least the coding was good.

Sana came out a little later. "My suit won't be ready until tomorrow either. Wait till you see it!" Then she checked herself, all this was new, but Sana had to admit it was all exciting! Bale smiled at her and was thankful everyone was treating her right. "What do we do now," she asked?

They spent the rest of the day touring the ship. Sana was getting used to transporting everywhere but it was an unusual experience. He showed her the observation deck which was available now that the AGAMEMNON III was in system. The star, B-621 shined brightly through the plasma field dome. There were children in the large room with them and their teacher, class was going on. Sana got to see the comfort center, essentially a small indoor mall with food vendors, clothing stores, a theater showing a movie she could not understand its theme and the Bodega where she could buy her own food if she desired. Engineering was off limits for now until her status was upgraded but Sana did not mind, that part of any ship did not interest her.

Bale finally took her to the library where they found some more students and others from the ship's company. There were not that many books available but then there were several study tables with screens in front of chairs. He sat her down in one and spoke to the machine, "Images of Earth, general. Edge of the Light, Jordan Critz audio."

Picture after picture marched past her eyes along with some of the most beautiful music Sana had ever heard. Snowy mountains, ocean shores, fields of animals, a rain forest with monkeys dancing through the trees and cities, large and magnificent cities somewhat familiar and yet different from her world.

As Sana had no implants Bale downloaded several files onto a small drive and gave it to Sana. "When you get back to your room, you can study them all you want."

She smiled up at him, "Pretty good tour guide you turned out to be. Thank-you!" The young woman was brash in a fashion after the pilots he had known. Bale liked her.

10

Commander Barnes was reading the report from Lieutenant Parks. The colony ship could survive a retrofit for the new engines that would take it up to TL 4. They would arrive in six months, but he still had a problem with what to do with them. There were no half-gravity worlds in this system and apparently, their ship would be susceptible to damage from the tides of the spiral gas as it had no real shields. The shields would not be a problem, they could give them that, but they would have no home to live on. A new ring might be the thing, but it would only support 3 million people and no one from Earth could live on it for any great length of time. It would be a waste of resources, and the commander already had plans for the asteroid cloud. A new ring world was not part of them.

They had found Explorer One on Beta Three in a high mountainous region. It had crash landed on the planet killing everyone on board. Why they dropped into the atmosphere and crashed was beyond the skill of the computer experts trying to find any data from the wrecked vehicle. They just did not know what happened. The bodies were burned beyond description, they had been in their acceleration couches when they hit the planet.

Commander Barnes slammed his fist onto the arm of the chair. *What the hell happened?*

There was no sign of Explorer Three, it may have fallen into a gas giant.

Fortunately, the captain of the Explorer was open to the changes in his craft. And he was surprisingly willing to accept that Terrans were their descendants. The man had no animus towards their cousins, but he was very disturbed that there was no half-weight world for them to settle.

Ring...ring...should he? It was a limited option, perhaps

for a hundred years...more than likely less as the ring world would be pretty much key-ready when they landed on it. No struggles to overcome and humans were pretty much prolific as lemmings. An ideal world they would fill quickly! They would eventually have to move. Earth would not tolerate the Teknomen for long on such an expensive station.

The battle-ready stealth ship ORION approached the Wolverines. There were two ships and a large freighter between them. The ORION was completely invisible to the beasts and spun-out nano ribbons onto each ship to determine their destination and purpose.

"Okay, let's see what we have here," said officer Billings. The Wolverine computer language was well known as it was completely Enki. Their spoken language was unpronounceable and considering their relationship with humans, no one cared to learn it.

Schematics of the three ships were brought up on his screens. Typical crew compliment, the freighter was empty so they must be after something, nothing special about the ships. Billings dived deeper into their computer to find their reason for being out here. He was surprised to find a computer firewall in the system, basically a locked digital door but his systems made short work of finding a key to open it. That was new for the Wolverines, they were learning so they must be aware of humans. This was a new crew that had some experience with humans, or knowledge of them at least.

Lieutenant Billings discovered the Wolverines had a small base about twelve light years to their stern. That was not good, he thought. They would have to investigate and possibly destroy it but that would only warn the Wolverines that humans were nearby. He frowned as more data was flowing across his screens. The beasts were indeed aware of Palisade and planned to visit in the future...they would not like what they found. Worse, their destination was a small planet filled with preindustrial talking fish, one of Palisade's neighbors. This was one of their new food sources and this was their third trip. That is what the freighter was for. Wolverines ate anything, sentient or not.

"Barry, we'll take out the first ship and the freighter. Better inform Charlie team to get ready for a boarding party on the third ship." He looked over at the man in the gunnery section, "They looked like they could use some exercise."

The midshipman smiled back at him, made a couple of adjustments to his station and said, "Firing in Three, Two, One..."

Sana and Bale had spent the next three days together and had not grown tired of each other's company. They talked about many things. Earth, her home world of Tekm, and more important to Bale was their reason for coming to Palisade.

"Our star is dying. The experts do not really know why, something to do with lower neutrino emissions. In about 100 years, it will turn into a blue giant, but Tekm will be frozen long before that." Sana looked down at her sandwich and realized she had lost her appetite. They were having lunch near the arboretum. She had been shocked again to find a small forest with plants and birds inside the ship.

Bale was surprised. He did not want to see Sana cry but then she had every reason to. He leaned over and gently touched her shoulder. Sana hugged his arm and buried her face against his uniform. She did not really cry as much as shudder at the pending death of her home.

"Do you have any family?" Bale was not sure it was a good question to ask but he had to know.

Sana nodded, "My younger brother went out on the colony ship Endeavor before mine. My older brother is with the Science counsel so he and his family will not leave until the last minute." She looked up at Bale, "My father died when I was young, an accident. My mother is now dead because of cancer...she would not be allowed on any ship. She put me on the Explorer and kissed me goodbye." Tears then welled up in Sana's eyes and she fell against Bale again and sobbed. "...I'll never see any of them again." Bale held her as long as she wanted.

He later learned that the siblings, being all adults were divided up into separate ships to spread their genes as all three had been specialists in one field or another. Sana was a top-rated pilot in her world so she got to leave her home too, but she had to work her passage, hence the survey crew allotment.

Sana realized that she and Bale had a lot in common as he had lost his family as well. Tracy had told her about Bale's home world of Orthos...what a horrible fate for a young man just beginning his life to suffer! As they walked and talked it became obvious to everyone around them, they were more than friends. Sana and Bale did not notice it but they touched a lot, laughed with each other and were quite the cute couple if a little odd in reach.

He was holding her on his shoulder as she reached for an apple from a tree planted in the main concourse. It was not illegal to eat one, but the seeds had to be saved! That was ship-law and was mandatory! Bale had thought to just hold her, but he was afraid he might crush her waist so up on his shoulders she went. Sana barely weighed 80 lbs. and Bale could bench-press twenty of her any day. He had to be careful with this special lady!

"Do you want one?" she called down. "Naw, I'm good." Apples were not his favorite fruit, and this was a Granny Apple tree, very tart. Sana did not care, she loved any apple regardless of tartness. She giggled as Bale carefully put her on her feet. She looked up at him and munched on the apple in bliss. "You don't have to be so careful with me, I'm a big girl!" Bale knew better. He walked over to a railing near some steps to a lower level. Some children just happened to be walking by. Bale grabbed the 4 cm. rail and bent it. It was solid metal so there was a screech as the metal complied with his desire. One of the boys in the group said, "Whoa!" Bale then rubbed his hands together to create some heat. People nearby could feel it. He then grabbed the bent rail and straightened it out as if new.

"Yes, I have to be very careful with you." Bale grinned at her, "You may be a big girl," he mugged at her. "But I am much bigger, and stronger too. Don't tempt me!" He pointed a finger at her and she jumped up to bite it." She laughed missing him. "Just you watch Mister, I'll have your number one day!"

Both laughed as the children walked away in awe. The children knew what a Marine could do to protect them but to actually see a demonstration?

Bale just got a notice, the Purser's office wondered why he had not picked up his suit yet. And where was Officer Abbicon? Bale stood still for a moment; he had completely forgotten about the suits. Sana noticed, "Are you all right?"

He looked down at her, "Wanna go outside?"

Sana grinned!

11

Bale was trying on his new suit. Cage had warned him that elbow and wrist joints were critical so to pay attention to them. Everything below the waist was not going to be a problem. The suit was like his other but smaller of course but the main difference was the fabric and joints were designed to handle someone much stronger than usual. It would not go well for the wearer to sneeze and blow out a gasket. He thought it felt good. The extra attachment points seemed a little unnecessary but then, this was a command suit. He might be required to haul some wounded with him and still be able to fight.

The door behind him opened and Sana walked in wearing her new suit as well. It was a gray and rose-colored thing with neon blue piping...and it was small, but she looked good in it. “What do you think?” Bale asked her.

She looked confused, “I think well.” Then she blushed, realizing he was asking about her suit. “It’s so light weight! Is it safe to wear outside?”

Bale nodded, “It has its own shield, you will be fine.”

Sana had tied her hair back into a bun. “They didn’t give me a helmet. Where do I get one?” Bale walked over and stood over the woman. “Push this button on your collar.” He pointed to the one on his and she got the idea. She found the button and pushed. A plasticine helmet unfolded out of the collar and covered her head. Sana could see clearly out of the helmet; it was like it was not even there and she could hear Bale plainly. “Like it?”

Sana smiled up at him and nodded.

“Good, let’s go stretch our legs. If you have any problems just tell me and I’ll get you back inside.”

They left the purser’s office and found another gate that took them to the hanger deck. Sana was going to have to get used to this new form of transport, all this zipping about the ship.

Bale found a Warrant officer and ordered a basic runabout, a small ship for tool supply and maintenance outside the ship. It was essentially a pickup truck with a bed in the back. Lt. Jackson got Sana inside the glass bubble in the front and put her in one of the seats. He had to jack it up for her to reach the controls...he had an idea for later she might find interesting. Once buckled in, Bale lifted the small ship and entered an airlock, no sense evacuating the air in the entire hanger deck for one little vessel.

He turned to Sana and said, "Don't be alarmed but the AGAMEMNON III is somewhat larger than the Explorer. We'll take it slow so you can get a good look."

Sana was getting used to the constant barrage of surprises from her newfound cousins. Artificial gravity, gates that took you anywhere in the ship, a library, trees and birds and food she found familiar and tasty. What was next? The Explorer was a massive ship, but Bale had just said this one was bigger still. How was that possible? It took nearly five years to build their ship and it had a single purpose. The AGAMEMNON III was a multi-use platform and they had kids on board!

Once they had cleared the airlock, Bale took the small vehicle out a few hundred meters, not too far because he wanted her to get the entire effect of the size of his small world. A wash of stars faced them, and the spiral gases could be plainly seen in the distance. Sana tried to look behind her, but her restraints would not permit that. Then Bale turned the small ship around and stopped. He looked over at Sana and was not disappointed by her reaction.

Sana's brain could not rationalize what she was seeing. The star behind them lit a massive wall of black and gray that faced her and raced away in both directions. Above and below, she could see stars, but the wall blocked out all else. Bale backed the maintenance ship slowly so that Sana could get the entire effect. "She is 1.6 km long by 400 meters tall. The AGAMEMNON III has a best speed of TL 18 but can reach speeds up to TL 25 for short durations, we have no need for hibernation but we can if we have to. Her crew compliment is roughly 560 people, 300 marines not counting children. She is part carrier, supply ship, colony ship if need be and a war platform."

Sana's mouth was open in surprise. What she saw appeared to be a large metal bar that was smooth with no protrusions like meteoroid cannon, guns or even radar masts. Either end tapered slightly so she could not tell where the front was. The name AGAMEMNON III showed near one end of the huge ship. Where were the engines?

"But your engines? Where are they? Did you drop them off?"

Bale smiled, "They are all internal. We don't use propellant for light speed, only for maneuvering near a dock or station, mainly hydrocarbon gas for the last."

"Let me take you around, show it off a little." Bale lifted the controls as Sana watched. She could tell these were made for hands like hers, but the controls were unfamiliar. She really hoped Bale would let her drive the small ship!

Bale moved back towards the AGAMEMNON III and began to rise above it. Sana could see lights running the entire length of the ship, but they were swallowed by its mass. The top of the ship was slightly curved running its entire length. As he flew over the dark side, Bale dropped down below the ship and rode under its bottom which was surprising to Sana as being very flat. *Could this thing land on a planet?*

"Why is the bottom flat?" She asked.

Bale was not sure what to say, it being a proprietary aspect of the AGAMEMNON III's function. But then, most races that ran into the Mother Ship AGAMEMNON knew why the AGAMEMNON III had a flat bottom.

Bale had studied the images and deep scans of Sana's Survey ship and immediately understood that the small explorer had not been held in a bay but rather a nest built to the side of the Explorer. Details of those grooves were provided by Lieutenant Parks and her team. Three were indeed empty. The other three still held drop ships for crew, supplies and other tasks once they had reached their destination.

"You know how your ship the Explorer Two mated with your mother ship?" Sana nodded. "Well, AGAMEMNON III is a support vessel for the AGAMEMNON, he emphasized the caps on that. "We have two sister ships that can mate with her too. The AGAMEMNON is over 16 kilometers long. It's our Mother Ship."

Sana started breathing hard, she had to quit fainting at every turn of events or new information. It was not proper for an officer! Bale got concerned, "Are you okay? Do you want to go back to the ship?" Sana shook her head; she continued breathing and held up her hand to Bale to make him wait on her.

"It's just...just, so much. Almost overwhelming!" Now how had she found that word and understood its meaning? "I'll be okay, just give me a minute." She slowed her panting and tried to calm down. Sana really hoped that these people, apparently her descendants were friendly. Bale was her friend, maybe more than that but she did not want her people to upset the Terrans!

Bale was worried but decided that a little fun might be in order. He turned to his side screen and toned down the power of the maintenance ship then he lifted the controls to neutral and called the station master. "MTL 14 calling. We are going on a short training mission a few kilometers out beyond the shield."

"Very well, Lieutenant Jackson but be aware that a spiral is heading for us in 64 minutes. Be inside before that or bubble up and we will find you later. OUT!"

Sana had calmed down and was able to catch the last of Bale's communication with home base. "Spiral?" Bale nodded, "It's what destroyed your survey ships. You had no shields, so your systems were damaged. Basically a gas and ice arm from the star that swirls about the system. It will not bother our main ship or its auxiliaries, but our little ship had no protection for that. Our suits will protect us, but it will not be fun and the ship will be destroyed. We'll have to bubble up to protect us if we're out too long."

Sana was too tired to ask what 'bubble up' meant. Her world was changing every minute of this week but at least

Bale had been a gentleman throughout it all. Maybe she should go in and sleep.

"Um Sana, would you like to fly this thing?"

Sana immediately brightened when she understood what he was asking. "Me? You trust me with this ship?" Bale smiled, "You are a pilot, right? Show me."

He showed her some of the functions of the controls and the nav screens. Bale was not worried about her going too far, the ship would shut down if it got beyond the AGAMEMNON III's range and the little ship didn't have that much fuel for an extended stay anyway.

Sana pulled down the control arm and gently brought the ship up to speed. It moved forward easily. She turned it gently to get a feel for the controls and what her body was telling her the ship was doing. There was a little jerking as she got used to the new system, but Bale said nothing, he just grunted occasionally.

The little ship seemed somewhat sluggish. Maybe this was an aspect of its design but then Sana noticed on her side screen its power was turned down to 30%. She looked evilly at Bale, "Oh, you did not turn down the power on me...get ready!" she teased. Then she took her finger and stroked it across the gage next to her like Bale had done to the screen on her arm. Sana was not sure it would work through her suit, but the gage rose up to 100%...she grinned!

"Sana! Noooo..." then Bale was pushed back into his seat. The ship shot ahead then flipped over and did a reverse barrel roll to aim at the AGAMEMNON III. Sana then did a spiral, another loop then pulled into a parallel course with the larger ship. A couple more barrel rolls, another loop then she slammed the ship into reverse, flipped over again and sped around the larger ship. A tight curl running the entire length of the AGAMEMNON III while avoiding other robots and maintenance vessels, then she stopped.

Sana was breathing hard. That was great! She looked over at Bale and finally realized what she had done to him. The man was panting now and was a little green. "You okay?"

He pulled down his controls and locked her out! He was huffing hard not to throw up. Now that the ship was running level and moving at a more sedate speed, Bale made it to the airlock...barely.

12

Commander Barnes thought about calling his Admiral. He had already sent a report of the Survey ship, its sister ship destroyed on Beta Three and the coming Colony ship, Explorer. Other reports gave a positive review of the system with extra benefits of material and surface conditions of the two planets they were to prepare for the eventual colonists. He left open the conclusions about the lack of half-gravity worlds for the colonists...let the admiral figure out what to do about that!

The ORION had returned yesterday, and Team Charlie was high fiving everyone that could stand their chatter. The boarding of the remaining Wolverine ship had gone as planned. After the crew was put down, computer experts removed the firewall Lieutenant Billings had discovered. The coding was not so difficult, it was just something they had never seen on a Wolverine vessel and it wasn't created by them. Wolves were smart but only with subjugation and mayhem. Barnes knew that there were other species that sold and maintained their digital equipment as nerdish skill was not a Wolverine talent. And firewalls were of an order well above their mindset. Who put it there? This worried Commander Barnes a lot!

All this went into the report to the admiral. Though the man could speak to him instantly, Barnes figured it might be another day before he received a message.

Other matters preoccupied him today. The condition of the ship in general and of the crew. Everything was going well. Studies of the biology on Beta Four were proving interesting in that the local fauna was primitive and would more than likely fall to the Earth based plants and animals. The insects were another matter as they were almost all poisonous. Odd in that they had no natural enemies, just each other, but a battle was going on in the Equatorial belt of the planet. Some of the researchers had been bitten and suffered mild irritation and occasional hallucinations. Nothing fatal but it was still annoying. Bug spray was being used lavishly.

Beta Three was more stubborn and was vastly different than its cold-weather neighbor. The planet was covered entirely in rain forest, swamps, high desert regions and oceans. All were teaming with life and they were hungry! Commander Barnes smiled at this one, the colonists would have their hands full taming this world! Were he younger and single, Barnes might have liked to work there and go hunting. Some of the troops had already discovered several new food sources, high in protein and attitude. Doesn't everything taste like chicken? It would be a fun world to conquer and for a game preserve. One of the biologists had discovered some new ingredients for medicine until he was almost eaten by a large plant. That brought him back to the ship for recovery but not before he laid out a plan for new research stations.

Ah well, each planet had its problems. Some good and some just boring but Beta Three was going to be entertaining!

Another problem was the pilot Sana Abbicon from the Colony ship Explorer. A real hot shot with the runabout, what would she be like in a fighter? He smiled when he thought about her. Vertically challenged or not, the woman was a top gun. 3rd Lieutenant Jackson got a real reaming from Lt. Commander Bayer for allowing the flyby stunt and he had it coming! But Commander Barnes did not worry about it, the young man was stepping into a new pair of shoes and this episode was a good reminder to be wary in the future. No harm but he had assigned Officer Abbicon to the pilot corps for additional training. The engineers bitched about adjusting the controls in one of the simulators for her size but it could be done. The other pilots watching her run through a few simulated tests were a little intimidated.

This whole mission to 'Palisade', a good enough name he thought, was becoming a headache and a welcome relief for the commander. The captain of the Explorer would be coming on board tomorrow to visit the commander and tour the AGAMEMNON III. He would also meet with Officer Abbicon and Mr. Bisset, the Geologist to ascertain their condition. Sana had no relatives on the Explorer, but Mr. Bisset did and he was having a hard time adjusting to the cultural differences of Terran life much less their obvious technological advantages. He would be going back with the captain, back to hibernation. And unless ordered otherwise, Sana wanted to stay on the AGAMEMNON III. But there was a problem. She had been separated from Lt. Jackson and was not happy about that! Lt. Commander Bayer tried to find her some new 'friends' and hoped that some of the flight crew would interact with her more but the diminutive woman was stubborn...she wanted Bale!

Hmm, it' only been a week but could it be...?

Commander Barnes had no problem with now Third Lieutenant Jackson waiting on his officer training. Perhaps as Ambassador Liaison between their two ships as well as an escort for Officer Abbicon was in order. And with his special augmentation, what better bodyguard would she need?

He laughed knowing full well where this was going to go...ah, to be young again!

Bale was not having a good time either. He was three days into his officer training, and it wasn't going well. For some reason, he just could not concentrate, and he did not know why. His instructor was not putting up with Third Lieutenant Jackson either. "Mr. Jackson! I realize that you are only in your first week of formal officer training but this comparative paper on the 100 years' war and the Mid-East conflict is poor at best. Your affirmative was awkward, and you completely ignored the negative. Bring another paper tomorrow and put some thought into it!"

Orbital mechanics was giving him a headache too, so Bale was being tutored in Calculus and Differential equations. In coding he was good, but Enki code required an expansion of his computer language skills, more than he realized. But history was the worst! And he still had light duty to fill out his day!

Cage met him in the gym as no one could spar with Third Lieutenant Jackson other than another Point guard, Gantry or the commander, all of them being the only advanced augmented on the ship. Bale never enjoyed the experience as Cage was truly the animal everyone thought he was, but Bale was beginning to realize that he was being trained and in a proper way. Cage enjoyed the training immensely! "C'mon boy, put some muscle into it! You're starting to hit like a girl," he laughed. Bale threw a punch at Cage's midriff, Cage dodged, then Bale jumped into the air and landed a blow to Cage's face. Cage grinned through a split lip, "Good move! Deception is always the key, like this!" He grabbed the younger man by his waist in a wrestling move, pulled Bale's left arm back, spun him around and threw him into a wall 20 meters away. The wall gained a new dent.

Bale got to his knees and stared at Cage, he was getting really angry now!

"Dude, that was too easy. You are weak! Wake up bucko, the Wolves sure as hell won't care if you're thinking about your girlfriend." He laughed at Bale again, "I heard you tossed your cookies after that joyride she gave you. Heck of a rocket jock I heard and damn pretty too. I might take her for a spin...OOF!"

Bale slammed into Cage and both men fell against the opposite wall. The thunderclap of their collision with the wall left it with a dent too, rivets flying across the floor. Everyone else in the gym stayed on their side of the large space. Though they continued to work out on various machines or loose weights, they kept a keen eye on the two fighting at the other end of the room. They were all augmented to various degrees but these two were brutes and were already proving what heavy augmentation was like.

"Oh ho! So that's what this is all about! You pinning for that Colony girl? Or is school just too tough for you, SIR?" Cage yanked a loaded barbell, about 450 kilograms and forced off the weights, grabbed the 5 cm bar and swung it like a pike. “Get ready kid, this is gonna hurt!”

13

Sana was in a mood and no one was going to get in her way! She walked down the hall from officer country and was about to enter the Marine's barracks. Karen and Tracy were in her wake for moral support if not out of fear for their new friend.

Tracy had met Sana through Karen and immediately liked the Colony woman. They had lunch a couple of times when they were all free. Sana had spent a lot of time with the flight corps and unfortunately with Mr. Bisset. The man was lonely and scared of being on the Terran ship away from his wife and sons. Sana had managed to get him to meet with the Terran Geologist, which Mr. Bisset said he enjoyed but otherwise he stayed in his room.

One day at lunch, Sana confided in her friends that she was unable to get or receive any messages from Third Lieutenant Jackson. Sana made it sound informal, but the other women were not fooled. "With your new status as 1st Lieutenant, perhaps you can just go see him?" Tracy giggled while Karen smiled at Sana.

"What? I mean sure, I miss him, but I just need more information about Earth from a man's point of view." Sana chewed her lip. What was she thinking? He was just another man, but he was so sweet...it would never work. *I didn't mean that did I?*

Tracy snickered, "Honey, you've got it bad! And if stories I am hearing from Cadet school and from the Marines is true, so does he only Bale doesn't know it." Karen smiled, "Let's get you some new shoes."

As they approached the Marine's entrance, Karen marveled at Sana ahead of them. They had bought her some elegant but smart shoes that gave Sana an additional three inches in height, but the outfit was almost dangerous as it was almost skintight like some of the other female officers wore for parties. Regulation to be sure but just barely. Tracy leaned into Karen and whispered, *"Well now we know she is all human. Work it girlfriend!"* she giggled. Karen elbowed Tracy and smiled but she had to agree that Sana was walking the walk and men were noticing. Lots of hip there *girlfriend!*

Sana was getting nervous, she had dealt with soldiers before, but Terran Marines were on a different order and they were no-nonsense about it. One of them had a gun strapped to his back that was almost as long as Sana was tall...never mind the other weapons he sported!

They both saluted her. Sana's commission was a gift from the commander, non-regulation but then all flight officers were Lieutenants. He had not received a chain of command chart from the captain of the Explorer yet, but the young woman proved that she had thousands of hours flying all manner of ships. That pretty much demanded 1st Lieutenant status even if it was complimentary from the commander. He hoped the captain would not be upset. Even though nominal, Sana received honors and respect from the noncoms.

"What can I do for you Lieutenant?" the young man asked. At seven and a half feet tall, he had to look a long way down into her eyes. Sana almost chinked her neck staring back up at him. "I wish to meet with the Master Chief." Stunned, the man thought about it for a minute while Sana waited, "Please, let me call him." He texted the chief through his implants, **What should I do, Sir?**

The Master Chief thought about it trying to ignore the noise coming down the hall from the gym. He shook his head, that is the last thing I need is that girl in here. But she might be the very thing to calm Jackson down, a Beauty and the Beast sort of thing. Another 'Bang' hit the hallway! He told the Sergeant to send her in but with a full escort...the girl was small and a half-grav. She could die in here!

The Sergeant in front of her nodded and spoke to her, "Just a few as we need to give you a full escort to the MC, please wait. I'm sorry ladies," looking over Sana's shoulders. "You can't come in. Have a good day!"

Tracy and Karen wanted to give Sana a hug and wish her well, but they nodded to her, smiled and walked away. Sana braced herself and turned to the door. Both Sergeants stood well back as more Marines faced her. “Come with me Lieutenant.” Six men faced her and then lined the wall to let the little woman walk in. Sana’s bravado left her then...she was in animal country.

One of the Sergeants put his finger on Sana’s shoulder, it felt like a brick was placed there. “Please Lieutenant, wait for a moment while we clear a path.”

Two of the front guards walked forward a couple of meters, one yelled out, “Hit the walls, hit the walls! Clear a path! Hit the walls!” Everyone ahead of them either ‘hit a wall’ or ducked into a room. The path was clear. “Forward, slow march.” And the men around Sana began a slow walk towards the Master Chief.

Sana was now fully nervous. What was she doing, demanding to see Third Lieutenant Jackson? She had thought of enticing him back to officer country, just for dinner and to talk but now, she didn’t know. Was this a good idea?

As her escort followed her pace, short as it was, they stared straight ahead and the rear was protected as well. Men on the wall stared at her as she walked by, her shoes allowing nothing but that swing, and they marveled that someone so short could be so...but she was a lieutenant and they all saluted as she walked by.

Master Chief Michael Green came out of his offices and looked at the young woman in front of him. “Hit the walls, gentlemen.” Her escort presented arms and put their backs to the opposite walls. He immediately saluted 1st Lieutenant Abbicon and asked, “What can I do for you, Sir?” At that moment, a large weight machine, more than 800 kilograms tore through the hall several meters away, a clang of shredded metal and pieces flying everywhere. Green had to admit the woman had spunk, she didn’t flinch. She just looked down the hall at the damage. Sana turned to look up at the Master Chief, “Where is Third Lieutenant Jackson? I need him for dinner tonight, Officer’s privilege.”

“Um, he’s in the middle of a discussion.” Several cylindrical weights shot through the same wall and past it through the next wall opposite of the hall.

Sana squinted her eyes at the man, “I want you to bring him to me now! Put a stop to it or I will!” When Mike hesitated, she turned and walked past the guard and entered the gym. Master Chief Green ran to stop her and only managed to shout, “Attend ‘chut!” Everyone in the room stopped what they were doing, the other noncoms huddling near a corner farthest from the action. Bale and Cage were in a chokehold on the other end of the gym and both were bleeding profusely. “ATTEND ‘CHUT!!”

Bale’s eyes were still feral, but Cage heard the command and pushed his tormentor back. He pointed to the door. Bale’s eyes finally focused and realized that Sana was in the room. His breath caught at the sight of her. Those eyes! Then he slumped to the floor.

Sana walked over to the two men, the smallest person in the room but everyone was watching. There was something about her bearing that screamed ‘Officer’! Cage saluted her. “Get him over to that bench would you please Sergeant.” Cage bent down and pulled Bale to a standing position then walked him over to the only undamaged bench in the gym. “Thank you, Sergeant.” She turned to Bale and studied him. Even as she watched, his wounds began to heal and close. Bruises faded. Nanos obviously, the man was riddled with them!

She took her finger and lifted Bale’s head by his chin, “Look at me Mister!” Bale opened his eyes and now knew his loss, his misery at Sana’s absence. He said nothing.

“You will clean yourself up Third Lieutenant and join me for dinner.” Sana pushed harder with her index finger and Bale got the message, he stood. “Does someone have a piece of cloth that I can clean this man’s face?” A junior officer ran over and gave her a handkerchief. Sana spit into it and rubbed Bale’s right cheek to clean the blood off. Then she pulled him down and kissed his cheek. She whispered, *Do not leave me alone again!* “Now get cleaned and put on your dress blues...I will wait here. Hurry!”

"I know we're short a point man but why him?" Lt. Commander Bayer and the commander watched as the ship's carpenters began cleaning the gym. Almost everything was broken, the walls too.

Commander Barnes ignored the mess and watched as the Master Chief walked over. "Yeah, we needed another to fill out the compliment but we both agreed, he is officer material. And as far as Point goes, I think we can see that he will not be a problem, at least not to us. The Wolves won't like him very much." Lt. Bayer shook her head but grinned, "Do you really think this is a good idea, Lt. Jackson being a Liaison? You saw how he looks at her, I mean damnit Jeff, the man is having a hard enough time concentrating on his studies!"

Commander Barnes laughed. "Can you imagine anyone else putting their undivided attention on 1st Lieutenant Abbicon? And who knows, she might just get him to focus on his career."

Lt. Bayer nodded, "She is cute, but..."

The Master Chief snapped a salute to the two officers and received one in return. "I apologize for the mess Sir, but the Master Carpenter assured me that this will be repaired by 1200 tomorrow."

Barnes frowned at the man, his 'other' right arm. "Mike, how could you let this happen?"

"Sir, Third Lieutenant Jackson has some issues that needed working out. Sergeant Daniels gave him room to let off a little steam." Mike looked around the damaged gym and understood that Lt. Jackson had a lot of steam in him. "I'm sorry that I allowed it to go on so long but the boy needed to vent."

"Where are they now?"

The Master Chief consulted his implants, "They are having dinner in the Marriot Lounge."

"Very well and thank you, Master Chief." He saluted them again. The Lt. Commander and the commander left the room.

As they walked back through civilian country to the Bridge, Barnes told Denise to give them a couple of hours of talk then to have them report to him by 2100 hours. "You're not going to do this, are you?" she asked.

Commander Barnes looked at Lt. Commander Bayer. "Do I have a choice? I cannot have the man turn her into a pair of Deuces! She'll need the strength and a couple of extra inches in height wouldn't hurt either."

14

Bale was still in a daze as he walked with Sana into the restaurant, and he was very sore from tangling with Cage. Sana's right hand was on his left arm, a custom of her people. The daze was from being without Sana for only a few days, but he now knew his fatigue and lack of concentration was a result of a lack of Sana. And now he was with her again!

Sana's mind raced with all kinds of thoughts. Was this man all that important? Why do I care about him? Does he really care about me?

They stopped at the Maitre d's stand. The man walked around, "How may I help you?" His English had a slight French accent, appropriate for the Marriot.

"I am 1st Lieutenant Abbicon, I have a reservation for two."

"Of course! Let me prepare a table, Mademoiselle and Monsieur. It will be just a moment."

The chairs were too large for Sana and the table was tall, so she sat on her knees to be eye level with Bale. She looked up to him and saw that he was nervous.

"So? 1st Lieutenant, I bet that surprised some people but then, you are a good pilot!"

Sana stared at her hands, "I just want to apologize for the way I treated you on the runabout. That wasn't fair of me. I hope you understand."

Bale did not want another trip like that but if he had to get away from Wolverines then Sana would be a good choice for a quick escape. A waitress brought them their menus. He helped Sana select from the French cuisine menu as it was different than common fair in the cafeterias.

Neither one spoke as they did not know what to say to each other. Bale just looked at her and Sana blushed. "I've...um, I've missed you. How is officer training going?" It was Bale's turn to be embarrassed.

"Not very well," he looked up at her and smiled. "I'm going to have to knuckle down if I'm going to stay in the program."

Knuckle down? Sana didn't bother to ask what that meant. English had so many metaphors sometimes it was hard to keep up, but she got the gist of what he was saying.

"You must work hard if you intend to achieve 1st Lieutenant. I'll help if I can."

"Sana? What did you mean...um, I mean," He didn't know how to ask the question? Had he heard her right about not leaving her alone?

She stammered, "Please...please tell me more about Earth.

Bale was a little surprised by the change in subject but was relieved too. The waiters brought their plates at that moment so now he could gather his thoughts.

Sana was astonished by how rich the food was. The wine was interesting too, but she had to be careful of the alcohol content, not too much for her! Bale ate with a gusto like any young man would and finished his meal early.

"Earth. I've only been there once for boot camp, so I didn't get to see much beyond the base. I was stationed in Germany for sixteen weeks. Marines of course but it does involve flight and space training."

"What is Germany?" She asked.

"Well, it's a country on the European continent. Quite beautiful! The language is difficult, but the people are friendly, and the beer is out of this world!" He smiled at Sana. Her beauty filled the room and his heart.

Bale had dated in high school on Orthos, but he didn't have the killer instinct to chase women. His sister chided him about that but assured him that one would be there for him, someday. He frowned and looked at his empty plate.

"What? Sana saw the forlorn look on Bale's face. "I'm just remembering my sister." Sana's eyes got wide. She knew about the loss of Bale's home, his entire planet to the Wolverines. "I'm so sorry, I didn't mean for that topic to come up. Please forgive me!"

Bale looked at her, "Nothing to forgive. She used to tease me about women, dating I mean. I was never good at it. But she said it would happen one day." Then he looked into Sana's hazel eyes, "Did you really say for me..."

"Yes!" She reached across the table and clutched Bale's huge hand. "Don't leave me again! I don't know what I would do without you!"

Bale's heart swelled, *was she the one?* He did not know what he would do with someone so tiny and a half-grav at that. He could hurt her! But damnit, he would try! She was worth it!

Sana jumped down from her chair and ran around the table to leap onto Bale's lap. She straddled him, placed both her hands on either side of his face and kissed him. She did not know if this was in keeping with Terran customs but she didn't care. Sana certainly could not fathom why she kissed him, but his green eyes beckoned and she followed.

Bale carefully put his arms around her and kissed her. This woman was very straightforward and maybe that was their way on her planet. He held her and cherished the moment. Bale felt he was home.

It was then that Lt. Commander Bayer pinged him that both Sana and Bale were to report to the commander at 2100, only 10 minutes from now. Sana could tell as Bale tensed up, "What?"

"We've been ordered to meet the commander, now! We've got to go!"

The Orange ship materialized near the debris field of the destroyed Wolverine's ships. Scattered bits and pieces drifted about spreading over a range of millions of miles, none bigger than a few centimeters in size. The destruction of the three ships was so thorough that a puzzle master would have to take centuries to put them back together.

Samples were taken onto the ship and analyzed. The interior was not a dark space but was not well lit either. Strange voices spoke and computers answered. The surrounding space was scanned. Only one ship about eight light years away appeared on their systems and it was moving too slow. It would not be the culprit of this destruction, but it might be worth investigating.

Their new soldiers would not be awakened for now, it would take three months to reach the colony ship if it was that. It was heading for another star two light years away. They would have to investigate that too.

Though this was an old neighborhood of theirs, they had been gone several thousand years. The ship powered up and jumped to TL 7.8 aiming for the other ship. Someone had destroyed an ally of theirs and that was unpardonable. There was a new power in this sector of space...they had to be conquered.

The Enki had returned.

15

Sana and Bale stood at attention in the commander's office. He looked over the tall young officer and decided that Third Lieutenant Jackson would have to continue his studies when he could. The young woman was merely a shadow of Bale, barely 5'-2" tall in heels but even petite, Officer Sana was all woman. He smiled at her. "Lt. Abbicon, your captain is coming onboard tomorrow for an inspection of the AGAMEMNON III and to meet with you and Mr. Bisset. He will also be returning with the bodies of your missing crew. I'm sorry to say that we have not found the other survey craft, we may never find it, but we will continue to look out for it during our surveys."

He turned to Bale, "How are you feeling son? The augmentation fits you well?"

"Yes, Sir!"

Commander Barnes walked around the room and sat on a corner of his desk. "At ease, gentlemen."

Bale and Sana relaxed and placed their arms behind their backs. "Mr. Jackson, you will remain an officer for His Royal Majesty's pleasure, but I am creating a new position for you. A liaison between our two ships and cultures along with protecting Officer Abbicon will be your new priority. Classes will have to be attended online but she will be your focus. Understand me, Mister?"

Bale swallowed and nodded, "Yes Sir!"

"Very well. I need to speak privately with Lt. Abbicon. Report to the lieutenant Commander at 0700 for your reassignment and Liaison orientation. Dismissed."

Bale saluted the commander, looked briefly at Sana and left the room.

Commander Barnes stood and looked down at the young woman. She was certainly 'cute' as Denise suggested. Her other assets intrigued him more because of the reports he received from the flight officer. Lt. Abbicon could expect to receive an official offer from the emperor and become a pilot in his Navy. Further study into Math and English symbology plus more flight training and she would be an official Navy pilot in two months. What her Captain would think of that, Barnes had no idea. The other compromise he had given the captain would probably bother him a great deal. Lt. Abbicon needed augmentation, or she could never fly one of their ships...they would kill her.

He led her to a pair of couches opposite each other with a low table in between. “Have you tried our coffee?” Sana sat down on the low couch and the commander sat opposite of her. “Yes Sir, it’s very much like our hot spice drink from home. We have it on all our ships. The caffeine helps!” She smiled at him.

Sana was so nervous, what was he going to talk to her about? The couch was low enough that if she bent her toes, she could touch the floor, barely.

“Lieutenant don’t sit at attention. You’ll hurt your back...relax.” Sana tried and almost fell back which would have been awkward so once again, she sat on one of her legs and let the other dangle over the edge of the couch. She was more comfortable but was still not at eye level with the commander.

A young man came through the door carrying a tray with a thermos of coffee, cups and assorted accents for the drinks. The steward put the tray down, saluted the commander and left the room. Barnes poured for both and handed her a saucer with a cup. “I have cream and sugar here as well. Help yourself.” She watched as he spooned two scoops of sugar and one dollop of cream into his cup. Sana considered it and decided a little cream would be nice. He studied the young woman over the rim of his cup.

Sana did not know this man much less any others except for Bale, but he was the commander. She wished she had time to change her uniform before this meeting. While she thought the outfit appropriate for her date with Bale, it was not a good look in a formal setting. The heels too suggestive, the uniform was skintight and the top was too revealing leaving no doubt as to her femininity.

"I assume you and Third Lt. Jackson get along well," the commander asked. Sana blushed. "Yes sir, he is a good comp...I mean, a man. He is always polite and careful around me."

The commander smiled; he had caught a little of her lipstick on the corner of young Jackson's mouth. "Good! You two will be working together for some time for the benefit of both our cultures." He could see by her blouse that she got excited at the idea. He smiled again, *ah youth!* The two officers were certainly healthy enough!

The commander put his cup down and leaned back into the couch. "Your Captain and I have spoken several times now and I am looking forward to him coming aboard tomorrow. I am happy that you have acclimated to the AGAMEMNON III and the Terran Navy way of doing things. You are a well-trained officer of your people. I compliment you and I have extended that report to your Captain. He told me he expected nothing less." Sana blushed again, "Thank you, Sir!"

Commander Barnes took another sip of his coffee and got serious. "I've heard from the admiral of our fleet. There are many aspects of Palisade that are positive for us and possibly for your people as well. Most of the issues do not concern you except for two. First, as you know by now there are no half-gravity worlds in this star system. You have nowhere to ground and settle. His Majesty's science division may have come up with a solution, one that is truly unique. You personally do not need to know that information currently as it is still under consideration. I will discuss this with your Captain privately tomorrow. Know this, you and Lt. Jackson will be placed in some position of responsibility in its execution. I sincerely hope that the two of you can get along for its duration as it will require more than a year of your time together."

Sana swallowed hard. She knew there were no planets suitable for Teknomen. Maybe the asteroids but that would require significant resources that they did not have. And they would need huge centrifuges to protect their people from bone loss and their overall health. She was not sure that the Terrans had it either but certainly now there was a plan. That she and Bale would spend a lot of time together would be a bonus!

"I understand, sir but you did mention there were two issues concerning me?"

The commander leaned forward and placed his arms on his knees and folded his hands together. He looked her straight in the eyes. "Do remember how you felt, physically after your jaunt around the AGAMEMNON III? You were sore, right? The medical staff responsible for your well-being reported to me that you had several bruises because of that joyride." The commander leaned back once again on the couch and put an arm across its back.

Sana looked down at her hands. She was embarrassed again and for good reason. Had they crashed, Bale would have been fine, but she would have died. It was reckless and dangerous what she did with that runabout...but she had not flown anything that fast before outside of translight. She did remember being a little sore but took it because of an unfamiliar craft.

"I'm so sorry Commander but I haven't flown in some time. I have no excuse. I apologize."

"You could have caused your death! Lt. Jackson has serious augmentation and multiple shields built into him and his suit. He would have lived. Your shield is barely on par with a robot. Had you crashed that runabout, you would have perished!"

Sana remained as still as she could, it would not have been proper for an officer to be shaking at a correct dressing-down as she was now receiving. She deserved any punishment the commander dealt out. She put both her feet forward and sat up straight and waited for what was coming. Would she still be able to be with Bale? What about this operation they would share for a year together? What was going on?

The man opposite of her ran his fingers through his scalp and sighed, "Were you a full-fledged officer of mine, you would be demoted. But I can't have that, and you don't really belong to this Navy...yet."

Yet?

"I've discussed this infraction of yours with your Captain. He laughed!" For the first time in a while, the commander smiled at her. "I have to admit that your Captain has a lot of faith in you. We discussed another topic in which he was not so jubilant, but he agreed that it might be the best result for both our peoples."

"Lieutenant, you cannot fly any of our equipment...fighters, freighters, survey ships, or even this ship until you are qualified. You are GROUNDED!"

Sana did not know the term, but she got the idea. She would never fly again on any of the Terran ships and would have to go back to hibernation aboard the Explorer as a half-grav, never to see Bale again. A lone tear began to form in her left eye. Sana had dated other men before, but Bale was different. Sweet, gentle, and well educated but with a warriors' heart. A man to be trusted in all things and he took his job seriously! But did she love him...or more important, did he love her?

Commander Barnes noticed her distress and stood to walk over to his desk. Sana took that opportunity to wipe her eyes with his back turned. She waited as the commander picked up a letter.

"There is a solution that your Captain and I agreed upon." He turned back to the lieutenant and saw that she was composed. Damn! I *need* more officers like her!

He returned to Sana and handed her the letter. "Sir?" The commander smiled down at the little woman, "Just read it, please."

To Commander Jefferson H. Barnes, Master of the AGAMEMNON III from

Captain Horacio de Verkon, Master of the Explorer.

My compliments to you and crew. Thank you for your support and welfare

of our surviving crew.

As to our discussion of Officer First Class Abbicon of the

Explorer Survey Team,

I instruct you to proceed with the operation on Officer Abbicon, with her

permission of course.

There were other notifications and a final numerical salute as both computers signed off with each other. Sana read the letter again, what operation?

"Lt. Abbicon, you cannot fly any of our ships nor can you survive an extended stay on a full gravity planet or station as you are. I recommend that you be augmented to enable you to pilot any of our vehicles. Your Captain agreed."

Sana was stunned! "Sir? I will be like Lt. Jackson?"

The commander chuckled, "No, that type of augmentation is permanent. He is becoming an officer but first and foremost, Lt. Jackson is a fighter and a very deadly one. That is his job and he has been well trained for it...I'm not kidding about deadly. You will be modified to fly any vessel of His Majesty's Navy. You will also be given a bit more height. All augmentation is reversable, but Advanced Augmentation is not one of them. You will be stronger, taller and enabled to handle multiple gees in any fighter. All of our ships have inertial dampeners but occasionally, a bump happens. The crew would be fine...you would be pudding on the floor without augmentation." He watched her very closely.

Sana was breathing hard! She would not be like Bale, but she could fly again in some of the best ships she had ever seen. Would this work? Her Captain agreed to it so it might be true! And after the operation, she could hold Bale like a woman should and not get broken in the process. *Yes!*

"Yes! I mean, yes Sir!"

Barnes grinned knowing full well her desire and was grateful for it. He needed more officers like Lt. Abbicon. Perhaps there were others like her on Captain Verkon's ship.

"You will report to Medical Enhancement now. The operation will take some time as you have not been fully integrated into our medical library. There will be a lot of tests, but you should be able to decant by 0400 tomorrow. There will be a short recovery time but once you are comfortable with your new body, I expect you and Lt.

Jackson for a late breakfast at 0900, Officer's Mess. You will see your Captain then."

Sana jumped up and crossed the table and hugged the commander, "Thank you!" Then she realized who she was holding. Sana let go and stood up straight, she saluted him. "I'm sorry Commander but I was overcome with excitement at the opportunity. It will never happen again."

"That's okay Lieutenant..." he started to say but the woman ran from the room with her new orders.

Barnes smiled, he got a new pilot, a real hot shot! And Lt. Jackson gets a real woman just like the commanders' wife...Lucky Bastard!

16

Tracy watched as the doctor injected some enzymes into Lt. Sana. Her screen lit up with the new trace of material racing through Sana's blood stream, along with hundreds of millions of nanos that were in the process of rebuilding her body. Though Tracy had completed this process on hundreds of patients over the years, it still made the hair on the back of her neck stand up when Sana's skin crawled like there were multiple worms squirming there. There were only a few minutes left for the operation.

Sana was now taller and much stronger, even moreso than a normal full-grav human. She would need it to fight on any ship. All Navy personnel received some augmentation, but Flight officers needed more to survive high gees. Tracy smiled as she thought Sana would need it if as she suspected, Sana and Bale did more than kiss.

After Sana had left the commander's office, she immediately called Tracy and Karen. They both met her at the hospital wing for officer augmentation. Tracy was off rotation so another bioengineer would be performing the procedure. She assured Sana the man was good at his job because Tracy had trained him.

"Will this hurt?" Sana asked.

Tracy shook her head, "Um, no but you will be a little sore for a couple of days. When you have breakfast tomorrow, eat a hearty meal because you will be starving!"

Karen leaned into Sana. "We have a delicate issue to discuss with you." Sana became alarmed. "What?"

"When you get enhanced, especially in your case you will be proportionately the size of a normal Terran female. No difference in appearance but you will be augmented. But there might be a problem concerning your, um...breasts."

Sana looked down at her chest and got worried. Tracy giggled, "What Karen is delicately trying to tell you is that your fun-bags will be huge unless we prepare for that. You don't want to walk around with a pair of cantaloupes on your chest, do you?" Sana had seen one on a food video and knew she did not want that additional weight.

Karen rolled her eyes, "Despite Tracy's irreverent image, some men do like that but it's a little uncomfortable. I would especially think so for a flight officer."

"So honey, do you want some bounce and wiggle in them jugs?" Tracy winked. Sana was relieved she had such good friends on AGAMEMNON III. She certainly could not discuss this with Bale! A little bounce would do.

Karen had given Sana a hug and went home to bed. Tracy drank her coffee and watched as most of the nanos were removed from Sana's body. The doctor was a little concerned about Sana's family history with cancer but could find no precancerous cells in her body. They would keep a watch on that for the future.

A technician was finishing the programming on Sana's new computer implants. She would not have access to them for now. Sana would need time to adjust to her new body, and use of her implants would come later.

Tracy took a nap after they took Sana to the recovery room. Sometime later a nurse woke her up in earnest. "Lt. Abbicon is having some trouble and is not cooperating!" Tracy figured something like this would happen. All patients prior to their first augmentation were given a lengthy orientation to the procedure. Sana had none of that, just her friends holding her hand and give her some advice.

Tracy rubbed the sleep out of eyes and walked into Sana's room. Sana was standing near her bed clutching the handrail and crying. Her other arm was brushing away the nurses who were trying to calm her down. "Don't touch me!"

With her hands on her hips, Tracy yelled, "Stop that right now!" Sana looked at Tracy and burst into a new set tears and moaning. "What did you do to me? I can't see right! And the floor is so far away!"

Tracy waved the nurses off, "I've got this, just give us a few minutes." The nurses nodded and left the room. She walked over to Sana and slapped the young woman as hard as she could. Sana's neck snapped to the right then she glared at Tracy. Then another burst of tears and she fell into Tracy's arms.

Sana was still wearing her hospital gown; she had not put on her uniform yet. "Ya know," Tracy murmured in Sana's ear as she wept. "If I had hit you like that yesterday, you would have had a broken neck."

In shock, Sana stood back and wiped her eyes. "You mean I'm human now?"

"Honey, you were always human but now you're taller than me and stronger too as I'm just now getting some feeling back in my hand." She laughed and Sana managed to smile.

"That's better, Dear. Put a smile on and let's get you dressed." One of the nurses walked in as Sana had put on her panties. There was no bra so Sana covered herself with her hands. "Oh honey, I've seen it all so cut the crap." The nurse was older and a bit crabby, but her smile was warm. She pulled out a stethoscope and checked out her heart, looked into her ears and frowned at the palmprint on Sana's face. She looked over at Tracy, "Some motivation, Doctor?" Tracy shrugged and ignored the comment. She continued to scan Sana with her own instruments. The nurse left and Sana finished dressing with Tracy's help.

"Okay, now the moment of truth. Ready to see how you look?" Sana panicked again but nodded weakly. "I'm not sure but okay."

She walked a little unsteadily over to a floor length mirror. Tracy held her arm as Sana caught her reflection. She gasped! It was like someone had stretched Sana for now she was taller than Tracy by a few inches. She was a little leaner but overall, Sana looked like herself. Blonde curly hair, hazel eyes on a heart shaped face but her body was definitely tall! As she looked back at the room through the reflection, it now did not seem so large.

Tracy could tell that Sana was shaking, "Let's go sit down

sweetheart, take things a little slow." She found a chair and Sana sat down near a table. Suddenly, the chair fit and the table was at the right height! With realization, Sana knew she was fully Terran, even the floor met her feet.

Tears started running down her cheeks. Tracy realized this might be a kind of body image rejection Sana was experiencing. If so, the surgery could be reversed but Sana would have to go back to the Explorer and to hibernation. "What's wrong, Sana?"

The woman leaned over and put her face into her hands and sobbed. "Maybe this was a mistake." *Uh oh,* thought Tracy. "I mean I love to fly but..." *This could be bad!* "...what will Bale think?"

Tracy blinked a couple of times and then started laughing. Sana looked up at her and then stood to glare down at her friend. Tracy embraced her and continued to laugh. "Oh sugar, you had me going there!" She pulled back from Sana and cupped the young woman's face in her hands. "Bale won't give a damn! He will love you just the same." Sana sniffed then smiled, "You sure?"

Tracy nodded. "Yep, now let's get some makeup on and practice walking and climbing some stairs. You have breakfast with your Captain and the commander in two hours. Bale will be there too so let us get you ready!"

Captain Verkon stood near the airlock with a brace of soldiers and Mr. Jeerish. They waited on Lt. Parks to dock with their ship. The docking collars were not compatible, so the lieutenant had nanos fabricate a new one for both vehicles. It would remain with the Explorer.

They could feel a small thud and some clanging on the other side of the door. From a nearby speaker, Lt. Parks could be heard. "Pressure is normalized, the air is good. Come aboard, Captain." Verkon could see green lights on his side of the door. Everything was good.

Once he and his men were inside the Terran ship, one of the crew assigned seats for his soldiers and Mr. Jeerish. "Come with me Captain. We have a special seat for you on the bridge. His Master Sergeant was alarmed but Verkon signaled him to stand down. They were being hosted by the Terrans, he doubted very much that anything untoward would happen out here.

They had somehow manufactured a command chair from scratch that fit the captain perfectly. As the pilot and navigator were on a lower floor, he could see out the window easily. He turned to Lt. Parks who was sitting next to him in her own command chair. "What type of glazing do you use for your ship's window. She looked over at him and smiled, "Actually, that is a screen. There are no windows on this vessel. The cameras outside are high resolution 3D and function much as a window does, they are also shielded from dust, debris and possible attack." Captain Verkon wondered about the last. Perhaps there was something he could trade to Commander Barnes for that technology.

"Gentlemen, let's take the captain for a spin along the Explorer to show him how the reconstruction is going." The ship gently pulled away from the docking ring and rode steadily down the side of the immense ship. Already several other ships from the AGAMEMNON III had unloaded additional shielding to be placed along the flanks of the Explorer. Men were crawling all over her and attaching devices and panels into place. More than half the ship was covered with the new material. The engines remained in place but were now useless as a new light-speed motor had been placed inside. A new bridge was being built to replace the old one. It would have artificial gravity like he was experiencing now on Lt. Parks' ship. How unique! With advanced electronics and detection sensors, Verkon and his crew and passengers would arrive in Palisade in just under six months. Extraordinary!

"Now Captain, I would like to give you the honor of Commanding our ship to return to Palisade." Verkon grinned at this, "How fast will we be traveling?"

Lt. Parks already liked this guy. He was not afraid of anything! "TL 8. We will arrive back at AGAMEMNON III in less than one hour. Now Sir, give the command!"

"Helmsman, bring us about." The ship moved away from

the Explorer to open space away from the work crews and the ship. "Is the plot laid in, Mister?"

"Aye, Captain!"

"Engage!" He braced himself for what must come but Verkon was still not ready. A hum started near the back of the ship and eventually filled the rest of the vehicle. The vibration was slight, but the power had to be enormous! "TL engaged in three, two, one...Now!"

Suddenly streaks of light ran past the ship. It shot forward and disappeared into another dimension.

Wow! And in just one hour, he would meet the commander of AGAMEMNON III. Captain Verkon smiled to the lieutenant woman seated next to him and could not stop grinning.

17

Bale stood next to the commander and visited Captain Verkon of the Explorer. Both men had to stare down at the older man, he was 5'-2" and the tallest man on his ship despite his 62 years.

"Mr. Jackson, am I to understand that you are now my pilot's bodyguard and Liaison between our two cultures?"

Bale had been thoroughly indoctrinated by Lieutenant Commander Bayer as to proper etiquette as a new Liaison. She was also the on-board Ambassador for any need of the same. Lt. Bayer was a harsh task master!

"You will speak only when spoken to. You will NOT volunteer an opinion! You will focus on Lt. Abbicon, and now the commander and the captain of the Explorer Mr. Verkon! Am I being clear, Mister?!!" Bale nodded his head and continued to stand at attention.

"Captain Verkon, as this is a new position for me, I will rely on you to guide me with the help of our Commander to perform my duties properly as a Liaison. As to my other skills, I am a fully trained and experienced Marine in His Majesty's Service."

The commander smiled at the answer. Denise had to have worked the boy hard, but she could not have put those words in Lt. Jackson's mouth. *Well done, young man!*

Marines! Or whatever the Terrans called them. Soldiers by anyone's standard but they were huge. Four of them stood at the corners of the large room, three men and one woman, all of them over seven feet tall. They wore nothing but fatigues, not a weapon in sight but Lt. Abbicon had warned him that each of these people could destroy an entire short platoon, even barehanded.

"Thank you, Lieutenant Jackson. I will trust that we are in your good hands." Bale nodded in appreciation. Then a chime sounded around the room, “This must be our errant people.”

The commander nodded to Captain Verkon, “Yes. Lieutenant Abbicon and Mr. Bisset are coming to join us for breakfast. A door to the rear of the commander’s Table opened and a brace of guards, another group of Marines walked in. Though the captain had his own guards fully vested with weapons, they did not compare to the Marines that walked in. Each over seven feet tall and festooned with every weapon Captain Verkon could imagine. None of the Marines at the corners wore a single weapon...he was not sure who to be more afraid of.

He heard a soft but femine voice, “Hit the walls, gentlemen.” The four that walked in turn and divided then saluted the commander, presented arms and stood at either side of the hallway. The rest, as Captain Verkon watched turned their backs to a nearby wall inside the hallway.

After the soldiers were placed, Captain Verkon could see a Terran woman holding onto the arm of a Teknoman, that had to be Dr. Bisset. The man was clearly agitated and wanted release; the woman would not let him go. They walked together further into the Dining Hall. She stopped and waited on the two Commanders. Mr. Bisset would not wait, he fell to the floor on purpose to be released from the officer. Then he ran, stumbled, fell on his face, got up again and ran to Captain Verkon. The woman did not bother to catch the Geologist, she stood where she was and waited.

“My Captain! Please listen to me! Take me back to the Explorer. You can’t imagine the horrors I’ve seen on this ship!”

Space! What a timid man! Captain Verkon shook his head and looked at the plump and useless person on the floor, posturing in front of him and the Master of this fine ship. The shame he was feeling now was beyond measure. “Were you tortured?” the captain asked him. “Um, no but...” “Then you were well fed, is that true, Mr. Bisset?” “Yes, but...” “They gave you adequate quarters, a bed, water, whatever you needed including medical care?” “Yes but they had one of these monsters follow me everywhere!”

"Master Sergeant De Marcos! Take this lump of lard back to the ready room. He is to be shackled and sedated until I finish my tour of the AGAMEMNON III!" One of his guards grabbed the man blubbering on the floor and marched him out the door. "Take all of your men with you! The Sergeant stopped and looked at the captain. "Sir?"

"I will be fine. Do as I say!" All the other guards followed the Master Sergeant and the puny excuse for a Teknoman out of the room.

Verkon turned to the commander, "Though I am responsible for every one of my colonists, I cannot help those that lack the Unity our people are required to share. I have no excuse. Please let me apologize for this pathetic display of humanity."

Commander Barnes was not surprised by Bisset's lack of 'Unity', he had pretty much displayed it the very first day he was awakened and every day since. Officer Abbicon was the only one to embrace her new situation. That the captain of the Explorer had no problem with his crew or the ship assured Barnes that not everyone on the Explorer was a xenophobe.

He looked over to the woman still standing near the entrance of the commander's Table. "Captain Verkon, I fully understand. We occasionally have people that cannot handle the requirements of space travel and the opportunities it offers. We place them in stasis until they reach their destinations so that they do not upset the crew or harm themselves. Dr. Bisset is clearly one such example. You have no need to apologize."

Bale was staring at the woman across the Dining hall. Was it Sana? He zoomed in with his sight and found out she was looking right at him...she winked! His heart was beating faster. Sana! Taller and just as beautiful as ever! What happened? Had she been augmented? Well, of course, he realized but...wow!

"Captain Verkon, may I introduce you to your officer pilot?"

Verkon looked at the woman across the room. He recognized her but was stunned by the transformation. "1st

Lieutenant Abbicon, please come forward to salute your Captain," the commander said.

Sana walked slowly over to her Commanders as she did not want to stumble in front of them. The room was at half-grav for the captain's sake, and she was having enough trouble walking in normal gravity.

Datsun in one of the corners 'pinged' Bale, **Dang! You're tagging her? My Man!** Bale blushed but smiled.

Sana knelt to her knee and placed her fist on her chest in front of her Captain. "In Unity, always Sir!" Then she stood and saluted the commander in Terran fashion, he returned the salute.

The captain smiled at the young woman. "Be still, officer Abbicon." He then walked around her studying her new physique. Though Verkon prided himself of his stature, officer Abbicon passed him by a few inches. Though she looked the same, Officer Abbicon was now a larger version of her old self. "Do you have any trouble with full gravity?"

"My Captain, I am fit and ready to fly with your permission and that of the commander."

Verkon turned to look up to the master of this ship. "Does she have your permission Mr. Barnes?"

"She is fully qualified on simulators. I will begin a training regimen for her next week. I believe she will more than satisfy our flight officer and of course will honor you as well. Isn't that so, Mr. Abbicon?"

Sana stood straighter in her new body, "Yes Sir!"

Bale was watching all this a few paces back. Sana ignored him and was speaking with the two masters about her pending career as a pilot. She was beautiful! Some of him missed the tiny version of Sana but the new version spoke wonders! Maybe he could hold her without breaking her. But was she still interested?

Commander Barnes turned to Bale. "Lieutenant Jackson. I believe you have some material to discuss with Lt. Abbicon. Breakfast is to be served in fifteen minutes. Hurry back. Dismissed."

Sana turned neatly on her heels and followed Third Lieutenant Jackson out of the room.

Captain Verkon smiled, “Well done, sir. And about time, I felt like I was caught between tuning forks. Do you really think...”

“Yeah, it was bound to happen with someone from your ship and ours. We are human afterall.”

Captain Verkon smiled. “Yes, and as with all youth, too many hormones!” He laughed.

Bale led Sana down the hall and around several corners. He stopped at a door, opened it and motioned Sana inside the room, apparently an unused office. Bale had just shut the door when his back was slammed into it!

Sana was heaving and breathing fast. Then she leaned into him and kissed him. He wrapped his arms around her back and pulled...nothing broke. “Easy big boy, I’m not an exercise machine.”

“Not yet!” Bale pushed her back and studied the new and improved Sana. 5’-8” tall, still a curly blonde with a heart-shaped face but the eyes...they had not changed. Bale pulled her in and kissed Sana again.

She pulled one of her arms in and leaned on his chest. “I was worried that you wouldn’t like me with my new body.” Bale tilted her head up to kiss her again, “It’s your eyes, baby. I do not care if they turn you into a turnip so long as you have those eyes. I will always love you!”

Sana leaned into his chest and purred, “I’m not a baby.”

“It’s an Earth colloquialism, meaning...”

“But I am your baby, right? I told you I would have your number.”

Sana wrapped both her arms around Bale and squeezed. He could feel her! Bale sighed and reached down to kiss this woman again. “What am I going to do with you?”

She smiled, “Anything you want, just don’t leave me again.”

18

Sevn was pulling some vines up from a road near the fence the Engineers had placed around the encampment. Only a few animals had been able to dig under the fence or fly over it. They were a nuisance but nothing more. Sonic vibrators in the ground and high-pitched speakers took care of the rest soundly enough.

A couple of drones floated above and around the surrounding area watching for any of the dangerous reptiles. Some were quite large, but the fence was very stout. So far, all the animals seemed more curious than interested in food within the compound. A shield would have been better, but they were power hungry and the fence was cheap. But there was one critter that made it through the fence, something with a lot of teeth about the size of a chicken and the sonic waves did not bother it. The darn things tried to eat up Petty officer Stanton's plants around the main lab. The plants were all earth-based and the idea was to see how they liked the soil on Beta Three. The plants did all right but the critters, they had not named them yet, all died after eating the plants.

Ah well, this was not going to be their world for much longer, maybe a couple of centuries. Eventually Man would have to build sanctuaries for any of the surviving species and plants.

Overhead, Sevn could see the daytime aurora caused by the spiral gas in this star system. Waves of brightly lit gas danced in the sky as the spiral went by. The gas was harmless here on the planet, mainly ice crystals and molecules of different gases spewed out by the star. It only passed through this area twice a year so Sevn and the others were fortunate to witness it.

Sevn heard a click on his headset, "Sevn? You there? We have got an anomaly happening a couple of klicks northeast of here. We are picking it up from the satellite. Do you see anything from your side of the camp?"

Sevn looked up at the nearby mountains some kilometers away. It was a sunny day and a little breezy but hot as usual. The rainforest covered the entire area except for the space at their camp. He could see the trees swaying with the wind but nothing else. "Naw, nothing here but a..." Then he caught a flash through the trees. It was not very bright but enough to dispel some of the darkness in the undergrowth. "Hey Neal, yeah something is happening about where you said. Some kind of flashing light. It doesn't look like fire, more electrical in nature."

He thought about the wind and decided it might be a bit much for a drone among those trees, plus there were vines hanging from them everywhere! "No fire you say?" Neal paused a bit talking to someone in the room, "Better get back over here. The Sergeant wants to send a group to check it out. Get your gear, you are going with them. Out!"

Hot damn! That beat picking weeds any day! Sevn ran back to his barracks to get his suit and testing equipment.

The Enki ship dropped back into normal space a few light years from the colony ship. Two of the Wolverine's ships met them. They reported the destruction of the other two ships of their allies and the cargo hauler. The Wolves were quite angry and wanted revenge! All three would proceed to the ship but would have to run at TL 3.4 as that was the best the Wolverines could manage. It would add another month to their trip but the Enki were nothing if not patient.

Sub-Commander Oliver finished his report for Lt. Bayer. All the heavy weapons were in place around the system. Six were outside the Oort cloud, three were within nearer Beta Three and Beta Four. It was the most AGAMEMNON III could carry on this visit. More would come later with the colonists. They did not really need the protection at this point because AGAMEMNON III was more than enough of a war platform by itself with its auxiliary vessels, each fully capable of defending themselves.

With a Wolverine base merely 12 light years away, it was the prudent thing to do.

Sevn rode with four riflemen and the lieutenant on a wingless carryall to the spot he had seen in the mountains. His suit was armored, and a helmet covered his head. He was only human; the marines were more than that! Though none of them wore their battle suits, each was armored more inside than out. Each was over seven feet tall and were fully loaded with weapons. Had they worn their armor the carryall would not have been able to carry them. Still, Sevn felt safer with them on board.

"Sir, could you drop us off about a half klick from the site? We want a lay of the land before we run into anything." The lieutenant nodded his head. He had worked with Sergeant 'Lucky Lucy' before and trusted her. The other two women and a man were recent recruits, but she would keep them in line. The Arboriculturist would have to fend for himself.

Sevn dropped to the soft ground with the others, the lieutenant flew off with the carryall to watch from overhead. The riflemen checked their equipment then 'Lucky Lucy' looked at Sevn. "Sir, your name is?"

"Sevn, um Sevn Odibossi and I'm Dr. Odibossi, thank you." She nodded her head and grimaced. "Just stay close with us and if we tell you to stop, hit the ground fast!" Too damn many PHDs on this trip but then that is what a planetary survey needed; the Sergeant did not have to like it though!

Most of the animals in the nearby forest disappeared as the carryall landed the troops. Some of the larger ones ignored the Men as they were vegetarians and frankly too big to be bothered. They walked through the forest stepping carefully over fallen logs, debris, and various insects. They did not have to worry about snakes because there did not seem to be any on Beta Three but there was one viscous mammal that resembled a Ferret from earth. Long of body though only half a meter and short legs but it had a temper and was very territorial. It barked like a dog, so the group knew when some were nearby.

The Sergeant watched everything and everyone had that skill. “Check your steps and watch the trees, remember the spiders.” It was not really a spider, more like a monkey with eight legs but it did have an exoskeleton for a body and resembled a spider including a web-like spit which they could ensnare prey. Sevn was a little freaked out by them, but they were rare and slow.

Light slanted through the canopy above. Sevn could see several of the trees he had identified and got to name. Most of them were tall like sequoias on Earth but their leaves were more fern-like. There were several varieties, and all were beautiful and easy to climb.

They were making good time up the mountain by using a trail made by some local hooved animal. Then Sevn heard a scream behind him. One of the women guarding their rear disappeared down a hole that opened under her. The Sergeant waited grinning; Sevn was freaking out now. One of their team had just died and the Sergeant just waited! Then two blasts from inside the hole and a gray and black shape jumped out and landed on a tree several feet away. He watched as the missing rifleman fired back into the hole. Then she dropped to the ground. “Just a weevil, Sir!” She was breathing a little hard while dirt and leaves fell off of her but the woman smiled.

The Sergeant grinned back, “Just don’t let it happen again.” She slapped the woman on the shoulder and the rest continued up the slope of the mountain.

Weevil! The thing was 300 kilos of underground rodent with teeth the size of bayonets! Sevn was shaken with what almost happened to the marine! And they were laughing about it!

‘Lucky Lucy’ came up to the Doctor and put her hand on his shoulder. “Watch your step, sir. There be dragons in these woods.” Everyone chuckled. Sevn just shook with fear.

An hour later, they stopped for a water break. You would think being in a rainforest, one could not get parched, but Sevn drank half of his allotment. Just as he poured some of the water on his head, he felt a vibration, seconds later a crackling sound very much like firecrackers on the 4th of July. All the riflemen brought up their weapons and looked about. Sevn did not have a weapon but he was not afraid. He walked forward and listened some more.

"Doctor! Sit down, now!" He ignored her. In the far distance he heard some more crackling with what sounded like broken glass. Then there was a bump on the ground, another explosion much larger than the imagined firecrackers. Sevn could see in the distance a tall tree fell in the forest with a loud crashing sound. Just as he was about to run forward, Sevn saw through the trees about 20 meters ahead a row of bright red crystals that begin to glow. They were getting much brighter. "Down! Everyone!" he yelled!

The red lights exploded much like firecrackers and there was broken glass flying through the trees. The entire strip of red lights lit off in a string, again like firecrackers thrown on the ground by a misbehaving child laughing at the display.

One of the riflemen grunted behind him. The other man was bleeding from his arm. The rifleman had not dropped fast enough and some of the glass caught him. Sevn crawled as fast as he could to the man. "Where's your med kit?" he screamed! One was handed to him. Sevn pulled out a scalpel from its wrapper and cut off the sleeve of the rifleman's uniform. "Doc, it's just glass..." then he started to shake.

"Hold him down!" Sevn searched through the med kit but could not find any Borax. He did find some sulfuric acid. Sevn found the piece of glass and pulled it out of the man's arm. Not much blood but it was coagulating strangely. He ripped open the tube of acid.

"Hold him very tight. This is gonna hurt!" All three woman fell onto the recruit. "I've got to clean the wound, or he might die!"

"Just do it, Doctor! Hold him tight, Ladies!!"

Sevn spread the wound and already saw some of the infection spreading to nearby tissue. He snapped off the cap at the end of the tube and stuck it down into the cut skin. Then he squeezed...the man did not do anything for about an eyeblink, then his entire body tensed up!

The roar that came out of him scared Sevn badly and he

crawled back and watched. The man's eyes opened, a man he did not know until today and still did not know his name yelled in immense pain. He managed to lift all three women off the ground. "Hold, HOLD!!" the Sergeant screamed!

The man panted hard then passed out. His body relaxed and though his breathing was shallow, he was *still* breathing. Sevn crawled back over to him and checked his wound. The opening was closing as he watched. Blackened skin from the acid flaked away. Sevn found a packet of bandages and cotton swabs and cleaned then dressed the wound. There was also a saline solution in the med kid. Sevn popped the needle then looked for a vein. "I'll handle that." One of the women said. She found a prearranged puncture mark on the rifleman's upper arm. "That needle won't go through his skin. Does he really need this?"

Sevn nodded, "Wrap him in one of the safety blankets and lift his feet higher than his body. He's in shock right now so the saline will help."

They could still hear strings of firecrackers in the distance and the occasional boom of something much larger. 'Lucky Lucy' studied the Doctor and found him tired but unconcerned about the explosions. He was looking for his canteen but apparently it was lost. She handed him her thermos, Sevn looked at her with thanks and took a drink.

"How did you know? What is it about that glass? And what is going on over here?"

Sevn sighed, "This planet is covered in crystals, mainly in the mountain areas. The red and pink ones are dangerous. Several weeks ago, we tested some of the quartz crystals for their properties. They are abundant near us. One day, Doctor Zimmer was walking by a small isotope tray. Nothing lethal but it was radiating. The red crystal slivers were small, but they all exploded ruining her hands and face. Small slivers of glass but each one was lethal to a human. She almost died until we found an antidote, a borax mixture with her blood. She was saved but your Sergeant needs a blood infusion quickly. I was able to close the wound with extreme measures but that won't fix the problem unless your augmentation nanos are that aggressive."

"So what made these explode?" she asked.

"If I had to guess it's the aurora above us. A couple of times a year, this forest and all the rest with red crystals have a 4th of July party. Nothing serious but those crystals are poisonous to humans."

Sevn leaned over his knees and placed his head unto his arms, he was so tired. 'Lucky Lucy' pulled out a power bar and another packet. "Here's some chocolate and some of my best apple pie."

Sevn turned his head and looked at the offer. "I could use some food now, thank you!"

'Lucy' said, "You saved one of my men. I'm grateful."

"Carry with you Borax in small packets. Just a little will inert the poison of the crystals. Even if you cut your knee by falling on one if it bleeds pack it with borax."

The Sergeant touched the man on the back "I've got the carryall coming back with three more riflemen. They will take Manchester back to the base and eventually to the AGAMEMNON III for hospitalization. She hugged him from behind then stood up. "Sir, I was wrong. We do need doctors out here." She saluted Sevn.

"Just so I can get a nap in. Thank you, Sergeant." He leaned back on the ground and shut his eyes. And then they sprang open again. 'Lucky Lucy' was about to turn away from the good doctor when she noticed his behavior. "What's wrong?" Sevn ignored her and turned over to look at the ground below him, then he took his hands and dug into the mulch. His fingers hit something hard like rock.

The Sergeant was getting very tired of repeating herself to this man, so she just watched as he cleared more mulch from what was clearly becoming a very flat surface.

"This isn't natural..." Sevn muttered to himself. 'Lucy' looked around and found what appeared to be more of the flat surfaces nearby. They did not notice them before as they were covered by dirt and little bushes and logs. They just never considered looking for anything like this.

"Ladies, pull back the dirt and let's see what we have here." One stayed on point guarding Manchester but pulled up the ground around the wounded man. The other knelt and moved a great deal of debris from another surface.

By the time Sevn had cleared his surface, there were three others that were cleared and flat nearby. They all seemed to follow a pattern going up the mountain. "It's a road!" Sevn breathed. All his exhaustion was gone as he looked up the hill spotting more and more of the pattern clearly delineating a road through the trees.

He looked down and brushed more of the dirt off the rock. The color was all wrong for this mountain. It was a light creamy gray. All core samples from the nearby hills were typical granite or dark gray with veins of marble in it. This rock did not come from here or anywhere nearby! And the more he dug around the edges, Sevn got the shock of his life. This was not chiseled, it was machined! Erosion wore down parts of the rock and other edges had broken due to logs falling on them, but the rest were clearly beveled!

The Sergeant watched as he jumped up and started running up the hill jumping from one tilted slab to another. "Doctor! Damnit, stop!" Sevn ignored her again and ran back and forth looking over the side of the ancient road. "Get him, private!"

The woman that had fallen into the hole with the weevil nodded, tucked her gun behind her back and ran after the short man. A few steps later she had him by his collar and quickly walked him back to the Sergeant.

"What the hell, Doctor Odi, ah shit...Doctor! What were you thinking of running off like that?"

"It's an ancient road, older than Man possibly!" He was breathing heavily.

"You mean there might still be natives about?"

Sevn laughed, "Of course not! You see the condition of the slabs? They have been here a long time. And considering the amount of natural erosion around here, they shouldn't be here at all! They should be all over the place, most of them down the mountain. No Sergeant, these are not only old but were built like old Roman roads that lasted over thousands of years...they were meant to stay put!"

He grabbed the Sergeant's arm and pulled her over to his original slab, she almost broke his arm for doing that but she followed. "Here! Look here! Look at the edges here and here. See the bevels? That is machine work. Even the Egyptians could not produce that level of skill and they were the best at working with stone of all types! And look at the color, it is not from this mountain or anywhere around here. These slabs were brought here by a high civilization!"

'Lucky Lucy' was getting a queer feeling in her gut. That this was important was obvious, but her immediate concern was where did this road lead?

19

The lieutenant that flew them here returned, this time with a freight hauler. In the back were three more riflemen with suits for the women and additional weapons. Manchester was loaded on the hauler and the lieutenant took him back to the compound where a doctor waited.

The women all stripped out of their fatigues and put on their armor. The other male riflemen thought nothing of it and studied the terrain around them. Sevn turned away a little embarrassed at their nudity. One of the women noticed and laughed, "Better enjoy the view, Doctor. There won't be another one." She winked at him. Everyone laughed and Sevn turned red.

More supplies were distributed along with extra ammo. The giants, now all dressed and looked down on Doctor Odibossi. "Sir, we directed the satellite to find this road and see how far it goes up the mountain." He turned to look at the commanding Sergeant, "This part of it stops about three klicks further up. Another one is lower and heading up to the same location opposite this position. There doesn't seem to be a structure at the intersection, but we'll have to see for ourselves."

She looked down at Sevn again, "Sorry Doctor, but you are our only expert with us. There is no one on the ship with any archaeological knowledge. You are pretty much it. We hope you have some experience to share with us."

Sevn understood and yes, he did have some experience as most of his studies of rain forests had many Mayan temples and other buildings in the jungles throughout Mexico and Central America. He nodded to the marines. "Let's go!"

As the day wore on, the air was becoming richer and heavy with humidity. All the troops were sweating in the heat despite the shade from the trees. The road was now easy to see as they knew what to look for. There were no more explosions as the auroras had passed not returning for seven more months, the planet completed a rotation in the Palisade system in almost fourteen months.

Sevn ran over to a tree that had fallen some years ago but was still hardly decayed. At its base was a small crater that must have had some red or pink crystals in it. They had blown up and toppled the tree. Inside the crater were new crystals growing but they were blue, green and some were clear...safe.

Lucky Lucy walked up behind the Doctor. “Earlier today, you ran up the road and kept looking over the sides. What were you looking for?”

Sevn looked up at her and brushed some of the sweat from his brow. “The Romans were one of the first ancient civilizations to put mile markers by their roads. Basically a ‘Here you are. This is how much further to Rome you must go.’ They were made from the same stone as the road and stood about a meter and a half tall out of the ground. If whoever made this road, there might be some made from this same material and planted in the ground nearby. It would be the same creamy gray as the road itself. So far, I haven’t seen any but, in this growth, it would almost be impossible to see one as I’m sure they all fell over. This road has been here for a long time.”

One of the riflemen pointed at the ground beyond the edge of the surface. “Um Doctor, is that one?” Sevn blinked then ran over to where the man was pointing. There on the ground was a lot of dirt and leaves but through patches of the stuff, he could clearly see the lighter stone. “Why didn’t you say anything?”

The man shrugged, “I thought it was part of a square that had broken off. This is the third one I’ve seen.” Another rifleman said, “I counted four.” Sevn wanted to pull his hair out! He grimaced and calmly asked the Sergeant, “Could one of you stand the thing up for me?” Lucky Lucy smiled, she could tell the Doctor was agitated. Serves him right, she thought. She pointed and one of the men jumped off the path, bent over and stood the stone up.

"Oh shit!"

"What?" The Sergeant asked.

The small stone was square but easily 2 meters tall and was tapered at the top like an Egyptian obelisk. All over its surface were markers that looked Sumerian.

"See these cuneiforms? They are Enki. It says we are about 12, somethings away from...another word I don't understand, some place of importance. I do not know if that means temple or storage house or hotel. I have never seen half of the symbols before. It definitely predates Man's recorded history."

Sevn looked at the path through the forest with new respect. "This road is thousands of years old!"

"Better get some pictures, Doc. Maybe someone back in linguistics can interpret it for us."

After several images were taken of the marker, Sevn put his camera away. It was clear, whatever message it carried was the same on all sides. The rifleman let the stone fall over to the forest floor.

They marched on and later found a gash in the mountain that a landslide had carved out in the distant past. Even the road could not survive that. There was a 60-meter span over boulders and trees plus a small stream running through the fissure. "Diver! Jump over there and scout the path." One of the new riflemen nodded, ran at the gap and jumped! Just as he was about to fall into the ravine his jets fired, and the man floated over to the other side.

Sevn had never been augmented so he had no experience with marines of any type that had been changed but this amazed him! "Looks good Sergeant!" Sevn could hear over his headset.

"Manners, you'll take the Doctor over." A huge man larger in his armor nodded, "Yes Sir!" With that all the other troops jumped and flew over the gap. Sevn looked around then up to the big man. "How are you going to..."

"Like this Doc." And he picked up Sevn in his arms like you would carry a child and jumped off the ledge. The rockets in his boots kicked in and Sevn and the trooper rose into the air and floated quickly over to the other side.

Once settled, Sevn hoped he did not have to go back that way. Maybe the hauler could come get him wherever they were going.

An hour later they had reached a level area that was quite large. The troops fanned out and looked for anything that resembled their destination, ruins, anything that gave reason for the road to nowhere. One of the riflemen found the other path leading away from the plateau. All around them the jungle screeched and howled with the business of the day unconcerned with the men below them. Brightly colored birds would fly nearby, but they were not like any animal on Earth. Beautiful but different.

"Base, has the satellite found anything at this locale?" Lucy asked. "Negative, Sergeant. There is too much interference from the trees and rocks nearby. We have you at the site but not much else. You will just have to look around. Out!"

Sevn brought out his ground radar and tied it to his helmet's monitor. He then took the radar gun and waved it at the rough surface moving this way and that. The radar was designed for tree roots especially taps as they went deep, sometimes into rock. The riflemen watched him then turned back to watching the forest around them. The large space created a permanent hole in the tree canopy above. As the sun was pretty much overhead there was plenty of light in the area.

In the distance they could hear thunder from a coming storm. Sevn thought they would not be much longer as there didn't seem to be anything around. As he walked away from the leading edge of the platform a fuzzy line appeared on his scope. It was buried in the stone about half a meter down and it was straight! It could only be an alloy to show up on his machine at all. A couple of steps over and he found another one running parallel with the other, about a meter apart.

"Hey! I've got something here!" The Sergeant walked over and tied to his scope. "Looks like tracks to me but why are they inside the rock?" Sevn shrugged, but he followed them towards a huge pile of logs and dirt near the back of the platform.

The marines fanned out and watched each other and the Doctor with his radar. The man had resources, more than they thought he possessed. At the base of the mound, Sevn found a pair of short stone walls coming out of the debris. They were several meters apart, but the tracks were evenly centered between them and ran under the pile. He looked up and saw the number of logs, sticks and mud covering the mound. There was something familiar about the whole setup, but he could not put his finger on it.

"What do ya think, Doc?" one of the marines asked. Sevn wasn't sure, the logs were old and dried out, but the mud was fresh. That was weird as there was no water on the ground other than general moisture. He pulled his radar up and pointed at the dirt pile that looked surprisingly like a beaver lodge. His scope picked up movement and a warm source of heat. Sevn backed up fast. "Run!"

Four of the riflemen pulled up their guns and the other marines pulled out electric swords, very long and very lethal. They could not cut through solid steel or carbon, but tissue was another matter. They were perfect for dealing with Wolverines in close quarters.

Logs and mud burst out of the mound flying in all directions. One of the marines grunted when a log smashed into him, but he cast it away shattering the wood with his fist. Out of the hole came a weevil, a big one. Four meters long and three wide with huge wood carving teeth long as a man's arm. It gave a deep growl and searched around for food walking near its nest. Though it was blind, its sense of smell might as well have been for a guided missile system. It ran for the Sergeant who was closest to the animal. She didn't have time to pull her sword so 'Lucky Lucy' shot it at point blank range. Blood flew from the monster and it stopped for a second in confusion. Another roar came from its mouth but was short-lived as one of the other women chopped off its head with her sword. More blood and gruel came out of the stump, but the animal was dead.

Sevn had fallen on his rump and had seen the whole thing. Had he been alone up here, the monster would now be dining on him down in its lair. He was shaking very badly but he shouted, "Check for cubs or pups or whatever you want to call them. They will be in there!"

The Marines looked at him confused at first but decided the Doctor might be right. One pulled out a smoke grenade and tossed it into the hole. A small thump and smoke began to come out. And then two smaller versions of their mother but as large as lions ran out and tried to eat the people in front of them. They were dispatched without incident by the marines.

"What the hell was that?" They all laughed. Sevn just shook his head, what was wrong with these people? Is it adrenaline?

The Sergeant pointed at two of the riflemen, "Go down that hole and find out what we've got to deal with. Be careful." They jumped in the hole like it was a holiday slide.

She walked over to Sevn who was nervously munching on the pie she had given him earlier. Squatting next to him she put her arm on his shaking shoulder. "You are quite the capable man, Dr. Odibossi! Did the scope pick it up or did you have a hunch?"

He looked up to her, "It reminded me of a beaver's lodge back on Earth That's where they give birth to their children." The Sergeant was from Mary's Ring, so she had never seen a beaver much less its nest. "They're that big?"

Sevn shook his head. "No but they build much in the same way, sticks, logs, mud and such." He stood up and looked back towards the hole the two marines were coming out of. "Nothing but bones and rotting meat down there, Sarge. Pretty big nest though."

"Sergeant, you'll find this is the entrance to an underground base of some sort. The weevil found the ramp leading down to the door or whatever they have and decided to build here."

She looked at him intently, "How could you know that?"

Sevn shrugged again, "Just a hunch."

20

Sana had managed to get all her lipstick off Bale this time. They arrived back at the commander's Mess and had breakfast. Captain Verkon had Sana sitting on his right with Sub-Captain Jeerish sitting on his left. The opposite side held Bale, the commander and Lt. Commander Bayer across from Sana.

The meal had been a success but embarrassing for Sana, she had to have seconds on everything. The captain watched as she put away all her food. "I'm sorry Sir, it's just that I haven't had anything to eat after the surgery."

Everyone chuckled, "Captain Verkon, augmentation puts many demands on the body for the change." He watched Lt. Bayer and listened with intensity. "How do these...Nanos(?) work."

Denise smiled; it was a question entering into propriety information which the Empire was not likely to share with anyone. And unless you were a PHD in microbiological engineering, it was unlikely you would understand the math anyway. "Captain, essentially these are microscopic machines, robots if you will that enter the bloodstream and do amazing things for whatever purpose the body needs. In Lt. Abbicon's situation, she needed to be able to manage Terran style controls and the gee forces that come with operating one of our ships. Also, we wanted her to be able to walk on our worlds and ships without discomfort."

The stewards removed their plates and coffee was served. The captain marveled at the taste but still preferred his hot spice drink aboard the Explorer.

Verkon turned to Lt. Abbicon, "You feel no discomfort, no illness?"

She shook her head. "Certainly I am sore but I was warned to expect that, Sir."

Looking at the commander the captain asked the obvious, "Would it be possible for you to convert all of our people?" The commander smiled and the captain shared the smile knowing full well the answer. "Our resources are limited but the main reason is the difference between our two cultures. We are all human here but if you were to sail your ocean and discover another people on a distant land, though human, they might have a different religion than yours, cultural mores and of course even a separation of technology. We have discovered five other human races out here since we left Earth 104 years ago. Some have been...difficult. Add to that some alien species that do not entirely accept Terran colonization near their space, well you can imagine our resources are stretched as is."

The captain nodded and fully understood. His world would soon be destroyed by their star. The Teknomen had raped the entire planet and their moons and asteroids to build the ships they would need to escape the impending doom of their world. And even with all that, over three billion people would remain to witness the event. "I understand Commander, it was just wishful thinking on my part."

Barnes wished he could give the captain a string of hope but at this time, the plan to save their people remained on Earth. He would be notified eventually.

Sana listened respectfully but occasionally stole a glance at Bale but he was occupied with a stirring conversation with Sub-Captain Jeerish. She looked down at her cup and realized that she did not want any more coffee. Sana was tired and wanted to go to bed even though it was still morning on the AGAMEMNON III. More than anything, she wanted Bale to hold her while she slept. *Be safe...be safe!* Sana could still hear her mother's voice even after all these years. She sighed and hoped that Bale would keep her safe.

Denise watched the young woman across from her. She was concerned that the girl was a bit over-emotional, maybe that was a trait of their people. Or perhaps Sana was still coping with Terran culture, a Terran man and being turned into a Terran. Obviously, that was more than anyone could expect of a person. But then Denise remembered a particularly difficult exercise on the simulators, a fight sequence that required split-second responses to a three-dimensional battle in space against a fictional Wolverine fleet.

Sana had run through the exercise just three times and came out victorious on the last. That was unheard of with a recruit! But then, Lt. Abbicon had more experience than any recruit. She had been in space as a fighter jock for over three years before she joined the colony ship. Sana was an Ace in her world! She always left the simulator exuberant though sweaty. Her instructors just scratched their heads.

Denise watched as Sana kept trying to get Lt. Jackson's attention. Perhaps she could do something about that. After a lull in the conversation between the two masters, Lt. Commander Bayer jumped in. "Commander, I've just been pinged by Navajo Base Two. They might have discovered an Enki Temple or storage facility on Beta Three. It's underground so we didn't pick it up in our first survey." All four men blinked. *Enki? Here?*

"Lt. Bayer, do we have someone on the ground looking at this base?"

"Yes, Sir and they have asked for a linguist to be transported to the spot right away. Apparently, there are a great many hieroglyphs to be interpreted. Corporal Dr. Ito will join them, but she is familiar only with current cuneiform symbols." Denise turned to Sana, "I believe you are more qualified to read any of the ancient Enki script. Am I wrong Lt. Abbicon?"

What did she want from Sana? Sure, an Enki base in this system demanded immediate attention but it had to be old. Sana had been reading Enki cuneiform all her life, everyone on her world did. It was used in their language. "Yes Sir, I am an expert in Enki cuneiform, it's not as rich as English but yes, I've used it every day."

"Very well. Commander, I request that Lt. Abbicon join Corporal Ito on the surface of Beta Three. I want them to look at this site as it is uncovered to aid the engineers I'll send along to open the base." Barnes nodded and thought that was a good idea...and he had to smile. What a sneaky woman Denise was!

Captain Verkon reached down to his satchel and investigated it a bit. He then pulled out a book, a tattered thing he had kept from his academic days. "You'll need this too, Lt. Abbicon. It is an old recovery of very ancient Enki text. It should help you and Dr. Ito. And I would like it back, if possible. I've had it for years." He smiled at her as Sana reverently held the book. "Thank you, Sir," she whispered.

"Um, Lt. Bayer? Aren't you forgetting something?" the commander asked. Denise pretended confusion, "No Sir, what do you mean?"

The captain hid his smile behind his hand and coughed a little as the commander continued, "The lieutenant needs her escort, isn't that so?"

Sana's head snapped over to Bale and his eyes stared at her, they were locked!

"Ah yes, Commander. I had completely forgotten your agreement with the captain of the Explorer. My apologies Captain Verkon, I was lapse in my duties." The captain waved her off and smiled behind his hand. He need not have bothered; the young Marine and his Lieutenant couldn't see the world except for each other. "If I can be so bold, would you chaperone these two to their posts?"

Denise nodded to the captain, rose and saluted him in Terran fashion. "Commander, if I may be excused?"

"Of course, Lieutenant Commander Bayer. Take good care of your wards and get them to the surface immediately!"

She turned to Lt. Jackson. "Lt. Jackson." She had to wait a second, "LIEUTENANT JACKSON!" The man finally noticed the sub-commander. He jerked out of his seat and saluted. "You will come with me and Lt. Abbicon to the wardroom and then to the gate. You are going to the Enki base with the lieutenant!"

Sana rose out of her seat and saluted her Captain and then the commander. Bale saluted the commander and the captain then followed Sana and the Lt. Commander out of the room.

Captain Verkon looked at Commander Barnes and started

laughing. Both men slapped the table and spilled water. "I thought I was going to go blind with that laser between those two!"

Commander Barnes wiped the laughing tears from his eyes, "God, that look would strip paint from a bulkhead!"

"With Love of course!" Both men fell into more laughter.

Sub-Captain Jeerish just sat in his seat watching the two men and wondered what had just happened.

21

Lt. Bayer stood near the entrance inside the officer's wardroom. Bale was on one side of a set of lockers and was putting on his suit. Sana was just over the wall on the female side doing the same. Both wanted to talk to each other very badly but with the lieutenant watching their every move, that was not going to happen. Sana's new larger suit had been manufactured during her surgery.

Sana was familiar with her armor now as she had to wear it during the simulations. Though lightweight and comfortable like her day uniform, it had its own shield. Bale was still getting used to his suit. He had worn it outside a few times and worked out in the armored gym, but it needed tucking in some places. His suit though was very flexible and heavily armored. He was a Point man so he would be the first to go into a difficult situation regardless of his rank. The suit carried multiple layers of shielding and a stasis field if needed. His insignia was stamped on the suit as Third Lieutenant, but it also included his cards and the gold hammer as well...fully augmented!

Sana walked around the corner and saw Bale standing there in his black and dark blue trimmed suit. He looked massive and deadly. She smiled at him. Bale looked at the newer and improved woman of his dreams in her gray and rose-colored suit with neon blue details. Her insignia was as 1st Lieutenant and was stamped onto her suit as well. Though she had no ground force experience for directing troops, technically she would be in charge on the surface. They stared at each other without saying a word.

Lt. Bayer looked back and forth at both lieutenants and rolled her eyes. "Yes, you are both very pretty. Now let's get your weapons!"

Sana was given a small but deadly energy pistol and a field

knife, "I don't want you to hurt yourself or anyone else." Sana smirked at her and holstered her weapons. Bale took a bit more time. Lt. Commander Bayer pulled Sana back, "We need to be careful here." Sana just watched and was amazed.

One combination pulse and sniper rifle, another general-purpose energy rifle, one energy pistol along with its companion Browning .45, an energy sword, an energy machete', various grenades and other devices that Sana could not identify but Bale knew each of them intimately. Another power pack was strapped to his back under the weapons nano-attached to his suit. Bale could walk into an explosion of significant force and all his weapons would be still on his suit even if he were dead. He put an additional knife in his calf holster then he dropped to the floor, did a few pushups, stood and rolled his shoulders. Bayer waited patiently and held onto Sana's arm as they both watched the man. Denise knew not to get in the way of a killing machine adjusting his weapons of war.

The Marines were trained strenuously to know their bodies and their weapons. If aliens or pirates waited on the other side of the reinforced door, it would require tremendous explosions for them to get in. Bale would just run through the armored door and kill anything outside of it.

Bale turned to her, "Ready Sir." Sana was stunned at the amount of gear Bale had put on his body, but he seemed to take it in stride. That he carried an additional 200 kilos of suit, armor and weapons did not bother him at all. She carried an additional 50 kilos and was not aware of it, nobody bothered to inform her of that fact. Her new body just did not notice any difference.

"Right, children. We are running a bit late, the engineers and Dr. Ito are waiting. And before we go, let's keep the fraternizing to a dull roar, shall we? I don't want you two to give the troops more than the usual gossip." She winked at them. Bale wondered was it that obvious? Sana knew they had been caught and she was embarrassed. But to be with Bale even if she outranked him was fine with her!

Sevn watched as the Marines pulled long metal rods from

a ruck sack one of them had carried. They snapped the poles together and built a large rigid frame five meters long by four meters high. As they stood the frame vertical, other riflemen attached guide wires to keep it standing up. What was this thing?

The wind was picking up and the sky was darkening as the storm approached. Two of the riflemen lit up their suits for everyone to see what was going on. They could work in the dark of course with their night-vision but something complicated like this needed all the light they could get.

Sevn walked over to the Sergeant, "What is that?" She looked down at him. "Ever see a portable gate? Well, now you have. More men, material and a plow are coming to help with the debris down that hole." Sevn was impressed. He had heard of portable gates before but had never seen one as it was entirely a military option only.

More of the marines were removing some of the heavier pieces from the mud pile. They would take their swords, cut up the logs and toss the chunks aside. Other riflemen knelt by the frame and attached a small power kernel to its leads. With a small control panel on top, one turned it on. The frame instantly shone with a light of its own and the gate formed.

Sevn smiled, he would get home that way and not have to deal with all this anymore. He would rather be pulling weeds from now on.

Lt. Bayer walked into the loading dock. There was already a large gate operating and waiting for the additional troops, the engineers, equipment and the loader/plow. The machine would remove all the mud with its shovel and tracked wheels. It was a small unit remotely controlled by one of the Sergeants.

"Attend 'Chut!" one of the non-coms shouted. Everyone in the room stopped what they were doing and saluted the lieutenant Commander. "At ease gentlemen. When will the gates be synchronized?" she asked the technician in the 'gate' house. "About two minutes, Sir!"

Sana saw Karen Ito and walked over to her friend. The Linguistic Doctor looked up to her and saluted. Sana smiled, "Don't give me that." She pulled her into a hug.

"Wow, now I can look up to *You!*" They both laughed at that. "Love your suit!" Sana laughed and turned around while Karen admired the look.

Two of the newer recruits brought on this mission barely knew anyone other than their commanding Sergeant. They 'clicked' to a private channel. "Who is the cupcake with the Lieut's pin? Damn! What a looker!" The other man nodded and pinged back, "Yep, she is that. But look over there at the punk in the Darth Vader suit. Who invited that shrimp to this party? Is it Halloween already?" They both laughed as they looked at Bale. He was a full head shorter than any of the other riflemen in the room though he was equally and powerfully built yet he had weapons that neither of the young recruits had ever seen.

Sergeant Cage was there as a staff for the departure. Though he was in fatigues, he was still a menacing figure. His headset caught the exchange. He casually walked over and looked at the recruits. They immediately stood straighter. Cage had a reputation as a tough trainer for the men plus he held a Master Sergeant's pip and a gold hammer for Point man...he was fully augmented.

"I caught a little of that." He paused for effect. "You might want to curb your enthusiasm for the lieutenant and marshal some respect instead."

"Yes Sir!" both men said. Cage then pinged Bale to let him in on the conversation. Bale was startled at first, but he did not move and did not look around as he recognized Nick Daniels' voice.

"As to the man behind the lieutenant, you'd best notice his insignia." Confused, both men magnified their vision and looked at Bale's chest. There was the Third Lieutenant pip but below it was a small gold hammer stamped into the suit, the man was fully augmented too! Below that was a small set of two cards overlapping each other, a pair of threes.

"Lieutenant Jackson got his cards while still a jarhead like you two but keep in mind, he has four years of experience before he became an officer elect." Both men were getting nervous. "You also need to know he is also a Taijutsu third level master and a Sword Master fifth level. He got his cards the hard way by close quarters contact with a Wolf. You can only get those cards by hand-to-hand combat...he ripped a wolf apart vertically."

Both men were now worried, they had practiced with robot versions of Wolverines but had never actually met one. Here were two men, the Master Sergeant next to them and the shorter man across the room. The Master Sergeant had several cards on his chest along with his insignia.

"Ya know," Sergeant Daniels continued musing wildly. "We have a tradition as Point men that when an officer or Sergeant gets his hammer, there is an initiation we all have to go through to be part of the club." The club actually existed but was for wounded and decommissioned Point Men. There were not a lot of members, most did not get to retire. "Among some of the silly rituals there is one that is vital. A man, with his shields turned off stands in front of a 20 mm Howitzer and takes a shell at point blank range." Totally untrue but these kids did not know that! "Once he gets up then he must disable the canon. Usually we just bend it." Another lie for the pipe was too strong even for a fully augmented riflemen...they might crimp it a little, but it was just easier to pick it up, tear off a few pieces and turn it on its side. "If he can't get to the tube to break it, then he has to cut it off with his sword." That was true, a Gold Hammer's swords could cut through steel! Regular swords could not, this was not taught at boot camp.

"So gentlemen, I would be a little wary around Lt. Jackson. He may only be a Third Lieutenant right now, but he *will* be a Commander one day. Vader would piss his drawers if he met Lt. Jackson in a dark alley." Cage clicked Bale out of the conversation. Bale took his cue and slowly turned his head and glared at the two young men standing next to Master Sergeant Daniels. Their eyes got wide! He then turned slowly back to Sana and Karen talking, ignoring the two marines.

"Oh, and a word to the wise," Cage continued. "1st Lt.

Abbicon is Lt. Jackson's boy-toy and he's rather territorial about it." Cage smiled and walked away. Both men shut up and minded their own business concerning the two officers. It was obvious that the Third Lieutenant could use all his weapons at once and still kill barehanded.

Though Bale wanted to laugh, he kept his face straight. **Hope you enjoyed that, lol!** Cage texted him.

Lt. Bayer heard the whole thing and did laugh. Cage, you are such a bullshitter!

"Lieutenant Commander, both gates are synced!", okay, down to business.

"Lieutenant Abbicon, take the troops through and good luck!"

Sana saluted her and walked into the water wall with Bale close behind.

22

Rain was beginning to pepper the ground that had been cleared when 1st Lieutenant Abbicon and her crew came through the gate. The loader/plow immediately rolled over to the mud pile with its attendant and began removing the dirt. Sergeant 'Lucky Lucy' met with the lieutenant and saluted her. "Your orders, Sir!" Sana sauntered over to the mess with all in tow. Bale and quite a few others noticed that the lieutenant had quite a walk, something on the order of Deaammmnn! "It's your show Sergeant, I'm just here to read a few glyphs with Dr. Ito." 'Lucy' looked over the shorter woman and wondered. Other than exceptional looks, there was definitely an officer in there, an experienced one!

Sana turned and looked at the man in black behind her. "Third Lieutenant Jackson, I will stay here with the Sergeant and Dr. Ito. Would you attend the men and make sure that ramp is cleared?" Bale saluted and she bounded over to the pile. He looked around and yelled at the other Marines and civilians then he walked over to a small boulder about his height, picked it up and tossed it into the nearby forest destroying a couple of trees as it rolled along.

Karen leaned into Sana, "Does he do windows too?" She giggled. Sana frowned. "I can't even get him to rumple the sheets. No one will leave us alone!"

'Lucy' was stunned! This man belonged to her? Sana, knowing full well the Sergeant heard that looked up to her, "Yes, we are a couple, but we are thoroughly compromised. I am an officer of the Flight Corps and he is a rifleman about to become a 1st Lieutenant, eventually. He is a Marine through and through. Bale is sweet and gentle, but he is also..." At that moment, all three women watched as Lt. Jackson pulled a 20-meter tree trunk out of the muck and tossed it aside like a stick. "...kinda strong. I'm thankful for my augmentation." She turned to look at both women and smiled. "I'm gonna need it!"

The Sergeant felt honored to be in their group, this ladies gossip Algonquin. "Sir, you will be fine. I have tangled with a Point before as a normal, I had to have a safe word. But you are augmented. It'll be alright." That she was becoming friends with these women proved their fellowship in the patriarchy of their military. That the lieutenant, a colony woman and another human felt the same meant a lot to her. 'Lucy' did a fist bump with the Lieut' and smiled.

Bale stopped and got a notice from upstairs; he viewed the readouts from the satellite. Something was coming and there were a bunch of them. He ran over to the women. "There is a group of bipedal animals heading this way up near the path. They are quite large. We need to get all the civilians down into the ramp now, Sir!" Sana trusted him completely. She turned to the Sergeant, "Assign your men as you would, Sergeant. Doctor Ito will go with Lt. Jackson into the hole."

'Lucky Lucy' smiled knowing what was coming.

"1st Lieutenant Abbicon, I will not leave you out here! Our Commander would not allow it! You will come with me even if I have to truss you up to get you there!" He then picked up Sana and Dr. Ito, put them on his shoulders and ran to the ramp. The Sergeant could see Sana grinning the whole while, Dr. Ito was not so happy.

The Sergeant yelled, "Squad one, hit the trees to the East. Squad Two, to the West. The rest of you cover the entrance to the base!"

Bale put both women down and turned to look up the ramp. The civilians and the two officers were behind him. He pulled his sword and the machete'. Both glowed a deep purple and steamed in the falling rain. Bale yelled at the three riflemen covering the ramp. "Don't bother with head shots, take out their legs! Helmets up!"

There was a burbling roar from an animal then Sana could hear shots ring out in the night. Bale tensed then jumped straight up into the storm. Sana pushed everyone back, pulled her pistol and toggled it to its highest setting. A large reptilian head dropped down on the ramp, its teeth still clamping for something, its owner not knowing it was dead. Another reptile passed over the ramp walls leaving its entrails all over the ramp and Bale too as he dropped back down to the floor. Bale flexed his muscles, and a brief but bright flash came from his suit...all the gore was gone as his suit steamed in the rain.

A large tail swept the three Marines at the entrance to the ramp. They screamed and disappeared. Bale was about to charge the monster when three shots shredded its head. There was a lot of screaming and shouts bouncing between the walls of the ramp, rife shots were flashing all over the place.

Bale turned and looked at Sana, "Protect the civilians! Don't move out of this ramp, I'll be right back!" Then he jumped into the fight.

Nick was watching the firefight. He did not have his suit, but he always carried his sword. "Get me down there NOW!"

The gate keeper shouted, "I can't! That gate is closed but the one on the heavy hauler is open!"

"Good enough!"

The gate operator barely managed to flip the keys when the Sergeant went in the gate.

Bale ran through a forest of reptilian legs cutting as he went. Large bodies dropped around him. The animals screamed at him as their legs were cut off. One managed to snag his sword arm but Bale cut its head in half with his machete'. Men were yelling all around him. Several bullets ricocheted off his shields as the men were killing the monsters on this paddock. Bale jumped into the air heading to a man that was being eaten by one of the beasts. He cut up another dinosaur and landed near the man. He shoved his sword into the monster's eye and pulled it out through the top of its skull. Bale then pulled its jaws apart and yanked the rifleman out of mouth. "Are you okay?" he shouted. The man nodded, his shield protected him but he had lost his weapons. "Then get a move on, Mister. Kill something!" The recruit would never criticize the officer again who had just saved his life.

Bale heard a thump behind him and turned to see Master

Sergeant Daniels coming up from a crouch in the broken stone. Cage had jumped from the heavy hauler thirty meters to the battle below. "Come to get some new cards?" Bale grinned at him. "You betcha'!" Cage answered.

Cage turned into the battle and started cutting up animals. Bale saw three of the dinosaurs running to the ramp. He put up his sword and machete', pulled out his rifle and killed all three. He could hear Sana screaming and her gun was continuing to fire at something down in the ramp, flashes of light bouncing off the walls. He jumped to the ramp and saw Sana shooting an animal that was gnawing on her left arm. She kept firing her gun into its head not realizing the thing was dead. Her shield saved the arm, but it was clearly broken. Karen pulled Sana into her lap and held her. "I've got her. Finish off the rest, Bale!" Sana had passed out from the pain. Karen handed her gun to Sevn. "Guard us!" Sevn had never fired a gun before but he stood point and looked up at Bale. "Shoot them in the face!" and Bale jumped back into the fight.

Some of the riflemen had jumped down from the trees and were doing a cleanup of the remaining reptiles. Cage had a rip on his arm and was about to dispatch another lizard. Bale shouted, "Hold! I need two alive! Hobble them!"

The dinosaur turned with the sound of Bale's voice. One of the Marines pulled out a zip line from his suit, attached a weight and whipped it about the monster's legs. It fell to the ground and screamed. Another screamed from the other side of the paddock, it was on the ground too. None of the other animals were alive.

Cage limped over to Bale, "What are you thinking, Sir?"

"We've got a queen below us. Those dinos didn't come for dinner, they were driven." Bale pulled out his long rifle and rotated the barrels to heavy ordinance. He fired three shots randomly into the trees below him. "I'm going to flush her out. When I give the word, kill them." Cage nodded and pointed to the guards over the two animals. He made a slashing move across his neck but kept his palm open.

Bale fired two more rounds further into the forest. Trees began to burn even in the rain. There was only one path down the trail and if the queen were smart, she would follow it.

He knelt and rotated the barrels of the gun, the sniper came into view. He uncocked the gun and captured the spent shell. Bale then pulled out a blue shell and inserted it into the gun. "Now!"

Cage closed his fist and both dinosaurs died. A scream was heard below them.

"There she goes," Cage said. He could see the reptile run down the path, the road.

Bale adjusted his calipers on the rifle. *C'mon baby, just one more turn.*

The animal looked behind itself every time it swung its head. It was fully a kilometer downslope, but Bale was ready. He had to gauge the timing. Bale saved his breath and waited. She turned her head to the right when he pulled the trigger. The queen turned to her left as the bullet entered her skull. The explosion from the bullet blew off the front half of the creature. Cage caught the entire video, "Good shot, Lieutenant!" Bale stood, folded his gun and placed it on his back. He looked at Cage, "We need to get the wounded out of here now, the civilians too. Bring the hauler down!" Cage saluted him and started yelling at the men. "You heard the lieutenant, get to it!"

23

Tracy held Sana's hand as she cried. "I can't let him see me like this!" she whimpered.

"Sana, he has been out there for two days. He took special leave just to be with you. You have to let him in!" Dan walked into the hospital room. He kissed his wife and started taking off his pants. "Dan!"

"Be still, Tracy! Young lady, you're about to get a new arm in a couple of days so it's time to grow up!" Dan still had his boxers on. He perched on Sana's bed and propped up his right leg. "See that? Can you see where the cut was on my leg? Of course you can't!" He then hit his leg as hard as he could. "Yeah, I felt that! You will not even know it was missing after they attach the new arm. And it is made from your DNA! So get over this nonsense and let the boy in. He's losing his mind out there!"

Tracy rolled her eyes, "Dan. Get your pants back on and get out!"

He grumbled about women and left the room.

"Honey, do you really believe Bale would think any different of you?"

Sana wished she could use her left arm, but the stump was strapped to the bed. "I don't know!" she wailed.

"Let him in, then you'll know." Tracy held Sana's good hand and kissed it. "Sweetheart, that man loves you! In our culture, this sort of thing is fixable...we are used to it. I know you do not have experience with this sort of injury but in our world, though rare for such damage, we do not even think about it. Honey, you will be fine, and Bale will not care one wit. He really wants to be with you! Please, let him in!"

Bale was sitting in the waiting room down the hall from

Sana. He stared at his hands folded in front of him. Cage sat next to him, “C'mon buddy, you know she will be all right.” Bale looked at his friend and mentor.

“I don't get this. Why won't she let me see her?”

“Dude, their technology is different than ours. We lose an arm, no big deal. They lose one, it is permanent. She is just lacking a little faith.”

Bale shrugged, “I just want to hold her, help her through this. It's not an easy thing to go through even with our tech.”

The gate near the elevator pinged and the captain of the Explorer and the commander walked into the room. Cage and Bale both stood and saluted the two men.

“At ease, gentlemen. The captain wants to visit with the lieutenant. I understand she is having a little trouble with her arm.”

The captain walked over to Bale, “Have you seen her yet?”

“No sir, she won't let me into her room. Please sir, anything you can do to convince her...” Bale stumbled, his words catching in his throat.

“Don't worry son, I'll take care of it.” He turned to the commander and smiled then he walked down the hall.

Verkon knocked on the door to Sana's room then walked in. Tracy stood and saluted him. Sana tried to sit up and salute him too, but he waved her down. “Don't hurt yourself lieutenant.” He turned to Tracy, “Thank you for being here with my officer but we need to talk in private. Please scoot.” Tracy smiled at the captain, “Yes Sir! Sana is also my friend!” She squeezed Sana's hand and left the room.

Sana pulled the sheet up over her cupped stump and tears ran down her cheeks.

“Stop that!” the captain said. “I understand they have a new arm for you in two days. The Terrans have technology we do not have. Soldier up, Mister!” Sana did not know what to do. She turned her head away and cried quietly.

“I have three daughters and their children I will never see again. I lost my wife and son to an automobile accident. You have lost your brothers, your mother and father. With the Terrans, you might get to see your brothers again and maybe I will get to see my children and grandchildren too. But that is in the future. Right now, you are getting a new arm."

Verkon walked over to Sana's bed. "Child, the Master of this ship lost three men and a woman to those monsters. You saved fourteen civilians because you stood your post! So you lost an arm and it's going to be replaced...better than losing fourteen souls!"

He reached down and held Sana's hand. "I had to spank my children to get them to mind me and their mother. I am spanking you now because you are not being the officer I thought I had. Don't make me put you back in hibernation."

Sana's eyes grew, "Please Sir, I'll do what you want, just tell me!"

"First off, I want you to quit whining about your wing. They tell me that you will not notice a difference after the surgery. Next, I'm concerned about your mental health."

Sana looked up to him, "Sir?"

"I am responsible for everyone's physical and mental health on my ship. Right now, you are performing poorly." He smiled at her. "There is a young man pining for you outside this door. You need him and he needs you, get to it young lady!"

"But what if..."

"Nonsense! If he does not hug you then be done with him! Otherwise, let the man in!"

The captain walked out of the hospital room and approached the commander. He looked over at Bale. "Does this young man have good character?"

Commander Barnes looked at Bale. "Second Lieutenant Jackson is exemplary in all his actions and stewardship of his position on this ship. I would not have promoted him were he not so, Captain."

He turned to Bale. "Young man, I'm going to put the same faith in you as does your Commander. Down the hall is one of my officers. She apparently has some faith in you too. I expect you to treat her with respect. Do you understand me, Mister?"

"Yes Sir! Do I have your leave?"

Verkon waved him off and Bale ran to Sana's room.

Jeffry laughed and Verkon winked at him, "That was too easy. Children! What are we going to do with them?"

Verkon chuckled too. "Spank them, kiss them when they get hurt and hope they give us grandkids...just so long as they don't move back home." Commander Barnes leaned over and laughed some more. "Amen!"

Bale gently knocked on her door.

"Come in."

He opened the door and looked in. Sana was sitting up in her bed and looking at him. He could barely walk into the room. "May I see you?"

"Yes." She was looking down at her lap then Sana looked up at Bale. She had a sheet over her left arm. "Bale, I'm hurt. Please forgive me..."

Bale did not care. He rushed to Sana, pulled her to him and kissed her! She fell into the embrace. Why did she make him wait so long? Sana now realized she needed him.

"I've missed you so much! I was so worried. Please don't ever shut me out." He kissed her again. They put their two heads together. Sana breathed on him, "Am I still your baby girl?" He cupped her chin, "Always!"

"Then hold me as I sleep. I've not had much lately, and I wanted you to hold me." Sana looked up to his eyes. "Hold me now. You are the only one I trust. Let me sleep in your arms."

Bale took off his shoes and laid down beside Sana. He pulled her in close as she laid her damaged arm on this chest. He said, "To sleep, perchance to dream."

"That's sweet." Sana smiled.

"You wouldn't like the first part. It is from one of our poets, Shakespeare. He wrote a lot of neat stuff."

"I don't care. You said it for me, that's enough." Sana snuggled into his arms and fell asleep.

24

Sevn was not too happy to be back down to this planet, especially away from his base. After his last experience, they really needed bigger fences! The loader had removed the bodies. Most of the animals were the size of ostriches but a few were bigger, on the order of a T-Rex. How had one small queen bullied all these creatures? And more important, why did she do that?

The loader was finishing up the work on the ramp. Sevn looked around and saw at least forty marines milling about, some were helping with the cleanup. At least they had more men this time to guard the place!

It was a bright morning four days after the attack. Drones were ranging all over the forest watching for any new threat. No more predators would get within a few kilometers of the base without them knowing! Bale was speaking with Master Sergeant Gantry who made an appearance to check fortifications. He would not lose any more men on his watch!

Bale nodded to him and walked over to the newly repaired gate. It pinged and Sana walked through with both arms. She looked around and studied the area. When she saw Bale waiting on her, Sana smiled. He saluted her, "Well look who made it back to the party? I guess you get your purple heart now."

"What's that?" she asked.

"An award for being wounded in battle and serving with distinction. You earned it!"

Sana gently grabbed her new arm. "I feel like a fool, I made such a fuss over nothing. I cannot tell it was ever hurt.

"Don't sweat it Lieutenant, we all get hurt one time or another...comes with the job."

She looked up at him in his black suit, "Do you have a purple heart?"

Bale nodded. “Fourteen or fifteen. I keep them in a little box in my room.”

“You’ve been wounded that many times?” She was shocked!

They walked over to Dr. Ito who was already in the ramp area. She turned and spotted Sana, “There’s my assistant. Feeling better?”

Sana grumbled, “I’m not your assistant.”

Dr. Ito laughed. “I’m just kidding. They gave me rank but I don’t pay much attention to that, or anyone else’s either.” She winked at Sana.

“So what have we got here? A temple or a storage locker.”

Dr. Ito frowned, “I’m not sure. Look at these symbols and tell me what you think. The door is definitely locked though.”

There were frescos lining both walls leading down to the door of the ramp. These resembled plenty of Sumerian and Byzantine images on Earth near all their Temples and city gates. But these carvings were different in content if not style. There were the usual gardens of plants and trees but like nothing on Earth, more like the ones found on this planet. The animals were quite different as well, most were your usual group of working animals along with ducks and birds but there were plenty of dinosaurs in all the images. There were cuneiform stamps all over the walls but they were so badly eroded they could not be read.

Sana and Dr. Ito walked down the ramp to an obvious door, Bale followed. Upon it were many cuneiform glyphs with a central figure carved into the door. What was interesting about the figure was it was a man in profile with the cross-impression of an Incan warrior and an Egyptian God. He was holding a cup to a carving of a small woman reaching for it. On the cup is clearly a glyph, just one symbol.

Dr. Ito turned to Sana, “Pretty, huh?” Sana walked closer to the door and read the symbols.

‘Enter to the Garden’...no, that’s not right, um Dr. Ito?” She moved over and shined a light on the pictogram. Ito traced her finger and knocked some dust and clay off the glyph. “Oh, it’s an old variant of ‘Lamp or Lantern’. I wish I had a better understanding of the older texts.

Sana reached into a thigh pocket and pulled out the captain's book. She searched through the pages until she found the glyph. "Lampus which does look like 'Garden and Lamp' but I don't know what that means."

Dr. Ito turned to look at the book and saw that it was filled with old text with modern definitions under each one. "Oh my God! Where did you get that?"

"The captain of the Explorer gave it to me for this project." She handed it over to Ito. The woman turned pages as fast as she could. "Do you think the captain would allow us to copy this? This is the most comprehensive dictionary of ancient Enki I've ever seen!" Sana smiled, "Sure but he'll want it back."

They stood back and looked at the entire figure again. The man in the image was riding a chariot with what looked like four horses. Sana wiped dust from the cup he was holding. She paused and stood back putting her hand to her mouth. Ito looked at Sana as she saw the woman had turned white as a sheet. "What? Are you alright?"

"What's wrong?" Bale asked.

Sana whispered something. "I couldn't hear you, honey. What did you say?"

Sana turned to her and Bale, "I said 'Helios'. He is the Sun God."

"I thought Ra was the Sun God." Karen said.

Bale stared at the figurine. "And let me guess, those are the four horses of the Apocalypse."

Lt. Commander Bayer was getting reports from Beta Three and Beta Four. Everything was looking good and there were no more casualties. She was ashamed that part of the team sent down to investigate the road had been killed. How could they have known some animals would attack the alien base? And why did they?

Denise read about some more roads scattered around the planet but like this base, the paths seemed to lead nowhere. There would be other underground structures near those roads but for now, they would concentrate on the one they found. Beta Four had no such structures or if any, the roads had broken up centuries before from natural erosion from the constant heat and cold...ice was a terrible thing for stone.

She promised herself and the others they would all be more careful in the future.

Bale focused his radar through the door. It was almost two meters thick! How were they going to open that? Sana walked back up to the door with a little trepidation. “How long do you think this has been here?” Sevn had been standing behind them and heard her. “Lieutenant, I’m not trained in archeology, but the trees around here are generations old. If I had to estimate, that base is several thousand years old...I’m just guessing of course.” Sergeant ‘Lucky Lucy’ looked down at the little man. *‘What an ingenious man you are!’*

Bale looked around the edges. The door was easily several meters wide and tall...it was a *big* door. “Ideas anyone? Bomb? Laser? A really big crowbar?”

Sana smiled, “It’s easy. We had one like this on our world in a museum, you just do this.” She turned, pushed the glyph on the cup. “Sana, No!” Bale yelled. She ignored him, the button pulled out and she rotated it 180 degrees and pushed it back in. “Helmets up!”

Sana stood back as a lot of sounds came from the door and inside the mountain. Then a huge puff of dust flew out of the frame and the door slid back. It took a while.

Nothing bad happened. Bale looked down at her and frowned at her. “We’ve really got to work on your Chain of Command skills.” She smiled up at him, “But Sir, I outrank you.”

At that moment, several honks came out of the forest below them, some were far away but could still be heard in the distance. It sounded like the distance was closing.

“Movement! We’ve got lots of movement heading this way!” the lieutenant in the hauler screamed over everyone’s headset.

Sergeant ‘Lucy’ yelled, “Not this time! Everyone in the

door! Grab equipment, weapons and the gate. Get inside now!!" As she ran by a frightened Lt. Abbicon she said, "I hope you know how to close this thing!"

Everyone ran around and gathered equipment, material and ran to the immense opening. Two men yanked the gate out of the ground, collapsed it and ran inside with its parts. The bellowing coming up the road was getting louder, and a vibration was felt in the ground around them.

Gantry yelled back up to the flyer. "What do you see?" A moment passed and they could hear heavy breathing. "They're the vegetarians. But they are a lot bigger than the other day and they look mad!"

Gantry told him to pull in the drones and rise to a higher altitude. The hauler flew up several hundred meters and waited. Gantry ran to the door with the last of the men.

Sana waited until all were inside, ran to another glyph along the wall of the door frame. She repeated the secret button affair like on the front of the door and it began to close...just as the men could see what was coming up to the platform. Huge lumbering beasts, more than four times the size of the reptiles that attacked them the other day.

The door was almost closed when one of the beasts found the ramp. It ducked its head and charged the closing door. Just as the last of the light faded from inside the base, the animal slammed into the stone portal. Inside, they heard and felt nothing at all. *Damn big door* thought Bale! No wonder they built these bases underground. The local fauna would tear everything up!

Master Sergeant Gantry yelled out, "Sergeant Danos, get your men to set up a perimeter. Lieutenant Jackson, get the engineers to set up some lights and do a preliminary radar and microwave reading of the space! Move it people!"

One out of three marines turned on their suit lights, the rest relied on night vision. Equipment was unpacked as Bale directed the engineers. In front of them was a huge, stepped ramp leading down into darkness. Bale pulled up his helmet and smelled the air. It was clean. He pinged the Sergeant, *Lucy, we've got clean air in here so there might be something other than us enjoying it.* She pinged him back,

Copy.

He looked up as one of the engineers pulled out four lights and tossed them into the air. They fanned out and switched on. The Entire space lit up, not brightly but enough that they could see the entire room...it was massive in dimension. The troops switched off their suit lights. Above them stretched a ceiling not much higher than they were on the platform near the door. It stepped up three tiers before it flattened and covered a space about as large as a playing field. In front of them were steps leading down into a dusky darkness where the floor could barely be seen. Huge columns rose from the ground and supported multiple levels and eventually the roof above. Though they were somewhat gothic in style, the serpentine nature of the columns was like nothing from Earth. No human had built this place.

As elegant as the room appeared it was in ruins. Several of the lower platforms had collapsed leaving open doorways along a blank wall. The steps leading down into the lower chamber were cracked in many places, but the entire staircase seemed solid. Though earthquakes were not common on Beta Three, it did not mean one had not destroyed this structure sometime in the deep past. Bale had no idea how safe the structure was but other than occasional mummers from the men and their footsteps, there was not a sound in the place. Maybe everything had settled inside.

Sana was about to touch some of the cuneiforms near her when Gantry came over to her. “Stop that right now, lieutenant!” She pulled her hand back and looked up to the massive man towering over her. He did not look happy.

“Come with me, young lady.” Gantry turned and walked along the platform away from the men and stood behind one of the massive columns. Sana stood in front of him and waited. Whatever was going to happen would not be good. She had screwed up...again.

Gantry folded his arms in front of him and looked down on the woman. “When we left Earth and went out into deep space, we had no idea what we would run into. Imagine our surprise when one of the first aliens we met was human. But there were others, and they were not so friendly. Our technology was superior, the emperor had seen to that! But we had little experience fighting in space, much less other creatures that wanted our tech. Then we ran into the Wolverines a few years later. We beat them but at a dear cost. Many men and ships died because of our ignorance. We lost an entire colony to them as well.

We have since corrected that mistake. We do not parley with anyone that wants to fight us, eat us or kill our people just because we don't look like them. Earth separates itself from their petty squabbles over resources, land or food. We accomplish this through extreme discipline...something you sadly lack."

Gantry reached down and picked Sana up by her suit collar and brought her face to face with him, her feet well off the floor. "You will not link Terrans in a chain for your foolish glory! We will not follow you into a hole for your death. We have worked too hard in this galaxy to give it up to the likes of you!

He dropped her to the ground. Sana grunted with pain and fear. He squatted next to her and was still taller by far. "Your Captain Verkon and our Commander Barnes reached an agreement prior to you coming to the surface of Beta Three and I'm about to enact it now...2nd Lieutenant Abbicon." She had been demoted. Sana felt so ashamed. "When one of my officers or noncoms or even a civilian tells you to stop, YOU WILL FUCKING STOP!! Am I clear, Lieutenant?" Sana ducked her head and nodded. "I can't hear you!"

"Yes Sir!"

"Good. 2nd Lieutenant Jackson will remain with you as your escort, but you are now subordinate to him. Dismissed!"

Though legally a Master Sergeant was subordinate to a Lieutenant, he or she had many years of experience more than the junior officer...they had to LISTEN when a Master Sergeant spoke!

Sana turned around and walked back into the main group. She walked up to Bale. "What are your orders sir."

25

Captain Verkon walked into the commander's office. Though he appreciated the suit he wore to keep him from collapsing on the one gravity floor, it was still inconvenient. Commander Barnes rose from his desk and saluted Verkon, the captain did outrank him after a fashion. Barnes then extended his arm, and they shook hands.

"I hope you don't mind but I requested Sub-Captain Jeerish to provide my Chef with some of your Hot Spice drink for your enjoyment. I've not tried it yet but I'm willing to." The captain smiled at his hospitality despite the reason for this meeting. The commander poured for them both and gave Verkon a cup." They both took a sip and Verkon was pleased to see it was prepared exactly right. He looked up at the commander and saw a frown on his face. "Interesting. It is certainly bold!"

The captain laughed, "I'm sure it's something you have to grow up with."

Barnes pointed to a pair of heavy chairs nearby. The captain sat down and placed his drink on a nearby table. "So my officer lost a bit of decorum, is that so Commander?"

"Yes Sir. She disobeyed a direct order to not complete an action that endangered the entire team on the planet." Verkon's eyes got very wide.

Barnes held up his hand, "Not to worry, no one was hurt but they could have been without fast action from my other officers."

"Sir, I apologize most deeply! Have her sent back to me and I will return her to hibernation. You will have no more trouble with Lt. Abbicon!"

"It is more than that. I have enacted our agreement. She is now a 2nd Lieutenant and will be watched most closely. Lt. Abbicon will receive additional training with our people in our form of discipline." He leaned back, "I don't want you to misunderstand but we still find her an exceptional officer especially when she held her ground during the reptile attack. I would expect nothing less from any of my men. But now we need to," he paused and frowned "reign in her enthusiasm a bit.

When we went into space, our technology was above par compared to other species but our tactical did not yet exist. We lost many men those first few years. It was a hard lesson to learn. So our mission statement in our training regimen is extreme discipline. Our troops are trained together to work as a team, in any environment, on any world and in space. Lt. Abbicon has none of those skills. She has not learned to coordinate with our flight officers, yet. That will change! Plus she will have ground force experience drummed into her until it comes out her ears. It's a difficult process but we will get it done."

He looked at the captain, "In short, we want to keep her, with your permission of course."

"You say she will be watched and trained, by who if you don't mind my asking?"

Commander Barnes smiled. "By her escort of course, 2nd Lieutenant Jackson. He is afterall still her protection. Others will help too with Lt. Jackson's support but now she will be subordinate to him."

Verkon laughed long and hard. "That should make for a new and interesting change in their relationship." Verkon shook his head, "In our culture, it is appropriate for all women to be subordinate to their men and other authority figures. I understand that in your culture women are afforded opportunities like being a doctor or an officer leading men but in our world, Lt. Abbicon would never rise above a troop carrier pilot. She is exceptional so it was a rare thing for a woman, for Lt. Abbicon to receive such a promotion as a fighter pilot."

Commander Barnes rose out of his chair and shook Verkon's hand again. "Then you don't mind if your lieutenant gets more training?"

"Certainly not Commander, you'll just be giving me back a

better officer!"

The men parted ways and the commander smiled after him. Yep, Lt. Jackson might find his hands full now! "Steward!" A young man walked in and took the commander's coffee cup. "Pour this crap out and bring me a decent cup of coffee."

Bale was now in charge though fortunately he had the assistance of the Master Sergeant and Sergeant Konos to fill in the blanks. He directed men to search every room they could find and to secure them. Bale pinged the heavy hauler above them. "Lieutenant Wilson, can you read me?" Static came over the line but then a broken voice got through, "Say...you're...up. Rep...you're breaking...!"

"Damnit! Ensign Javis, we need a hole straight up for an antenna." The man pulled out his radar and looked at the ceiling. Near a column at the back of the room was a thinner section of the ceiling. "There's only about 30 meters above us there. I can drill through it!"

"Lucy, get all the men back to the landing platform. Engineering is going to drill a hole for an antenna." She made motions and the men on the lower floor and platforms either jumped up to the next level or flew up to the door's platform. "All set, Sir!" She saluted him. "Get to it Javis!"

The man flew over with his suit carrying a half meter disk. He punched a few buttons on the device, it then floated slowly up to the ceiling and attached itself there. He flew back and punched another button on his arm. The device lit up and started spinning fiercely. Then it rose into the roof of the space and disappeared. The whine of the drill could still be heard in the chamber but faded as it rose higher into the rock above. Once it had cleared the surface, it fell back down the hole and flew over to the engineer.

Then Javis and another engineer picked up a meter squared device and flew up to the hole, bolted it to the ceiling and turned it on. Inside a four-centimeter rod began extruding up the channel to the air above. Once out of the hole it rose another ten meters and stopped. It was nano made and nano protected, not even lightning could hurt it.

Javis turned on the Lan and looked at Bale. "Lieutenant Wilson, can you read me now?"

"Five by five, Sir! You are clear!"

"Prepare a drone to go through your gate, I'll control it from here." Bale turn back to Javis, "I need a two-man gate set up and matched to the hauler's gate."

At that time, Sana walked up and saluted Lt. Jackson. He had caught part of the conversation with the Master Sergeant, pretty much everyone in the room did. "What are your orders, Sir?"

"Just a moment, Lieutenant." She watched Bale and wondered if they were through as friends.

"Coming through!" As the two-man gate shimmering on the floor of the chamber, a drone flew into the room and stopped in midair. "Javis, reverse the gate to the Agamemnon, please."

He talked to the gate master on the Agamemnon, got a good ping and sent the drone back through the gate. "We've got it, Sir!"

Bale then turned to Sana. "Lieutenant, you will continue to assist Dr. Ito in interpreting these glyphs. I will expect a report in two hours. When you write your report, you will tell me what you know. I do not want an opinion. If you do not know then put that in your report too. Dismissed!"

Sana walked over to where Dr. Ito stood at part of a wall near an entrance to an empty room. She was photographing the pictograms with her tablet. Sana did not smile but asked, "How can I help?"

Ito looked at her with a prim mouth, she was angry! And then she whispered to Sana, "Look bitch! I have got a granddaughter back on Earth I have not seen in three months. I was hoping to go back on the supply ship but now I am stuck in this tomb with you! And quit crying, you do that too much!"

Sana sniffed quietly and nodded her head again. *"I'm sorry!"*

Ito turned away from her, "Look at these glyphs and tell me what you see."

She looked up at the little cuneiforms, "It's just an office for someone. And this is not a tomb, it's a staging base."

Dr. Ito whipped around. "How can you know that?"

"Well this glyph gives the room number, the officer's name and a button to open the door." As there was no door there, the button was pointless. "Damnit girl! I meant the other thing...staging or something. What a minute. Lieutenant!" Ito yelled out. Bale heard her and ran over. He was not especially fond of being near Sana again.

"Lt. Abbicon tells me this is a staging base or something." Bale looked down at her. "Well, Lieutenant?"

Master Sergeant Gantry walked over and listened. Sana sniffed again, "We had these all over Teknoman. The Enki masters used them for storage of seed, food and weapons. Below us will be several large chambers with any of that or nothing in them. But there might still be ships there. I don't know." She looked up at Bale, "The hieroglyphs inside the door gave the reason for the base, it's purpose and I could read them. They're like the ones at home...*Sir*." She whispered. Sana looked down again.

Master Sergeant Gantry looked at Bale and then around the room, "I'll be damned!"

26

Sana was running through a rough course built on Beta Four and the cold was searing her lungs. Bale was ahead of her and did not mind the cold at all. The other men and women were keeping pace with him but were having a difficult time of it. They all had been running over the course, through snowbanks, over cold and broken rocks and around the few scrub trees in the area for over ten hours.

It was two months since they had found her and then the Explorer. Her mother ship was on its way with the new engine and would be in Palisade in just under three months at TL 4. Everyone on board the Explorer was happy even if it was only a few people, the rest were still in hibernation.

Bale stopped ahead and called a halt. “Build your camps here. We’ll have food tonight!” That was good for none of them had eaten in two days except for crackers and the occasional power bar.

Sana dropped her load and began helping everyone put up their tents.

Bale turned to the two Master Sergeants with him. “Gentlemen, I don’t recall anything about tents. Did I mention that in the brief yesterday?” Both men grinned, “No Sir!”

“Parkas and change your socks,” he ordered!

Fires were built instead, and the recruits got to warm themselves on the hill with strong winds coming up the mountain. It would be a long night but they would get food!

An hour later as the temperature had dropped below -7 degrees Celsius, a hover flew over and dropped a package just outside of the camp. One of the sergeants walked over and picked it up. “MREs, two for each of you.” Everyone groaned but tore into the packages as if they were their last meals.

Once she and Dr. Ito had finished all the pictograms in the base, Sana had been transferred back to the AGAMEMNON III for intensive training with some new recruits, 20 of them fresh from Earth. She could not be known to be an officer. That she had never had any formal training on ground force deployment surprised them, but Sana kept up. She was even becoming something of a star in that she never gave up and helped the other members of her troop to keep going on. Sana had already saved a couple that just wanted to quit. They were all augmented to different degrees, but she was still the shortest of the bunch but made up for it with stamina.

Dr. Ito got to go back to Earth on the return shuttle. She and Sana had finally made up...Sana was going to miss her. The latest news was that AGAMEMNON was coming to Palisade to look over the situation. They had a plan for the new colonists, but no one knew what it was.

Bale would not talk to her either. Sana could not be sure if he was still mad at her or if it was his status as lead officer for the new recruits.

A week later, all the recruits were sworn in as enlisted men serving the emperor. Sana made new friends and renewed some old ones, mainly in the flight corps where she would begin coordinated flight training in about two weeks. She was on Leave.

Dan and Tracy Reynolds threw her a party for her official entry into the Marines. Sana even got her 2nd Lieutenant bars back. She was happy but missed Bale a great deal. She had seen him every day for eight weeks but had not spoken to him privately in all that time.

"You haven't even talked to him, like in private or anything?" Tracy asked.

"What a prick!" Dan bellowed. "Shss...the kids are asleep." Dan was getting drunk while watching a football game on the vid. "Hey! I was yelling at the quarterback, but Bale is being a douche too!"

"Don't worry, I'll put him to bed in a couple of minutes." She jumped up and ran over to catch his beer before it fell on the floor. The man was already asleep when his team won the game.

Sana smiled. “Thank you for being my friend.” Tracy reached over and hugged her. “You want, I’ll call him and setup a blind date with you.”

Sana shook her head, “Thanks but no, I’ve got to work this out by myself. I better go. Thanks again for the party!”

She transferred over a couple of gates within the huge ship on her way home when Sana decided she wanted an apple. Sana walked through the mall and found the small forest with some apple trees right outside. She picked one, found a bench nearby and sat down. As she munched on her apple, Sana could see several couples going in and out of nearby restaurants and some going into a theater for the late-night movie. She and Bale had attended one, a romantic kind of story but she still did not get it. The female lead was too bossy, but her boyfriend finally got her love. Tears started rolling down her cheeks as she ate the apple. What was she going to do about Bale? He promised to be with her!

“You know, you have to save the seeds. It’s a ship rule.”

Sana turned to look behind her and Bale was standing there. She dropped the apple and waited. He smiled and sat down beside her. Bale bent down and picked up the fruit and put it in his pocket. “If this apple didn’t fill you up then we can go to dinner...Officer’s privilege.” He smiled again then leaned into her.

Sana pulled back, “You just can’t go around and start kissing strange officers.”

Bale smiled again, “Yep, you’re about as strange as they come.” He pulled her in and kissed her.

Sana lost her mind, wrapped her arms around Bale and kissed him back. Bale pulled back and wiped her eyes then kissed her again.

After a long moment she asked, “Does your place come with room service?”

“Nope but that hotel right over there does.” He pointed at the Special Visitors Hilton.

Sana smiled. “Goodie!”

Javis was down in the bowels of the Enki base. Once the entrance to the underground bunkers was discovered a team went down and found the entire place empty. There were scraps of seed in several storage lockers, but they were incredibly old, thousands of years old. The base had been empty a long time.

Some of the engineers thought it might be interesting to trace the internal wiring of the place before they left the ruins behind. “Reed, try x-201 next.” He got a ping back and attached a pair of leads to the exposed metal in one of the walls. The Enki did not have outlets or electrostatic transfers like on an Earth ship but rather vertical power strips throughout the structure. The Engineers mapped all they could, but they were running out of time to test them all, the place was just too big!

Javis had a small hand-held kernel in his hand and fired a shot through the cables. Nothing ever happened. Reed pinged back he did not get a signal.

“Mr. Javis, hurry up in there! It is getting dark out here and the hauler is loaded. Move your ass!” The officer upstairs was not the usual lot, a little too impatient. “Okay, just one more. Reed, let’s try y-391 this time.” Reed pinged back that he was ready.

Javis held down the trigger and fired a low voltage shot across the cables. This time there was a spark. Huh? That had never happened before. He reversed the polarity and fired another round. This time the room glowed. The current had gone through but to where?

“Reed? Did you see that?” The lights coming from the walls flickered then died out. Should he try that again at a higher amperage? Just as he dialed up the juice a noise came from deep inside the base, something heavy was winding up to speed. The lights on the walls flickered again then stayed on and got brighter.

“Javis! You better get up here, something is happening!”

He grabbed his tools and ran from the room. Everywhere there was light, and the vibration underground was gaining strength! Javis thought it sounded like a generator. As he reached the main floor of the chamber, he could see Reed waving at him from the entrance's platform. "Hurry, the door is closing!"

Javis cut in his jets and flew upwards. He and Reed barely made it out the door before it shut.

"What did you do in there?" The lieutenant ran over and stopped before the two men. On the walls outside the ramp, several panels had lit up and shone brightly on the floor. "Get in the hauler now!" They did not need any encouragement. They jumped on board just as the hauler took off.

Looking back down they saw that the entire complex was lighting up, some through nearby trees and further up the mountain.

27

"I only count 12 scars," said Sana as she watched Bale pull on his pants, "where are the rest?"

"Inside where they belong." He turned to her, bent down and kissed her then he slapped her bottom. "C'mon, get dressed. You may be on Leave, but I have got to report for duty in three hours. I'm hungry and I have to get breakfast!" He pulled on his shirt as Sana danced into the shower. Bale looked around the room for his boots. Clothes were everywhere, empty food plates on a rolling table, two empty wine bottles and the sheets were definitely rumpled. *'What a fun night!'*

Ten minutes later, Bale was still looking for his socks when Sana came out of the bathroom. She was fully dressed, makeup and her hair except for her shoes. He looked at her stunned, "How did you do that?"

She sauntered over, picked up her boots and socks, found his as well and threw them at Bale. "Well, ya see I had this really mean Lieutenant that wouldn't let me sleep in during boot so I figured how to get dressed fast so I wouldn't have any mess duty." She grinned at him and he smiled back as he put on his boots. They finished with their jackets then Sana folded into his arms. She looked up to him, "I promise, I won't FUBAR another situation again."

"We've apologized to each other enough. I love you but now let's eat!" They ran out of the room as Bale paid the bill and pinged the door 'Vacant'. They were still laughing when they entered the lobby but stopped immediately. There was Lt. Commander Bayer standing there with two military police. They saluted her and stayed at attention. She walked around them both nodding at the incredible health of these kids. Bale was ramrod straight as usual but so was Lt. Abbicon. Sana looked a little lean but was also clearly on the bounce! Denise liked that!

She turned to the two men, “That will be all, thank you for your help.” They saluted her and left the Hotel lobby. “At ease, gentlemen.” Bale and Sana lowered their arms and waited. Were they in trouble? Sana was worried!

“Well, I see you’ve kissed and made up...perhaps more than that, I imagine.” She smiled at them both then approached Sana. Sana went back to attention and stared straight ahead. “This man I trust. He has proven himself in battle many times and does not give the commander any trouble. But if you do any of that shit again, I will drive you back to the Explorer and slam you into hibernation myself even if I must fold you into it. Do you understand me, MISTER?”

“Yes Sir!”

“Good, now that we have that out of the way, you both need to get back to the surface. Apparently one of the engineers pushed the wrong button and turned that base on. Since Dr. Ito is on her way back to Earth, that leaves you 2nd Lieutenant Abbicon with the skills to read the glyphs that lit up like a tree at Christmas. Suit up!” With breakfast forgotten they ran to dress in their battle armor. Sana found two power bars in her locker and ate one quickly. She walked around the corner as Bale was putting on the rest of his vestments. “Here, eat this. It’ll hold you until lunch.”

“I doubt it. I got a good workout last night.” He winked at her and shoved the bar, paper and all into his mouth and chewed while he finished. Sana looked at him in shock! He looked back, winked again and swallowed, “Good ruffage in there plus I won’t have wipe later.” Sana blushed but she had heard much worse during boot from her comrades in Pain. The lieutenant was the blunt end of many of the crude jokes, mostly about his childhood.

They got their weapons and marched to the gate house. “What’s the jig, Lieutenant?” Once on duty, she followed his lead as he was now her superior.

“You’ll know when I know, Lieutenant.” Bale looked over and noticed Sana now carried a pulse rifle along with both pistols and her field knife. She looked great! And he knew she was a crack shot with the gun.

"Attend 'chut!" Master Sergeant Cage yelled. Everyone in the room saluted Bale including officer Abbicon. "At ease. Cage, what have we got down there?"

"No people as of yet but a warrior drone went through the two-man gate we left there. It looked around and found no ETs but it did see this." A video played across Bale's eyes. What the hell?

In the middle of the room was a hexagonal tower that rose four meters from the chamber floor. It *was* lit up like a Christmas Tree! Several lights were flashing on most of the glyphs covered by the thing and there were screens about head height for a normal human being on all six sides.

Right now, the drone was pointing to a hall adjacent to the floor chamber. It was not moving but it was armed. Something was coming up the hall but was still out of sight.

"Any ideas Master Sergeant?"

Cage shrugged, "That's what you and I are here for." Bale nodded. He looked at the other men in the room, thirty including Sana. He pointed to two men, "Stay with Lt. Abbicon. Bring her in when you get the all clear."

Cage brought up a shield on his arm and a gun. Bale grinned and pulled out his sword and another pistol. The gate room took on a ghastly purple hue from their swords. "You block and I swing, right?"

"That's the drill, Sir. Ladies first!"

Bale jumped through the field and disappeared, Cage counted two and followed. Sana feared for them both. The other men in the room were afraid too but were ready.

Bale jumped into the room and saw all the lights were on. He moved over and linked up with the drone. Indicators on his HUD said the room was warmer now but still contained fresh air. Cage popped out and linked to the drone too. Down the hall, they could hear a scaping sound with an occasional thud approaching them. Bale sent the drone high over their heads to keep post as Bale looked around the corner. There on the floor was a robot pulling itself to the chamber, but it was so rusted and its joints had mostly failed it was a wonder that it worked at all. It pulled itself along with one clawed hand dragging the rest of its body with it. Bale zoomed in on the target. It was armored and had weapons, or at least did at one time. Most everything seemed to have fallen off, parts of it were strewn along the floor behind it.

"Hold Cage, I'm going to negotiate with it." Bale jumped high and cut off the gun the bot was trying to raise. The gun managed to fire but a weak fizzle came from its nozzle. Some kind of electrical charge, lightning gun perhaps. The gun separated from its body and the robot collapsed on the floor unable to move more than a claw or two. "Sir, there's another one coming from further down. Let me have it!" Bale bowed with his sword and let the Master Sergeant pass. The huge man turned the corner and a bright flash erupted; Cage flew back with his feet still on the floor sliding to the wall behind him. "It's got a little more sizzle to its fizzle," he laughed then he fired his gun to something out of sight. There was a small explosion, but the damage was done. "Clear!" Cage said. "Pull back, I'll send in the drone." Cage holstered his gun and started humming, *send in the clowns*. Bale grinned, "Very funny."

The drone shot around the corner and sped on. Soon they could hear it firing at every single bot coming up from the lower regions. Bale and Cage watched and almost felt pity for the little things. Most did not even make it past their nests in a hidden wall. The drone shot them all, even the lockers that had not opened. The bot pinged back *Clear*. It came back and rose to its post position guarding the two men.

Bale and Cage ranged around the chamber floor and up to the platforms. They returned to the floor and circled the hexagonal tower near them. "Got any ideas, Sir?" Bale shrugged, "Looks like a welcome center to me." He could not know that at that time, he was right...but on a galactic scale. "Sergeant, send them in. Hold on the lieutenant."

Everyone upstairs had seen the whole thing on their displays. The little robots got some laughs until one fired at the Master Sergeant. They all admired the man for the zeal he gave to his work but to take a blast like that on purpose and laugh about it?

"First squad enter now. Second squad enter in thirty seconds. The lieutenant stays put until the all clear." After the men were sorted out, Cage sent eight men down the right-hand corridor to see if there were any robots there. A few minutes later they could hear shots bounce around up the hall, but the short squad was laughing over their headsets. Cage held Bale back, "Bale, this is their first time on an alien planet...most of the men. Let them have a little fun."

"Sure thing Cage but when one of the real things show up, I don't want to see any tears."

An hour later, the all clear was made. Sana came down with the two riflemen with her. They parted and went to the Sergeant for orders. Bale walked over. Sana though excited to see a working Enki device kept her face in check. She touched nothing and consulted her tablet as there was one thing that needed doing. She turned to Bale. "Sir, I have found the security links to this base. There are more robots the base is trying to activate but none of the others are responding yet. I would like your permission to turn them off." Bale nodded at her new professionalism. "Carry on, Lieutenant."

Sana walked up to the machine and found the icons she needed. She verified they were the ones controlling the security. 'Measure twice, cut once' she had heard one of the Staff Sergeant's say during her training. She checked again and was satisfied. She reached up and pushed two buttons in sequence. Nothing seemed to happen, but her tablet confirmed the base was not going to attack anyone again inside the base.

Then her eyes grew wide. "Sir, we may have another problem." Bale listened hoping that Sana had not made another mistake. "When I shut down the robots and other security auxiliaries, a signal was shut off too. It was going off-planet! It must have come on when the rest of the base was activated by the engineers."

He looked at her, "Standard procedure lieutenant. If I had a base that was overrun by unknowns, I would let home base know too. But Homebase does not exist anymore, does it?" Bale said matter-of-factly.

Sana looked at him, "But a Wolverine base is nearby, 12 light years out. Might that count?"

Bale paused and thought some more. "Lieutenant Abbicon, you are just a fount of information."

28

Lieutenant Rose Parks on the LEXINGTON and Lieutenant Nathan Parks on the BELMONT both caught the ships behind them with their sensors. Both ships immediately went to stealth mode and vanished from sight. Captain Verkon on the Explorer caught them too but there was little he could do about the ships. So far, his new sensors declared the three ships were moving much slower than the Explorer but they were still only a light year behind them.

"Rose? Do you think they saw us," her husband asked? Parks studied her instruments and called back, "I don't think so. I have got no TL scan activity from any of them, but they are coming. Perhaps they are out of range."

Nathan rode the heavier ship, and it was loaded with multiple weapons and shielding. Even in stealth mode, the ship was dangerous. "Gate the AGAMEMNON III and inform the commander. I'll hit the Explorer's six, you unload your passengers. Have them set up a gate in the passenger compartment near one of the locks. I will send my people over then. Belmont Out!"

Parks pursed her lips, "You heard the lieutenant, call the AGAMEMNON III. Get me a direct line to the commander, now!"

The Lexington drifted over to an airlock on the colony ship. Parks met the Sergeant in charge of her men. Eleven Marines saluted her and she saluted back...she did not know if she would ever see them again. "Sergeant, we've got three Wolverine ships trying to close with us. So far we are out-running them but that could change. You are the rotation defense, but the others will have to stay as well. Take all your equipment with you and any food stuffs you need, even from us for an extended stay. Inform the Master Sergeant to build a gate near this airlock inside the ship. He will take charge once you and the other team from the Belmont are on board. We will stay on point and provide any intel we can get to him. Protect that ship!"

Lucky Lucy saluted her, "We're on the bounce, Sir!"

The Enki ship was about to slip ahead of its two allies when it received a call from the planet ahead. There was a base there! And it had been breached! That was unforgivable!

They searched kiloyear-old records and could find nothing about a base on this planet. That did not mean it did not have one just that their data was old and fragmented. The signal was pure Enki though, so they decided to fly onto the planet and secure the base from intruders. They would disable the colony ship as they went by. The Enki informed their partners of the new plan and ramped up their speed.

Bale materialized from the gate to the bridge, saluted the flag and ran over to the commander. "Sir, one of the three ships is apparently Enki. We don't know if it's an old ship used by the Wolverines or if possible," Bale swallowed, "they might be back."

Commander Barnes rolled his eyes. This whole mission should have been a cakewalk even with a possible Wolverine base nearby. The AGAMEMNON III could destroy it easily, but he had to stay here to coordinate ships and crew. Palisade was beginning to be a hotbed of trouble. Barnes would not contact his Admiral yet but the time was coming near.

The commander held up one finger and Bale grew still. "You were saying, Lieutenant Parks?"

Parks was one of his best new flight officers. She did not falter under pressure. Nathan was no different and he had trained her personally, they were a good team on and off the ship. Barnes had to smile at that, they were very much like Lieutenant Jackson and the colony girl Lieutenant Abbicon. Fraternization was originally forbidden between officers and non-coms but was discarded decades ago. Everyone knew it happened so why worry? If they were professional while serving the emperor, they could let their hair down after hours...or clothes, whatever. These two had eventually married.

"All the Marines are in the Explorer. Master Sergeant Davidson has assigned duties inside and outside the ship. The Belmont is riding Point on the Explorer's six. We are 10,000 kilometers off her bow. TL at 4.0. So far, we've received no pings from the vessel, but they know we are here."

"Connect me with Master Sergeant Davidson, please lieutenant."

"Yes Sir. Connecting...Oh shit!"

Lieutenant Parks while on a ship heavily armored was also filled with significant long-range sensors. She saw the Enki ship push ahead at TL 7.8...no species other than human had that kind of speed!

"Sir, one of the ships just jumped to TL 7.8! It will be here in," she paused and looked at a screen one of her crew pointed to. "47 minutes. We are powering up. I will send the information to the Belmont and to Master Sergeant Davidson. Lexington Out!"

Barnes turned to Lieutenant Commander Bayer's station. Denise said, "I've got the relay and three more ships leaving Palisade in two minutes. They will arrive at the Explorer in twenty-five minutes at TL 12. They will back up the Belmont and the Lexington. I have brought online 50 more Marines. They will decant in 42 minutes. Weapons are hot on all the platforms. I've directed each base on-planet to go to black stasis until either you or the AGAMEMNON arrives to relieve them."

Denise looked at Jeff and breathed heavily. Barnes grinned, she was at her best when Denise was scared but then the rattle did bother her. "Very good, Lt. Commander. Meet me in my office once you get everyone settled." Bale just stood and waited.

Barnes read Lt. Jackson's report. The ping on a base or something out beyond Beta Seven bothered him. Depending on how the engagement with the Enki ship near the Explorer worked out, he was about to put the AGAMEMNON III to battle stations. Barnes opened one of his screens and dialed the admiral on the AGAMEMNON in route to Palisade. They were two weeks out but maybe they could hurry a bit.

A moment later Admiral Kai Nakamura appeared. Commander Barnes bowed briefly, "Sir, thank you for answering. We have a situation developing right now."

The admiral was tall for a man of Asian descent and though his hair was dark, there were streaks of gray in it, all well-earned. He had taken command of the AGAMEMNON after Admiral Hobart committed suicide. Hobart had overseen destroying a Wolverine colony world in retribution for the destruction of Orthos. Though Admiral Hobart had asked for the assignment, he could not stand a life without his wife and children all of whom had been on Orthos when it was attacked. After the Wolverine colony was destroyed, he killed himself.

The effect was not missed by the emperor. From that day forward, all military personnel with lost loved ones from Orthos were subject to therapy where necessary and were generally watched by supervisors. Lieutenant Jackson was one of the rare success stories from that debacle. There had been several suicides like Admiral Hobart, but most carried on.

Admiral Nakamura frowned, "What's going on, Jeff?"

A knock on the door and Lt. Commander Bayer and Lt. Jackson walked in. They waited patiently as the commander continued his conversation with the admiral.

"The Explorer has been retrofitted and is proceeding on to Palisade at TL 4. A few minutes ago, three Wolverine ships appeared a lightyear to her stern. Though they are traveling at TL 3.4, one just jumped to TL 7.8. I just sent three more ships to aid the two escorts at the Explorer. They should arrive in about 15 minutes before the other ship reaches the Explorer. Sir, it's possible the faster ship is

Enki."

Nakamura blinked in surprise. "And you suspect this because..."

The commander turned to Bale and motioned him forward. "Here is Second Lieutenant Jackson. He will explain as he was the officer at the base on Beta Three."

Bale swallowed and saluted the admiral. He went on to explain the discovery of the base, that some engineers had accidentally turned it on even after 12,000 years and a beam or signal had gone out from the base, a warning of some sort. Of the three ships trailing the Explorer, only one responded. The theory by their scientists was that it was an Enki ship. They would know more during its flyby of the Explorer.

The admiral questioned the lieutenant further then turned to Commander Barnes, "You've taken appropriate precautions, I assume?" Barnes nodded, "Yes Sir."

"Very well. I will leave AGAMEMNON II with the tugs." The commander smiled. "Yes, Jeff, we're going to build a ring for the Teknoman race. The emperor ordered it and by the way, His Majesty is on board. I will give you details about the ring later.

The AGAMEMNON and the AGAMEMNON I will proceed at best speed to Palisade. We will be there in three hours. Hold the fort, Jeff! Nakamura, out!"

The commander saluted one more time then turned to Lt. Commander Bayer, "Lieutenant, I need..."

"Yeah, I know. I'll call Housekeeping to get this place spic-and-spanned." Commander Barnes grinned at her.

"That's a good idea but what I wanted was a ship and crew to take Lieutenants Jackson and Abbicon to that 'ping' out by Beta Seven." He turned to Bale, "Have you burned that impulsive streak out of her yet?" Barnes didn't have to wait for his answer. It was rare that a new Second Lieutenant knew what he was about but with this kid, the commander liked having him at his back.

Bale grinned at the commander. "Yes sir! It took a bit of doing but Lt. Abbicon is on the bounce!"

"Good man! Lt. Commander, who do we have on

reserve?"

Denise consulted her pad, "I've got Manchester, the one the tree doctor saved, Turner and Datsun." Bale smiled at that, he really liked working with Datsun. "The other seven will be recruits from Abbicon's class." She turned to look at Bale. "Do you have a problem with the Master Chief Green being your right arm on this cruise? He has got an itch that cannot be scratched, and I am tired of it. I want him to get out and stretch his legs a bit."

"No Sir! I would be honored to have him with me!"

She looked up to him. "Yeah, well this isn't a bromance. You will be his boss but if you have a question, he is the one to ask. He's got twenty-five years on you kiddo in the emperor's Marines!" Denise slid her tablet in a leg pocket and placed both her hands on her hips. "You better keep track of that girlfriend of yours because if you don't, the Master Chief will! Am I clear, MISTER?"

Bale stood up straight and saluted, "Yes Sir!"

"Scoot." She pointed her thumb at the door. Bale rushed to leave the commander's office.

As soon as the door closed, Barnes started chuckling.

"Denise! You are a real ball-buster!" He sat on the edge of his desk, folded his arms over his chest and continued to laugh.

The three ships appeared where the Explorer should have been. They dropped out of subspace and began scanning for the ship. The Enki finally found it almost a light year away moving at TL 4. This could not have been the same ship! At their current speed, the allies would never reach it but the Enki were intrigued now. They checked their instruments again and found that the colony ship was moving at a constant rate. There was also no residue, a trail to follow. This was new technology indeed!

Had they been detected on an intercept course with the ship? If so, that was more technology to gather. The Enki directed their allies to push on, it would go ahead and disable the ship.

On board the AGAMEMNON III, alarms began to sound!

Once the base had been cleared again and locked up, they grabbed robot samples and transported back to the ship. The samples were sent to the Lab. After debriefing, the commander immediately directed them to Dr. Tamore for further analysis in his labs. Bale and Sana marched down the halls in the science section, all business. Sana knocked on the door to the main lab entrance. “We’re looking for Dr. Tamore, is he about? The commander sent us.” The woman behind the desk directed them down several halls to the main lab.

Sana was still impressed with the size of the AGAMEMNON III and the technology it contained. Also, all the people about and everyone had a different function. Her ship, the Explorer was little different in that everyone also had a different purpose, but the ship was mostly filled with people frozen in hibernation. Colony supplies, animal embryos, artificial wombs, construction material, food and other medical supplies filled the Explorer. It was not a war platform, nor a research vessel and it could only go one speed until recently. Explorer was a fancy but simple transport ship.

They found Dr. Tamore studying various parts of alien robots scattered on a long table. “Fascinating! Would you look at the linkages? How they survived 12,000 years is incredible!” Bale stood behind the Doctor and waited to be noticed. Sana did not say a word but waited too.

“Doctor! Lt. Jackson and Lt. Abbicon are here as ordered by the commander,” Bale said. “Um...” the Doctor turned around and looked up to the two officers. “Ah yes! Sorry, I am consumed by the samples you brought back from the surface. Fascinating! It is little wonder that they fell apart. Their lubricates basically turned to dust...” Bale held up his hand.

“I’m sure that is important to know for the sake of the Federation, but we have another topic to discuss with you. Were you not informed?”

"But you must understand. To find a lubricate that lasts for thousands of years would be a great boon for us!"

Bale sighed dramatically.

"Oh, yes, yes you mean the beacon. I apologize, I do tend to get caught up in new things. Come over here with me." They walked over to a large screen on the wall. The Doctor pushed a couple of icons and a series of graphs appeared. "I analyzed the beam, but I couldn't really find it until I thought of TL or gate communications." Bale's eyes narrowed. "Are you telling me Doctor, they have the same communication tech that we do?"

Doctor Tamore looked up at the tall man. "Why yes!" Then he saw the look on the lieutenant's face. "I mean not exactly. Look at the graphs. It does not have the same frequency as ours. It is not Laser and certainly not microwave but it does jump interdimensional. But the main difference is that their signal requires a great deal of power to send, ours takes little and is capable of more information. They do basically the same thing, but the method is vastly different." He could see that the lieutenant was not satisfied. "Okay, another difference is range. Only about six or seven light years then it fades away. Ours can go on to Earth and beyond and is stable the entire distance. So, in a sense, this was a beacon for help but of a limited range."

Sana and Bale were relieved. The signal was limited and could not reach the possible Wolverine base 12 light years out. Doctor Tamore looked at Sana strangely. "Don't I know you?" Sana smiled at him.

"Doctor, don't you remember? You found me on my wrecked ship. I was the pilot." She smiled prettily at him. His eyes widened, "Yes, yes, you were the young girl we found but..." he paused, "my, how you have grown!" She told him of becoming augmented and joining the emperor's Navy with the consent of her Captain.

"Well my dear, we are sure glad to have you with us. You sure gave me a good scare back on that ship. That anyone could live that long in ancient hibernation tanks is beyond me." Sana frowned at that, but the Doctor meant nothing by it.

That was when the alarms went off.

Bale called in to the bridge. "Lieutenant Jackson here. What's going on?"

"Three ships just appeared a lightyear off the Explorer's stern. They are on the chase at TL 3.4...Wolverines, Sir! The commander needs you on the bridge as soon as you're finished with the Science lab."

Sana turned to Bale. "Sir, with your permission, I would like Dr. Tamore to use his systems to check out a theory I have." Bale stared at her wondering where she was going with this. "Very well Lieutenant."

Sana turned to Tamore, "Do you have a way of tracking that beacon to see if it 'pinged' anyone in the neighborhood?" There was no way that signal would reach anyone much less a Wolverine base 12 lightyears away. It was of a type that was specific to its owners. "I might, I might." He moved another set of icons and traced the wave coming from the beacon." Sana could clearly see four other pings on the surface of Beta Three. "Those must be other bases," she said. The Doctor nodded. "But what about this one?"

Beyond Beta Seven, another ping came back. Was it another base? Then the Doctor grew very still. "Um Sana..."

"Doctor, you will refer to me as Lieutenant or Lieutenant Abbicon while I'm on duty!" Bale smiled at that. Sana was taking all this very seriously, as she should.

"Yes, um...okay, lieutenant. When did you turn the beam off?"

She consulted her tablet and quoted a time reference.

"Apparently, you didn't turn it off soon enough. I just got a ping off a ship heading to Palisade, about two lightyears out."

Bale jumped in. "Doctor, according to our long-range sensors there are three ships heading this way. They are moving at a Wolverine speed of TL 3.4."

Tamore turned to Bale, "But sir, the beam is specific. Only one caught the call." Dr. Tamore got very worried. "The beacon was created by Enki and can only be received by Enki...that's an Enki ship. They are back."

29

Lieutenant Rose Parks on the LEXINGTON and Lieutenant Nathan Parks on the BELMONT both caught the ships behind them with their sensors. Both ships immediately went to stealth mode and vanished from sight. Captain Verkon on the Explorer caught them too but there was little he could do about the ships. So far, his new sensors declared the three ships were moving much slower than the Explorer but they were still only a light year behind them.

"Rose? Do you think they saw us," her husband asked? Parks studied her instruments and called back, "I don't think so. I have got no TL scan activity from any of them, but they are coming. Perhaps they are out of range."

Nathan rode the heavier ship, and it was loaded with multiple weapons and shielding. Even in stealth mode, the ship was dangerous. "Gate the AGAMEMNON III and inform the commander. I'll hit the Explorer's six, you unload your passengers. Have them set up a gate in the passenger compartment near one of the locks. I will send my people over then. Belmont Out!"

Parks pursed her lips, "You heard the lieutenant, call the AGAMEMNON III. Get me a direct line to the commander, now!"

The Lexington drifted over to an airlock on the colony ship. Parks met the Sergeant in charge of her men. Eleven Marines saluted her and she saluted back...she did not know if she would ever see them again. "Sergeant, we've got three Wolverine ships trying to close with us. So far we are out-running them but that could change. You are the rotation defense, but the others will have to stay as well. Take all your equipment with you and any food stuffs you need, even from us for an extended stay. Inform the Master Sergeant to build a gate near this airlock inside the ship. He will take charge once you and the other team from the Belmont are on board. We will stay on point and provide any intel we can get to him. Protect that ship!"

Lucky Lucy saluted her, "We're on the bounce, Sir!"

The Enki ship was about to slip ahead of its two allies when it received a call from the planet ahead. There was a base there! And it had been breached! That was unforgivable!

They searched kiloyear-old records and could find nothing about a base on this planet. That did not mean it did not have one just that their data was old and fragmented. The signal was pure Enki though, so they decided to fly onto the planet and secure the base from intruders. They would disable the colony ship as they went by. The Enki informed their partners of the new plan and ramped up their speed.

Bale materialized from the gate to the bridge, saluted the flag and ran over to the commander. "Sir, one of the three ships is apparently Enki. We don't know if it's an old ship used by the Wolverines or if possible," Bale swallowed, "they might be back."

Commander Barnes rolled his eyes. This whole mission should have been a cakewalk even with a possible Wolverine base nearby. The AGAMEMNON III could destroy it easily, but he had to stay here to coordinate ships and crew. Palisade was beginning to be a hotbed of trouble. Barnes would not contact his Admiral yet but the time was coming near.

The commander held up one finger and Bale grew still. "You were saying, Lieutenant Parks?"

Parks was one of his best new flight officers. She did not falter under pressure. Nathan was no different and he had trained her personally, they were a good team on and off the ship. Barnes had to smile at that, they were very much like Lieutenant Jackson and the colony girl Lieutenant Abbicon.

Fraternization was originally forbidden between officers and non-coms but was discarded decades ago. Everyone knew it happened so why worry? If they were professional while serving the emperor, they could let their hair down after hours...or clothes, whatever. These two had eventually married.

"All the Marines are in the Explorer. Master Sergeant Davidson has assigned duties inside and outside the ship. The Belmont is riding Point on the Explorer's six. We are 10,000 kilometers off her bow. TL at 4.0. So far, we've received no pings from the vessel, but they know we are here."

"Connect me with Master Sergeant Davidson, please lieutenant."

"Yes Sir. Connecting...Oh shit!"

Lieutenant Parks while on a ship heavily armored was also filled with significant long-range sensors. She saw the Enki ship push ahead at TL 7.8...no species other than human had that kind of speed!

"Sir, one of the ships just jumped to TL 7.8! It will be here in," she paused and looked at a screen one of her crew pointed to. "47 minutes. We are powering up. I will send the information to the Belmont and to Master Sergeant Davidson. Lexington Out!"

Barnes turned to Lieutenant Commander Bayer's station. Denise said, "I've got the relay and three more ships leaving Palisade in two minutes. They will arrive at the Explorer in twenty-five minutes at TL 12. They will back up the Belmont and the Lexington. I have brought online 50 more Marines. They will decant in 42 minutes. Weapons are hot on all the platforms. I've directed each base on-planet to go to black stasis until either you or the AGAMEMON arrives to relieve them."

Denise looked at Jeff and breathed heavily. Barnes grinned, she was at her best when Denise was scared but then the rattle did bother her. "Very good, Lt. Commander. Meet me in my office once you get everyone settled." Bale just stood and waited.

Barnes read Lt. Jackson's report. The ping on a base or

something out beyond Beta Seven bothered him. Depending on how the engagement with the Enki ship near the Explorer worked out, he was about to put the AGAMEMNON III to battle stations. Barnes opened one of his screens and dialed the admiral on the AGAMEMNON in route to Palisade. They were two weeks out but maybe they could hurry a bit.

A moment later Admiral Kai Nakamura appeared. Commander Barnes bowed briefly, "Sir, thank you for answering. We have a situation developing right now."

The admiral was tall for a man of Asian descent and though his hair was dark, there were streaks of gray in it, all well-earned. He had taken command of the AGAMEMNON after Admiral Hobart committed suicide. Hobart had overseen destroying a Wolverine colony world in retribution for the destruction of Orthos. Though Admiral Hobart had asked for the assignment, he could not stand a life without his wife and children all of whom had been on Orthos when it was attacked. After the Wolverine colony was destroyed, he killed himself.

The effect was not missed by the emperor. From that day forward, all military personnel with lost loved ones from Orthos were subject to therapy where necessary and were generally watched by supervisors. Lieutenant Jackson was one of the rare success stories from that debacle. There had been several suicides like Admiral Hobart, but most carried on.

Admiral Nakamura frowned, "What's going on, Jeff?"

A knock on the door and Lt. Commander Bayer and Lt. Jackson walked in. They waited patiently as the commander continued his conversation with the admiral.

"The Explorer has been retrofitted and is proceeding on to Palisade at TL 4. A few minutes ago, three Wolverine ships appeared a lightyear to her stern. Though they are traveling at TL 3.4, one just jumped to TL 7.8. I just sent three more ships to aid the two escorts at the Explorer. They should arrive in about 15 minutes before the other ship reaches the Explorer. Sir, it's possible the faster ship is Enki."

Nakamura blinked in surprise. "And you suspect this because..."

The commander turned to Bale and motioned him forward. "Here is Second Lieutenant Jackson. He will explain as he was the officer at the base on Beta Three."

Bale swallowed and saluted the admiral. He went on to explain the discovery of the base, that some engineers had accidentally turned it on even after 12,000 years and a beam or signal had gone out from the base, a warning of some sort. Of the three ships trailing the Explorer, only one responded. The theory by their scientists was that it was an Enki ship. They would know more during its flyby of the Explorer.

The admiral questioned the lieutenant further then turned to Commander Barnes, "You've taken appropriate precautions, I assume?" Barnes nodded, "Yes Sir."

"Very well. I will leave AGAMEMNON II with the tugs." The commander smiled. "Yes, Jeff, we're going to build a ring for the Teknoman race. The emperor ordered it and by the way, His Majesty is on board. I will give you details about the ring later.

The AGAMEMNON and the AGAMEMNON I will proceed at best speed to Palisade. We will be there in three hours. Hold the fort, Jeff! Nakamura, out!"

The commander saluted one more time then turned to Lt. Commander Bayer, "Lieutenant, I need..."

"Yeah, I know. I'll call Housekeeping to get this place spic-and-spanned." Commander Barnes grinned at her.

"That's a good idea but what I wanted was a ship and crew to take Lieutenants Jackson and Abbicon to that 'ping' out by Beta Seven." He turned to Bale, "Have you burned that impulsive streak out of her yet?" Barnes didn't have to wait for his answer. It was rare that a new Second Lieutenant knew what he was about but with this kid, the commander liked having him at his back.

Bale grinned at the commander. "Yes sir! It took a bit of doing but Lt. Abbicon is on the bounce!"

"Good man! Lt. Commander, who do we have on reserve?"

Denise consulted her pad, "I've got Manchester, the one the tree doctor saved, Turner and Datsun." Bale smiled at that, he really liked working with Datsun. "The other seven will be recruits from Abbicon's class." She turned to look at

Bale. “Do you have a problem with the Master Chief Green being your right arm on this cruise? He has got an itch that cannot be scratched, and I am tired of it. I want him to get out and stretch his legs a bit.”

“No Sir! I would be honored to have him with me!”

She looked up to him. “Yeah, well this isn’t a bromance. You will be his boss but if you have a question, he is the one to ask. He’s got twenty-five years on you kiddo in the emperor’s Marines!” Denise slid her tablet in a leg pocket and placed both her hands on her hips. “You better keep track of that girlfriend of yours because if you don’t, the Master Chief will! Am I clear, MISTER?”

Bale stood up straight and saluted, “Yes Sir!”

“Scoot.” She pointed her thumb at the door. Bale rushed to leave the commander’s office.

As soon as the door closed, Barnes started chuckling.

“Denise! You are a real ball-buster!” He sat on the edge of his desk.

30

Lieutenant Commander Bayer walked over to the bar and poured two shots of bourbon. She handed one to the commander, they clinked glasses and drank them down.

"My wife tells me that too."

"You get off just before Thanksgiving, got some plans?"

"Yeah, Robin is already planning for Christmas and it's only June! Damnit Jeff, what am I going to do with fourteen grandkids?"

Though they were good friends he knew not to touch her even though Denise really needed a hug. She had been abused as a child so today Denise had no truck with men. She and Robin had been married for over forty years. Robin was her ground, Denise needed that.

"Crack a beer, take your shoes off and let Robin rub your feet for you. Kimberly does that for me. As to the grandkids, make coo-coo noises and smile a lot. You know you love them."

Denise shook her head. "But one of them is learning the violin. I hope she's gotten better."

Barnes chuckled, "Comes with the territory."

Denise looked up to the tall man, her friend and mentor. "You're really going to kick me off this boat?"

He looked at her and shrugged, "You made the short list. Denise, you are almost over-qualified. Take the THOMAS MORE and sail her for a few years and try to have some fun."

"Jeff, that's a lot of ship plus three auxiliaries! What do I..."

Barnes waved her off, "You'll do fine. I know it and so does the emperor. The admiral backed me on this too. Time to get out of your comfort zone but please, be gentle to your second. Let him or her do their job without you hovering over them."

Lieutenant Commander Bayer walked over to Barnes and wrapped her arms around his waist. He was startled at first then he dropped his arms over her shoulders and returned the hug. He was the first man Denise touched like this in sixty years. Jeff bent down and kissed her hair, "You'll be great, Denise. I have faith in you."

She pulled back and wiped her eyes. "You do know that I will out-rank you if I take over the THOMAS MORE?"

"Grandpa wants me on a short leash. I am good with that because I get to meet and train people like you. Now, get out of here and get my wayward kids moving!"

Denise saluted her Commander, turned and walked out of the room.

Though Bale wanted to run to his apartment he shared with Sana he had to take it slow. He may only weigh 260 lbs. but it was all muscle and augmented too, people would get hurt. When he opened the door, Bale heard laughing and some weird century-old song about Staying Alive. Rounding the corner, he saw two half naked ladies dancing to the song, Tracy and Sana. They pirouetted while holding hands and laughed until they saw Bale standing there. Sana squealed and jumped into his arms. Tracy screamed, grabbed some clothes from the couch and ran to the bathroom. Bale watched her go.

Sana grabbed his chin, "It's my butt you're supposed to look at!" He pulled her up, kissed her girls then found her mouth and kissed that too. "Yeah, me and all the other men on this ship. And when did Thursday become a lesbian holiday?"

Sana squirmed out of his hold, landed on her feet and thumped Bale on his chest. "Tracy brought over some clothes. We are about the same size in the chest, and she thought they were cute. I agree! See this one?" She held up some pink thingy and displayed it over her breasts.

"Well, put that on later. Right now you need to suit up. We've got a mission by the commander."

Sana gave him a hard stare, "Okay, I'll be right back." She

ran to their bedroom as Tracy came out of the bathroom. She was blushing but looked up to Bale.

"If you tell Dan you saw me in my skivvies, I'll mess with your suit!" Bale smiled at her. "If you decide to tell Dan, tell him I'm ready to swap anytime."

"I heard that!" Sana yelled from the bedroom.

Tracy pulled Bale down and kissed him on the cheek. "Honey, I'm too married for that, and Dan would die young even thinking about it, I'd make sure of that. Tah! Later Sana!" She walked out of their apartment.

Sana came out of the bedroom and barely managed to tuck her breasts into her flight suit while zipping it up. She strode over to Bale and slapped him in the face.

Bale grinned while rubbing his face, "Love you too, babe. And by-the-way, you just struck a superior officer."

"We were just having some fun and you don't get to proposition my friend. I will give you lip service when you suit up. But in this house, I rule!"

Bale grinned harder, "C'mere." He pulled her to him and forced her to kiss him. A normal woman probably would have died by the crush of his arms, but Sana was augmented too. She gave in and kissed him back.

"Dan's a lucky guy and yes, she has a nice butt plus Tracy gave him children. I have one woman and you are handful enough. Now be nice." Bale kissed her again.

Sana slid to the floor, "Okay, but no more of that with one of my friends." She went looking for her boots. "So, what's the jig, Sir?"

"You'll know when I do, Lieutenant."

Sana rolled her eyes, "I so hate when you do that!"

Enki ships were quite different than other species' ships and were avoided at all costs by those that had long memories. Other species without that knowledge did not usually enjoy the experience when meeting the Enki. Terran ships were avoided too. It was not a good idea to tick off a super-power.

The Enki ship did not fly so much as roll through space

like a comet with a long tail behind it. In the Enki's case, the tail was a collection of tentacles for propulsion, weapons and grapplers. It was an attack ship by any definition, fully a kilometer long.

As it approached the colony ship it released a squad of boarders to the surface of the fleeing vessel. These were not Wolverines but something much more dangerous. About the size of a man but all teeth and tentacles racing over the ship looking for an entrance, an airlock.

The Enki had discovered this species several thousand years ago and had modified them considerably from their amphibian beginnings. Not especially bright but they took orders well and could eat anything they caught.

The Enki fired a shot at the engines at the rear of the ship. The Explorer did not slow down as expected with its engines destroyed. The Enki were surprised and intrigued. There was a power source but no discernable exhaust to explain its propulsion. How was the huge ship still moving at light speed? Just as it was about to fire at the obvious crew compartment at the front of the vessel a huge blast blew off a third of its tentacles. Two more blasts fired on the Enki ship.

"Take that asshole!" Nathan shouted. "Bring us about! Hornet, Texas and Churchill...fire at will!"

The other three ships fired at the alien vessel shearing off more tentacles. Lieutenant Parks waited for it to get closer. The alien ship fired at the Belmont, the only ship it could see. The Belmont took massive blows to its shields then bubbled up, the ship becoming a giant shiny egg. Parks held her breath, for that to happen, the ship had to be heavily damaged. She turned to her station and brought up several icons and pushed them on. "Sir? What are you doing?" one of the flight officers asked.

"Program a collision course with that ship, now Mister! I have armed everything we've got and set the ship to explode upon impact. We will bubble up shortly. Make it happen people!"

31

Though they could not hear anything inside the passenger compartment, the Marines could tell the aliens were trying to enter the airlock, they could feel it through their boots. Of the 40 monsters dropped from the Enki ship, the five marines outside managed to kill ten of them before they died. Two of the aliens missed the ship entirely and continued to their deaths in deep space. One of the marines managed to send images of the weird looking attackers. They had no suits but were sufficiently armored for vacuum, their air supply was part of their backs under their skin...and they were fast. Their weapons were electrical or lightning devices that could fire a charge without missing the enemy, but they only had three shots. Then they would attack with teeth and tentacles ripping the marines apart.

Davidson called out. "Lucy, place three men outside the hall on the sides and one overhead, swords only. Chop them up! The rest of us will space around the passenger compartment and shoot them. Shields on high! Charlie and Wallace, down to the engine bulkhead and work with the other men there. Everyone get ready!"

Lucky Lucy flew back into the hallway opposite the airlock door. She took two anti-personnel mines and attached them to the door. At that moment, a laser started cutting the door from the outside. The beam grazed her arm and hurt like hell, but her shields saved her. She flew back out of the hall and waited. Once the door was cut open, she pushed a button on her sleeve and the mines exploded. Nothing could be heard in the vacuum of the passenger compartment, but the blast pushed the door out of the ship. Several more of the intruders were shredded by the blast, others were blown off the ship by chunks of the door. The rest came in.

The three marines surrounding the hallway entrance

started cutting up the aliens with their swords. Some lost their heads while the others lost their tentacles. One of the unwounded monsters reached around the doorway, grabbed a marine and threw him across the large space. The man was unharmed but landed on several hibernation capsules crushing them instantly. Other intruders entered the space as the marines opened fire.

Five of the tentacled threats raced for the far end of the passenger compartment, running for the engine. Two were destroyed by the marines but one marine got too close to one of the monsters. It grappled with the man for perhaps two seconds while the man screamed and fired his weapon at point-blank range, then he was ripped apart by the alien. The creature had waited too long and died by other marines. The last two raced for the bulkhead firing their weapons and killing five of the men waiting there. Wallace was the last survivor. He had to defend the engine no matter what!

Lucky Lucy and Davidson flew after the last of the aliens but might show up too late. Wallace pulled his sword and short-sword and prepared himself. Just as the two aliens were about to hit him, he jumped straight at the leader and cut it in half, turned and sliced most of the tentacles off the second as it went by. The thing grabbed him and pulled him close for the kill. They slammed into the metal of the bulkhead and Wallace lost his swords, so he did the next best thing, he grabbed the jaws of the monster and pulled. It took all his strength even with augmentation to pull the jaws off the monster but it died.

Lucy and Davidson arrived and helped Wallace stand up on the metal floor. He was covered in green goo but at least he was alive if a little sore.

They took stock of the survivors. Of the 40 men Master Sergeant Davidson started with, fourteen were dead with three wounded. Worse, the exchange of fire inside the huge passenger compartment resulted in 31 deaths, three of them passenger children.

Davidson looked up at the expanse of the chamber and looked to the open airlock. He hoped things would go better outside with the Enki ship. He knew they would not survive another attack by the intruders.

Lieutenant Parks prepared the ship for collision with the Enki ship. Her instruments noted that the Churchill had not been able to bubble up before being destroyed. The other two ships continued firing at it but the Enki had slowed and was growing more tentacles as it fired upon the other ships. It had not seen the Lexington yet.

"Gentlemen, time to save yourselves. I'll be right behind." The men protested but bubbled up individually, shiny spheres surrounding their bodies with an impregnable shield. They could be dropped into a star and still survive.

She made a couple more adjustments to her ship then Lieutenant Parks took a breath. Just as the alien ship was about to fire on the Explorer, Parks turned off her stealth mode and fired her ship at the Enki. It immediately noted the ship in front of it and tried to turn away, but the Lexington cut inside the Enki's turn and slammed into its shields. The ship erupted in a huge plasma blast, every weapon and both engines ignited at once. The Enki ship was taken apart!

The Belmont came out of its bubble and Nathan could finally see the battlefield surrounding the Explorer as it continued at TL 4 heading to Palisade. Debris from the Churchill could be seen flowing past the receding edge of the Explorer. The Hornet and the Texas were making recovery of the Marines on the vast ship. Nathan could hear chatter and knew that things were not good there. His people were dealing with damage control on the Belmont. Had their shielding not been sufficient, they might have very well ended up like the Churchill.

He turned his sensors ahead to where the Enki ship should already be, but it was gone...along with the Lexington. Nathan would not know for several hours that his wife rammed the Enkie ship with her own.

32

Bale received the report of the disaster at the Explorer. Several good men and women had died there. He knew all the Marines personally and grimaced to hide his grief. He did not know the crewmen on the Churchill, but Sana remembered one, a burgeoning friendship blooming there and now gone forever. She wept quietly. 1st Lt. Collins looked over at her while he flew the heavy transport to Beta Seven. "Table that Mister, I knew them too so save it for when you get home. We've a job to do and no time for that."

Sana sniffed and nodded her head, "Yes Sir."

Bale and Sana had met Lieutenant Collins and the other Marines in the launch bay. There were not many ships left in their hold, only a heavy transport and four scout ships. All were heavily armored, but would it be enough for them if they ran into any trouble at Beta Seven?

The Master Chief walked over to Bale and saluted him. Sana walked over to the crews of the transport and two of the scout ships supporting them. They started talking quietly, the flight crews knowing all the dead on the Churchill. The four members of the Lexington had survived the explosion with the Enki ship because of their bubbles and were being rounded up now.

"How is she doing?"

"Lieutenant Abbicon is doing well."

"That's not what I meant. Their race has never encountered another species before us and now they have had a taste of the real world. We lost a lot of good people there, more than any other recent engagement with the Wolverines. This is going to be difficult for anyone."

Bale sighed and looked down at the deck plate, "Yeah, it

came as a shock to me too. But Sana had a friend on the Churchill. I've seen men die before and tossed back a couple in memory." He looked back up to the Master Chief. "It's the only way to do a good send-off."

The chief nodded knowing full well what the young man meant, having tossed a few for lost friends himself over the years.

Lieutenants Collins and Abbicon walked back over as the flight crews entered their ships.

"Sir, what is the situation?"

Bale told the Master Chief about the signal that came out of the base on Beta Three that got this whole mess started. The man had read the reports as any Chief would, but he did not know about the 'Ping' off something beyond Beta Seven.

"We're going there to inspect it. The AGAMEMNON will not arrive for another 15 minutes and will still require time to meet with the commander. It will then send support craft to follow us. We do not know what is there but it's our job to find out. Load up everyone!"

They all picked up their gear and headed to the heavy transport. There were heavy weapons loaded inside and the space was large enough for the Marines not to have to scrunch down for the three-hour ride.

Sana rode copilot with Lt. Collins as she was qualified to fly the ship. She was beginning to doubt again. What had she gotten herself into? Was this to be her life from now on? Even with Bale, this mission now had teeth on it, and she was frightened.

Everyone else on the transport was frightened too.

They had left Beta Seven behind and were out in open space. There were a few moons nearby but all tested negative to the 'ping' the transport ship sent out. "Where is this base?" Collins looked at his instruments and could detect nothing. Sana made some adjustments and scanned around. **Got anything yet?** Bale texted the crew. "Not yet sir."

"Rotate 47 degrees to starboard and let's take a sweep there," Sana directed.

"Copy." Collins turned the ship and Sana fired off the Enki signal again. A 'ping' immediately came back, about 20,000 klicks ahead. "Gotcha!"

"Lieutenant, you might want to come up here and check this out."

Bale pushed past the Marines and entered the cramped cockpit. "What have we got, sir?"

Though Bale was the Mission Commander for this trip, Collins outranked him especially as he was a flight officer. He was one of Sana's trainers.

"Looks like an asteroid and a damn big one." Collins got within 300 kilometers of the rock and stopped. He looked over at Sana, "Check it."

Sana reviewed her screens and passed them over to the lieutenant. "It's clean. No radiation other than background and no debris either. It's cold, sir." Collins nodded. He liked this newer version of his flight officer. Apparently her boyfriend had knocked some sense into her.

Bale read the numbers over the lieutenant's shoulder, he whistled. "Damn! 500 kilometers long and 122 wide. That's a lot of real estate!"

Collins nodded again, "Five, take the high road but stay close. Two, grab our six." Both scout ships acknowledged his order.

"We're going to take a slow tour if that's all right with you, Lieutenant?"

"Mapping?"

"Already on it, sir." Sana responded.

Collins leaned back and looked up at Bale, both men grinned. Sana was going to be all right!

Sana punched a couple of more icons, "I'm right here, gentlemen." Snickering could be heard coming from the back. She turned in her seat and yelled, "Shut up!"

Bale slammed the door to the cockpit. "Step down, lieutenant." He turned to Collins, "Let's see what we've got here."

The Master Chief switched to a private channel and started laughing. "Oh, he's gonna catch hell when they get home." Datsun leaned over and slapped hands with the chief.

"You got that right, sir." They all laughed.

"Has he bought a ring yet?"

Datsun sobered. "He's...shopping around."

A couple of women from Sana's group gasped. "Are you sure sir?"

Datsun nodded. "Yeah, he's pretty serious about this gal though for the life of me I don't know how he'll handle her."

The chief grinned, "My Nancy was the same, short fuse and all. But a fine woman! Bale will manage. And no one is to say anything to 2nd Lieutenant Abbicon or you will be washing toilets with toothbrushes for a month! Understood?"

"Yes sir." "Copy."

The transport circled the asteroid from a safe distance. So far there was nothing to see. "Give us some light, Lieutenant."

One million lumens ran over the surface of the asteroid. Just your basic floating rock but a big one.

Sana was mapping the surface when they came around to the end. As they were making the turn, she said, "Whoa!" Everyone in back tied into her images.

On their screens they could see a huge hole, like a broken egg on an otherwise rough surface, and the light from their ship could not penetrate the darkness beyond.

"Something damn big hit this rock some time back."

Sana zoomed in on an object. "Look at that!"

Near the entrance to the hole stood what looked like a man or a statue. One of its arms was missing and part of its head too.

Bale looked closer. "A robot, sentry perhaps. Any heat there, lieutenant?" Sana shook her head, "Cold as the stone it's standing on. Looks like it has been there a while."

Collins pulled the transport closer. The robot or statue, whatever it was would not move as they slid past. The hole was darker still. "Put a flare in there lieutenant."

She pulled a lever, and a bit of fire flew into the space. They could see a huge cavern as the light went further into the cavern. It died out into the depths.

They waited but nothing happened. Collins pulled the ship

back. "Ping it hard!"

Sana pushed another icon and ramped up the frequency. "Here goes..."

Though they could hear nothing inside the transport, the sonic vibration was massive.

Mapping and radar showed a monstrous cavern inside that went deep into the rock. It was not natural. Something or someone had carved it out. The rock was hallowed.

"I think we've found our base. Load up everyone! Get us as close as you dare, Collins. Lt. Abbicon, you stay here with Turner until we give the all clear."

"Yes sir."

Just as he was about to assign the drones to Datsun...*click* *Attention heavy transport, AGAMEMNON III. This is Captain Castillo from the AGAMEMNON, we are AGAMEMNON I. We will be on station in five minutes. Come in."*

Bale signed into the signal. "Welcome Captain Castillo. We were expecting some company, but you decided to bring the whole party."

Captain Castillo on board the AGAMEMNON I smiled, "We thought you might be lonely. Who am I speaking with?"

"2nd Lieutenant Jackson, Mission Commander assigned by Commander Barnes unless that has changed, sir."

"You've still got the reigns but one change by the admiral himself. You are now provisional 1st Lieutenant Jackson for the duration of this mission." Bale felt his chest vibrate and his insignia changed from 2nd Lieutenant to 1st Lieutenant. He now outranked everyone on board. Sana looked up to him, "Congratulations." He patted her shoulder, "Provisional is the operative word here, lieutenant." But he smiled back at her. Collins grinned.

"We will stay on station after we give you additional personnel and material. What do you need lieutenant?"

Bale thought for a moment. "Another squad if you can spare them and three more points. The space is a lot bigger than we imagined so more lights and another kernel would be good. Got any K-9s? We're good on drones."

"Traveling light, Mister? I can give you four K-9s. 10,000

meters okay?" These were killer satellites.

"That should do us. You might have your squad bring another puptent. Give us an hour to check out the interior then we'll build a gate for your people to come over."

"Copy that lieutenant. We will be ready. Over and out."

Bale floated back to the marines. "Datsun, you've got the drones. Everyone ready?"

The chief smiled, "I do like working with professionals. Congrats on the promotion!"

Bale grinned, "Just don't bury me with it."

33

They left the transport and approached the broken edge of the huge opening. "Datsun, one up high and another about to go in. Keep the other on standby."

The walls of the darkness were at least twelve to twenty meters thick but once they entered the space it was clear that the interior was carved out, the inner walls were smooth. Datsun sent one of the drones further into the chamber. Its lights could only brighten the nearby walls. "Infrared people. Let's look sharp!"

Bale pulled himself over the edge and held onto the broken crag and waited on the drone. Microwave and radar began to fill a picture of the interior. Though tubular, the volume had several flat areas like pavilions that followed the curve of the circular wall. Another feature that became visible were the spokes crossing through the center of the mass. Like bicycle tire spokes, these large stone columns reached from the floor to a central tube running the length of the camber. But to call it a chamber diminished its size. Bale remembered the old 20th century football stadiums that were massive. This space could hold three of them including their parking lots like back in the day when cars still ran on wheels. The word gigantic was barely adequate to describe the cavern.

"Wake up people! I need motion sensors all over the place. Get to it!" The Master Chief was in awe too, but he had seen other bases just as large only they were human and floated out in space for all to see. This one was completely inside an asteroid. They were going to need more lights.

Bale called the transport, "Collins, look for airlocks or some kind of doors wherever you can."

It was clear the base was abandoned. Then he heard a scream!

"Sorry, sorry...Darnell here. I just found a body. Kinda freaked me out."

The chief and Bale moved over to the specialist and looked over her find. Buried under lots of rocks from the catastrophe was a humanoid body missing its head. It was clearly alive at one time as they could see arteries and bone, long fossilized protruding from the severed neck.

"Sir!" Datsun called out, "I've more bodies, some just lying about on the floors and along the walls!"

"Condition?"

"All fossilized, some embedded into the walls, and some buried in ice a 1000 meters below the opening. But the weird thing, they are all different species but humanoid." The drone showed many bodies lying around the huge space. Whatever happened here was sudden and they were unaware of their pending demise until the moment that it occurred. "And sir, their heads are all different, some even animal-like."

It was clear most of the residents were still home. Some would have blown out the opening when decompression occurred, but the rest just stayed home and died.

"Chief, how did this happen? I mean they were an advanced species if this is the Enki. How did they get caught off-guard?"

The Master Chief, Michael Green shook his head, "Sir. I cannot imagine, but there is a bunch of water in here, ice I mean. I do not think they were attacked or that another asteroid hit them. I think it was a comet. Maybe Beta Seven was pulling it in from the dark side and they did not see it before it hit. I have looked around the rim and there are no blast marks anywhere. This was not a fight they lost. There are ice crystals all around the rim and beyond but not anywhere else on this rock. It had to be a comet but how they missed it...I just don't know."

Lt. Collins called in, "Sir, I've found three airlocks, two blown out. The third is shattered but wedged in the surrounding boulders. But the most important thing is I found a pair of big doors, hanger doors under the asteroid. They are out of alignment but still closed. This base lost all its air at once with the crash."

Bale nodded his head, that made sense. The collision sent shockwaves throughout the structure. He looked around the chamber as it was slowly lighting up, but most was still in the dark. Even then, there were shattered columns, broken structures like small buildings, toppled statues and other debris all over the place. Most of it was against the wall of the circular space.

"Chief, I think this thing rotated to emulate gravity. Notice the rocks and the bodies? Most are against the walls. Even after a collision and the wobble it caused, this rock was still spinning. Everything not tied down hit the walls!"

Mike grinned in his suit. He really liked the way this young officer thought. Bale's observation skills were proved by Gantry, his Master Command Sergeant, second in command for the Marines. "And since the thing no longer rotates, it has been out here a long time. Even sunlight will slow it down eventually."

Bale grinned back, "Yep, 12,000 years can do that to anything this size. Collins?"

"Yes sir!"

"Send Master Sergeant Turner over with Lt. Abbicon. The navigation lights should be along the rim by now. With the captain's permission, I will send you over to get us another squad and more material. Bring them back then dock with the AGAMEMNON I and take a siesta for 12, I will see you tomorrow. Get some rest."

Lt. Collins grinned, "I'm up for that. I love Mexican food! Be right over with the lieutenant." The AGAMEMNON I was largely Hispanic, so their food was ethnic. The emperor liked diversity in his crews, and they appreciated his choice.

Sana heard all this and got up out of her seat. Collins turned to her, "Sana, risk might get you lucky but more often it will get you killed. Pull your head out of your ass and listen to the lieutenant and do your job." He paused for a minute as Sana stared at him.

"Please be careful, I don't want to think I wasted my time with you. You're a fine officer, don't disappoint."

Sana leaned over and kissed Mark on his cheek, "Tell

Mary I love her too. You are the best! I won't let you down."

She closed her helmet and walked into the storage part of the transport. She looked up at Master Sergeant Turner. He was the blackest man she had ever seen but the man did have a sense of humor even though he treated all her team of recruits like dirt. "I'm ready, sir."

"I'm to call you Sir, sir." He grinned with brilliant white teeth. "It'll take time, but you'll get used to it. But do not call me sir again, okay?" Sana thumped him on the arm and waited for the clamshell doors to open. Time to jump into the void.

34

Bale was managing a lot that was going on. Motion sensors, lights what few they had, the navigator lights, and most important his people. The Master Chief helped a lot and now that Master Sergeant Turner was back with Master Sergeant Kono Nakamura (no relation to the admiral, at least by 100 years) otherwise known by his moniker 'Datsun', Bale had plenty of help. But he was busy.

He took a pause, "AGAMEMNON I, come in please."

"This is Captain Castillo, I read you lieutenant."

"My compliments, Captain, by myself and of course by Commander Barnes. Do you have some time?"

Janet Costello smiled; this boy ran by the book! Lieutenant Commander Bayer had given her a heads up about the man. He would do what he was told but he would be creative about it. His bio and record were exemplary! A man that followed orders, made them happen and adjusted for current conditions. Barnes had warned that Lt. Jackson was a rare breed. Certainly, Commander material...maybe even Captain! Lt. Jackson may never be able to finish as a cadet...he would be going Old-School! Learn by attrition. And that he was a Hammer at such a young age suggested that others were already following his career. She would give the young man what he needed.

"Thank you, Lieutenant. What can I do for you?"

Bale took a deep breath. This was going to be hard to ask of a Captain especially when she knew how limited his resources were. "Captain Castillo, with your permission could I have docking privileges for my transport with the AGAMEMNON I? I would like Lt. Collins to pick up your next squad, bring them here and come back for another squad if you have any available." Bale knew very well that the captain had plenty of suits. "It's going to be at least several hours before we get a gate up. We are still exploring just this one chamber. I need all the help we can get."

"I've been watching your progress. We are building a digital map of that rock as we speak, information from the drones. I have got two deep survey drones just collecting dust in my holds. Would you like them?"

Bale grinned. As the chief said, it was nice to deal with professionals. "Yes sir! But I have a shopping list also."

The captain and Bale talked for several minutes. She made him accept another squad plus one to rotate the other three every eighteen hours for R-and-R on board the AGAMEMNON I. A gravity generator, once the gate was built there would be air pumped into the puptents, food, medical supplies, additional weapons, more lights and kernels to power them. Bale and the captain dallied about the amount, but she refused to slight this officer one bit. This man knew what he wanted but did not dig for more than necessary. She had to practically beg him to take another squad!

"I also want to send over my Second. Dia Terashita is Commander-elect. She still needs some experience with Marines. Is that agreeable with you, lieutenant?"

Bale was a little surprised at that. How can a Commander-elect be shy of Marines?

"Certainly sir. The more eyes we have the better."

"Very well, 1st Lieutenant. Carry on. Over and out!"

Sana waited out of the light for Bale to finish his instructions to the ground crew. Though this was a weightless environment all the troops were standing, their boot grapples holding onto the floor inside the asteroid. She took the time to look around the space. Spokes reached up into the darkness with only a lone drone lighting the central axle or shaft that ran the length of the chamber. Inside was like a large city but abandoned long ago. She could see some of the bodies nearby and they were weird, twisted shapes no longer corporal to this plane and time.

"Murkowski, Dickens, the captain has found a tunnel leading further into this rock. The main shaft goes right through it. Captain Castillo tells me there is one large platform near the tunnel. I want sensors just inside that tunnel. I don't want any surprises so get it done!" Both men saluted and grabbed ruck sacks full of motion sensors and flew down the chamber to the hole at the back. It was 200 meters across, a big hole leading into the darkness beyond.

"Datsun, park one of the drones near the entrance to that hole. I want it armed at all times."

"Yes Sir!" Datsun directed 'Shelly' to follow the two men. Kono liked to name his drones and this one was trigger happy. It reminded him of a mean-spirited woman he had known at boot, hence the name.

Sana heard the rest of the commands and saw that Bale was finished. She walked into the light slowly to give her boot grapples a chance to grab the surface. Generally, everyone walked slow but for a woman, it was a different experience. Not that they had any trouble with the gait, but a woman has more gears from the waist down than men.

Sana approached 1st Lieutenant Jackson with a walk that any woman would practice if they knew how. A skintight suit, a lithe form and Sana without intent or even knowledge captured every eye in the place.

"Shit!"

"How does she do that without gravity?"

"Deammmn!"

"Lucky bastard!"

Sana stood up straight and saluted Bale, her chest out. More mutterings and a few coughs from the peanut gallery. "Lieutenant, where have you been? I've just finished my assignments and you weren't here!" Bale glared at her.

"Sir, Master Sergeant Turner and I have only just arrived. I was waiting on you, sir." Bale looked at Turner. The man shrugged.

Bale almost laughed and he had heard the comments too. *Lucky me!*

"Lieutenant, I want you to explore that shaft above us. Take the chief and Master Sergeant Turner with you."

Sana saluted again, "Yes Sir, I'm good at shafts." She meant it in all seriousness but the laughter coming in over the coms embarrassed her. Bale turned red in his suit. "Move it, Mister!"

Sana took off up into the night. The chief and Turner came over and slapped Bale on his back and took off too.

They texted him on a private channel.

Yeah, I bet she knows all about large poles.

Turner followed, **Yep, the lieutenant knows how to ride a shaft. Look at her go for that big one!**

Damn that woman! He watched as sure enough Sana began to spin around the large central shaft. He knew she was flying in her mind, but did she have to touch the darn thing?

Bale could hear both men snickering but then they stopped in mid-vacuum and watched Lt. Abbicon sail around the spokes and the shaft. It was like a dance and some serious gymnastics.

What no one knew until the data started coming in was that Lt. Abbicon had a gravimetric and material sampler strapped to her wrist. She was getting samples of the columns and the shaft as she flew by. Sana was also taking pictures and radar images of each spoke she touched. But she was having fun too.

She giggled as she flew. Sana was just in her suit, but it was a type of flying and that was all that mattered. Work was just a by-product. She rarely used her pulse rockets, Sana would just push off the surface, flip in the air, slide by another one, grab a flange of a spoke and circle the thing doing her job...but it was fun!

Her last trick was to let go of the spoke and with her momentum Sana arched her back, shot a few more pictures while her legs were spread like a ballerina then she tucked into a roll and landed on the central shaft without engaging her magnetic boots. Sana stood there for a few seconds and transferred the data to Bale. Once finished she looked up at the two men who were there to protect her. “Ready to go? I’m done here.” Sana smiled at them. They both nodded dumbly...how the hell?

Sana jumped down to the floor well below them and the men followed.

The chief started laughing. **Lucky bastard indeed!**

Turner just shook his head, **Do you know how many beds that man will have to replace in his lifetime?**

35

Emperor Lucas Barnes entered the Command deck of the AGAMEMNON and walked over to Admiral Nakamura. There were no guards with him but then, he did not really need them on His ship. Kai watched the man approach. Everyone in the room kneeled. "At ease, gentlemen." They all rose and went back to work.

Lucas was about as eclectic an Emperor as they came. A sport coat and tie on over a paisley shirt, blue jeans and cowboy boots. The man broke his own rules of decorum at a moment's notice. But despite his appearance everyone knew who he was with those piercing blue eyes, a Vandyke beard and grayish blonde hair. He was over 140 years old and had changed the Earth forever all by himself.

In his early twenties Lucas had discovered a sunken Galley full of gold, silver and precious gems. Well over 20 billion dollars at the time, he had managed to steal them out of Columbian waters and start his own business or rather a trove of businesses that lead to what the Terran Empire enjoyed today. Then he bought a castle in England and discovered more treasure buried in the catacombs under the keep. Add another five billion and the young man was the celebrity of the world. Cash strapped England decided to Knight him so they could keep the taxes from his booty several centuries old.

But Lucas had no interest in being a celebrity, he was a very private man. His first wife is still unknown but his second, or third there being some rumors, was Mary Stewart of New Amsterdam. They produced three children and lived a quiet life.

But between his first and second wives, Lucas was anything but sedate. While everyone else on the planet was developing stem-cell research, Lucas pursued nanotechnology. Using his many cottage industries scattered around the world and always in rural areas, through his scientists he was able to grow a new industry in home cleaning supplies using safe nanos. These bloomed into military contracts cleaning barnacles off Navy ships. Later he used the nanos to remove old buildings throughout the rust belt, factories, piers and other late nineteenth and early twentieth century industrial buildings rotting on the ground. His fortunes grew.

By his early thirties, Lucas was slowly becoming the first Trillionaire in the world, but no one knew it but the IRS. He paid his taxes, he had his own bank and rarely played in the stock market. That he was able to maintain his huge company, BARNES Ltd under sole propriety ownership is a study to this day in economics and banking history. Lucas kept a low profile most of his early life.

And then on his 35 birthday, his team accidentally discovered Gate technology through nanos. Like most great inventions, this accident led to medical nanotechnology, faster than light drive and eventually the Ring or Maul development...nanos used on a massive scale. Since any new medical discoveries were forbidden without government oversite, Lucas moved to the moon, Earths' one satellite.

He had purchased a company that developed satellite cell phones. Lucas placed several telecommunication spheres in orbit much to the smiles of his investors, then one of them blew up. The company he purchased was ruined by the fallout of such a catastrophe. He sold off all his stock in the phone company and absorbed the loss the whole while a chunk of the exploded satellite crashed unto the moon...it was full of nanos.

Once the nanos burrowed into the rock about 70 meters down, it found a large cavern, built a gate and phoned home. Lucas was now in business on the moon.

Two heavy cargo haulers and a starship later, Lucas conquered the moons of Mars and the moons of Jupiter and Saturn. He had bases all over the Sol system and no one knew it but him and his people. Lucas held the high ground!

To say he was unconventional would be an understatement.

"Damnit Kai, fourteen dead along with thirty-one colonists? How did this happen?"

"Fifteen now, we couldn't save the last marine. She died on the table." Kai grimaced. "We expected boarders, but we thought they would be Wolves, not these nasty little buggers."

Lucas nodded; he had seen the pictures. Nasty was right!

"Do we have samples?"

Admiral Nakamura nodded, "Yes and they are being analyzed now. Extremely fast and strong. They were able to overcome our rifleman in hand to hand and crush their shields. We are taking a different approach and increasing field strength, but it will limit energy time. Our team is working the problem."

"The Hammers?" the emperor asked.

"None were on board the Explorer. The outcome would have been different. We will need more to convert. I'm drawing from the rosters to find out who would be willing to make the final transformation."

"I want two Hammers on every mission! I don't care if they are shepherding an ambassador; two at least!"

Kai nodded, "I would rather have four Hammers for every mission. I hope you will agree with me Sire."

"What about the Enki ship? Did we get anything from the debris?" Lucas was very worried about that ship. It was not so fast but then they did not know how fast that ship could slip.

Kai shook his head. "Lt. Parks did a thorough job of destroying it. We did get some of the tentacles from it but nothing else. I hope Lieutenant Jackson can find a similar ship on the Enki base beyond Beta Seven. He found some hanger doors, but they were shut. We can only hope."

At that moment a nearby gate 'pinged' and Commander Barnes and Lt. Commander Bayer walked into the control center. They walked over to the admiral and the emperor and knelt before them both.

"Enough of that." the emperor said. "I'm sorry about your

men, Commander. They will be missed by friends and family alike. This was a tragedy!"

Denise spoke up without permission, "Sir! It is all my fault. I did not send enough men and munitions to handle the job. Those men and women died because of me!" Tears ran down her cheeks.

The emperor walked over to the woman and pulled her hand to him. "Denise, you had no idea what we were running into. I know you did the best you could, no one could have done any better. Now enough, Mister. I depend on all of you, Earth certainly does! I'll have no more of that." Then he pulled her into an embrace, a second man she had ever allowed that honor...and shuddered into his shirt.

Denise pulled away and sniffled and saluted her Emperor again, he nodded to her.

"Sir? We have a memorial tonight onboard the AGAMEMNON III. I was wondering if you could attend and say a few words for the troops." Commander Barnes said.

"I'll be there. I'll have Scotch but have available any other spirits to toast our fallen brethren."

Jeff nodded and thanked his grandfather.

Though Lucas was the commander in Chief of the entire Federation, he was barely a military man. Several decades ago, after his second rejuve, Lucas had joined the Navy to learn what his men and women were doing for him and for Earth. He had survived boot and a year as a noncom only to learn how difficult it was to be a rifleman. Shortly after, he was dragged into becoming the emperor...something he never wanted.

Lieutenant Bayer left the AGAMEMNON to return to her ship. Lucas spoke with the admiral and then pulled Commander Barnes to a lift. "Walk with me."

Commander Barnes was nervous. Not of his grandfather but what the man might tell him...he had a rather good idea what that would be.

Lucas had gated them to the portside mall. With over 10,000 crewmen and family on board the AGAMEMNON was a crowded place. People did not bow or kneel; this was one of the emperor's rules. Except for special events, no one would openly recognize the emperor in public, but many stared just the same.

They walked for a bit without saying a word. Lucas brushed some leaves from a nearby tree, smelled the perfume on his hand and walked on, his grandson stayed with him.

A girl gasped across the walk, waved her card at a nearby flower merchant, grabbed a clutch of flowers, picked up her younger brother and ran to Lucas, her mother in fear and shock. "Anita, NO!"

The girl was maybe ten. She knelt in front of the emperor and placed her brother on her knee. "Here Sir! These flowers are for you. We need a bigger apartment. My mother has asked but housekeeping won't answer, Sir. Um, I mean Your Majesty. One with a window would be nice. My brother likes to look at the stars as they go by, Sir!"

Lucas smiled at the girl and started to get on his knees in front of the children...

Anita L. Townsend, brother Robert M. Townsend, Mother Jennifer D. Townsend, Father Robert Montgomery Townsend-deceased. Formerly Navy Engineer, M. Sergeant. Died building a bridge on Antellon. Enemy fire was cause of death. One bedroom apartment for three, one bath. Pension ends in three years. Jennifer Townsend, radiological technician in science lab, level four.

He settled on his knees. Lucas looked at the entire ship's roster and found five other widows living in one-bedroom apartments with children. He also found 14 men living in two and three-bedroom apartments, without spouses or significant others. All these men were the walking wounded, they got the space according to their rank and pensions. Three were drunks and one had a three-bedroom apartment around the corner from Mrs. Townsend, he lived by himself and the apartment had a window. Then Housekeeping tried to lock him out. The emperor overrode the computer, a man came online *Whoever you are, we are about to send the police to pick you up. Get off this site right now!*

Lucas signaled back, *0100 and get your boss online RIGHT NOW!*

He could hear the man swallow when he heard that call-sign. Only the emperor could use it, anyone else was shot even if they thought it was just a prank. *Yes, your Majesty!*

Lucas finished kneeling before the children and took the flowers offered to him. Their mother ran up, "I am so sorry your Majesty. I won't let them bother you again!"

Lucas looked up into the woman's eyes, "Just wait for a minute, if you please?"

He smelled the flowers and smiled at the children.

Your Majesty, I am so sorry I was not in my office. How can I be of help? a woman's voice asked over his link.

You will clean out your desk, return home and tomorrow, you will turn yourself into the local magistrate. I am hereby ordering you to serve hard time for three years on Beta Three, Palisade. You will learn a new profession and you will excel at it. Your family can stay on AGAMEMNON, or they can join you on Beta Three, your choice. You are fired!

Lucas thanked the children and stood up to address their mother. "Just a moment more, Mrs. Townsend." He contacted the admiral knowing full well Kai had heard the exchange. *I will not have Widows or Widowers with children sleeping in one-bedroom apartments on any of my ships! Is that clear, Mister? You will take those men, clean them up, rejuve them and put them back on the front lines. If they have mental issues, send them back to Earth! They can keep their pensions, but I will not have the walking dead on ANY OF MY SHIPS! Those who have lost spouses with children in the service of Terra will Forever have priority!*

He did not wait for an answer. Lucas looked up Jennifer Townsend's bank account and deposited an additional $20,000 credits from his own account. He also extended her husband's pension to her son's eighteenth birthday.

He looked down at the little girl who was holding her two-year-old brother, a child that had never seen his father. "You will have a new apartment with a window in two days. Thank you for letting me know."

Lucas turned to her mother, "Ma'am, you won't have to pay any more for a three-bedroom apartment than you are paying now, I've seen to it."

He bent over to tweak the boy's face, but the child turned away and hid in his sister's shoulder. Lucas smiled. "He is just shy," Anita said. "I'm ten! Can I join the Navy when I'm eighteen?"

"I certainly hope so! I like the way you think! But the man you will have to talk to is my grandson. I am going to retire."

Lucas pointed to the tall man behind him. Anita stood up tall with her brother in her arms and saluted Commander Barnes. "I hope you'll accept me when I'm old enough!"

By now a large crowd was surrounding them and their phones were taking pictures.

Jeff Barnes walked over to the girl, "Are you in the Explorer's Club?"

"Yes Sir!" Anita proudly announced.

"Very good. As far as I am concerned, you are in the Navy now." He pulled one of his pips off his shoulder. "Kneel before me, please." Anita gave her brother over to her mother and dropped to one knee.

"This is a Commander's pip, I worked extremely hard to get it. You can wear it now, but I will be there when you finish boot. And if you study hard, take care of your mother and brother, exercise and stay heathy, I will be there when you become Commander. Am I clear, Mister?"

Anita beamed up at him and put the commander's pip on her shirt. She stood up and saluted again. "Look mommy! I'm in the navy now!"

Emperor Barnes and his grandson walked on. "See? That is how it's done. A little bit goes a long way and engenders good will all around." He paused and looked up to the younger man. "Just remember, you can't help them all. When this crisis is over, you will take Command as Supreme Leader of Earth, but I will maintain it for now. But Jeff, you serve these people, not the other way around."

Jeff patted his elderly grandfather on the back as they walked. "Thank you, Sir."

That went better than I thought it would, both men thought to themselves.

36

Commander-Elect Dia Terashita was not working out well.

She transferred to the Enki base without any retinue, but then she did not need one as she considered everyone on the base belonging to her and at her beck and call.

Bale was dividing up the men and material to set up two bases inside the shell. One was the Command center with medical, food service, and bunk beds for the troops. The other base was on another flat platform with an enclosed room that had been sealed like the Command center. It served as a garrison and bunk room for strategic forces. Both rooms were as large as warehouses so the troops had plenty of space, but the Command center was in full light, the garrison stayed in the dark far away from the broken end of the asteroid. The puptents were never used.

Sana was spending her time flying all over the cavern, mapping and taking samples of the city-wide space. She accomplished more in one day than other teams surveyed in two. Her aerial acrobatics were a pleasure to watch when she was near. Everyone's tension lessened when Sana let out the occasional 'whoop!' or giggled as she flew by. The commander-Elect thought she was a buffoon!

Everyone helped move supplies around the area and when time permitted, they could explore. Commander-Elect Terashita did her part but it was clear, she had complete distain for the Marines. The troops from the AGAMEMNON I knew her well and avoided her at all costs. The rest just got bossed around...a lot!

Though she out-ranked everyone else, she could not hassle 1st Lieutenant Jackson. He was Commander-in-Theater and thus out-ranked her. She hated that! *Let me get him back on my ship and I'll show him who's boss, he and that damn girlfriend of his!*

Bale had looked up her bio and found out her father, a short Colonel in the Marines had been killed in an engagement by friendly fire when she was about twelve. In the fog of war, this sort of thing happened though it was rare. It was obvious Terashita blamed the entire Marine Corps for her father's death.

He shook his head and wondered how she had made it this far. The woman was talented, her specialties being logistics, flight and engineering. That she had little to do with the Marines was not a negative for starship officers dealt very rarely with ground forces. That is what Master Chiefs, Master Sergeants and various lieutenants and Sergeants were for. But the commander had absolute authority and ultimate responsibility for all her troops, regardless of station or position. Terashita could not avoid the marines for they were all around her!

Unfortunately for 3rd lieutenant Gardener, she had made him into her personal attendant. Terashita was also part Royal to the Japanese elite so training Gardener to be her servant was not difficult. Getting her food, setting up a private room for her use and groveling to go to the can when she allowed it. The man would wash out if Bale did not do something about this!

He was outside and finished his report to Captain Castillo he then put his tablet in a thigh pocket. Sana landed neatly beside him and finished her report on the samples, photos and mapping. She tucked her tablet away and saluted him. "Sir, we are 92% finished with this chamber. Another day then we can proceed further into the asteroid." He nodded to her and smiled.

"Very good lieutenant. Send my compliments to Commander-Elect Terashita and have her join me outside the pavilion." Sana frowned knowing how well that was going to go over with the princess. Most everyone had a taste of 'Her Royal Highness' by now.

The Master Chief came over to Bale along with his staff. A planned exploration of the inner workings of the Rock, as they were now calling it was being arranged with staggered troops lining the Subway, the big tunnel leading into the depths of the asteroid. They had not found any kind of control room much less the generators that originally powered the Rock. They were also hoping to find a hanger near the rear of the artificial structure perhaps with ships inside. As they talked, Sana came over and stood demurely waiting on Bale.

He looked down, “Lieutenant? What is the problem? Where is officer Terashita?”

Sana looked at the ground then back up to Bale, “Um sir, she said she was off shift and was doing her hair...um, and uh,” Bale stared at her. “Spit it out!”

Her lips trembled but there was anger in her eyes. “Officer Terashita said if you wanted to talk to her then you were to come to her private quarters...sir!”

Mike looked at Bale, he could see the growing anger there. No officer treated another like that!

“Sir?”

Bale turned to him, “Chief, I want her here in cuffs. Do it NOW!”

The Master Chief turned to the men near him. “Cage! Datsun! Take three men with you and destroy her ‘private quarters! I do not want to see any evidence that it even existed at my next inspection! You two bring her back for the commander’s pleasure. Go!”

Sana stood very still and tried to melt into the surrounding rocks. Over the coms, she could hear the woman screaming as she was trussed up and brought to Bale. Sana had seen other officers get angry but not Bale. This time it was different, and she was scared.

A moment later Commander-Elect Dia Terashita was dumped unceremoniously at Bale’s feet. “Uncuff her.” The woman thrashed around and then stood up. “How dare you kidnap me!”

Her hair was indeed wet and plastered around the inside of her helmet, some of it was outside the helmet, had frozen and broken off and stuck to her suit. Vacuum was hard on hair much less anything else.

“Officer Terashita, you were...” Bale was interrupted.

“YOU PIG! I’LL HAVE YOU EXECUTED FOR ASSULTING

A SUPERIOR OFFICER!!!"

On board the AGAMEMNON I, the first officer looked over at his Captain. "Sir! Are you getting this?"

Captain Castillo nodded, "Yeah, I'm watching. Let's see how it plays out."

"But Sir, he has the legal right to kill her!"

"I know, let's just see..."

Sana stepped forward. "You have no right to talk to a Commander-in-Theater like that! Apologize right..."

Dia slapped Sana's helmet. The younger and shorter woman bounced off Bale and landed on the floor next to his feet. Her helmet fogged up briefly but the nanos in the suit fixed the cracks in her face shield. Other men around Terashita moved in but Bale held up his hand. He looked down and saw blood on Sana's left face, her ear was bleeding along with a split lip from her microphone. The blood was already caking on her skin by the suit's air. "Are you all right?" Sana nodded looking up at Bale. She crawled on her back away from the woman.

Bale looked up at Terashita and glared. The woman was holding up the offending hand in horror and realized what she had done. "I didn't mean to...I mean..."

Then Bale did something no other officer or enlisted man knew he could do. He remotely turned off Commander-Elect Terashita's shields. He then reached over and grabbed her chest plate and crushed it with one hand. He pulled her up and stared into her eyes. Her suit was not compromised but it could never be used for battle or protection again. She held onto his arm with both hands desperate to get away!

On board the AGAMEMNON I, the captain grimaced.

Her first officer did a facepalm, "Here it comes!" Everyone on the Command deck was in fear.

"Just wait," Castillo said.

"There is not one of these men and women who wouldn't die for you! I WOULD DIE FOR YOU! They would die for each other!! But I will not suffer anyone striking another officer or enlisted man by a Coward...2nd Lieutenant Terashita!" Though her chest shield was crushed, she could feel a vibration as her insignia turned from Commander-

Elect to 2nd Lieutenant. “Nuuooooo!”

Bale turned and faced a nearby wall, he threw 2nd Lieutenant Terashita ten meters as hard as he could. Her bubble flickered as she hit the wall. When it turned off, she and several chunks of rocks fell to the floor, a neat curve shaved out of the wall above her.

Captain Castillo sighed with relief, he had demoted her, not killed her...and that was his Right!

“How did you know, sir?”

“I didn’t but I know this boy. He will be a great man someday.” She turned to look up to her First standing behind her. “You would do well to stay in favor with him.” She turned back and smiled.

37

Sana was hurt badly and the ringing in her ears was way too persistent. Sergeant Sabastian would not leave her alone. “Hold still while I give you more medical nanos!” He slapped his arm against hers and fed her some new nanos. Sana began to feel better almost immediately. Then she saw a body fly past her, it was Dia Terashita. Vibrations in the ground made her look up. Bale was moving towards Dia and the look in his eyes meant death!

Sana pulled away from Sabastian and scurried through the crowd to get in front of Bale. “Stop! Please Stop!!” She looked behind her. Terashita was a broken woman surrounded by rocks. Her vitals said she was still alive but one look in Bale’s eyes told Sana that Terashita would not be for much longer.

Bale looked at Sana and his heart broke. Her face was covered in blood though some was beginning to flake off. “I’m not going to kill her but she is definitely going back to the AGAMEMNON I. I won’t have a weak link among my men!”

Okay, he’s not going to kill her. “Sir, I can save her! Give me a chance, give her a chance!”

Bale’s eyes flickered to Sana and then turned red when he looked at Dia. Sana could tell he would not kill her, but she would not be in any condition to fly a ship when he got done with her. And none of the men would interfere. They hated that woman!

“Remember how many times I FUBARed a situation? You and others gave me three or four chances, then you had to drive it home! I was arrogant! I was foolish! I had no idea there were other species out there to kill us!”

Sana looked up at him, “Give her a chance. If it does not work out, then send her home but don’t hurt her. Let me and others fix her like you fixed me...Please!"

Bale clicked to their private channel, "But she hurt you!"

Sana looked up to him and saw those amazing green eyes through his helmet. "Not that much so I'll live." For a moment, Bale could not help himself. He pulled Sana close and hugged her.

"About Face!" The Master Chief yelled. Everyone turned and Sana and Bale had some peace.

"She touches you again, I *will* kill her," Bale whispered. Sana knew he meant it and accepted the condition.

Bale took a deep breath, "I want you with me tonight. Datsun takes over while four of the Points, the chief, some of the troops and you and I sleep. Six hours from now...please come to me."

"She's not going to be ready to talk until tomorrow. I'll sleep with you against the rocks." Sana smiled at him. "I'm glad you are my friend."

Sana turned away and helped Terashita to a safe room. Sebastian would need a couple of hours to get her square.

Bale walked away from the men and approached a ledge. The chief ordered the troops to duty and got them away from the lieutenant. The man was troubled right now, and no one needed to get hurt. They scattered eagerly.

He kicked a large boulder meaning to send it to the bottom of the asteroid, but it shattered. Bale yelled and grabbed a large rock, bigger than his head and threw it at the far wall, ten kilometers away.

The chief yelled, "Incoming!" Everyone on the far wall radared the rock racing at them. Fortunately, no one was nearby as it hit the wall and continued through. Part of the wall shattered and slowly fell to the ground with what little gravity the asteroid generated.

One of the men flew over and peeked into the space. He looked back at Bale and the chief, "I'll be damned!

Sir! You just found the Control Room!"

Sana struggled with Sabastian, "Will you hold still? Damnit woman, you are the most difficult patient I've ever had!" She had taken a shower and put on a new-under suit, but Sana still hurt, and Sabastian was not helping one bit. "I have to get ready. The lieutenant will be here in a couple of minutes!"

They called him a Medic but in fact he was a doctor, the other term came with being in the Navy. Sabastian put another bandage near her eyebrow and then pulled her left earlobe again. Sana was surprised that really helped the tinnitus, the ringing of the ears. It was pretty much gone now.

"How did you know to do that? She asked.

"Modern medicine can do a great many things but sometimes the old-school works just as well and faster too." Sabastian smiled at her. "I guess you'll do." Sana grinned up at him...and that is when all hell broke loose on the other side of the lockers.

Clanging, metallic parts being thrown around and heavy footsteps met her as she ran around the corner. Men and women, riflemen in the middle of dress and undress ran with their uniforms away from the man stomping to the showers. Bale was in a mood!

The chief was running behind him to gather Bale's weapons, grenades and swords. Bale ripped his under suit and threw it to the floor as he stepped into the shower room. The man glowed purple as his inner shields kicked in. People ran out of the shower naked, but they did not care, they had to be away from their Commander!

"Chief, please put those weapons on the floor. I expect he will want them. Put his suit in the dryer and pull out his clean one. We are going to hit the wall in an hour, he'll want to be dressed!"

The Master Chief did not question or balk at being ordered about by Lieutenant Abbicon. He did the work hoping this woman would calm the man down.

Sana walked over to the shower and watched as Bale turned off the water. "Wash your hair again. I want you clean in every way." Bale rolled his jaw and turned the water on again.

Later Sana watched as Bale got dressed. No one was in the

room with them. His liner went under his armor. She glared at him when Bale did not reach for his weapons. “I won’t sleep with you if you’re not fully dressed.”

Bale grunted, flexed his muscles and all his weapons jumped to him. Swords and guns on his back, grenades and other sundries around his waist and two pistols in their holsters. He caught the knives and shoved them into their sleeves on his calves. Sana always smiled when he did that, *Show off!*

Sana walked around the lockers to the women’s side and finished dressing. Before she turned on her helmet, Sana looked at Bale who still had not said a word.

“You need to calm down. I’m a big girl, I’ve been hit before...I’ll live.”

Bale’s eyes got wide, “*When?*” he breathed.

She shrugged. “Before I got on the Explorer. If I met him today, I would bend him in half. Or I could just give him to you.” Sana winked at Bale. “Don’t worry, he wasn’t on the Explorer, I made sure of that!”

Sana reached up to Bale’s collar and pulled him down to her level. She kissed him. “All better now?” Bale could still taste some of the blood from her lips. He frowned, “If she...”

“Yeah, I know. But I promised to fix her, you let me worry about that.”

They walked hand-in-hand through the force field that kept the Command Bunker airtight. Bale did not worry if anyone saw them like that. “Datsun!”

“Yes Sir!” Kono, Nick and the chief had waited outside just in case things did not work out, but Beauty had calmed the Beast. They were relieved.

“You’ve got the Watch. 0500 for me,” Sana grabbed Bale’s shoulder. “Um, I mean 0600, no later!”

The men watched as the couple walked away. “Deeeammn, even in armor she still has a nice ass!”

The chief jabbed Nick in his side while Kono rolled his eyes. Nick wheezed, “I’m just say’n...”

“Shut up, Cage!”

The nurse ran as fast as she could but the grapplers on her boots would not allow that. She could have flown to the Command Center, but flying was not her forte'.

"Sir! There's something wrong with the commander and his, um, I mean...the lieutenant!"

Datsun jumped up from his desk and ran through the force field door, the nurse tried to keep up. Several men passed her on the way to the commander.

When she finally got to the wall where all the sleepers were waiting, the nurse heard the Master Sergeant laughing. "It's okay." She looked at the other sleepers, all were fully weaponized, and their suits grabbed the walls behind them. The Master Chief, two Master Sergeants, four Points and all the rest slept on the rock wall, all of them ready to fight a battle upon wakening.

"But sir? Is that normal?" She pointed to the commander and Lieutenant Abbicon. The woman was folded over the commander and had her knee slightly on Lieutenant Jackson's thigh, his hand held her back and his other hand cupped her fist. They were asleep but their suits were not.

Tendrils came out of their suits and entered the other. Like thin wires they were connecting the two sleeping officers. One of Bale's fibers pulled off Sana's neck and snaked up to her damaged ear and went in. The nanos of her suit did not interfere in any way. Several vine-like wires came out of Sana's suit and were plugged into Bale's legs. He did not seem bothered at all.

Kono smiled, "It's called a Marriage Web. Quite the phenomenon shortly after nanos were invented. Married couples that had nanos in them traded information and medical nanos while they slept." The nurse had never seen or even heard of such a thing! "But Sir. They are not married."

Kono looked at the woman and laughed. "A marriage license is just a piece of paper. As far as they are concerned, they *are* married."

He turned away with the rest and walked back to the Command Center. *And the two shall become one!*

38

The two remaining Wolverine ships made it back to their base a couple of months later after the attack on the colony ship. They were sorry to report to their masters that the one Enki ship escorting them to the prey had been destroyed, they had witnessed its destruction from a light year away. Their ships turned for home being uncertain who had caused its demise. The colony ship had gone on to the system ahead of it apparently unharmed. The Wolves were scared but they had suspected who had caused this disaster...Terrans!

The Enki waiting at the Wolverine base had no clue who the 'Terrans' were but with description by their allies and a data dive into their thousand-year computer files, they recognized the race. Of all the subjugated species the Enki had taken from other worlds as slaves, this one was the most robust. They had not been called that at the time of their capture, just a number in a file and the location of their home planet 27 light years from here. Not impossible to reach but it would take time. No, it would be better to send part of their fleet to the nearest planet and capture technology and information. The Enki, while being arrogant were cautious as well.

Millennia ago, the Deities had decided this part of the galaxy had lain fallow long enough and it was time to inspect what their subjects and their overlords had accomplished. But then they had run afoul of a new and terrible enemy. They were a dreadful species that lived in gas giants and their technology was horrible indeed. Many convoys would travel to a system to use resources from those same gas giants. The enemy waited in the clouds for their tankers to skim the surface gases. They would rise and destroy the tankers then went after the rest of the convoy. They were not indestructible, but their weapons were devastating! Most convoys died with no idea who had caused their end. The enemy had no name and no language that the Enki tried in desperation with which to negotiate. They just killed the Enki and disappeared back into the clouds.

This began a three-thousand-year war. The Enki would not be dominated by an inferior race of gas bags! Whole systems had been destroyed to get to the enemy. But many Enki died just the same, their race population almost cut in half.

After sufficient time, the Deities decided to abandon that section of the galaxy and return to their previous hunting grounds. Centuries later, they got another shock. Of the subjugated species, few remained or had devolved to their primitive beginnings, the bases on such planets abandoned by their overlords. Of the few human worlds at the edge of this sector, most were advanced with a few that had star drives. Their overlords and their bases destroyed. What had happened?

The Enki killed all the humans they could find, they had no desire to have anyone following them to their hunting grounds. But now they had an apparent formidable enemy ahead and their allies said they were human. Were they previous slaves, were they from their home world? The Deities decided to send an Attack ship to the planet ahead. It would require three months to get there at its highest speed, but they would be able to communicate with the Wolverine base upon arrival. It would be a larger ship, more heavily shielded and with more weapons. The Deities knew it would have no trouble with what it found there.

This would give the rest of the fleet time to stock up and prepare their allies with newer ships and faster drives. The Armada would wait on the Attack ship, the ship and crew could handle this new enemy simply fine.

They were about to find out how wrong they were.

Bale and several riflemen entered the Control Room or rather a Throne room by the looks of the main chair in the place. It was a massive stone structure that sat on three rising daises in the center of the room. Whoever had sat on the chair was now crushed beyond recognition by part of the ceiling above. The comet or whatever hit the asteroid had thrown everyone and everything not tied down, the room was a mess.

They had found the entrance deep under the ice connected to the frozen pond outside. It was little wonder they never found the door. The ice was removed, and the door opened. Lights were brought in, fortunately the space was not all that big. The room gave up its details under the harsh HID lamps. What they saw stopped everyone with awe.

There was a pile of bodies slammed against a wall behind the Throne. Whether these were the god-king's retinue or petitioners was not known but they were not Enki soldiers, their finery gave up that notion. The soldiers were scattered all over the place and though humanoid, they all had dog faces and weapons. It was obvious even to the uneducated in such things that some of these people survived the crash but soon died of asphyxiation as all the air rushed out of the asteroid. Several positions of death spoke loudly of gasping for air, a commodity taken for granted then but all too precious and now gone. Most had died gruesome deaths, but the rest entered the next life, according to their religion without a guide much less a proper burial.

Captain Castillo had brought with her several archaeologists, a few cuneiform experts, and an ancient civilization historian one who's specialty was Sumerian, Byzantine, and ancient Egyptian. They could all read cuneiform, but this type was older than any in Earth's recorded history. Bale needed Sana here as soon as possible as she was the only person on this mission used to incredibly old cuneiform.

Sana had her hands full with Dia Terashita. The woman was fully broken and might not come back. She wanted to go back to the AGAMEMNON I for her punishment, but Sana would have none of that! "I deserve to be drummed out of the Service. My Uncle will be so disappointed, I may be banned from the family!" Dia leaned over and touched her 2nd Lieutenant insignia on her uniform, her tears dripping on it.

For two days, Sana had used every trick in the book and some Doctor Sabastian recommended. They were screaming at her, Dia never responded. Talking did little help either. Sana forgave her, but Dia would just nod, "Thank you. I don't deserve that but thank you anyway."

Sana wanted badly to get to the Throne room. Bale wanted her there and she was jealous of the head start the other experts were enjoying though it seemed they did not fully understand what they had. Dia started speaking only in Japanese. Sana did not know if she was praying or speaking to her ancestors. Sabastian was getting worried. "If we don't stop this now, she's going to go catatonic!" Sana had enough!

She ran out of the garrison and flew to where the chief was. She landed, "Chief, I need Master Sergeant Nakamura right now!" The chief stopped his conversation with his logistics people and waved them off. "Sir, what is going on that you need one of my best men?"

"I believe 2nd Lieutenant Terashita is almost over the hump," Sana lied, "but she is starting to drift. I can't have that!"

The chief frowned at her, "Why do you care? That bitch almost killed you!"

Sana squared her shoulders and looked up to the big man. "Gantry and Bale set me straight, and you and Turner have watched me ever since. I hope you know I am on the Bounce now, but it took time." She sighed and shook a tear out of her eye and looked back up at the man. "Please...Mike. She is a bitch perhaps, but she is or was a good officer, just not around Marines."

The chief did a facepalm to his helmet. "This is because Kono is the only other Japanese here, right now, am I correct Lieutenant?"

She nodded through her helmet and waited on the chief. He muttered, "I can't believe I'm doing this. How long will you need him?"

"Maybe just an hour or maybe," she hesitated, "a day. If

this does not work out, then she goes back to the ship. I will not waste any more time on her. Let Captain Castillo deal with the problem, Sir!"

"Will you quit doing that? You are my superior!"

"Mike, you're my friend and I trust you, but you are kinda...old. My mother always made me respect senior citizens." Nearby officers and enlisted men were snickering but stopped when the chief glared at them.

"Oh Ho! That is the way of it then, girly girl! But I want that in writing! You can have Datsun for one day, not one minute more. That man of yours wants down the Subway in two days and I'll be damned if I make him wait!"

Sana transferred a file to the chief. It was everything she asked for and promised in return...in writing. The chief pulled it up and read the thing. "*Ah shit!*...Datsun!!"

Sana and Kono stopped outside the Garrison. "Really sir, I have no idea what you think I can do. She out-ranks me and if she gives me any airs, I will just leave. I have permission from the commander."

Sana looked up at the tall man. "Kono, this isn't about you being the only other Japanese citizen in billions of kilometers, but you do speak the language. My interpreter program cannot keep up. I mean no offense, but she is lonely and alone. I do not expect you to get along but please try. I think she is worthy of saving."

Sana pulled up a file and sent it to Kono. "Please, what is she saying?"

Kono listened for a bit and frowned, "It is a prayer to her ancestors. This sort of thing takes a while especially if one knows his or her lineage. Um wait, this part is about her father. OH SHIT!"

Datsun did not bother to explain to Sana but ran into the garrison shouting in Japanese. Sana ran after him through the field and throwing back her helmet to its sleeve. She turned on her recorder. Kono burst into a room and found Dia Terashita kneeling on the floor with a very sharp Chef's knife held in both hands. She was naked from the waist up and held the knife pointed at her stomach.

Kono stood tall and did not move but he yelled something in Japanese at the woman, it was deep and guttural but rose in volume to the point he was screaming at her. The look on his face was of anger and shame. She cried at him in the same language; tears were running down her face. Kono spoke again, demanding something from her. Dia held the knife firm as if she were about to plunge it into her gut. Kono slowly walked around the room nowhere near Dia. He yelled at her some more then stopped and laughed. More words but they affected Dia Terashita instantly. She screamed at him! Kono continued to laugh, his words though unintelligible had a profound effect on Dia. Her lips were trembling. Kono was being cruel to her, he waved his hand at her like he just said 'Go ahead, kill yourself. No one will miss you!' The knife wavered in her hands. Then Sana caught one word from Kono, 'Terashita', the prefix must have something to do with her father. Did Kono insult her with her father's name? The woman screamed at him again and reached up to wipe the tears from her eyes with one hand. That was all Kono needed.

Sana was always amazed how fast a Marine could move, certainly faster than a normal human. Kona grabbed the knife out of Día's hand and broke it in half with his fingers. Día's hand had not even reached her eyes. He pushed her back and threw the two pieces of the knife to a stone wall, they shattered into multiple pieces. Dia tried to cover herself but Kono would have none of that and would not allow Sana to kneel next to her in support.

Kono said something gentle but commanding to Dia. She looked up to him and held her broken fingers where the knife had been stricken. Another command and she stood up, covered herself and looked up to him. Kono spewed out a long and determined speech to Dia, he was calm but firm. When he finished Dia looked at the ground "Hai."

Kono snapped at her! More words and Dia looked up to him, "Hai, hai!"

Doctor Sabastian rushed to her to mend her hand.

Sana looked at Datsun, "What was that all about?"

Kono pulled her away from the other two and glared at the men and women eavesdropping on the drama, they moved on to other business. "It's called Seppuku, a ritual form of honorable suicide. But that sort of thing is reserved for the Samurai. She is not but her father was. This was to honor him and save face with her ancestors. But in our culture, if a woman attempts this sort of suicide, it brings great shame to the family. This was not something she knew. Only a warrior like me would know that."

Sana's eyes widened, "I don't know what a Samurai is, but does this mean you are one?"

Kono nodded, "Who do you think taught this fleet how to use swords? We have been doing it for select races for over 700 years. I did not train him, but Bale is one of the finest swordsmen I have ever met. The Samurai have trained many nations since we went into space for the emperor. I serve the emperor as do you but, in my case, were I to disgrace Him in any way, that would be my only honorable way out to save honor for my family."

"Kono? Is she safe?"

"I've got her for the next 23 hours, after that it is up to her. Yes, I think Dia is now over the hump, the shame of what she did to you and to her career. But I will train her in ways you will not understand. She needs to grow up!"

Sana leaned in and hugged Kono, she did not care if anyone saw them. "Thank you, Kono!"

Kono held her then let Sana go, "Return to Bale, your husband needs you."

"But...but we're not married."

Kono smiled, "Not yet."

39

Several ships arrived from Earth along with the AGAMEMNON II. Three huge tugs each ten kilometers square and five deep were put into orbit around Beta Three. These machines had little in the way of crew quarters as they were almost entirely engine. A Maw joined them.

Imagine a child's toy where you stick a doughy substance in one end, squeeze a handle and out the other pours out shapes through a plastic die. The Maw was exactly like that only it was beyond massive. Almost 30 kilometers wide by 17 kilometers tall. A three-kilometer opening in the rear enabled chunks of asteroids to be shoved in. Out the front, the Maw converted the material with nanos at a furious rate and rolled out a huge, curved panel 1600 kilometers long. Side walls were connected to a floor. Mountains, valleys, lakes, and other landscapes could be programed into these panels. The tugs would then take each panel and stick them together to eventually form a large ring, big enough for three million people to live on. It was a gigantic undertaking, but the emperor had already created five rings by this method. There were only two rings much larger than the diameter of Earth and they were called Arcs. These were formed from gas giants and created in the clouds, pulled out and set into place somewhere in a system. The process took years to complete but someday, Palisade would have a ring spinning at one half gravity for the colonists of the Explorer.

The last ship to arrive was the NAUTILUS. This was not a colony ship or an exploration vehicle, it was a Dreadnought, a killing machine, that was its only purpose. Fully eight kilometers in diameter, the huge sphere was nothing but guns, shields and very determined crewmen. It had only been used twice, once against another Wolverine base that was hassling a nearby Earth colony, but they were run off by the gun platforms. The NAUTILUS arrived at their base, a small moon and destroyed it completely. The other time was more vicious but at least human life had been saved.

Antellon was another fallen race set up by the Enki. They had managed to overcome their master's several centuries before but for some reason they kept their idols and bases as places of reverence. Antellions were discovered to be pre-Roman tribes captured by the Enki three thousand years before. Their religions spoke of a return of the gods, so they were a very superstitious lot. When the first Earth ship arrived, they welcomed it thinking that the gods had returned. But despite the larger size of their Earth cousins, the Terrans were revealed by the ruling council on Antellon to be blasphemous creatures imitating gods. The first scouting party to meet with the Antellions were captured, tortured in ways that had not been seen on Earth in thousands of years and eventually killed, their bodies desecrated. The rest of the ground party were dispatched by sniper fire. Master Sergeant Townsend died this way trying to help the Antellions.

The Earth ship ran off not wishing to destroy the planet but to report to the emperor of the horror their people experienced by these lost humans. The emperor was furious! So the NAUTILUS arrived as a show of force. It destroyed one of the space stations from half a lightyear away just to prove that it could. The people of Antellon were informed that all other stations and bases around the Antellon system were to be abandoned and for them to return to the planet's surface. The Antellions refused and tried to start a war with the NAUTILUS. It was a short war.

Everyone returned as ordered. All stations, bases and artificial satellites were destroyed. Ground-based lasers were destroyed along with any nuclear rocket bases. The military was reduced to ashes and many of their support industries joined them. All the Temples were destroyed too.

Antellon had been intentionally clocked back 200 years and became an agrarian society. The emperor warned them when next a Terran ship appeared in their skies, they would be welcomed and treated with respect or their world would be blasted from this universe. The Antellons believed him!

Commander Barnes folded his arms over his chest and frowned at the image of the NAUTILUS. “Don’t you think this is a bit of overkill, sir?”

“Of course it is!” His grandfather retorted. “Jeff, just one of those Enki ships killed a lot of people before we destroyed it and we had to sacrifice another ship to do it. You and I know that is not the only one and any others are probably back at that Wolverine base. I am having Admiral Nakamura order you and the NAUTILUS to that base to destroy whatever is there. If you must use the final solution then I want you to make the order by my command, make it happen. This will not be the first time we run into these clowns. We don’t need any false gods coming back to enslave or kill people just because they think they can!”

Lucas was incredibly angry, more than his grandson had ever seen in him. “I don’t need to remind you how many Terrans the Wolves have killed plus an entire world! And these overgrown rodents work for the Enki. Don’t have any moral compunctions about leveling the playing field...wipe them out!”

Sana landed at the entrance to the Throne room. She walked in with other technicians and stared about her. The room was large and well-lit even if the floor was tilted a bit. All the walls were smooth with Sumerian carvings all over. The ceiling high above was adorned with Helios’ God Symbol, a large sun with rays that reached out to every corner except where Bale had thrown that rock. The colors were still brilliant after all this time, there was even gold embedded in parts of the relief. “Lieutenant Abbicon, report to the commander!”

She jumped up in the air and followed the icon to Bale. Sana landed neatly next to him and other officers and some scientist types. “Here as ordered, Sir!” She saluted him and smiled brilliantly. Bale looked at her, “Are you high?”

“No, just happy to be here and to serve.” She kept grinning stupidly at him.

"Hmph, how is Lt. Terashita doing?"

Sana continued to smile but was a bit more subdued. "She's over the hump. Dia has accepted her demotion and thanks you for not killing her. The lieutenant is with Master Sergeant Nakamura for the next few hours. He's retraining her, in what I don't know but it's a Japanese thing."

"Yeah, I heard about that. I'll need my man back tomorrow."

"No problem, sir."

Bale turned to the men and gave additional orders. As they left, he turned back to Sana, "Lieutenant Abbicon, I want you to meet Dr. Warring and her assistant Mr. Roy. They are part of the Archaeological survey team that came with Captain Castillo on AGAMEMNON I. Doctor?"

"Thank you for coming," Dr. Warring looked Sana up and down and wondered at the age of the young woman who supposedly had more experience than her in cuneiform. "I understand you are from the Explorer?" Sana nodded. "And your language from your home world was based on the original Enki pictograms?"

"Yes ma'am." Sana was getting a little ticked at this patronizing attitude from the friendly doctor of language and archaeology. Why was she being so snooty to her?

Bale could tell the doctor was a little upset that she was no longer the foremost authority in the room, but he decided he would let Sana handle it...this should be good!

Dr. Warring continued to grill the lieutenant to ascertain her credentials like for a job interview that Sana did not want. "I understand that you accidentally woke up the base on Beta Three."

"That is incorrect, ma'am." The doctor bristled at the correction. "Two engineers accidentally started the base, I was aboard AGAMEMNON III at the time. When I returned to the base, I was able to interpret every single glyph at that base. It took some time. I was also able to turn off the distress signal the base was sending out and to disable the remaining robots still trying to attack our men.

Doctor, I grew up on a world reading cuneiform that predates yours by a few thousand years. I also have a copy, a dictionary of Enki glyphs that predate Tekm' by at least 10,000 years. I am sorry the emperor did not see the need for you to have a copy. Perhaps His Royal Majesty felt he already had an expert on site. I would give you a copy if you asked the commander politely and he authorizes it, of course he will have to ask my Captain as the manual belongs to him...that could take some time."

The Doctor was furious and excited at the same time. She had no idea that there was a document that held ancient Sumerian pictograms, that it even existed! These military boobs were keeping it from her!

"Lieutenant Jackson, I instruct you to tell this young woman to give me a copy of that text so that someone on this rock will be fully qualified to interpret them correctly," she turned to Sana, "no offense dear." She sneered at Sana, "None taken Ma'am. In the future you *will* refer to this gentleman as Commander as he is the commander-in-Theater. It's a military term, not a civilian one but if you don't use it correctly, the commander will ignore you and then you will be escorted from this 'Rock' back to Captain Castillo so that she can explain it to you in complete detail."

Sana turned to Bale, "Sir, I'm sorry I was delayed but I would like to do my survey now. I certainly hope no one has disturbed the site."

"Carry on, Lieutenant."

People nearby laughed quietly as the mad doctor sputtered. Lt. Abbicon had put that woman in her place, and they loved it!

40

Sana put the self-important nutjob out of her mind. She brought up her camera and began taking pictures of fallen control panels. Some were crumbled on the floor of the Throne room while others were still standing. The fallen ones she would just float over and snap away, the others she stood in front of and to the side to get highrez images of the raised glyphs. "Here, I brought a tripod for your camera."

Sana turned and saw Dr. Warring's assistant. The man appeared about thirty in his helmet but there was no telling how old he was. Sana ignored him and continued to examine the control panels.

"Um, if you don't mind my asking, why are you taking pictures of these stone tablets? Aren't the real artifacts over there on the walls? I mean, the controls of this base?"

Sana turned to the man. "Mr. Roy, that's just decoration. It celebrates the Sun god Helios. These are the real control panels, 22 in all by my count, Enki loved prime numbers. Why use 17 when 23 was better? But for some reason, one is missing."

Gerald studied the young woman and even in a suit she was the most beautiful woman he had ever seen but she was an alien. Oh, he knew that she was supposed to be human but there was something different about her. "But all these panels are the same and they're all made from stone. How can they be in control of anything?"

Sana sighed, "Don't you have anything better to do? Each panel *Is* the same and for good reason, but each serves a different purpose. We design our computers to change faces for different controls as we need them but sometimes, they break and then you are on your own. Except for the catastrophe this asteroid experienced, these panels would still work. The base on Beta Three proved that, even 12,000 years later. And though they are stone, have a good look at their bases. They were wired. The cuneiforms light up! How the Enki did that we are still trying to figure out. Now sir if you don't mind, I have a lot of work to do before dinner."

"Um about that, I was wondering if I could invite you to sit with me for dinner. I would enjoy your company and of course your expertise in cuneiform. My name is Gerald, and I would be honored to have dinner with you tonight."

Sana was bending over and taking more pictures of the crumbles on the floor hoping the man would go away. As she stood up, Sana caught him staring at her butt. He blushed.

"Isn't that sweet! I would accept your offer, Mr. Roy but I am having dinner with a friend, a previously arranged engagement. I'll say 'hi' at dinner."

Gerald shrugged and walked away with his tripod.

Bale buttoned up his shirt and put his jacket over that. All his metal was on including his cards. He did not know what Sana had in mind, but she made a fuss that dinner would be special tonight. Something about service from the captain of the AGAMEMNON I. He could not let his men be out of uniform much less without weapons in a hostile environment, but they could eat a nice dinner with their chest plates and sundries on the walls behind them to use at a moment's notice.

He thought about it some and like so many times before, he put the object in his pocket. *Maybe tonight, in front of everyone? What if she says no?*

Cage knocked on his door and of course just walked in as Bale was buffing his insignia. "You're not going to believe this!"

Oh Lord, what now? Nick was now one of his best friends. "Well, first off Captain Castillo is here and brought an entire contingent of troops to guard us during dinner." Bale smiled, that was nice, and he was glad she was here as she had brought the first real hot meal they had had since hitting the rock two weeks ago. He wanted to thank her personally for the hospitality, and of course the backup. He finished up in front of the mirror. "What else?"

Cage grinned wickedly, "Your ladylove is dressed to the nines! And it's not regulation." *Uh oh.* He looked in the mirror and wondered if he was dressed enough for Sana. What was she wearing? Then he chided himself for acting like his sister just before a date.

"C'mon, you look great! Let's eat, I'm hungry!"

Cage and Bale walked out of his rooms and down a hall when they ran into the captain. Both men stopped and saluted her. "At ease gentlemen. Master Sergeant, if you don't mind, I would like to speak for a moment with the commander." Cage saluted again and left them alone.

"I'm sorry to crash your soiree but I wanted to meet you. I have read the reports from you and your team and I have to say I am impressed! Commander, I'm going to recommend to the emperor that your 1st Lieutenant status remain permanent." The woman had a strong Texas accent with Hispanic overtones. She was not short but was slim in an aristocratic way. Her eyes smiled at him and were surrounded by thick blonde hair tied into a French braid that ran down her back. The woman was elegant in every way.

"Thank you, Captain. I appreciate that but do extend your thanks to the rest of the men. They all have worked extremely hard on this project. And thank you for the food! Beans and ham with eggs on occasion only go so far."

She laughed and grabbed his arm with both of hers, "I'm sure you've eaten better than that, but I will admit my Chef has prepared something special for your crew. Let us go and enjoy our dinner!" Bale escorted the captain to the main hall inside their Command Center.

Sana was nervous in that she wore less than the other ladies in the room. Her blouse was navy blue and a very loose affair with a scalloped neckline that was a bit too low, scalloped sleeves, a matching short skirt with a slit on her left side almost to her hip and thigh-high leather boots that were wrinkled and more of a suede in texture, the heals were four inches high. Her eye makeup matched her blouse with coral highlights and her lips were dressed in dark Pink. She did not need to do anything to her hair, it remained curly and bounced like her blouse did. Sana was surrounded by her friends and all were having a good time, the ladies complimenting her outfit, the men just staring and thinking *Lucky Bastard!*

"Attend 'Chut!" Everyone sitting instantly stood up and the rest all faced Captain Castillo as she walked into the room on the arm of the commander. They all saluted. The civilians present did not know what to do but stood anyway. "At ease," she said.

On one wall was mounted the Terran flag. Captain Castillo shouted, "Salute and Pledge!"

Everyone recited the Pledge and finished. The captain was glad that the commander kept up traditions.

Mary Conners a new friend whispered to Sana, "You just had to let those girls go free-range tonight."

"Shhh, I want Bale to notice."

"Oh, he noticed and so did every other man in the place," Mary giggled.

Captain Castillo practically had to drag the commander over to Sana, the man stumbled at almost every step. Any other officer, she would have him tested for drunkenness while on duty. She smiled as Sana came near. "Here dear, I believe he belongs to you." Bale just stood there and stared at Sana. She was magnificent but all he saw was her hazel eyes. She stared up at him and put her hand on his chest, "Breathe..." She pushed his stomach in and the man finally gasped. Bale coughed a little and though embarrassed turned to the captain. "May I escort you to your table, Sir?"

Captain Castillo smiled, "I think I'll find my own way, thank you." She winked at Sana and walked away. Sana looked up at Bale. "Do you like it?"

Bale nodded, "Yeah, and the clothes are nice too!" Sana pouted but smiled at the compliment. "Where did you get them?"

"I ordered them from a shop on the AGAMEMNON I, they have terrific stuff there!"

She placed her arm on Bale's left and they walked over to

the long table, one of two for the fifty plus men and women having dinner in the large hall. The captain wanted Sana on her left so Bale pulled out her chair and she sat down. "I wanted us to have some time to talk," the captain smiled at her. Bale sat next to Sana, the chief and Cage sat opposite. Cage could not keep his eyes off Sana's blouse. She wanted to kick him with her silver tipped boots, but the large man probably would not feel a thing. Servers brought over plates for the five of them. Everyone else hit the buffet line.

They enjoyed tortilla and corn soup, Ox tail and brazed chicken thighs on Spanish rice, fish and shrimp tacos with a mango salsa, beef fajitas, steaming Sopapillas and for dessert Pay de Queso with strawberries. The men ate with gusto. Mike and Nick sent back for seconds and thirds. Sana could not eat that much as she was just not that big a girl, but she tried everything and loved it all! They could hear others around the room making yummy noises as they consumed a cornucopia of new tastes.

The captain wiped her mouth, "So my dear, how do you like our neck of the woods?" the Texan twang clearly in her voice.

Sana had never heard that colloquialism before, but she gathered its meaning. "It's frightening but never boring!" Everyone laughed at that one.

"I've been following your career too. I heard you had a rough start besides your obvious skills."

Sana ducked her head in shame, "Yes, I was difficult, and I made a lot of mistakes." She looked up to the captain, "But with these men and others not present, they brought me through."

The chief leaned in, "She has become a real asset to the team and on board the AGAMEMNON III. We are all real proud of her." Cage even jumped in with a compliment. "I've known the commander for a few years but in just a few short months, the lieutenant tamed the Baywolf. It needed doing, he paused and looked at Sana, "and you did it Sir!"

Sana blushed and squeezed Bale's hand under the table. "Thank you," she smiled.

Small talk continued and everyone seemed happy. Down

the second table in civilian country Gerald sat next to a couple of technicians and some non-coms. He looked across the way at the commander and Sana. “So she and the commander are a couple?”

“Yep,” one of the sergeants said. He looked over at the little guy, “You didn’t make a pass at her, did you?” Gerald blanched. “No, no of course not. We’ve only just met!”

The sergeant belched and said, “That’s good because if you had and the commander found out, you would be crawling home.”

“Crawling, sir?”

“Ya can’t walk with no legs!” All the other troops along the table burst out laughing!

41

Mike leaned into the captain. "As it seems we're almost done here I thought a little entertainment might be in order, with your permission Captain."

She smiled, "Of course!"

The chief turned in his seat. "Lieutenant Darrell, front and center!"

A tall spare man with long fingers came over and saluted. "None of that Mister, we're off duty due to the grace of our hostess. Now go get your guitar and play us a tune." The man smiled and left the room for his bunk. Cage smiled too, "Captain, this will be good! That man can sing so well that rocks cry."

Captain Castillo smiled at Cage. The man was gritty, but she liked him in that he reminded her of home, the ranch where she grew up. The ranch hands spoke just like he did, not nasty but certainly crass. Cage made her feel homesick. "Would anyone like coffee?" Cage eagerly nodded.

Lieutenant Darrel came back with a wonderfully designed guitar. It was considered an historic asset and he owned it, having been passed down to him, father and son for five generations. Mike stood up and whispered into his ear. Darrel's eyes widened, "But Sir, that would be cruel!"

"Just do it and make it romantic. The girls will love it!"

People moved the tables out of the way and cleared an area in the middle of the hall. Darrel plucked a few notes then waited on the chief. Mike walked around the table and held out his hand to Sana. "With Bale's permission, I would like to have this first dance." Her eyes watered and looked at Bale, "I haven't danced since my father died."

He cupped her chin. "You'll do fine so long as the chief doesn't break you." Sana stood up and carefully took the chief's hand and walked out onto the improvised dance floor.

Darrel had been warming up a tune but had yet to begin singing. Sana curtsied to the chief and he bowed to her...and hit the floor. "Damn! There goes my trick knee again!" Everyone knew he did not have a trick knee, but they played along. "Bale, you're going to have to finish this for me." The chief dramatically limped back to the table. Bale passed him going to Sana, "*Trick knee, my ass!*" Mike winked at him.

Sana was worried, "Is he going to be all right?"

"Yeah, it goes out once in a while," Bale rolled his eyes.

He was nervous. Bale did not dance except with his sister. He hoped he remembered how to do it. He bowed to Sana and she curtsied again. Darrel picked his guitar a little louder and began to sing.

♫Tale as old as time, true as it can be... ♫

Most of the women swooned when Darrel began singing, and not just because of his voice but also the song was one of the most romantic tunes well over a century old and still popular with young girls. They had all been young once and still remembered the tune from their childhood.

Bale began to lead Sana with her right hand held in his left, he held her waist as she kept her other arm free. His feet were moving in conjunction with hers. How was he doing this?

♫Both a little scared, neither one prepared...Beauty and the Beast♫

Bale jerked his head up. "Hey!" He knew who the Beauty was.

Sana pulled him back down as everyone laughed.

Three women walked over and started to sing the chorus along with Darrel.

♫Certain as the Sun, Rising in the East... ♫

Bale turned Sana marveling at how his feet moved without losing balance or dropping her.

Sana was lost in the moment. Bale was dancing with her! And the song was beautiful!

The song seemed to go on forever and that's exactly where Bale wanted to be, with this beautiful woman...forever!

♫Tale as old as time," Darrel slowed down. "Song as old as rhyme..."♫ Bale pulled Sana in then dipped her to the floor and pulled her up. She looked up at him and smiled with tears in her eyes.

♫Beauty and the Beast.♫ Darrel let the last note follow his fading vibrato.

She leaned into him then pulled his head down and kissed him in front of everyone.

"Awwww...!" Bale blushed in colors no one had ever seen.

Sana smiled, "Our first song." And everyone heard her. Men and women smiled, some snickered. It was obvious that Lieutenant Abbicon did not know this was a children's story. Bale realized he would have to download at least the first two versions of the movie for Sana. But the music was good.

Lieutenant Darrel started playing a different song, the Blue Danube. "C'mon everyone who can. This is a Waltz so join in. Several couples joined Bale and Sana on the Dance floor and began the slow but beautiful dance centuries old. Captain Castello grabbed Cage, "Let's see if you can cut a rug!" Cage smiled, he really liked it when a woman took over.

Sana was amazed at the intricacy of the dance, the swirling, raising and lowering of arms and the interplay between couples just missing each other as they danced by. It was all too fun! How Lieutenant Darrel could play such an intricate song on a guitar with only six strings proved his genius.

When it finished, Darrel moved into an intricate and fast-moving solo on his guitar. That his fingers could strum so fast amazed everyone. They applauded him as he finished.

He stood up, bowed and said, "Just one more tune so everyone, please wait."

Everyone took a break and talked. Darrel walked over to the captain and spoke to her in Spanish. Her eyes widened, she had no idea the man could speak her native language but then she realized, he would have to speak many languages to perform his musical talent. They spoke for a few minutes and she nodded to him. She called over to the Master Chief and spoke to him. The chief 'pinged' a female on the floor. "Darn! Sana, I must trade places with one of the troops outside. Save me some of that cheesecake!"

Cage got a 'ping' too and started putting on his gear. Bale

wondered what was going on. One of the men inside guarding the captain walked away from the wall and took off his gear. Another man came in from outside, his armor steaming in the heat of the hall and discarded his gear as well. Darrel walked over and spoke to the two men then all three left the hall to a smaller back room.

Servers were cleaning the tables and stacking them away. Sana turned to hug Bale again, "I'm having the best time! I wish I could do this with you forever!" Bale smiled down at her, *not yet, not until the last song*.

The captain was sitting at her table as it had not been moved for her convenience, Cage in full gear stood next to her. They could hear the men distantly singing in the next room. It was barely legible, but the captain began to cry.

"Captain?" She reached over and grabbed his hand. "Please, call me Janet." He reached over and covered her hand with his other. "What's wrong, Janet?"

She sniffled and wiped her eyes. "It's El amor es para Siempre, a love song. My parents sang it to each other at their wedding and after my mom passed, he sang it at her funeral to her...he died six months later from a broken heart. This song has special meaning for me. I hope it does for your Commander and his lady." Cage teared up over that story. "I guess I'm sentimental too."

Darrel and the two marines walked back into the hall. Darrel leaned his guitar against a nearby wall and walked forward. Everyone got quiet and pulled back. Darrel walked forward and stopped Bale and Sana from melting into the crowd. "Please Sir and Ma'am, stay right here." Sana looked up at Bale and was confused. Bale shrugged as he had no idea either. They were the only couple on the dance floor.

Darrel rejoined the two men and all three began humming. Both the backup singers began a song in Spanish. It was low but stirring then rose to more dramatic moves. They sang for several measures building up the audience then Darrel joined in. All three men were tenors, and they sang acapella.

Sana did not understand a word, but she could feel the emotion. Darrel rose with the song but the men behind him pulled him back down into a minor key. Sana's heart swelled. There were tears in the song but joy too!

Sana leaned into Bale and put her arm around his back or tried to as the man was so big. Bale pulled her little hand to his chest and stood there transfixed by the song. There was hope, fear and happiness in the song. He could not figure out why a song he did not know a single word to affected him this way.

Darrel and the two men rose and fell in pitch and harmony. People were crying, the captain was holding on to Cage and he was gently holding her. Bale was losing his mind! This song!

Sana swooned, smiled with tears and held tightly to Bale. He pulled her to his front, and she leaned back against him. Bale wrapped his arms around her, and Sana clung tight to him as the three men slowly walked to them. The song rose and then climbed some more. Darrel and the marines raised their arms and reached a new height in pitch and power! People were clapping now. The men finished in a harmonious celebration and stared at the ceiling on the last note they held for several seconds. Then they dropped their arms and bowed to the couple in front of them.

The room exploded in applause! Whistles, hoots and laughter along with a lot of tears being wiped from their collective eyes. It was so beautiful!

Sana turned and cried into Bale's chest, he held her close. Somehow that song was meant for them and for so many others over the centuries. But what did it mean? He pulled Sana's head back and bent down to kiss her again. *It was time.*

The three men pulled back and waited. Cage bent to the captain, "You don't want to miss this." Janet turned around, wiped her eyes and looked at the commander and Sana. "Do you think...?"

"And about damn time too!"

Bale pulled back from Sana but held onto her left hand...then he knelt in front of her. There was a hush in the room and all eyes were locked on Bale and Sana. Sana was lost, *could it be? Would he?*

"Sana de Verico Abbicon, we met for the first time seven months, 16 days, 8 hours and 37 minutes ago. Never in my mind would I have imaged this day to come or that you would be the woman of my desire. I...I can't even begin to understand how you, um, I mean ever thought to kiss me. What do I mean to you? But for me, it is all too simple. I love you!

You are a pill, extraordinarily pretty but your eyes captured me first. You saved me and I saved you. We're a team, um not like a military thing but, um...well," Bale swallowed. He was screwing this up! Then he looked up into her eyes again and remembered the first time. All fear was gone, he would not part with her again. "Sana, I can't live without you. Will you marry me?"

He reached into a side pocket and pulled out a small box. Bale opened it and showed her the rings. Sana put her hands over her mouth, tears were forming on the lids of her eyes. And then she looked into those brilliant green eyes that had captured her soul that very first day. Everyone waited on her response.

"Yes, Yes! I will marry you! I love you too! I always have. I will marry you! You are my best friend! Oh yes, Bale! I want to be your wife!"

Everyone cheered!

Bale stood and took one of the rings from the box. "This is an engagement ring. It's simple but you can wear it under your gloves." He put it on her finger. "The other is a wedding ring." It was fully adorned with diamonds, silver and gold. Completely gaudy but it was appropriate. The little thing flashed the entire room. "The last ring is our wedding band, it is armored. Simple but you can wear it anywhere."

Sana looked at the rings on her finger and then placed her hands on Bale's chest. "Will I always be your Baby Girl?"

Bale grinned, "Always!"

Sana leaned up to kiss her future husband.

Everyone cheered and clapped!

Sana ran over to her friends and showed off the rings. Mike walked over to Bale, "You sure about this son?" Bale glared at him, "Yes! You got a problem with that, Chief?"

"Nooo, no no but she is going to put you through the wringer. My wife worked me hard and she taught me a lot about myself. Son, when the kids come along, she will be a barracuda. You won't mean a damn thing!" He laughed and slapped Bale on the back.

The captain walked up, "Well that was a nice finish to the evening. Now I am going to take your future bride-to-be back to the ship."

"Wha...?" Bale stuttered. Sana's head snapped around, "But I don't want to leave!"

The captain looked over at Cage. "Master Sergeant? Would you be so kind to deliver this young lady to my state rooms on the AGAMEMNON I?"

Cage grinned wickedly, "Yes Ma'am." With that he picked up Sana and ran for the gate. "Baallllee..." And her voice shut off as she disappeared into the gate with Cage.

Janet looked back up to Bale. "And since you won't be getting any sleep tonight, I expect everything to be ready for tomorrow's junket down the subway."

"But Sir...why?"

She reached up and patted his face. "Young man, I've buried two husbands, not by choice but I loved them both and have children from each. This is a strong commitment the two of you are taking. I want you to be sure. I will deliver officer Abbicon in the morning. Have a good night!" She grinned at him and walked away through the gate.

Then Mike Green walked over and put his hand on Bale's shoulder. "Well, I guess you didn't expect that?"

42

The AGAMEMNON III and the NAUTILUS had left Palisade two days before and would reach the Wolverine base in 17 hours. They were traveling at TL 18 and under cloak from their shields. Commander Barnes did not know if the Enki and their flunkies could detect them but there was no point in taking chances. All unnecessary crew, spouses and children had been removed from the AGAMEMNON III. They would not be risking them too if a battle broke out between the Terrans and the Enki. Surprise would be on their side, at least for a short time. Enough for the NAUTILUS to unleash damage to any ships in the area and if necessary, to deploy its ultimate weapon.

"Sir?" Jeff turned to his navigator. "We've detected a ship heading in our general direction coming from Star 998. It must be Enki for it is moving at TL 7.8." Taylor looked up to his commander.

"Heading?"

"Straight for Palisade. At its current speed it will reach Palisade in three months."

Another voice came over the Comm. "Commander. Do you wish for us to destroy it?" It was the captain of the NAUTILUS. Commander Barnes did not much like the captain even though he outranked Jeff, it was not that. The man had no empathy for others and thus was cold as a fish. He and all his crew shared this trait, and it was a desirable one to operate the NAUTILUS. They took no joy in killing an enemy, but they had no qualms about doing it either, conscientious objectors were not allowed on the NAUTILUS.

"No, we will pick them up on the way back. Stick to the mission for now. We do not want it to warn anyone at their base."

They trained cameras on the Enki ship as it flew 100,000

klicks away. It never noticed death passing them heading for its base.

Commander Barnes sent a message back to the admiral warning them of the coming Enki ship...just in case something was to happen to the AGAMEMNON III and the NAUTILUS.

Sana woke up and stretched on the comfortable bed. Then she realized Bale was not next to her. *What a stinker Captain Castillo was!* They did not talk about the wedding, was she doing the right thing or not, or anything! The woman just sent her to bed. Sana stared at the plain engagement ring and wondered about her future with Bale...as far as she was concerned, it was not in doubt!

She found a robe next to her gear and weapons. Mary Conners had brought them over the night before and hooked them up to the rechargers. They had talked some, but all Mary did was console Sana as she cried. Happy for the engagement to a man she loved and damn pissed off that they didn't get to celebrate the night together! Mary nodded and smiled. "Honey, everyone within a Parsec knows you two belong together. Just be patient." They hugged and Mary went back to the Enki base.

Sana rubbed her eyes and wondered where the kitchen was. Coffee was in order and she needed it now, but the apartment of the captain was a spacious thing. Then she heard soft voices and laughter coming from around a corner of a wall. She staggered in and found the captain leaning into Cage with her robe open. Fortunately, he was wearing boxer shorts. "There's the sleepy head," he pronounced!

"Shut up!" Sana pouted.

"Morning Joe is over there." Cage pointed with his free hand and drank from his coffee mug with the other. Janet just smiled and stared at Sana, her head leaning on Cages' chest fully two feet below the top of his head.

Sana found a mug and poured herself a cup. Cage finished his and put it down. "I'd best be going. His nibs is going to want an early start." Cage bent down and kissed the captain then walked out of the kitchen.

Janet closed her robe, “Had time to think about it?”

Sana sipped her coffee and closed her eyes. “You are evil and should be destroyed!”

Janet chuckled, “I’ve got three daughters and two granddaughters that would agree with you.”

Sana put her hands around the cup to warm them. “Why? We’ve got to plan this wedding and...our life together!”

“Lust is one thing, a marriage is entirely another. As to your futures, Bale is going to be a great man in our military. You will follow *him*!”

Sana’s lips trembled. “You mean I have no say in his career, or mine?”

Janet smiled broadly. “Oh Yes! You will have a great deal to do with his career! Our military is quite different than that of a century ago where a military wife clipped coupons and played Rummy with the other military wives.”

Sana looked confused, “Rummy?”

“It’s a card game, dear.”

Sana put her cup down and frowned some more.

“I understand that your society or culture is very patriarchal.” Sana nodded. “Ours isn’t so much but in the military, it is entirely Patriarchal.” Janet walked over and started plucking at Sana’s locks loosening stray ones to fit back into the intricate puzzle of her hair. “You will stay in flight and Bale will stay as 1st Lieutenant and eventually become a Commander. When the kids come along then your roles will change. You will have unimaginable power over Bale and the military knows this.” Sana let go of her cup and hugged the captain. Janet pulled her in and cupped her beautiful head of hair and Sana cried into her shoulder.

“Honey, everyone knows that boy loves you.” Janet wiped Sana’s eyes and kissed her forehead. “No one can stop this, not that we would but you do need to know and learn how he is to proceed. It will take time and if you need my help, I’ll be there...just don’t muck this up for both your sakes!”

Sana nodded, “Thanks! I have made so many mistakes that I am not sure where one ends and another one begins. But I promise, I will do better!”

Janet grinned. “This mission should end in the next week or so. I’m offering the AGAMEMNON I as your Chapel and the Presidential Suite in the Hilton for your Honeymoon, my treat!”

Sana smiled, wiped her eyes and said, “How do I get such good friends like you, Cage, Tracy and all the others?”

Janet pulled back and stared at the woman. “We’re just jealous and happy we get to meet a princess in love with an armored beast!” They laughed together and hugged again.

“Um, uh...I have to go.” Cage stood at the kitchen doorway a little embarrassed that he had heard the last of that. He was fully armored, but his helmet was not lifted yet. Sana walked over and pulled his collar down.

“You take care of my boy, okay?” Then Sana kissed him on his cheek. Janet did not want to waste this moment either. “You heard the Lady!” Then she kissed his other cheek. Cage turned around and looked at his image in a hallway mirror. “Damn! I’ve got to get this tattooed on! No one will believe me!”

He looked down at Sana, “Don’t be late...you know how he worries.” Cage winked at the captain and ran through her personal gate.

“Go take a shower dear and get ready.” Janet stumbled against the cabinet. “Are you okay?” Sana asked.

Janet held on to her hip, she looked at Sana and smiled. “I’m going to feel this later this morning.” She sucked in air, “There is a difference between fully augmented and ‘Really Fully Augmented’! Be careful with Bale.”

The AGAMEMNON III and the NAUTILUS dropped out of TL half a light year from system 998. There was nothing special about the blue dwarf star and its planets. Not many planets, no gas giants but lots of asteroids. The only full gravity planet the Wolverines used had a methane atmosphere and was uninhabitable except for the domes used by the wolves. What made the system special was the fleet of ships scattered throughout the small system and near the base. It was huge and mostly Enki. The ships had tentacles attached to spheres. The larger ships had to be carriers and their tentacles were as large as some of the smaller ships. There must have been over 800 ships in that system!

Captain Dillon did not wait on the commander of the AGAMEMNON III to advise him. "Spin up the BB!" He switched to another channel, "Commander Barnes, I am warming up the weapon. There is no possible fight here. We would lose!"

Jeff agreed. "I need intel first. Make ready and find a suitable spot near the base for transfer. There appears to be several shipyards in orbit around it and one carrier nearby."

"Commander, when we deploy the weapon, it won't make any difference where the carriers are in the system!"

Commander Barnes nodded, he did not want to do this, but his grandfather insisted. With the size of that fleet Earth could be in jeopardy! He had no choice. He would deploy the BB.

The BB as it was known was a humorous metaphor for the horror it caused. Several years ago, a scout ship found an old *Scientist* ship adrift. Scientists as other races called them were a species strictly interested in knowledge. But they had found a way of supporting themselves with that knowledge. They flew around in generation ships that were huge but were essentially large research vessels. They had no weapons, little shielding and slipped at TL 1.2...terribly slow ships. Everyone knew not to destroy them but to swallow some pride to get what they needed. The Scientists were not without pride and gullibility, their egos inflated since their magnificent skills almost demanded it!

The Scientists were plied with food, energy, fuel and other creature comforts along with lengthy compliments as to their worth to the galaxy. The pliant race would run off with their loot, the Scientists thinking they had made a good deal. This time it did not go well for the Scientists.

The ship was punctured in many places, part of it was missing too. It had been dead with its crew for several centuries. The scout ship found that the generation ship had been stripped like a car in a bad neighborhood. What few bodies they found had been tortured, the rest had blown out when the ship had been blasted postmortem. But the boarders missed something, something especially critical.

There were eight fuel tanks along the main axis of the ship near the engines, four on each side. All were 100 meters in diameter. The boarders found them and drained all the fuel but two were already empty as far as their sensors could determine. The raiders were in a hurry, so they did not bother confirming that those two tanks were in fact empty. They were not, instead they held star destroyers. The casings over the devices held a little fuel to make it look like it was almost dry but inside was a machine in each tank that could destroy an entire system when the star blew up.

Earth picked up the machines, read the manuals that were connected to each and learned how to make new ones. That the Scientists left digital manuals for these horrors spoke loudly of their hubris, everyone should have a star destroyer but at a cost!

The Nautilus held two in its hold. Each was 50 meters across and did not need to be dropped into a star to activate. This device had been tested once...just once, and that was enough. The shock wave had destroyed two of the testing ships several light seconds away. The rest managed to escape the forming nebula from the exploded system. This was not a weapon used lightly.

Commander Barnes sent two drones into the system to lace the Enkies with nanos. Their shields resisted the lace, so he had his men direct them to the shipyards. One of the carriers was tagged to it and a small Wolverine ship was in the grapples of the yard being refitted. The nanos were able to enter the carrier through the yard and began exploring its database. What the commander and his men found was frightening! This was one of three armadas now in Terran space!

More information was gathered but for the location of the other two fleets, they just did not know where they were. Most of it was in Enki pictograms some of which they could understand but the rest was up to Lt. Sana Abbicon to interpret. The commander nestled the two drones to ships nearby, their explosives armed.

"Captain Dillon, deploy the weapon on order of His Imperial Majesty Lucas Barnes. I want you to puncture as many carriers as you can after the weapon is transferred. Then we escape at TL 25."

"Yes, Commander but I want you in my shadow before I transfer the BB. I will give it a thirty-second window. I do not want the emperor's grandson to be harmed. You will leave as soon as I deploy the weapon. Is that clear, Sir?" The commander agreed.

The BB was spinning at a furious rate in its cradle, the gate built around the large cargo space activated and waited. The AGAMEMNON III moved behind the NAUTILUS and fired up its engines for a high TL speed, all hatches were closed and everyone inside belted up. This was going to be a rough ride.

The invisible NAUTILUS moved into the system slowly to get as near to the Wolverine base as possible. "Pinhole those seven carriers with a double tap." The captain indicated which ones he meant, and his gunners entered the data. Once the weapon was deployed, they would be visible as the gate transferring the BB would drain the cloaking device.

The Enki never noticed the smaller sphere in their midst, but they did fire on the larger sphere that appeared out of nowhere. The barrage had no effect on the NAUTILUS. It then fired on the carriers. Two were destroyed, the rest damaged with many Enki onboard killed by the plasma shaft running through their ships. Then the NAUTILUS ran with the AGAMEMNON III. The few survivors were shocked that the ship could slip at TL 25. Then the BB exploded.

There was little need to wait for a result, the NAUTILUS and the AGAMEMNON III raced for home. It would be years before the blast would be seen on Palisade.

43

Sana transferred back to the Enki base. Bale was working on strategy with his team leaders. He paused and looked over at her and waved off the men. They smiled and left his office.

"Sir, I'm sorry I'm late but the captain wanted a few words with me." She saluted Bale. He nodded back and whispered, "*Sleep well? I missed you.*"

She pulled her glove off her left hand and showed him the engagement band. Sana smiled, "Missed you too. We will talk later. I need to get to the throne room and find that last control panel."

Bale smiled at her, "As you were, Officer Abbicon...carry on." Then he bent down and kissed her.

Dr. Warring and her two assistants were already in the Throne Room. They were pretending to study glyphs but were waiting for 2nd Lieutenant Abbicon to move to the far side of the room. The doctor already knew where the twenty-third control panel was and had hid the fact from everyone but those on her team. It ticked her that the young woman knew there were 23 panels. She had been studying the manuscript all night and was scared. Most of the document negated over half of her observations from the last ten years. Her PHD was in jeopardy! Well, the doctor would show this tart and her Jackass Commander who the real intellect was on this mission!

Sana ignored the pretentious professor over on the other side of the room. She checked her map and made a few calculations. That panel would not be over here but at the other end of the space away from her. Sana looked over at 2nd Lieutenant Terashita, "What do you think?"

Sana had managed to snag the woman away from some mundane chore Bale had assigned to her. Dia was grateful and was glad to be with Sana. It may have been a small thing, but any redemption was worth the effort. Dia checked Sana's calculations and confirmed it should be on the other side of the rest of the control panels. "Yep, this is not the place." She smiled at Sana and both looked over to where Dr. Warring and her associates were lifting some heavy rocks off something.

Sana was confused and narrowed her eyes zooming in on the trio. Something was under that pile. Dia saw the same, "Sir, I don't think they need to be doing that. I see something sticking out of the floor just a few centimeters. Is that important?"

Lt. Abbicon knew it was. "Stop that right now!" All three people looked up and then hurried to finish uncovering the pile. Sana turned to the nearest rifleman, "Stop them right now!" The man did not hesitate but immediately flew over to the Doctor and her men. One of them pulled a small gun and fired at the noncom. The bullet ricocheted off his shields and flew off in the distance. The man's head soon followed being swept by the marine's arm. Mr. Roy threw a rock at the rifleman and died instantly when his chest shield was caved in by the private's foot. He then grabbed Dr. Warring and held her for his lieutenant.

Sana landed by the man and watched as the pile began to rise on its own. "Lieutenant! Thompson! Stop that panel from rising!" The rifleman pushed the doctor down and placed his hands on the rising panel. Dia joined in but it seemed to be no use. "Lieutenant! We can't stop it!"

Sana turned to Dr. Warring, "You idiot! You may have killed us all!"

The doctor sat on her rump and sneered at the little bitch. "It's not harmful. I read the manual! It's just another panel for my research, it means nothing!"

Sana kneeled in front of her, "Have you seen any of the other panels move?"

Confusion struck the woman. That was when fear broke the glass of her confidence, weak as it was. "But I didn't think, I mean...it shouldn't do anything!" she wailed.

Sana leaned over and snapped her fingers. A stasis field formed over the doctor. Unfortunately, one of her feet did not quite make it into the shield. It flopped once on the ground and froze instantly.

"Thompson! Get two men and get the rest of the civilians through the gate. Contact the captain of the AGAMEMNON I and inform her of your intent. I've got to call the commander!"

The man nodded and flew off to the Command center to gather the pain-in-the-ass civilians. He had no regrets of killing the two men...they were stupid and may have killed him and the rest in their ignorance.

Dia stood by and waited on Sana not quite knowing what to do.

"Commander Jackson, Now! Priority One!" Sana waited while the panel cleared the rest of the rocks and climbed to its eventual height. It stopped.

"Report!" Bale said on the Comms. Everyone could hear and they got worried quick.

Sana stiffened her spine, "Dr. Warring found and activated the twenty-third panel. She knew where it was and did not inform you or the rest of the team. She just now uncovered it from under a pile of fallen ceiling and it rose out of the floor on its own. I think it's about to..." And that is when the lights on the cuneiforms lit up. She read the lit icons at the top of the panel and took a deep breath, "Sir, it is the Systems and Security panel for the Rock."

Bale grimaced back near the Subway. His teams were ready to enter it when this happened. "What have you done with the civilians?"

Sana responded, "They are on their way back to the ship, the last were giving the men some trouble so they went as cargo." Which basically meant they were bubbled and sent through the gate without a choice.

"Have you tried to..." Sana interrupted him. "Sir, I'm trying to stop it right now, but things are moving at a fast pace! The cold-fusion reactors are now on-line, three out of five are working."

That was when the lights in the huge main chamber started to flicker. The main axis shaft was the source, a massive and long light tube. It put out no heat, but the lumens were climbing in brightness and color. Sparks began to fly off the shaft at every juncture of the spokes supporting it. The thing was obviously bent to some degree and the light dimmed there just a bit, but the light ran all the way into the Subway.

Sana ran through as many subroutines as her tablet had from the Enki base on Beta Three. None were working this time. "Sir, it's shutting me out. Right now it is testing all environmental systems on the rock. Now it's trying to apply spin, but all the gages show empty on fuel!" Sana watched as system after system was being queried by the panel and coming up negative. Airlocks were being shut all over the asteroid and, what was that? Crap! A field was forming over the broken crag at the top of the rock where they initially entered the city. Somewhere in the huge rock, subterranean canisters were pumping air into the living spaces. They must have been huge, but why didn't it protect the citizens the first time thousands of years ago?

She looked around the floor and saw massive rocks that had fallen from the ceiling at the time of the crash. Some must have slammed this panel back into its nest turning it off. The air went out and everyone died.

Bale could feel pressure returning to the chamber. What was happening in the Throne Room? "Lieutenant Report!"

"Sir, this panel managed to secure this facility and seal it. Air is being pumped back in! Heat too! A signal is being sent out, but it is very weak and sporadic. I can't stop it, but I doubt it will make it out of the Palisade system." Uh oh, "Sir, I see that the panel is sending robots up the subway shaft, lots of them!"

A sergeant near Bale called out. "I've got movement four klicks down the shaft heading this way!"

"Okay, you and Lt. Terashita get up here on the horn. We're going to need every gun we've got!"

The captain had just sat down in her Command chair on the bridge of the AGAMEMNON I with a fresh cup of coffee when the call came in from Specialist Thompson. The rifleman informed her that all civilians were being evacuated from the Enki base. Several were bubbled up but a designated one being Dr. Warring was to be incarcerated for treason according to Lieutenant Abbicon. The doctor would need medical treatment as she had left a foot on the Rock.

Serves that bitch right! Thought the captain. The woman had been a pain ever since they left Earth.

"Comm, get me the commander now!"

"Sir! Check out the Rock. Something is happening!"

She turned to the screens at the front of the room. Several were focused on the outside view of the huge asteroid. Lights were beginning to turn on. Not many but some of them blinked like navigation lights. She switched views from one K9 to another until she found the one focused on the broken entry. There was a shimmering field covering the hole now. Apparently, someone had turned the base on, and the captain had a fairly good idea who did it!

"Commander Bale here sir. Glad to hear your voice, we thought we were locked in without communications." Janet frowned, at least they could talk. She hoped the gates still worked otherwise she would have to make a hole to get her people out.

"Report!"

"Sir, at approximately 0930, Dr. Warring and two of her assistants uncovered the last operations panel. It awoke and fired up the rock. Her assistants are dead, and the doctor is in your possession. Lt. Abbicon tells me that it was the Systems and Security control for the entire Asteroid. Right now, we are getting air, light and heat. It is building slow, but the rock is renewing itself. We are also anticipating several robots of some type coming up the subway. They are moving slow but they are coming just the same. My men are ready. We are about to meet them."

"Very good Commander. I will have another squad ready here if you need them. Stay in touch and keep me informed. Out!"

44

Sana and Dia arrived at the Horn, a flat rock several hundred meters above the floor. It was flat and exceptionally large, enough for Bale's team and some drones to operate. The floor of the Horn looked right down the shaft of the subway. Light was brightening around them, but it was more like dusk of early morning.

"Datsun, you've got the drones. Chief, manage the troops and spread out the snipers. Master Sergeant Daniels and I will go down the shaft. Squad one you will follow 100 meters after us. Squad two, 100 meters after squad one. Squad three and four, protect the Horn and do not let those robots out into the Chamber! Lt. Abbicon and Lt. Terashita, you will protect Master Sergeant Nakamura as he will be busy with the drones."

"Copy!" Sana's eyes grew. He was going down there alone with only Cage as his backup? All the other men and women behind him were Points too and dangerous but still...

Cage landed near Bale. "What do you have in mind, sir?"

Bale looked over at him and smiled, "Mayhem of course!"

"My man! I thought you needed a little exercise. So you got some tunes for us to dance to?"

"How about Stairway to Heaven?"

Cage rolled his eyes, "Yeah, it picks up later, but I don't want to waltz with this bunch!"

Bale laughed, "Um," he ran through his playlist "how about Cricket's Dream?"

"I hate techno! I never know when they are going to change the beat. Something else, please!"

Everyone around them laughed but Sana was losing her mind! What were they talking about? Killer robots were coming, and they were discussing music?!!

Bale scrolled a little more. "Perfect!" He grinned wickedly

at Cage.

"What?"

"How does Welcome to the Jungle by Guns N' Roses grab ya?"

Cage gasped, *"Which version?"* he whispered hoping beyond hope.

"1987, Live!"

Cage was bigger than most Points but even at 600 lbs. he was dancing around like a little kid. "Please, please! Give me a copy...gimmie, gimmie, gimmie!"

Bale pinged one over and Cage settled down. "Well? Are you going to cue us up?"

"Weapons check first sir." Cage could not stop smiling. Christmas had come early this year!

Sana was struck with disbelief. Both men were nonchalant about their possible deaths as they checked their weapons. Then she saw them do something Sana had never seen a Point do before. Both men extruded a purple lit whip with chainsaw blades on them out of their arms. They dragged them across the ground sending up sparks and deeply gouging the floor of the Horn. Then they spun them in the air like whips they appeared to be. Both men reeled in the chains with blades on them and looked down into the shaft. Movement could be seen in the distance. Sana was truly frightened.

"Okay, let's go," Bale said.

"Wait, I've got to hear the opening riff from the guitar." Both men lit up like purple monsters, Bale with his sword and machete', Cage with two swords. Purple light flashed across the Horn and the rim of the subway. Sana thought it was beautiful and eerie too.

"You do realize this is now our song," he grinned.

"Up yours, Cage!"

The song began and everyone could hear it. A guitar banged out a few notes, waited half a second and strung out more notes building. Then a howling scream could be heard building in power. In the background the audience of the live performance from over a century ago could be heard shouting their enthusiasm. Drums landed the final blow...

"Now!" Cage and Bale jumped into the shaft and headed for danger.

♫ *Welcome to the Jungle, we've got fun and games!"* ♫ The song moved to a dangerous beat throbbing in everyone's head! ♫ *We got everything you want honey, we know the names!* ♫

Bale and Cage met the enemy and plowed into the robots like a hot knife through butter. Both men broke pieces off the machines, ceramic and metal/plastic parts flying everywhere and yet the song with the heavy beat played on.

♫ *We are the people that can find whatever you may need.* ♫

Smaller robots, no more than 20 centimeters across fired needles harmlessly against their shields. One jumped on Cage and he grabbed it crushing the poor thing. That is when his shield got a darker shade of purple. "Sir! Shield candy!" Bale grabbed one off the wall and crushed it too. His shields jumped 15%. What a rush!

♫ *If you got the money honey, we got your disease!* ♫

The drone behind them and slightly above caught all the action and everyone could see these two killing machines wrecking the Rock's defenses. Sana could not help herself, she started dancing. First moving her hips then she started moving in a circle spinning about herself. The beat drove her and watching her man tearing apart the enemy was too hot!

"Sana! What are you doing?" Dia was really confused and worried for the young lieutenant. Sana ignored her and waved her gun in the air. Then she turned to Dia and grabbed her hand. "Let's dance for the boys. I can see your hips moving too."

Dia did not know what to do but the beat was too hard to ignore. Sparks flashed around them as they spun around, then they did a hip bump to the beat of the song. Not a single robot made it past Bale and Cage.

♫ *In the jungle, welcome to the jungle*
Watch it bring you to your shun n-n-n-n-n-n knees! ♫

Bale spun around the axis grabbing spokes as he went by. He was doing some acrobatics like Sana would do. How? He did not know or care, he was having fun. Shots from some of the farther robots were going past them now. The drone fired back. Cage and Bale were too busy with the up close and personal robots to notice.

Bale saw a large humanoid robot heading their way, easily four meters tall and it was moving fast. It had no guns but a sword and a spear.

"Ya know boss, I've always had a thing for drumsticks," Cage commented. Bale responded, "Good! I prefer wings myself." Both men slammed into the big bot. Bale shattered its right arm and spun out his chainsaw whip, wrapped it around the head and left arm and pulled. Cage scissored the legs with his swords. The robot exploded in three directions. The men went on like nothing had slowed them down.

♫*Ohhh ah, I wanna watch you bleed!* ♫

By now everyone was either moving their heads or tapping their feet to the beat of the song and to the beating of the robots by the commander and the Master Sergeant. The two women kept dancing around each other backlit by falling sparks from the light axis above them. Squad one jumped into the shaft and followed the two men ahead of them. Other than killing the occasional little bots, there was really nothing for them to do.

The captain onboard the AGAMEMNON I was doing a butt dance in her seat and smiling while everyone else tapped their feet. This was Awesome!

Her FIRST said, "This is..." And both people said, "'Epic!'" Janet looked over at her younger Commander and grinned. "Yes!" She winked at him and continued to watch the show.

Cage had just sliced a bot diagonally when something came out of the wall near him, and it was all teeth. It swallowed his arm up to his armpit, sword and all. Cage yelled and punched it in the snout. The machine released the arm and Cage went on, did a back flip and reached out with his hand, snapped his fingers and the bot's head shredded as the sword raced back to his hand. Bale heard the yell and spun around to help Cage but something grabbed him too and yanked him into a large hole.

"Commander!" Sana yelled! But then she smiled and kept dancing... "Never mind."

Several explosions could be heard through the tunnel walls and then a few meters down part of the rock wall exploded! Bale sailed out and a huge gout of flame followed him. “Not now lieutenant, I’m busy!”

Dia yelled, “Did you see that?!!”

Janet’s FIRST yelled, “Did you see that?!!”

The chief just smiled. *Show off!*

More ribbed robots came out of the walls, teeth and all but the two men were now warned. Purple whips ripped off heads, their bodies oozing fluid and thrashing about.

♫ *Welcome to the jungle, we take it day by day*

If you want it you’re going to bleed, but it’s the price you pay! ♫

The beat of the song drove everyone into a frenzy. Everyone grinned as they watched Bale and Cage mangle everything in their path down the subway. Squad two jumped into the subway but realized there was nothing they could do but they would get closer to the show.

Sana and Dia spun their hips and torsos with gears a man did not have. Occasional shots from the robots sliced past them but the women ignored them as none were close. Just streaks of light joining the flood of sparks flashing around them.

♫ *And you’re a very sexy girl, very hard to please*

You can taste the bright lights, but you won’t get there for free! ♫

Kono already had one of the drones filming the entire attack when Bale and Cage jumped into the subway. He let the other go with the second squad, but he kept the last one focused on the girls dancing. *This is going to go viral!!* Other men and some women let part of their cameras catch the tableau around the two women. They kept their guns ready and watched the front, but the cameras caught the rest.

♫ *In the jungle, welcome to the jungle, feel my, my, my, my serpentine.*

Ohhh ah, I wanna hear you scream! ♫

Squad one spent more time brushing broken parts out of the way than dispatching the occasional live robot. They did not mind, they were catching up to the masters of this disaster for the Enki base.

Bale flipped over and sliced another bot as it got close then he pointed his sword behind him and decapitated another. He did not know how he knew it was there, but it did not matter. And the drone caught everything and sent it out.

♫ *Welcome to the jungle, it gets worse here every day.*

You learn to live like an animal in the jungle where we play. ♫

Cage could not remember the man's name but he sure as hell could sing! He would look it up later and buy every album the man and his band produced! He placed his left-hand sword on his back and pulled the heavy pulse rifle and fired it down the line one-handed while dragging his right-hand sword through a wall to slow him down. Robots exploded!

Bale flitted around the axis using the spokes to give him momentum. Robots died. When they fired at him, he was able to deflect their shots with his sword and machete' into the nearby walls. Cage was firing behind him and blew up several robots down the line, but these were slower and much more aged and damaged. They all had guns though and were using them. Some fizzled out and some exploded in the hands of the bots which would look at their missing limbs in confusion. Bale swept through them all.

♫ *If you got a hunger for what you see, you'll take it eventually.*

You can have anything you want, but better not take it from me! ♫

Then Bale saw something he only dreamed of in nightmares. Three huge spider-like things covered the last kilometer to the entrance to the hanger bay. He was not sure if they were maintenance bots until one fired at him. The shot bounced off his shields, but it hurt! Cage fired more shots to little effect. The drone was joined by the other one and both fired a continuous barrage at the spiders. They were getting damaged, but the drones were getting battered too.

Cage raced up to Bale, "You okay sir?"

"Yeah, they've got shields but a couple of their legs are broken." Cage looked down the shaft. The mechanical spiders were coming closer, slowly but getting to their position.

Bale was sweating in his suit, "Remember that summer when you taught us how to play soccer and you tricked us with that slider move?" Cage nodded not understanding him.

Bale pulled some heavy ordinance from his belt and handed them to Cage. "I'm going to skip a small PK along the axis. When it explodes it will get their attention. It will not hurt them, but it might distract them for a second. You toss these PK 10s, mine and yours under the spidies. That will finish them off!"

"But sir!"

"Yeah, best get behind one of these spokes and hold on for dear life!"

Bale reached down and crushed a few of the mini robots that were trying to pinhole him. His shield strength went up to 110%. His suit was getting hot, but he figured he would need all the shielding he could stand. Cage copied and grabbed a few too and slammed them into his suit.

Bale flew up to the axis and skipped the small PK down the pipe. The robots immediately fired at him, but his shields held...barely but he made it down behind a spoke. Cage had already slid three pairs of PK 10s under each spider. The smaller explosion did get their attention!

Cage jumped behind a spoke and welded himself to the frame and held on.

♫*And when you're high, you never ever want to come down.*

So down, so down, so down, Yeah!

You know where you are?

You're in the jungle, baby! You're gonna die! ♫

Squad one jumped behind spokes too even if they were still 50 meters behind the two men. Squad two jumped into holes left by the ribbed robots they had killed. Everyone knew what was coming.

The PK 10s proximity sensors noticed the enemy above them and went off.

Men at the Horn grabbed Lt. Abbicon and Lt. Terashita and flew away with them off the Horn. They flew as fast as they could to get away from that hole. Kono was right behind them with his last drone.

There was air in the tunnel now, not much but the blast could be heard.

The first pair of PKs destroyed the shields of the spiders, the second pair destroyed the spiders shredding their bodies, the third pair destroyed the subway almost half-way to the entrance. Fire and debris raced past the men screaming in their suits as they held on through the torrent.

Flame shotgunned out of the subway entrance and melted the Horn turning it to slag as it slowly fell to the floor below. Rocks and robot parts on fire raced out into the gloom of the Chamber. The axis flickered and went off. While everyone was getting their bearings, the light came back on again. The chief shook his head in fear. How could anyone survive that?

Sana screamed and writhed while being held by two augmented riflemen. Dia held onto her frame facing her. “I’m sure he’s okay!” Sana ignored her and thrashed about. The two men were barely able to hold her, even her suit was beginning to turn purple. How was that possible for a flight lieutenant?

He called out. “AGAMEMNON I, this is Master Chief Green. I need immediate evacuation and medical teams available. Over!”

The captain was already on the move. “I’m sending a ball through the Master gate. Tell me if it gets to you!”

A couple of minutes later, “Yes Sir, it came through alright!”

“Send a man over here right now, Mister!”

“Jones?”

“I’m good sir,” and he stepped through the gate.

“We’ve got him! I’m sending men and medical over there now!” The captain wanted so badly to be there to help the chief deal with this situation but she had to stay there to prepare all her stations for the survivors.

Bale coughed some blood inside his helmet then realized he was seriously hurt. He released his helmet and breathed. The air was thin but it was available. *Damn! There's still air here?*

He heard Cage struggling near a pile of rocks and crawled over to him or tried to when he realized his lower right arm was missing. His suit had cut off the broken pieces and sealed the wound over. *Well shit! That's all I need!*

With his left-hand Bale pulled Cage out of the gravel. There was blood and vomit inside his helmet. Cage was looking wildly about and choking. Bale hit the button on Cage's collar so it would flip back. It only made it so far. Bale grabbed the rest and yanked it off Cage's head. The man breathed and then threw up again, there was more blood this time. Both men were in serious trouble.

"Damn Baywolf," he spit some mucus and blood on the ground, "you sure know how to throw a party!"

Bale checked his own vitals and did not like what he saw. He took command override and checked Cages' too. "You're down to 7%. C'mere." Cage tried to brush Bale off, but he would not be denied. He slapped his arm against the older man and gave him half of his power and nanos.

"Aw damn! How am I supposed to explain this to Sana?"

Bale ignored that, "Sorry that you lost the tune. It was rapture time for me!"

Bale passed out. Cage pulled him up and stretched him across his lap.

"Help!!!" Cage held the man close then ran through his playlist and ramped up the end of the song.

Dia heard it first, then others. She flew over to where Sana was helping survivors. She touched Sana's hand then called. "Master Chief! I need a medical team and four Points to follow this signal!" She played it back for the Master Chief. "They are alive!"

45

The hottest part of a flame is near the tip, the blue part.

Sana was slowly banging her head against the glass separating her from Bale and Cage. They were both in nano tanks being repaired. It was a lengthy process as both men nearly died. As they were both Points, it was their magnificent bodies, hardened by nanos, that saved them.

Bale's new arm was not grafted on but grown inside the tank. Layers of skin and muscle, plus some internal organs, were being replaced as well. Cage lost both his legs due to the explosion. His suit had melted into his legs and could not be safely removed, and his entire ribcage had to be replaced as well.

They would be in the tanks for another two days, their injuries being so severe.

2nd Lieutenant Terashita walked up behind Sana and put her hand on her shoulder. "Please don't do that. Do you want the commander to wake up and see a bruise on your forehead?" Sana looked up and stared past her ghostly reflection into the room. Fortunately, she could not see into the tanks except for vague shapes floating in the milky nano solution. Masked technicians walked around the room checking their tablets and the wall monitors near each patient.

Sana frowned and turned to Dia. "I feel so useless right now." She wiped her eyes again, then hugged the woman. Dia held her and then pulled back. "They are going to be all right, you know this."

Sana nodded. "Yeah, I know, but it's the waiting that is killing me." She looked up to Dia. She smiled at Sana and was thankful she had a new friend in her.

Kono walked up to them. "Sir, it's time for your deposition." Sana got a real angry look on her face. "Right!

Let's do this!" Kono turned to Dia and said something in Japanese. She bowed briefly, "Hai, Sensei." He and Sana left the hospital.

The tall and dashing JAG turned from the video and looked at Sana. "Do you agree with the recording, officer?"

"Yes, I gave the command to stop, and they ignored me."

He turned to the Judge. "Let the record show that the witness confirmed the video of the event. Also, I submit documents signed by the prisoner and her assistants clearly stating that any officer or enlisted man or woman can and will be obeyed by every civilian for the safety of the crew and for their own safety. Testimony given today has demonstrated that this order, signed and recognized by the prisoner, was ignored intentionally."

Sana looked around the Courtroom and recognized almost everyone. Newly promoted Sergeant Thompson would go far under the tutelage of the Master Chief. He had been cleared of the killing of the prisoner's assistants. Thompson had responded immediately to Lt. Abbicon's command, without hesitation. That was his job, and he did not question the lieutenant as to why.

The captain of AGAMEMNON I was prim and extremely angry! That this accident by intent fell on her watch was unforgivable to her. Commander Barnes was not happy either. He was not a witness but to be a witness to what came next. The emperor just looked at the desk in front of him. Not happy but not sad either, just being there. Other officers present had given testimony as to the outcome of the prisoner's actions. Everyone else in the gallery, either as friends of the Court or friends of the missing, sat in anticipation...they were all angry.

"May it please your Honor that the actions of the prisoner justify this petition of Treason. All testimonies, documents, and video records state that this is true. Thank you, your Honor. I rest my case." The man sat down.

"The witness may step down." Sana rose and went back to her seat. The prisoner was nearby, so she walked well around her.

The Judge looked at the bound prisoner and said, "The

serious nature of this petition is not trivial and should not be swayed by individual emotions regardless of the actions of the prisoner. In this case, the evidence is overwhelming as to Treason in the First Degree. It is the decision of this court that the prisoner is guilty of this charge. Her criminal actions have spoken for themselves. Doctor Olivia Warring, you are found guilty of High Treason against the People of Earth and her agents and to the emperor."

She banged her gavel. The trial was over.

Emperor Barnes rose from his seat and sighed. He straightened his coat and walked to the front of the Courtroom.

"Doctor Olivia Warring, this is the last time you will hear your name. It will also be the last time your name is ever mentioned. These court records will be sealed for all time. Your current and previous projects, thesis and related documents are being scrubbed as we speak. Any records of your education, identity, and even your birth are being destroyed right now. Any surviving members of your family and associates have been informed by me not to mention your name on penalty of death. It will be like you had never been born.

You have caused the death of three of my warriors, the mutilation of two of my best warriors, the deaths of both of your assistants, and the wounding of so many others. Your avarice for recognition rises above sedition. You sacrificed others to gain popularity among your peers; that is unforgivable! But to cause the deaths and mortal wounding of so many for the same ambition tops the high bar of Treason! By evidence presented to this court and having been found guilty of Treason, your sentence is death."

The woman was crying, her head bowed over her chest. She was in a wheelchair. Her left foot had never been replaced as there was no point in wasting resources better used for others. Her mouth was taped shut. "Look at me!" said the emperor.

The woman looked up at him. Lucas Barnes pulled a pistol and shot her in the forehead. Blood, brain material, and skull fragments hit the wall behind her.

The emperor turned to the Master at Arms and handed

him the hot gun. "Burn her body but leave it in the mortuary furnace. Remove the furnace and any other applicable devices and drop them into Star 1056. I do not want her bedding, robes, medical gear, trash, even that chair or the wall behind it on this station, much less in this system. Am I clear, sir? Return the gun to my rooms."

The man saluted the emperor. Everyone filed out of the courtroom.

The emperor spoke with Captain Castillo for a moment, then went out with his grandson. Janet turned to Sana. "Our men have cleared the subway and have reached the hanger doors, but they can't open them. I need you to return to the Enki base and see if you can open it like you did at that base on Beta Three." Sana frowned. "But Bale..."

"He's not going anywhere and will be out for two more days. There is no sense in you sitting around. Now do as I ordered."

"Yes, Ma'am. Sir? Why did the emperor execute the prisoner himself?"

Janet frowned. "That's always been his way. He refuses to let others take that chore for him. He says it is his burden to bear. Now go suit up. I will hold the fort here. Take who you need and check in with the chief when you get down there."

The chief met her at the Master Gate. "How are Bale and Cage doing?"

Sana shrugged, "You know as much as I do. He and Cage will be in the tanks for two more days. We will just have to wait." Mike walked over in the feeble gravity and hugged the young lieutenant. He turned to Lt. Terashita. "You'll keep an eye on her for me?" The woman saluted the Master Chief. "Yes, Sir!"

They flew up to the rim of the subway, the light axis glowing as it plowed down the tunnel. Four Points were waiting for them with some tools to open the door if needed.

The walls of the subway had been polished from the flames of the blast. They were quite smooth. As the group drifted down the shaft the walls got darker, but the axis shone brightly. There was no soot on it. At about the halfway point, the walls began to show fractures, but the spokes still held. Further on the walls were broken in several places. With less than a kilometer to go the walls of the subway were gone. Fortunately, the spokes ran well past the walls to the adjoining rock of the asteroid. The tunnels the robots had traveled were revealed now. They had all been cleared by teams of marines. Some of the robots were still working but were vacuum frozen in their bays. They were all destroyed.

The last Spoke in the wheel was fractured but was hastily reinforced by manmade devices. This was the spoke that saved Bale and Cage...barely.

The last 40 meters were completely open where the bombs had gone off and killed the spider-like robots. The blast had opened the entire area. Machinery could be seen a couple of kilometers down in some cavern dug out by the Enki. No one knew what they were for, but they apparently did not work anymore.

Sana and her crew landed on a metal grate stretched across the chasm and mounted to the wall where the obvious door was. The Points immediately tied strong cables to each other's back and to the two women. The cables were then clipped to large bolts mounted on the walls. Dia asked, "What are these for?" One of the men answered her. "In case there is vacuum beyond that door, sir. This will keep you from flying off into space."

Dia looked up and saw that the axis ran right through the wall above the door. All around was jet black from the explosion. Sana walked up to the door and started brushing off soot from the glyphs imprinted in the door. To the side was another set of pictograms she recognized. She pushed one, and it lit up along with all the others. A flat panel of stone lit up, too, and became a screen with instructions and questions. Sana smiled. "There's air inside. No robots either." Everyone relaxed; they had all been worried about that. She pushed some more buttons and made additional queries. "I'll be! There are ships in there!"

One of the men asked her, "You can read that, sir?" She nodded. "I've been reading it all my life back home and on the Explorer. These glyphs are older than ours, of course, but the manual my Captain gave me, Captain Verkon from the

Explorer, has copies of all these going back thousands of years." She turned back to the door.

"Okay, I know how to open it. I want all of you to back up a ways, weapons ready just in case. You too, Lieutenant Terashita." The men pulled back and waited. Dia got back as far as she could. Sana pushed a couple more glyphs on the side panel and then pushed another on the door itself.

At first, nothing happened, but then machinery down in the hole below them started up. The door jerked, and some dust flew out. Then the door slid back a couple of meters and then moved to the side into a pocket for it. Another airlock door was already open a little further down. There was no vacuum beyond the door, only the subway continued with the lit axis above. The floor here was flat. The tunnel ran another 100 meters and then opened into a huge chamber much like the one at the other end of the tunnel. The whole space was brightly lit.

Everyone stood in awe at what they had found.

46

Sana waited impatiently outside the hospital rooms. Bale and Cage were fixed, but they were not being released yet. “Don’t bite your nails dear, it’s unseemly.” Sana started to rise, but Janet pushed her back down. “We’re both off duty, so stop that. Just a couple of girls waiting on their men.”

The captain sat down and crossed her long legs. “Waiting. It sucks!”

Sana smiled and agreed. “Do you think this will change things between Bale and me?”

Janet plucked another errant lock and folded it to Sana’s hair. “No. He probably wants out of there as much as you do. I’m sure he wants to be in your arms right now.” Sana smiled at that possibility. “Keep in mind, he will be very sore. More than usual after such a long time in the tanks. He will want to sleep, so don’t press him for any extracurricular activities.” She smiled at the younger woman. “I’ve looked over his record. Bale did not get 15 purple hearts, now 16, for no reason. He has been hurt before, terribly in a couple of cases, but I agree, this is the worst any man has ever suffered. I am glad he is back, but we will have to watch him. That will be your job. Physically, he is in perfect health. The doctors assured me and the emperor of that! Mentally...we will have to wait and see.”

Sana leaned over and placed her head on Janet’s shoulder. Janet held her hand. “Cage is all right?” Janet nodded. “He will be fine, too. He is older and has suffered many mishaps over the years. I believe he will be okay. I just hope he doesn’t mind being a bit shorter.”

“Shorter?” Sana sat up and looked at the captain.

Janet smiled, “During our tryst, he commented that he wished he were the same height as the commander. I agreed in that I had to, um...just to kiss him. So I took Officer’s

Privilege and gave him what he and I wanted. I hope he'll understand." A tear beaded on her eyelid. "I hope."

Bale sat on the locker room bench and felt like hell. The other man in the shower had to be Nick as he sang so badly. "Welcome to the Jungle, I want to hear you scream!"

It had to be Cage; no one else would sing that song again and again and so badly.

Bale rubbed his hair with a dry towel and leaned over again. He felt like a recruit that had completed boot camp twice! He was so exhausted!

The shower shut off. Humming followed a large man out of the shower. "C'mon, Baywolf, walk it off!" Bale was stunned. The man that sat next to him was his height now, six foot six. "Nick?" He looked over the man as who was much shorter now. And his tats were gone too!

"Janet and I discussed this our last time. See, um...she had to undock just to kiss me. Well, you know me; I do not like having things interrupted just for a kiss. Don't get me wrong, I like a woman's lips but, um..."

"What about your tats?" Bale looked at his dark arms, already missing some of the more creative ones. Cage shrugged, "I'll get new ones maybe, but really, been there, done that. Janet kinda shies away from that sort of thing anyway. She's not much into ink."

Bale grinned, "Pussy whipped already?"

"You're one to talk. You bought an engagement ring, and she is wearing it right now! Don't talk to me about pussy whipped!"

"By the way, thanks for saving me." Bale hung his head in shame but was glad his friend made it out alive. "Saving You? Son! You gave me half of your juice! Neither of us would be alive had you not done that. Don't thank me, I should be thanking you!" Bale looked up and gave Cage a high five. The slap rang around the room. Cage smiled at Bale, "Cut that sentimental shit out. Let's go see our ladies!"

A nurse walked through the door from the hospital. "They are coming out right now." She smiled at the women and went back to her station down the hall. Janet felt the need to squeeze Sana's hand. She returned the squeeze and then started bouncing on her toes. “Don’t be inappropriate, dear.”

Sana just looked at her. “Yeah, sure, Mom! Your man is coming out too, and I can see your nipples in anticipation! So shut up!”

Just like one of her daughters, always telling Mom off. Janet shook her head and laughed.

The door opened again, and Bale and Cage came out. Both men looked fabulous but pale. Cage was now the same height as his friend. Sana could not wait anymore. She shrieked and ran to Bale and hugged him. He gasped, “Easy, easy.” Sana backed up and put her hands over her mouth. “I’m so sorry. I forgot, but I was so excited to see you again!”

“Just take it slow,” he smiled at her, “Okay?” He bent down and kissed her gently. Sana touched his face. “Oh, my poor baby!”

They looked over and watched as Janet and Cage kissed. He had his arms around her, Janet’s hands on his chest. She pulled back. “Are you sure?”

“Yeah, baby. I was tired of always ducking doorways. This is perfect!” Then he got a little paler and more, then stumbled some. Bale tried to reach him. “I’m starving!”

They managed to get the men into an electric cart the captain had arranged. Cage got in front with Janet, Bale and Sana got in the back facing the rear. “I know a place nearby.” Neither man heard her as they had fallen asleep. Sana held onto Bale as he slept on her shoulder. “Are they going to be all right?”

“Yeah, this happens every time a rifleman is injured. Usually, they can get around, but sleep is definitely the second order of business, food the first. These young men have been through a crusher. We will feed them up and put them to bed. Don’t be surprised if Bale sleeps for 24 hours.”

She pulled up to a stylish restaurant near the Starboard Mall. It was empty except for the Chefs, servers, and the hostess. It’s good to be the captain; they had the whole place to themselves!

The men immediately woke up when they smelled food. The girls laughed as they got out of the way of the two men rushing the door. “Steak, I’ve gotta have steak!” Cage breathed. “Oh yeah, steak is good!” said Bale.

Later, Janet and Sana nibbled on their salads and bread rolls while watching their men devour everything put in front of them. Porterhouse steaks, they even ate the bones, baked potatoes, fish, salads, soup, bread, milk, tea, and coffee. “Veggies, dear, both of you.” They sulked; they ignored the carrots and green beans. Janet curled her finger and slowly unrolled it to stand up straight. “They are good for you for many reasons.” Both men’s eyes widened then they attacked the veggies. Sana snickered and leaned over the table to whisper in Janet’s ear. “Veggies do not help with that!” Janet shrugged, “You and I know that, but they don’t.”

Janet ordered some sliced fruit and made the boys eat that too.

“Beer! It’s Miller Time!” Cage yelled out.

“Okay, but just one each!” Sana was firm about it.

“Cage, I didn’t know you could look like ash, but you managed it,” Bale said.

“Well, look at you, all high and mighty. You look like a blank domino!” The two good friends slapped hands again and drank more of their beer.

Sana laughed; both men were getting their color back. Food was the answer!

Cage changed the subject. “Hey! Hey, you remember that four-meter job? We took that apart, sweet!” Bale jumped in with his own story, “I liked the one whose gun exploded in its hand. The look of confusion was priceless!”

The men regaled their ladies with stories of the subway melee. Janet and Sana traded winks, knowing this could go on for hours. “And one of those sharks grabbed your Lilly white ass and sucked you into a hole.” Cage slapped the table, making the dishes dance; he laughed hard. “Nothing that a couple of grenades couldn’t fix. Besides, one got you too! Sucked your arm and sword to your pit. Bad hygiene I guesse.” Cage smiled. “At least I got my sword back!” Both men laughed!

Janet could tell they were slowing down. Cage’s elbow slipped off the table. Bale did not even notice, as his eyes were about shut. She called over the hostess and paid the bill. Sana lavishly tipped all the servers and the rest of the staff. “Please thank the Chef for us. It was a fabulous meal. Thank You!”

“Let’s get these boys home before we have to drag them there.” Sana agreed and managed to get Bale out to the cart. Both men fell asleep again. Janet dropped Sana and Bale at the Hilton. She made good on her promise of the Presidential Suite. “Let me take him up, then I’ll help you take Cage home.”

“Never mind, honey. I can manage my man, and you take care of yours. Later!” And she drove off.

It took a while, but Sana got Bale into bed with only his underwear on. She looked down at his sleeping form. Not a mark on him, not a scratch, yet the man had almost been torn apart. Tears formed in her eyes as she watched muscles roll over his flat stomach, two six-packs, and other muscles that a man should not have, but Bale and Cage did. He turned over on his side and started to clutch at the air. Sana pulled the blankets up over him. Bale settled down and slept.

She turned out the lights and shut the door. Then she walked over to a couch, sat down, and cried.

47

"Twenty-six hours? Damn!" Cage was incensed! "And Bale is already over at the Enki base?"

Janet smiled as she put his third helping of eggs, sausage, and fruit on his plate. "Yep, he woke up seven hours ago. Youth wins," she giggled. Cage pulled out his chair and grabbed Janet and put her on his lap. "Woman, that doesn't help." She smiled and speared a section of orange and stuck it in his mouth. "You wasted part of your sleep on me, I've got the bruises to prove it!"

He chewed the orange, swallowed it and said, "Ah damn. Did I hurt you?"

Janet leaned over and kissed the man tasting the orange in his mouth. "No, you did not, Rough Rider!"

Cage eyes widened with glee then he laughed. "...Rough Rider! I like that!" The captain smiled and kissed him again.

She fed him the rest of the plate by hand. Cage ate every bite while looking at this amazing woman sitting on his lap. How does this sort of thing happen? She was a Captain of an auxiliary to the AGAMEMNON, and he was just a grunt, a Master grunt but still...just a simple man. And maybe that is what it was all about. They found each other and discovered their mutual need. Was it lust or was it something else?

She stood up and pulled Cage to his feet. They walked into the bedroom. Janet turned to Cage, "You are to be on duty in thirty minutes." She dropped her robe and leaned against him.

"I can get dressed in five minutes," he breathed.

"Ten after you have a shower so get busy Mister!"

Cage bent down and kissed the captain.

"What the hell is she doing?" Bale asked.

"Running me ragged." Collins said as he wiped his face with a paper towel. A suit could get hot, so he was sweating but no one took off their suits. Air may be abundant now, but vacuum never ended, they kept their suits on just in case.

Sana was flying all over the larger ship, a pink and orange sphere with tentacles four kilometers long. Hatches were open all over the ship and one of the tentacles was detached. "Couldn't you take her for a long lunch just to give us a break? She has been at this for over three days! She's killing us!"

Bale smiled as he watched his wife to be flit all over that monster. There were three ships but one of them got crushed by the larger one when the collision happened. The other smaller scout ship survived but the attack ship was the prize. He could hardly see the end of the ship's tentacles reaching the other end of the brightly lit chamber, the perspective was that extreme.

"Okay, I'll grab her. You and your men take the rest of the day off. I'll post a guard through the chief."

"Thanks Commander! We all must sleep sometime. I hope you're feeling better."

"I'm getting there, lieutenant. Have a beer on me." Bale pinged a charge for a free beer for all the men.

Sana spotted Bale on her HUD and raced over. "Hi honey, um...Commander!"

Lt. Collins smiled and shook his head. He flew down the subway with all the other men. "Hey! Where are you going? I didn't..."

"I gave them leave for the day. You've just about killed them with overtime." Sana frowned then put her hands behind her back. She was not wearing armor, so her chest stuck out prominently. Bale looked down, "Trying to distract me, Lieutenant?"

She tilted her head and winked at him. "You betcha'! Wanna be the first to do it in an alien vessel?"

Bale rolled his eyes and laughed, "You ever think of anything else?"

Sana pressed her breasts against his chest plate, "Nothing else when you're around. And c'mon, it has been almost a week since the last time!"

He smiled, leaned down and kissed her. "I was indisposed." Sana hugged him then thumped his chest. "And don't do that to me again! Send ten troopers to do your job, you just stand back and watch next time!"

"Oh I'll definitely watch next time. I saw the video." Bale smiled. Sana blushed, "I couldn't help myself. Dia and I were having some fun and you and Cage were doing all the dirty work. Someone had to make it special!"

And special it was with all the sparks dropping around the two girls, shots screaming by from the robots and then followed by an epic blast out of the subway. The vid had gone viral all over the net. Donations were made in the name of the two men and one woman that had died during that campaign, their families already compensated by the emperor. The video was dedicated to them. How Kono put that together Bale would always wonder.

They both had a moment of silence remembering the three people killed. Sana laid her head against Bale's chest. "Please, don't do that to me again. My heart almost burst when that blast came out of the subway." Bale held her close.

Cage showed up and landed near them. "Sorry I'm late sir but I was...Whoa!"

Sana stood there in her practically sprayed on suit. "I'm gonna tell Janet what you just said."

"Well, sir...you can't really blame me. I mean..."

*I heard and saw. Really Lieutenant, couldn't you wear some clothes while on duty? * Janet said to Sana. *I am off in four hours. Let's go shopping! I would rather Master Sergeant Daniels stare at my ass than at your obvious assets. * She clicked off.

Bale grinned, "Dude, you are so busted!"

"Yeah, I'm in trouble now. But I'll work it off!" Cage grinned and Bale laughed. Then both men got quiet as Sana started putting on armor from her locker near the entrance to the hanger. She wiggled into her armored pants finally pulling it up over her butt. Sana heard the silence and looked back at the two men. "What?"

Both men turned away as she grabbed her chest plate and

backing. “Really? You were checking out my ass? You two are perverts! Are your brains between your legs?!!”

Cage leaned into Bale, “Do you know what God said after he made Adam?”

Bale smiled and shook his head.

“I can do better!”

Bale burst out laughing and slammed his open palm on the nearby wall; it cracked.

Sana rolled her eyes and finished dressing. “I’m ready if the two of you jokesters are done.”

Bale responded, “Sorry Lieutenant, we were just admiring your asset.” Cage grabbed his mouth and fell to the floor of the tunnel. Peals of laughter were coming through his hand as he kicked his legs about. That was too funny! Sana rolled her eyes again. “I am So going to tattle on you both with the captain! Now let’s roll. You need to see the inside of this ship.”

The Attack ship lost all contact with the Enki base and their allies. The crew onboard had no idea the base no longer existed. A few cycles later one of the carriers contacted it. The carrier had been on a long patrol and witnessed the blast. The entire fleet and the system were now a giant expanding cloud of gas. They had also witnessed two ships leaving the area at a high velocity unknown to the Enki until now. If they were Terran then the Enki indeed had a powerful enemy. The Attack ship was warned to hide until the carrier could arrive.

The Enki had no such weapon in its arsenal. They wanted that weapon!

Bale, Cage and Sana flew up to the entrance of the attack ship, its door ironically right in front. “How did you get it open?” Bale flew past the entrance and on into the large ship.

“That’s the one thing that bitch did right.” They did not have to guess who she was referring to. “When power came on these three ships lit up with backup power. I found the door, punched a couple of icons and she opened. I managed to turn off the crushed ship but this one and the other scout are working fine. Hard to believe after all this time." Cage looked around. "I take it no one was home."

"Nope, no robots either but there sure are a lot of weapons!"

They floated through a tunnel and rose several levels. There were workstations that could be seen, something like a galley with several tables neatly bolted to the floor. The chairs were stacked in a corner, they seemed normal enough. Sana told them the chairs were all over the place, so they moved them out of the way. There was a slight stench in the air. "Bad food?" Sana nodded, "Quite a bit. It was all flash frozen with the vacuum in the containers but began to rot as soon as the air hit it. Can you believe it? They actually had apples, the rest we didn't recognize."

Other tunnels led off to different parts of the ship. "What about its power plant, engine, whatever?" They found their way to the bridge or at least one that looked like a control room. "Cold fusion, two reactors. As new today as they were thousands of years ago when they were installed. The engineers are excited about them. Me? They scare me to death! This thing could blow up if we started them. I'm not doing a thing until we drag this away from the rock, far away." Cage thought that was an exceptionally good idea!

Bale looked around and saw a few manmade computer terminals connected to a couple of stations. "Having any trouble figuring out the glyphs?" There were lights on all over the room. Familiar icons flashed and occasionally a beep would sound. Some language was spoken every now and then. "The glyphs, no. But the language is hugely different. It is not in any of our databases. I do not recognize any part of it. I sent samples of it to Captain Verkon, and he doesn't recognize it either so we just don't know."

Sana walked by a terminal and pushed a couple of keys. The display lit up and glyphs were marching past the screen and were being assigned definitions in English and Teknoman. "So far Lt. Collins and I have figured out about

80% of the controls and systems. Navigation, environmental, radar though we are not sure how it works, engine, communication, even their medical library. They do not have nanos but these guys with the weird animal heads were not born that way. Their brains are in their torsos so if you meet up with one, shoot them in the gut." She turned to the two men, "Essentially they are human like you and me, but they live a long time. Why the weird heads," she shrugged, "must be part of their religion or something. Let me show you the throne room and harem."

They floated down another tunnel that was larger and ornate. Through a pair of doors, the men found a large room with a throne on a short dais and a huge bed against a wall. The wall was painted and etched in an orgy of images...literally an orgy of people with animal heads in various positions. "Kinky..." said Cage. "His nibs enjoyed a good time, huh?"

Bale was a little nauseated by the pictures, but they could not be avoided, they covered all the walls in the room. "Was this Helios' ship?"

"Yes. There is plenty of room in other parts. We also found bays for the Wolverines and a bunk house for soldiers. Several staterooms for guests and slave quarters. This is a war ship but it's his personal yacht as well. Look, I've got to go and meet the captain."

"We'll look around some more, but we won't touch anything. See you back here tomorrow."

Cage smiled, "And don't let the door hit you on your asset on the way out." Sana stuck her tongue out and left the ship. She could still hear the men laughing on her way.

Sana was still fuming when Janet walked up. She sat down next to the younger woman, "What's up sugar?" Sana looked at her. "If you did not already know, men are pigs! They are ruled by their hormones! How did we let them live so long?"

Janet pulled Sana's hand to her. "Well, there is the issue of children and a good push and pull with a strong pelvis helps too. But as crude as they can be, these men will defend an entire city with their lives! Their boys will follow, it is bred into the men of our race. Cage was just reacting, Bale joined in and you were the object of their amusement and protection. But in your case, you get to marry Bale and have children with him. There is no greater honor for him than when someday you carry his child.

"I can make my own kids with their raw material and an artificial womb." Sana grumbled. Janet laughed. "We're not going to milk them for that, besides it's more fun the old-fashioned way! Just swat Bale on his butt next time you see him in front of his men, see how he likes being embarrassed. I would do that to Cage but more than likely he would enjoy it." Sana giggled, "You're right about that." She stood up. "Let's go get you one of those nifty skin suits for Cage."

"I better get three. I won't be wearing them long and Cage isn't that careful with my wardrobe."

Sana beamed at her with gleaming eyes. "Captain!"

48

Captain Verkon along with the crew and passengers of the Explorer finally entered Palisade space. The crew were tired but relieved to make it to their new home. Unfortunately, there was no home to settle. They gently sailed through the spiral gas coming from the star, their newly installed defense fields protecting them all.

The captain was worried. He had ordered two of the ship's councilors, several engineers and some medical people awakened. The Explorer's crew compartment was too small for them to meet with the Terrans, so Commander Barnes had offered the use of one of his Conference rooms and adjoining offices for the Teknoman. All the spaces were set at one half gravity for their comfort. Furniture had been provided to their dimensions and was very lush. This meeting was important, but the councilors were not impressed, and neither were their soldiers. Horatio was not thinking of mutiny, but it wasn't absent from his mind either.

Technically the captain was still in charge of the mission as they had not grounded. He could not retire until a planet could be settled. There was no planet for them to colonize but the Terrans had a workable solution but one that would take time. He was not sure the crew and passengers would wait.

The counselors had insisted their soldiers be present at the meeting. All fourteen stood with their backs to the wall behind the Teknoman contingent and all were armed. The Terrans only brought in one Marine but he was intimidating enough. A large black man, a race the Teknomen had never seen stood to one side of the Terran's table. He was much taller than any of the Teknoman soldiers. He had no weapons, but he was armored. What the councilors did not know was that every man and woman in front of them were riflemen too. There was also a short platoon outside their door. The Teknomen were outnumbered.

The emperor sat in a slightly larger chair and faced Captain Verkon. "Thank you for coming. The purpose of this meeting is to give you a visual demonstration of the Ring we are building for your occupation and to answer any questions concerning it." The lights dimmed and a hologram appeared in the air. One of the Terran engineers began speaking. "The next habitable ½ gravity planet nearest us is 23 lightyears away. In discussions with your engineers, we all agreed that the Explorer would fail if it were to continue that course. Your medical people confirmed that more than half of your passengers would clearly suffer brain damage during the trip even if you arrived safely. We do not have the resources to put all 30,000 passengers into stasis so that option is not available. Though we have the ships to transport you to System 861, it would require many trips and a period of seven years to complete. This would vastly reduce our safety from the Enki and the Wolverines. The emperor has decided against that plan."

In the hologram a large ring appeared against a background of stars. "This is one of our ring worlds near Earth. All our rings spin at full gravity like Earth's gravitational pull. The emperor has built five ring worlds, four of which are over a century old. There have been no mishaps or failures on any of the rings. This is a very safe technology."

Another image formed and showed the Maw as it currently was with two 1600-kilometer curved floor panels nearby. Another was extruding from the large machine. "As you can see, we have already begun the process of building the ring. It will be approximately..."

"LIGHTS UP!"

Cage spoke slowly and clearly to the soldiers in front of him, two of which were starting to draw their side arms. "Stop where you are, gentlemen. Another move and I will kill all of you!" The interpreter computer spouted out his words in Teknoman. One of the councilors sneered at him. "You may be impressive in height and strength if the traitor in our midst's is correct, but you cannot defeat fourteen armed men without a weapon." All the other Teknoman soldiers pulled their weapons and pointed at Cage. One pointed at the emperor, he sat in his chair unconcerned.

Sana stood up. "I am not a traitor! We are here to help you! Captain, tell them!"

The other councilor laughed, "We will be taking over this ship with the help of your precious Emperor as hostage."

Lucas Barnes was saddened but he gave the command. "Do your duty, Master Sergeant."

13 men fired on Cage, lasers that had no effect on him. Several of the shots ricocheted off his purple armor and splashed against the fields of the Terran officers including 2nd Lieutenant Abbicon without harm to any man or woman. One of the shots took the top half of the laughing councilor's head off. Captain Verkon lost an arm and fell to the floor in agony.

Cage moved...

To Sana's horror, his purple chainsaw whip came out of his arm. The man swung the chain at the soldiers. All fourteen soldiers were cut in half! Cage flared his suit and chain cleaning off the blood then reeled it in. Cage raced over to the other councilor and with the edge of his hand he decapitated the man dropping his head in the lap of the already dead councilor. Then Cage bent down to dispatch the captain.

"STOP!"

Cage stood back as the emperor came forward. Captain Verkon was unconscious from the pain of his burnt arm. "I don't believe this man had anything to do with this attempted coup. Wouldn't you agree, Commander Barnes?" Jeff was stone-faced, angry, and broken-hearted at the same time. "No sir, I don't think he knew anything about it. He has helped us in every way. No...he was not part of this."

Lucas turned to Sana, "What about you, young lady?"

Sana knelt before him. She turned off her shield and wiped her eyes. "No Sir! The captain always put his people and us first! This would not be like him! I'm sorry...I am so sorry!"

"Commander Jackson. Do you trust this woman who is to be your wife?"

Bale answered him the only way he knew how. "Sire, if you want me to drop this woman, return her to a natural height and have her put back aboard the Explorer, I will not stand in your way."

"You have not answered my question." Sana looked up at Bale and worried, her lips quivered.

"Sir, I love this woman with all my heart. I trust her completely!"

Emperor Lucas Barnes nodded. The rest of the squad came in and secured the medical and engineering crew with a tried-and-true method, zip-ties. He pointed to Captain Verkon, "Take this man to the hospital and make sure he gets a new arm. I will question him in three days. And clear up this mess," he pointed to the bodies of the Teknoman soldiers.

He walked over to Bale. "Don't you find it interesting that your fiancé' said 'His people and Us?' Bale blinked; he had not considered the comment by Sana.

Commander Barnes came forward. "I think he was worried, I could see that on the captain's face."

"That doesn't make him guilty only that he suspected this ruse by the councilors. Two less men I would have killed. Good in my book." The emperor turned to Cage, "Well done Master Chief!" Cage had just been promoted! "The Master Chief on the AGAMEMNON I is retiring. The admiral and I were looking for a new man to fill that slot. Up to it Mister?"

Cage was speechless for the first time in his life. "Um...um, yes Sire, your Majesty!" Sana rose on Bale's hand and rushed to Cage and gave him a hug. Then she realized what she was doing. Sana turned to the emperor and saluted and tried to kneel. "Stop that right now, silly girl." Lucas lifted her with her free hand. "Would you do me a favor and take the new Master Chief and the commander out of the room?"

"Your majesty, I am so sorry for this incident! I believe we are all human even if some do not follow that reasoning. In defense of Captain Verkon, I will not apologize when I say 'Us'. We are all human!"

Lucas walked up to her and placed a hand lightly on her shoulder. "I am restoring your status as 1st Lieutenant as of now." He said to Sana. "Commander Jackson and Master Chief, you are commemorated to the new rank I have authorized." All three people felt their insignia transforming on their chests.

Bale thought, *I am a Full Commander now?*

Cage thought, *I am a Master Chief now?*

Sana thought, *I better watch my ass!*

Emperor Lucas Barnes turned to the frightened engineers and medical personnel from the Explorer. "Now what am I going to do with all of you?"

49

The carrier caught up with the Attack ship that was hiding in an asteroid cluster half a light year from the given path of the human ships to the system ahead of them. Supplies had been transferred to the Attack ship as it had to wait two months for the mother ship to arrive. Even at TL 7.8 that both ships could slip, there would be another week before they arrived in human space, the enemy.

There were three Deities on the carrier each with his own suite of rooms for their wives and children and slaves. They had little to do with each other as they were rivals but three were required on any Capital ship to make a quorum. And now they were worried.

They had spent the trip debating and setting new policy for the coming invasion when they could agree on anything at all. The humans, once slaves now owned terrible weapons, huge ships that could fly faster than their own and something that could destroy an entire star system. Once part of one of the larger armadas that arrived in this sector of the galaxy, they were now reduced to two ships and sortie vehicles, small fighters that could do some damage but were limited in speed and agility. The Attack ship was more heavily armed and shielded but it did not have the power of the carrier.

The carrier would have to carry the battle but there was only one. It was too far to reach another fleet in time to secure the system in front of them. The attack by the humans on their fleet and allies demanded revenge even if they died trying to achieve that goal!

Bale, Cage and Sana waited three days for the captain to regain his arm and some dignity. "Your Majesty, I thank you for the new arm. Your technology is beyond belief!" Lucas stood at the end of the hospital bed and stared at Captain Verkon. "Sir? Can I safely assume you had no knowledge of the attack by your men?"

Horatio shut his eyes and sighed. "The two councilors were elected by the Ship's Council before we launched. They were to be awakened first by me upon arrival in Palisade. Normally they were quite efficient in their duties and decision making. But after learning of the situation here on Palisade, they were jealous of you Terrans. They became bold and xenophobic that Earth even existed outside of myth. I heard rumors but wrote it off as scuttlebutt. I had no reason to doubt these men...I was wrong. I have no excuse. I apologize to Your Majesty for my lack of judgement. I certainly had no idea they had compromised my men. I suspect there were some feelings of inferiority to your Marines. They wanted to prove themselves and died for choosing that option." Verkon looked up to Commander Barnes standing next to his bed. "Your Commander has assured me that all future protection will be handled by your men. I will not be releasing any other soldiers until the Ring is completed."

Lucas nodded knowing all this from questioning the prisoners. None of them were involved with the coup attempt but two, an engineer and a doctor were in full agreement with the attempt, they just did not know about the pending attack. Everyone confirmed that the captain of the Explorer was kept in the dark. The doctor and the engineer were returned to hibernation onboard the Explorer.

The rest of the prisoners were excited by the Ring the Terrans were building for them! They wanted to help with its design and construction.

"Captain, how many other passengers might be infected with this xenophobic attitude?"

Horatio shook his head, "I don't know but it would not surprise me if fully a third were upset and culturally shocked by their predicament. This was not what we expected and to meet our descendants from Earth. No, our religion is loosely based on your Catholicism and does not tolerate anyone else in the universe but us. Most people ignore that philosophy but here you are as proof that we are not alone. Some will not take that so well. Add to that other species that would kill us for no better reason than we are not like them, that some also consider us food. That will be a huge hurdle to overcome, your Majesty."

"Captain, heal up and we will speak again before I go home." Lucas turned to Sana, "I believe you have a request for the captain?"

Sana swallowed nervously. She was in the presence of three great men, not counting Bale who mattered the most to her. She approached the bed and reached for Horatio's hand. "Sir, do you see this ring on my left hand?" He looked at it and nodded. "I am now engaged to this man behind me. This is their custom, to place an engagement ring on the woman of their desire, to share a life with and to share children as well." Rings were not uncommon on Tekm' but were merely for personal taste, an ornament. Married couples shared cloaks and scarves as a symbol of their unity or marriage.

Horatio stared up at Bale and smiled. "Well done young man, well done indeed! Your Commander and I knew this was going to happen. Congratulations!"

Bale was startled. *They did?* "Thank you, Sir. I promise to take good care of her Sir!"

"You better Mister or I will have your butt on the line!" Horatio stopped and winked at Sana who blushed. "I can't think of a better way to unite our two races and cultures than for the two of you to marry. When is the Unity Celebration to take place?"

Sana looked at the emperor who smiled back at her. "Um sir, would you marry us? With the emperor's permission of course!"

"No trouble from me. I'll be here another month or so."

The captain smiled brilliantly. "I would be honored!" He stared at Bale, "And you and I will have a long talk about Teknomen women, okay?" Bale swallowed and did the only thing he could think of, he saluted the captain in his bed. "Yes Sir!"

Everyone laughed and Bale wondered why.

On the flight back to the Enki asteroid, everyone was still in a state of shock at their promotions. “Have you told Captain Castillo yet?” Cage shrugged, “I’m sure she already knows, that Chain of Command thing. But if not, I’ll tell her tonight.”

There were several new men and women on the supply ship with them, but one was rather young and sitting across from the three friends. He was not a Marine but a specialist engineer. He was being transferred to the Rock for the time being. The man was fidgeting in his chair and looking at the three across from him. Cage had enough. “Sit still! What’s got a bug up your ass?”

“You are Points, right?” The young man smiled at them. Bale nodded but Cage did not say a word. Sana knew he was referring to the two men either side of her, the Gold Hammers clearly on their breast plates. Hers had a Flight insignia.

“Did you fight the squids on the Explorer?”

Bale responded. “No, we were not there. The outcome would have been completely different.”

“Yes! Yes! Because of your whips and overall strength, the general augmented do not share.” He started bouncing again. “I designed your whips!”

All of them were stunned. “Impossible! We’ve had these for three years now and you’re just a kid!” Cage was angered.

The man looked down in embarrassment. “I know I’m young, but I designed those when I was in high school. The patents took a while plus the Navy had to approve them.” Then he looked up and smiled again. “And now you have them! I have got new one’s regular personnel can use on the squids! They will cut the tentacles right off those suckers!”

Bale and Cage sat there in shock. If this fellow could be believed they had a new weapon for every man in the service. The squids as they were being called now did not stand a chance!

Sana leaned forward and touched the young man’s knee. “What’s your name, honey?” The freckled-faced boy blushed in shades a rose would appreciate. “Um, uh Mason Dillon, Ma’am.”

“I am 1st Lieutenant Abbicon, here is Commander Jackson and Master Chief Daniels. We are glad to meet you!” The man almost fainted from the blood rushing to his face. “I know you. You are the woman from the Explorer. How did you get so tall? I thought all the Teknomen were shorter.”

“I’m augmented sweetie. They made me taller and stronger so I can handle flight and full gravity.”

Bale leaned in. “Tell me about this new weapon.” Mason swallowed, the man was a Commander, and he was really big! “Sir, it’s a device that can strap to the arm of a Marine and be deployed much like yours only yours are built in and longer too. Yours are much more powerful but these beauties can reach five meters and cut through carbon and concrete, flesh is no problem. They can be worn by a righty or a southpaw, no problem. No problem at all!” he repeated himself.

Cage joined in. “What about training?”

“That’s going to be the hard part. I intentionally reduced the power of these whips. They will deflect off static defense shields, so no one gets hurt. Your whips will go through anything. Static fields, steel, poly steel, sides of ships no problem! But you and the other Points are already highly trained in many martial arts and sword skills. Plus no one wants to be around when you deploy your weapon. I made them that way knowing your skill level. It will require practice for noncoms to use this new weapon, but they can use it! That is why I am here! I’ve got a trunk load of the things in the hold.”

Cage and Bale sat back. They were flabbergasted! They looked at each other and grinned. The wolves would not know what hit them, the squids would not care as they would be dead!

“Aren’t you sweet! Let me guess, you’re a genius, right,” Sana asked? Mason lowered his head to keep from fainting. He had never seen hair like that on a woman especially one so pretty! The only time was in his mom’s fashion magazines she looked at online. And her eyes! He thought he was falling in love."

Sana smiled, she had seen that look before mainly from Bale and other men, but Teknomen males did not send out messages of lust. Terran men had no problem with that! Terran men had no problem defending their turf either as she saw Bale glare at the young man. She took off her glove and showed him the armored black and gold spiraled engagement ring. "Now do not go there, Mason, I'm spoken for. But do not worry honey, I know a lot of girls about your age that would Love to meet you, I'll make sure of it!"

Cage banged his head against the bulkhead and laughed long and hard. "Son, better say goodbye to your virginity. One of Sana's beauties will cure you of that!" Sana took her fist and rammed it into the Master Chief's crotch. He blew out air and clutched his armored balls. "Sana...I was just sayn'..."

"Shut up!" She turned to Bale who was doing his best not to burst out laughing at Cage. "And don't you start!"

Bale wiped his eyes and managed only to chuckle. "Mr. Dillon, by chance do you know Captain Marshall Dillon of the NAUTILUS?" It was a long-standing joke that the captain of the most dangerous ship in the Federation was named after a sheriff in an old black and white TV show from the last millennium, something about a town in the old West during the late 19th century. Captain Dillon was always confused when the emperor made a joke, "I'm gonna rip your liver out Marshall Dillon." Then the emperor would laugh and say he was kidding. Captain Dillon never bothered to understand the joke much less look up the reference.

They all three looked at the young man waiting for an answer. There was a long pause.

"Yeah, he's my dad and he is an asshole."

Lieutenant Collins had made good progress while Sana was gone. The Attack ship was lowered through the hanger doors and was being pulled out of the asteroid. All systems were fully understood by now and new terminals, human style was synced to the Enki controls. Man could now run this ship! The engines had been removed and replaced with human Translight motors; the reactors worked fine with them. They could only reach TL 12 with short bursts to TL 16 but that was the best the Enki ship would ever make. Not that the ship was not stout enough but the hold for the engines was not large enough for a usual TL Drive. The Engineers replaced a few components and linkages but overall, the ship was sound. Sana still did not trust it. She attached grapples to the larger ship from her scout and began the maneuver to pull it one billion kilometers away for testing; it would take a couple of days to get there. When testing began, it would be by remote from the scout ship she and Lt. Collins operated. Collins was impressed that Sana could operate the scout without need of a human terminal...she was also having a good time!

Cage screamed at the men, “Counterclockwise! You want that whip to hit the right wall! C’mere you!” The men were very scared of their new Master Chief.

Bale was having problems of his own. He had received forty new Points. They were all experienced men and women, but they were still getting used to their new bodies. He had them in a gym and was trying to teach them some basics to Jujitsu. None were armored any more than he was and if Tracy was right, they had the same capabilities as Bale in a battle...but Bale was experienced. It was not a fair fight by anyone’s measure.

“HALT!” Master Chief Mike Green walked over to Bale. “Hit the wall, Sir!” Bale did not question the man. He walked over to a nearby wall and parked himself with his back to it. The Master Chief turned to the men and women in various forms of attention and distress, they had been worked hard by the commander. “At ease but stay here, then you will be dismissed.” He turned back to Bale. He hit him as hard as he could...Bale spit out some blood but did not fall away from the wall. He glared at the Master Chief.

“See that Sir?!! You are used to punishment. These people do not have your knowledge of pain! I know Master Sergeant

Stevenson, Sword Master Keyano and all your martial arts instructors. You were well trained! You cannot compress four years of demanding, painful training into these people in a few days.

You have forty-five engagements with an enemy, forty-six if we count the disaster of Enki Rock. That you and Cage survived that merits another metal." He turned to the men and women behind him. He pointed to them, "They all have at least eighteen campaigns under their belts. Benson had twenty-one and you sent him to the emergency room!"

All the Points in front of him were ashamed that their Commander was training them and yet they fell short. They tried so hard, but it was of no use. The Man was too instinctive about hand-to-hand battle.

Mike turned back to Bale. "Let me finish their training, I will deliver a crew that will make you proud. But do not get in my grill about it. You're in a timeout!" Bale ducked his head. "Please Sir, I've done this for over twenty-five years. I am good at it. Let me put these children to bed with a beer and I'll see you in two weeks."

Bale sighed. "Don't let me down, Chief. I fear for our Federation. I need all the help I can get." He turned to the men and women behind the chief. Mike saluted him and all the others followed. Bale saluted back, "Dismissed!" Bale walked out of the room wondering what to do now.

50

Molly De Vries was careful around the other humans. She was so short that even the slightest touch could hurt her. The Terrans were so tall and used to a full gravity with which she had no experience. They were so strong! Even their children could break her bones without meaning to and some were taller than her.

Molly was a nurse in training. She was already a nurse but for Teknomen. Terrans were another matter. She had to relearn their ports for injections, how to mount a blood pressure clamp that weighed more than she was used to, measure their temperatures with tools she had never seen and manage to learn other weird devices for medical treatment. Her manner was exemplary to a profession she had already excelled. Molly could calm down any patient with barely a word and a smile. That was enough for them.

"De Vries! I have a patient coming in who is exhausted. Check out his stats and report them to me. Room three." Doctor Ambry yelled at her. He meant nothing by it just that he was busy.

Molly walked along the hall to examination room three. Two other Teknomen nurses and one Teknoman doctor gave her dismissive looks. She saw her reflection in a nearby window and sighed. Molly was very dark complected, she was a mutation as far as other Teknomen were concerned.

She opened the door and found a short man crying as he looked out the window of the medical unit. She was amazed that there was any Terran only a few inches taller than her, a man at that. She looked at his chart and discovered he was not military. "Mr. Dillon, would you come over here please?"

He knuckled his eyes to wipe away his tears. "I'm sorry doctor, I am just so tired." He kept his head bowed like he was almost about to sleep. "Take off your uniform so that I can examine you. You can keep your underwear." Mason complied but almost fell over a couple of times. She managed to get him on the padded table. His head was still bowed, the man was falling asleep again.

"Lay down and let me look at you."

She then saw the bluest eyes she had ever seen before he closed them. Blue?

She let the man sleep. He was muscular but in a threadbare way, slightly augmented but he was very thin. Molly checked his chart again and found that Mr. Dillon had just finished a two-day regimen of suit training. He had not closed his suit properly on the way to the Rock and had suffered some radiation poisoning. His doctor, after chewing him out royal had given him over to the military for some very rough retraining on suit management. Mr. Dillon could now put on his suit properly while being naked in a leaking room in the dark without gravity. They had been very rough on him!

His electrolytes were low, lactic acid was still high but diminishing, his blood pressure was fine if not robust, but his skin color was not good. The man needed food and rest. Food would have to wait as he was asleep. Molly finished his chart and mailed it to the doctor. She found a sheet in the medical locker and covered him then she held his hand. Human contact was especially important to any patient. Molly smiled; she liked being a nurse.

She checked his background. Mr. Dillon was an engineer, something to do with weapons. He was three years younger than her and only five inches taller. Maybe this Terran had not finished growing, he appeared to be an older adolescent, yet he had a PHD after his name. Molly did not know exactly what that meant but he was a man of some authority.

He sighed and rolled over on his right side and faced her. His eyes opened briefly, and Mr. Dillon looked at her...he smiled. "My nightingale, thank you." Then he closed those amazing blue eyes again. She reached over and clasped his hand. He entwined her fingers with his but did not hurt her. Though his hands were rough, he was easy with her. Oh Unity! Would this man remember her tomorrow?

Nathan and Rose Parks walked into the cafeteria with their two teenaged children. "Honey, your roots are showing," as Lt. Parks picked at her daughter's rainbow-colored hair. She slapped her mother's hand away, "Not now, MOM!"

"Okay, okay..."

Nathan chuckled, "Leave her alone will ya? Her friends are here."

His daughter stood on her tiptoes and kissed her father. "Thanks Daddy!" and gave Rose an angry look then ran to her friends. "Some veggies this time," Rose called out. Her daughter ignored her and ran on. Their son smiled. "Hey Dad, there's Dickhead!" His mom frowned. "I'll grab a burger and yes, a salad too." He ran off to the food line, grabbed both, waved his card at the cashier and ran to his friends.

"I wish he wouldn't call Chris a Dickhead. He is a nice boy. I like his mother."

Nathan laughed, "Look at his haircut. He looks like a dickhead!"

They got in a line and chose their food. Rose kept bumping her husband of many years playfully. "Move along, horsey!"

"Hey, I'm deciding here!" She walked around him with her tray and headed for the salad bar.

Once they had paid for their food the two walked out to the tables. Rose spotted a young black Teknoman sitting by herself far away from the other people of her group. Rose's blood began to boil.

Teknomen were primarily white so this short person of their race was ignored. Terrans came in all colors, shapes and sizes. This poor young woman was excluded from their presence because she was different. This would not do! Rose stomped over to the young woman.

"May we join you" Rose asked. Molly looked up at the two Terrans in front of her and did not know what to say. The man was completely white, bleach white with ice blue eyes and he was very tall. The woman was shorter, and she had the same skin color as Molly, her hair was frizzed. Molly did not know what to do. She stood, "Yes, please. I would be honored!"

The white man smiled, "Don't be so formal. I am Nathan and here is my wife, Rose."

They all sat down. "I've never seen another person with my skin color. Is that normal with Terrans?"

Rose munched on some lettuce and swallowed. "Honey, humans come in all colors just like you!"

"But your husband...is white normal?"

Nathan laughed, "I'm what you call an albino. It is a skin disease; I have no pigmentation. No protection from sunlight."

Rose bumped him again, "This man can get a sunburn under a lightbulb!" She laughed and Nathan laughed too as he bumped her onto the floor.

"Hey!" Rose got up, "That was mean!"

Molly giggled, their interplay was special. She wished she had a man like that.

Sana had just come through a gate when the rarely used elevators opened. A short and thin man stumbled out. She caught him, "Are you okay, sir?" Then she recognized the kid. "Sweetie! What happened to you?"

He recognized her, "I didn't have my suit properly closed on the supply ship, I got a little radiation. They cleaned me up then put me through two days of suit training." He huffed and put his arm against a wall. "I'm a little hungry. I was told my doctor, um I mean my nurse was having breakfast here. I wanted to thank her for the attention she gave me."

Sana almost picked him up but instead walked him into the cafeteria. Mason looked around and found Molly. "There she is!" He pointed to a couple of humans but behind them on a bench sat a Teknoman woman, small but very pretty.

"Mr. Dillon!" Molly jumped out of her seat and ran to Sana and the man she was helping into the room. "Come here and sit down. I will get you some food!"

"I'll take care of that, you get him settled." Sana said.

"Anything greasy, gravy too and pickled beets, he needs as many antioxidants as he can get. Also get him a dark chocolate bar!" Sana watched as the young woman sat Mason down, brushed his hair then laced her fingers with his. *Hmm?* This was not the actions of a concerned nurse. She smiled and went and got Mason's food.

It was 0630 so she pinged the captain. *You guys awake yet? How about breakfast?*

Janet called her back. *'Just a minute sugar...get off me!* Sana heard a crash. She heard Cage say, *'Hey! I ain't paying for that this time!'* Sana grabbed her mouth and squeezed her eyes shut with laughter. *'We'll be there in ten. Cafeteria two, right?'* Sana clicked twice and closed her phone.

Sana got the food and put it in front of Mason. "Is there any coffee?" She ran back to the food line and got him a large cup with sugar and cream mixers on the side.

Molly rubbed Mason's back as he ate his breakfast. She leaned in and cut up the beets. "I know you don't like them but they're good for you. Please eat." Mason smiled and did as he was told. Nathan and Rose smiled as the young woman took care of the young engineer.

Nathan checked the data base and found this young man already had a PHD at eighteen. "Son? When did you finish high school?"

Mason swallowed some chicken fried steak. "I was twelve then. Fifteen when I got my master's in engineering. The Doctorial was a natural so I did it. Got that when I was eighteen, no problem. I'm nineteen now."

He reached down and clasped Molly's hand without hurting her. Molly smiled and took a napkin to wipe his lips. He bent down to kiss her and then realized what he was doing, he pulled back in embarrassment. "I'm sorry. I didn't mean to, I mean...um."

Molly did not care. She reached up and grabbed his neck and pulled his head down. She kissed him. It was a long kiss.

"Lt. Abbicon, is this what we were to expect?" Janet and Cage came over with their trays and sat down. Molly quickly wiped her lipstick off Mason. "I'm sorry Captain. It was a spur of the moment."

"A kiss after breakfast. That is the beginning of a good day!" Cage said. Janet rolled her eyes and started eating her eggs.

Sana sat down and started eating her bagel when a large biscuit hit Molly on her head, crumbles going everywhere. Mason brushed most of them off, "Are you okay?"

Laughter was coming from across the room. The few Teknomen were slapping their legs, "You can keep her, Terran! We don't need a mutant in our crew!" Molly was tearing up. "It's okay, they treat me that way all the time." Mason glared at the men and women who accosted Molly.

The captain started to rise. "Let me deal with this, Janet. Um, can I kill them?"

Janet looked up to Sana. "Legally no, only if you are attacked. But you can hurt them a little. Don't give me too much paperwork Sugar."

Sana turned and walked over to the Teknomen. She grabbed a table and yanked it out of the floor, bolts flying.

"Damn! I didn't think she could do that," Cage said.

Sana spoke in Tekm'. "You have no idea what it's like to live in a prejudice free world! Color, size, ethnicity doesn't matter to us!" The captain raced to get the feedback of Tekm' to English. Sana pulled another table from its grips. The teenagers ran from the room. *Mom!* There was an angry adult in the building.

Just go, we'll be alright. Nathan reached down and clasped Rose's hand. She smiled up at him, *I love you too!*

Mason grabbed Molly and ran to a corner of the room. He put her down and braced his hands against the walls over her. Molly hugged him, she was scared and worried. "What's she going to do?"

Mason glared back at the men, "What should have been done from the beginning. She is going to teach them to give a little Respect!"

Sana leaned over and slapped her hands down on the table in front of the men. She continued to speak to them in their native tongue. "You will go over there and apologize to that young woman. She is a Teknoman nurse. Do you really want to have her mad at you?"

One of the men stood up and still had to look up to Sana, he was not even five feet tall. “We know you, Bitch! You are the traitor that abandoned us to this useless system. You went over to the other side without a thought! And I hear you are going to Unify with one of these animals. You are useless to us like this system and that lousy Captain that brought us here!” With that, he grabbed a dull butter knife and plunged it into the back of Sana’s hand.

Everyone else in the room stood up and their internal shields rained purple. Sana held up her other hand and waved them off. She reached down and pulled the bloody knife out of her hand, dropped it to the floor and lifted her hand for the Teknomen to see. Ligaments knitted themselves together, a broken bone fell back into place and the wound closed. She then plunged her hands into the table and ripped it apart. Screaming, Sana grabbed the man that had stabbed her and threw him into the wall behind her. The other Teknomen ran but were gathered up by the Terrans.

She reached down and pulled the broken man up. “Your life is forfeit!” Then she threw him across the large room shattering his already broken body against a column. The man died instantly.

51

Sana paced the small cell, “I just can’t do anything right, nothing...not a damn thing!”

Bale watched through a camera as she paced. “How much longer? Sana has been in there for several hours.” Her testimony was the last. All the witnesses were already deposed. The Provost Marshall, the Judge, JAG, Captain Verkon and Captain Castillo were talking. Cage put his hand on Bale’s shoulder. “Bale, Janet told me last night it’s a done deal, they’re just going through the motions. It all must be legal you know!”

Bale reached up and touched the screen where Sana walked back and forth. She was like a caged animal. Though she still had her height everything else was stripped from her. The rank, her uniform and her Nanos. A tear stole down Bale’s face as he watched Sana pace. To see her in a prison uniform offended him greatly. “I hope she is not broken by this.”

Cage turned him around and switched the screen to the officers trying her case. He could see that his friend was having a hard time here. “Bale, she’s going to be all right. You sent her to boot, Sana made out like a bandit! But damnit Bale, she is from a different culture! You have a long road ahead of you.”

“I can’t part with her Cage.”

“I know.” Cage worried for his friend. “Have you got the rings?”

A large man burst into the emperor’s apartment and pushed the young assistant out of his way. “Move it kiddo!” The young adjunct to the emperor got out of the way, he knew who the man was. The angry man rushed to the bar and poured a large snifter of Brandy and a small glass of whiskey. He turned to the emperor, "You promised!"

He walked over and handed the emperor the glass of whiskey. "It's a little early for alcohol don't you think?" Lucas said.

The large man checked his watch. "The bars are open at 4:00. It's now 4:30 in Australia. Cheers!"

They clinked glasses and drank them down. "Plonk!" Lucas coughed a little; a couple of fingers of whiskey was always early any time of the day.

"By the way, Tammy liked the new carpets on your ship. I liked the new uniforms on the women. Lots of cleavage there! I take it you're not getting married again."

Lucas grinned. "Mary just got a rejuvenation. She clocked back to 30 years and invited me to visit."

"Oh ho! She wants to play?" He looked around for a fireplace and could not find one, so he sent his glass into a corner. It shattered quite satisfactorily. He filled another snifter and accosted the emperor.

"Damnit Luc', you know damn good and well you promised me my retirement! I am not building another Ring! And you better stay clear of Tammy. She wants your balls in a sock!"

"I'm sorry Russell. I've got a situation here that needs solving."

The Ring Master as everyone called him tossed off the last of his brandy, grimaced and threw the glass into the corner with its neighbor. "Yeah, I heard. One of these Tekm's tried to kill one of their own, one that you augmented to be a pilot. Yeah, that was a fair fight! Damn near broke the man in two! And did I hear right? You promoted an E7 to Commander in only a few months? How the hell does that happen?! And he is going to marry this Tekm? Have you lost your mind?!!"

Admiral Dean found a seat and plopped into it. "And you want a Ring spinning at half a grav. The R-channels alone have to be redesigned to make that work. It took me three years to learn how to build the first Ring and we damn near lost it on Saturn! And you want to give an expensive piece of hardware to a bunch of bad-tempered Munchkins!"

Lucas knew his friend would be mad. He shewed the adjunct out, the admiral was about to get angrier. He shut the door and got himself another drink. Admiral Dean's eyes narrowed. He knew the emperor did not drink much so whatever was coming was going to be worse. "Admiral Nakamura and I have already discussed this. The Teknoman woman in question is extremely intelligent and has fitted into our culture quite well despite her obvious passions. Her operations on the two alien ships have been invaluable and she does know her own people."

Admiral Dean interrupted the emperor, "Don't say it! Oh no...don't you dare!"

"I want you to train her and Commander Jackson to build this Ring."

The large man slumped in his chair. "...shit."

52

The Enki sat half a light year from the human system. They had found a large gas cloud drifting by on galactic tides. It might hide them from observation, but it also made viewing a little difficult. They had sent out a small probe with a long scope. The probe had gone beyond the edge of the cloud and observed the spiral star. It was unusual and they had no record of it in their Kilo year data base.

They had been recording data about movements within the system and outside. Human ships left and arrived at tremendous speeds, much quicker than any Enki could slip. The technology was unfathomable to them. How did their ships just disappear like that? Another would reappear a few days later. It just appeared suddenly then coasted into the system. And one of the ships was a monster, almost as large as a common asteroid. Altogether there were five large ships and several smaller ones. There were also huge gun platforms that floated about the system. This was a heavily guarded station for humans.

But the reason was obvious. There were two full gravity worlds worthy of colonizing, many asteroids for mining and three gas giants for fuel. There was also an assortment of moons. The entire system was a cornucopia of resources!

The Deities on board the carrier lusted after the Palisade system and imagined building huge and elegant palaces on the planets. They wanted this system!

But how to take it with only two ships?

Sana sat in her chair handcuffed. She never thought she would be back here in court again, certainly not as a prisoner. Her hair had not been washed in a couple of days, she smelled, and the prison food was horrible! Sana was miserable. She hung her head in shame.

Captain Janet Castillo sat next to her but did not touch her. She could sit with her friend but mainly, Janet was there to help Sana keep her mouth shut!

"They are almost done. The verdict will be announced soon." Janet leaned in, "Don't worry honey, we'll find something for you. You'll marry Bale, time will pass, and all this will be forgotten."

Sana sniffed, that was all she could do as she had cried herself out. "I don't want to embarrass Bale anymore. I will go back to the Explorer and wait for the Ring to be built. Just send me home." Sana never lifted her head.

The four men up front nodded their heads and spoke a little more then the Judge leaned back in his chair and looked at Sana. "Young lady, please stand for the court." Sana managed to stand but she could not look at the Judge.

"Miss Abbicon, it was originally desired by certain factions in particular your Captain Verkon that you be charged with Manslaughter according to our rules." Sana's head jerked up and her lips trembled as she looked to her Captain. *How could he?* "There would be some jail time and then probation. Under Teknoman Jurisprudence, you would be executed." Sana's eyes widened at that. Her Captain had saved her life...maybe.

"Then there is the matter of self-defense which clearly all witnesses testified to that effect. But it is this court's opinion that you took matters to an extreme in killing the man.

Right now, you are a woman without a country. Neither side seems to want you, yet you must belong somewhere. The emperor of the Terran Federation, of which the Teknomen now belong whether they like it or not, has a third option for you. All rise for Emperor Lucas Barnes!"

At the back of the courtroom, the doors opened and the emperor and his Grandson, Commander Barnes walked in. Everyone stood and saluted the emperor. Sana wanted to but was not allowed. She shook in fear! Where was Bale?

"Your Majesty! I believe you have something to say in defense of the prisoner?"

Lucas smiled, "May it please the court, I do have a

suggestion."

The marriage of Commander Bale Jackson and Miss Sana Abbicon was rushed to completion. The bride was not made to wear her prison uniform, but she could not wear her wedding gown either, one that she had paid so dearly for. The groom wore a plain uniform with his cards, Gold Hammer and Commander's pips on his shoulders. The Judge officiated the nuptials and they were quickly married.

Sana was then rushed into another office with the emperor, Commander Barnes, the Judge and another Admiral they did not know.

Bale fidgeted out in the waiting area of the office and stared at his new wedding band. "What's going on?"

Janet and Cage sat across from him in the plush anteroom. "Bale, Captain Verkon could not take her back. The other councilor members, much less the crew and passengers would be horrified by the idea. We could not really accept her either for pretty much the same reasons. She *was* an officer for the Federation, but she lost all that when she killed that man. The Judge was right, Sana was a woman without a home. Because of that, she could not be charged with anything under either form of law. Now that you two are married, she belongs to us!"

Bale squared his jaw. "Are you telling me you are going to charge her with murder this time?"

Janet smiled, "Easy big fella. The charges were dropped for all the reasons I gave you. Double Jeopardy now applies. It is like it never happened. Captain Verkon notated his logs that Self-defense was the cause and that closes the book on Mrs. Sana Jackson. The emperor sealed the records too. No one will ever know for the rest of time."

She stood and Cage with her. "You need to come with us and grab some dinner. They are going to be in there for hours. Don't worry, they will feed her too but what is coming is especially important for both of you."

"But..."

Cage spoke, "Dude, I told it would work out. Now let's eat

then you can come back and worry some more."

Sana sat on her bed in her robe. She had finally had a descent bath the night before and another one this morning. She was starting to feel normal except for the shock that she and Bale were now married. Not exactly the way Sana wanted it but the deed was done.

They had not consummated their marriage yet. Sana had been so exhausted from the long meeting that went well into the night, she had taken a shower and Bale poured her into bed. He was already gone this morning to a meeting of his own. She could only imagine how surprised he was going to be at his reassignment. She still could not wrap her mind around her reassignment either.

There was a new uniform draped over a chair across from her. It was a deep Navy blue with Lieutenant Commander pips on the shoulders and it was hers. *How did the emperor come up with that idea?* Her flight pin had been attached to it as well. Sana was also given back her nanos for strength and medical reasons. She would never fly again with a team, but her status was no longer compromised. She was an officer again and an important one.

She was going to build the Ring for the Teknomen.

Bale remembered his first Sergeant, a seasoned professional. Sergeant Adler almost killed him when Bale misfired a gun into another Marine. The case was cleared when the gun was found to be defective. The man he accidentally shot was fine, Bale was in the infirmary for two days. The Sergeant was not found at fault for almost killing a recruit, that was his job. Bale never forgot it.

He steeled his nerves and waited for what was to come regardless.

Admiral Dean started the meeting with a royal chewing out. "Astronomic, 2.7. Math in general, 3.2, History, 1.8, Lord Son! Economics, psychology, sociology, health, Engineering, shit! I know monkeys that can do better than that!" He consulted his pages, "I'll give you Medic training and Computer languages including Enki, 3.9." Then he threw the pages at Bale. "You also get good-housekeeping skills, or you wouldn't be a Marine! Ever used a toothbrush to clean a toilet lately? Whatever possessed you to consider being an officer?"

An aide ran over and picked up the pages on the floor, sorted them and gave them back to the admiral. He took a swipe at her and she ran back to her corner clearly afraid.

The admiral shuffled through the pages. "Ah, now we come to the fun part! Your military career!"

"Lance Corporal in your third week of boot. Impressive but then you fucked up and got bumped back down to recruit with that gun mess.

Sword Corporal upon release from boot.

First engagement with Wolverines, nine dead by your weapons fire, Ace!

You have served on six ships of His Majesty's line, 45 engagements all told.

Your knowledge of weapons, hand-to-hand and Tactical and Strategic arts is unmatched.

You coordinated the attack on Nevorall and the Black Nine group.

Leading our troops in various and difficult situations and having them come out alive, Outstanding!

In five years you have saved the lives of 97 men and women all while under fire.

E6 by the time you were 20 years old.

16 purple hearts.

203 dead wolves, one that gave you your first set of cards...a pair of threes!

You destroyed the rebels on Mars station Five by yourself while vacationing on that station.

You have led men and women into action with their complete confidence in you.

You have trained Marines, guided them and fought with them.

Fourteen Commendations from three Captains, six Commanders, four Master Chiefs and others.

Then saving your crew on the Enki base here in Palisade. That merits another medal.

Your reputation precedes you Sir!"

The admiral dropped his pages to the floor and walked over to Bale. "I wouldn't have another man, any Marine protect this system while your wife and I build another Ring for the Teknomen."

He saluted Bale and Bale saluted back!

What the hell?

53

"There! You did not have the priorities right."

Bale leaned over her head, "But, when I want to..."

Sana grinned and touched the screen. "I've already organized every Point under your command. Records, facials and including recommendations. Home, family and children if any, it's all there!"

Bale let out a breath of air. He had been working on this for over eight hours. 200 men and women that had converted to Points. He had to know each of them. Two companies! Sana had reduced his work in less than twenty minutes!

"How did you do that?" Bale asked. Sana stood up and turned to him. "I'm quick."

Sana started unbuttoning his suit. She pulled it off and then lifted his shirt over his head. "Am I still your Baby girl?" She dropped her robe and leaned into him.

"Baby. I almost lost you, I was that scared!" Bale huffed and swallowed; tears were in his eyes.

Sana reached up and grabbed his shoulders, pulled herself up and wrapped her legs around his waist, Bale barely moved.

She gently brushed off his tears then kissed each eye. "I would be nothing without you." Sana stretched out her left arm.

"See this ring? In my culture, it would be a bauble, a trinket. In our world it means a lot!" Sana swallowed, "It means a lot to me! You bought it to show your love for me! I get it!" Sana squeezed out some tears on his shoulder. "I promise never to embarrass you again." She looked at him. "Just never leave me, please!"

Bale kissed and held Sana for a long time.

The Enki were running out of time, their supplies were running low, and tempers were beginning to flare. It was time to attack or abandon the whole operation. Then something interesting happened. Two of the largest ships and another somewhat smaller were leaving the system. One of the auxiliary ships detached itself from the larger one and joined the other two staying in the system. They were not near as large as the Enki carrier but there were three and the Enki had no knowledge of their capabilities. Were they formidable or merely troop carriers?

They had mapped the entire system and found an asteroid out beyond the seventh planet. There was a lot of work being done there. What for, they had no idea. Also there was something being built. Extremely large, curved panels, hundreds of kilometers long were being forged from some monster device that took in asteroids at one end and pushed out the panels from the other. This was technology the Enki never imagined. This was becoming a trove of jewels for the Enki. They had to have this technology! But how? And once taken, how would they hold on to it? The transmutation device alone was worth the effort, but they would die in the process of taking it. No, it was decided. The Attack ship would have to take a long journey to bring another armada to this system. They could hold it then and nothing the humans could do about that!

The Attack ship was made ready with plenty of supplies and fuel. It would take several months for it to reach the nearest subgroup and more to return. The Deities had everyone, but a skeleton crew put down for suspended animation while they waited for the armada to arrive.

The Attack ship took a circuitous route away from the spiral system to avoid detection by the humans. The carrier went dark in the gas cloud.

The emperor, newly promoted Captain Bayers and Admiral Dean's wife slipped back to Earth. She did not want to shepherd her husband while her grandkids were back home. Tammy had been through this trial five other times and did not want to enjoy another five years watching a stupid Ring being built. Especially for some ungrateful fallen humans!

Cage and Bale floated in space and watched as the AGAMEMNON escorted the emperor's gig and the NAUTILUS leave Palisade. All three ships disappeared as they jumped into TL drive. "Well, I guess you're the boss now, huh? And why the hell do you have to be outside when a ship slips?"

Bale shrugged in his suit, "I think it's neat. And no, your girlfriend is the boss, she out-ranks me."

"Well, let's get back inside. I'm cold and your wife is getting antsy, she might accidentally kill Collins." **I heard that!** Bale grinned. "If you're cold you might have a leak."

Cage spun around, "What? Where?"

Bale pushed his friend and Master Chief towards the airlock of the small Enki scout ship. As soon as they were inside, Sana buttoned up the ship and flew towards the Attack ship she had named Tulip. It was not its official name, but she liked it as it had the colors of a tulip. With the newer engines Sana made good time to the Enki ship.

"Did you really have to call this one Rosebud? What's with you and flowers?" asked Lt. Collins.

Sana giggled. "I like flowers. You should give Mary some, I'll bet she likes them too!"

Lt. Collins rolled his eyes. He had had a long and interesting career but this last year was almost too much. Mary wanted him to retire, and he was fielding some requests that he become a lay flight instructor at the Academy on Earth. His wife would like that and being closer to the grandkids would not be bad either.

Bale and Cage entered the bridge of the little ship and sat in two folding chairs bolted to the walls that would support their weight, they strapped in. Sana pulled the small ship up next to the much larger one. "Are we synced yet?"

Lt. Collins hands ran over his terminals. "Give me a sec...Okay! We're matched!"

"How much range do you think?"

"Lt. Commander, I want at least a million kilometers. You better have the brakes on this thing working!" Sana nodded, she made some adjustments to her terminals and the small ship pulled back. Cage started tapping his foot, Bale was worried too. The Tulip disappeared. "We are good, Commander. Whenever you are ready."

Both ships were well beyond the boundaries of the Palisade system. "Warm her up, Mister!"

"Reactor one, online! Spooling...okay, Reactor two, online. Spooling. It's all good."

"Warnings?"

"That's a negative Lt. Commander."

"Let's give it a minute," Sana paused, "okay. Torch it in ten seconds on my mark. Now!"

"Affirmative...in five, four, three, two, one."

The Tulip disappeared from their screens. Rosebud followed. Light was racing by at fantastic speeds! "Close it up Commander. I don't want that kill switch to kick in." Sana made some adjustments and Rosebud groaned. Cage looked like he was about to throw up.

"Systems!"

"In the green. Wanna take her for a spin?"

"Oh yeah!" Sana grinned. "We'll start slow...a little to the left, a little to the right."

"And everything will be alright!" Lt. Collins laughed as he finished the song.

Cage and Bale turned white.

"Commander, Tulip is getting a little vibration."

"Not made for this slip."

"Affirmative. Drop it down to TL 10 and let's see what we get. Gentlemen, there are barf bags behind you." Lt. Collins smiled and Sana winked at him. Cage grabbed his and promptly filled it. Bale held on as long as he could then grabbed a bag too.

Sana looked behind her as the two toughest men she knew puked into their bags. "Pussies!" She high-fived Lt. Collins and kept looking at her terminals.

"How's the vibration now?"

"Good Commander. I doubt she will ever meet TL 16 without a breakup. Just not strong enough."

"Okay, let's go home. A couple of barrel rolls but keep us level. I don't want to upset the ladies behind us any more than we already have."

Lt. Collins grinned. "But you promised we could follow Tulips' maneuvers! I was really looking forward to spinning this sucker!"

Bale and Cage grabbed another set of bags and gagged into them. The stars swung by as they returned to Palisade.

Sana turned to look at Lt. Collins and smiled. **You are cruel!**

Yep!

Back on AGAMEMNON I, Captain Castillo laughed hysterically as she watched poor Commander Jackson and her boyfriend the Master Chief toss their cookies.

The next day Lt. Collins ran into the commanders' office. He saluted everyone that needed it, the rest saluted him. Bale just stared at him. "What do you need Lieutenant?" Collins swallowed. He knew he was still in Dutch with the commander over that test flight.

"Sir, you need to see this! I also need Lt. Commander Jackson to interpret for me and for you of course, Sir!"

Bale took the tablet and looked at the screen. The spatial coordinates were well off Palisade boundaries, but it was clear there was a trace of something. It was a ship leaving at TL 7.8...Enki!

"You got this from the scout?"

"No sir, it came from the attack ship. She picked it up when we were returning to Palisade."

"Can we track it?"

"No sir. This trace is now over a day old. We have no idea where it went."

Bale took off his office suit and flexed his muscles. Everyone stood back as his armor and weapons flew to him. Once every piece was clamped on Bale tightened his muscles and purple flared out of his armor. Twenty members of his personal guard were pushed back by his shields. They could do that too, but it took a lot of time and experience to do it. Their Commander had that in spades.

Bale clicked a link to the AGAMEMNON I. “Captain Castillo, I require your presence on Beta Four at Admiral Deans’ residence where Lt. Commander Jackson is taking a lesson. This is an Emergency! Red Alert on all ships! There are Enki nearby!”

Janet did not doubt Bale for a second. She peeled out of her uniform down to her undersuit. She flexed her muscles, and her armor flew out of a locker and clamped itself to her. “Lt. Commander Wilson, you have the Conn. I want all three AGAMEMNON ’s at battle stations!” She held up her hand with all her fingers spread wide. Five Points joined her and pulled their weapons.

Lt. Commander Wilson dialed in the admiral’s address then pointed to the captain. “Go!” She and the five Points ran through the gate.

“Lt. Vickers! I want all ships at battle stations until further notice! Smaller ships are to return to their hangers. Ground forces to return to base and go to Black Bubble until further notice. Notify Fleet as to our situation but not to reinforce at this time.”

“Yes Sir!”

Aditsan *Walker* Wilson pulled his hand back behind his chiseled features and touched his wife’s feather, an Eagle’s and his two daughters’ feathers, both blue birds entwined into his braid. He was large for an American Indian, well over six feet tall. He owed the captain a life debt as his gang had taken the life of her first husband.

It was supposed to be a simple mugging, the woman knocked out and her man beaten when he tried to defend her. They did not know that Mrs. Castillo was augmented. The woman woke up while they were trying to take her clothes off. She killed the four boys with him. Mrs. Castillo beat him senseless, trussed him up, threw him over her shoulder and picked up her husband then ran to a nearby hospital...it was two miles away.

A week later, her husband died.

Lt. Janet Castillo and a few of her friends broke into the prison hospital. All were armed with high-end military equipment and armor. No one was killed but a few doors were broken beyond repair. She found Aditsan in a bed, pulled him up and screamed at him. "My husband just died. He was not a military man but by God, you will become one! You owe me a life...Yours!" She handed the teenaged boy to her Master Sergeant, Aditsan's feet never touched the floor.

He looked into those blue eyes of the huge blonde man and knew real fear for the first time. "Sweetheart, you just dropped into Hell!"

Aditsan was drummed into the Navy, the emperor never said a word.

Aditsan touched his braid once more while thanking the captain for saving his life. He would never betray her again.

"Sir! We are ready!"

"Blackout now!"

Every ship except for the Tugs and the Maw vanished.

54

Captain Castillo found Admiral Dean, Commander Jackson and Lt. Commander Jackson looking over a tablet. She directed her men to go outside and protect the property with the commander's men. Bale saluted her.

"Talk to me!"

Admiral Dean waved his hands, "You don't want to talk to me. I don't want any part of this!"

Janet fumed. Admiral Russell Dean had proved himself in battle, three purple hearts! But his love was engineering. That is why he became the Ring Master. The man could tell you about electrons and then make them do things they were never meant to do. He was the Expert!

"Commander Bale, tell me!"

He turned to his wife. "Lt. Commander Jackson will explain this to you."

Janet glared at Sana. "Sir, the attack ship detected a trace of a small ship slipping at TL 7.8. That is a typical speed of an Enki ship. We have no idea where it is going, we can't track it as this event happened yesterday."

Bale spoke out. "Sir! It is going for reinforcements! There is still a ship somewhere around us, perhaps many ships that weren't destroyed at the Wolverine base."

Sana changed her tablet's menu and scanned the area with long-ranged detection satellites. There was not much to see but then she found a gas cloud. There was a hard object inside the cloud, and it was huge!

The Enki was finishing his lunch of nectarine and spiced meat when his panel shrieked with new data from the star system. He punched a few icons and got his answer. Every human ship just disappeared! Where did they go? He debated waking the Deities but decided to wait. This might be a ruse but even then, their ship was in jeopardy! The humans must be hiding. Were they moving on to the carrier? Had they detected the scout ship?

He warmed up the carrier's armaments.

Gun platforms were moved gently to locations in the system, all were focused on the direction of the cloud half a light year off. It was too far out of range but if any ship other than theirs approached, it would be fired on.

The AGAMEMNON I and AGAMEMNON III approached the cloud from different directions, their shields hiding their ships on full alert. "It appears to be dormant." Commander Barnes called back from the other ship.

"Yes sir but I'm getting readings from several of its guns as being active. I think they saw that we disappeared. They're worried."

Captain Castillo nodded. "Commander Jackson, when we get within the cloud you will have only a few minutes to board that ship after all hell breaks loose. Wait until we disable the engines and las a hole through the cloud. Commander Barnes, once you burn a hole through the gas put a MAC round through that ship. Try to avoid the command center which appears to be on top. We need all the information we can get from these clowns! Out!" Captain Barnes didn't mind taking orders from Captain Castillo as she was the Defense coordinator for Palisade; she did out rank him.

She turned to her navigator, "Take us in slow. Weapons, be ready with three torps for the engines. Slow in on TOW then at 1000 meters sink them in!"

The AGAMEMNON III waited just outside the gas cloud nearest the Enki ship. They could not see much detail, but the ship was larger than any of the AGAMEMNON 's Auxiliaries. It had to be a carrier. They could not fire the MAC round through the gas. It would penetrate but would lose most of its momentum thus doing little damage to the ship. Initially Commander Barnes would have to Laser a hole through the gas. Timing was everything in this operation.

"Torps One, Two and Four away Sir." They could not use the third torpedo as it was nuclear. "Easy does it Ensign, we don't want to wake the neighbors, not yet."

"Copy that sir." The weapons master brought the torpedoes as close as he dared. "Ready when you are Sir."

The Enki commander aboard the carrier was getting nervous. It had been several hours since the human ships had vanished. He had woken more of the Dog Soldiers but left the Mori still in their tanks. They were dangerous to have wandering the interior of a ship. The Wolverines were not so difficult, but they were hungry. If something did not happen soon, they would want to stop and eat.

He directed the little probe outside the gas cloud to look around. Nothing, not a thing registered to its sensors...wait! Some of the gas behind it was moving! Something must be there!

"Now Ensign!"

The three torpedoes went to maximum drive, rammed into the rear of the carrier and exploded!

Bale and 40 Points waited just outside the carrier, several hundred meters. They saw the explosion at the back of the massive ship. "Filters up, Now!"

Commander Barnes fired the huge laser and the gas dispersed.

The Enki fell to the floor along with his soldiers after the rear of the ship was destroyed. He tried to stand up and give the enemy alert when a bright light flooded the front of the ship.

"Fire!" The depleted uranium shell turned to plasma and struck the carrier in the front. A moment later the entire back third of the ship exploded shredding Enki, metal and fuel into space, the MAC round having gone through the entire length of the ship. The Mori had been instantly killed by the MAC round. They had been boiled alive in their tanks. The ship was hulled, and air escaped. Its guns were automatic and fired into the space around it. Their targeting did not work as there was nothing to see but the guns fired anyway.

Commander Barnes yelled, "It's still not dead. Hit it again!"

Another round tore off the keel of the wounded ship. All the lights went out and the guns stopped firing. "Now Commander Jackson!"

Bale and his men raced for the top of the ship. He directed three men forward. "Open her up, gentlemen. The rest of you stand ready!" They found an airlock. One of the men placed a sensor on the door and moved away. The other two placed metallic caulk around the edges of the door then they moved away too. Everyone else fanned away from the airlock. "Sir, there is air inside."

"Not for long." Bale pushed a button on his sleeve and the caulk blew up sending the door into space. Several Wolverines blew out with the air, but they had no suits on and died instantly.

Six men entered the hole and went in different directions. "Clear!"

The rest followed with four standing guard at the door. There was debris everywhere. The ship had been yawing to the starboard when the artificial gravity went out. The Marines did not need gravity and apparently the wolves did not either. Several floated around a corner of a hall and began firing at the humans; they had on suits. Bale stood back and waited on his men.

The Wolverines weapons had no effect on his men and women, their suits now stronger and all of them being Point assured that. The wolves died slowly but finally. "I've got a Duce!" "Four of a kind!" "Hey! I shot it first!" "Yeah but it wasn't dead and you weren't here to rip it apart." Everyone laughed.

"Cut the chatter! Move forward and up. Find the bridge!"

Bale felt something bounce off his suit. He was standing at the juncture of two halls and five wolves were coming for him shooting their weapons. He pulled out his chain and snapped it forward. The point of the purple chain pierced all five wolves. He yanked it out and floated over to the aliens. He grabbed the arms of the first one and pulled.

"That's another Pair of Threes," his Master Sergeant said

behind him. Bale ripped the head off the next one. "An Ace in the Hole!" The third wolf was trying to bring up a weapon, but Bale pulled three of its arms off before it died. "Three of a Kind!" Bale was not going to let the fourth die on him before he got his full house. He quickly pulled each leg off before the eyes in the monster rolled up. "Royale Flush! Good job, Sir!" The fifth one had a chance to die before Bale got to him.

"Behind you Sir!!" Bale pulled his chain out and lit the small space with its deadly purple light. He whipped the chain behind him. He felt it grab something and pulled! When he spun around, he found himself facing his first Enki. The bird-faced thing was cut in half but was trying to grab Bale's throat. Its hands kept sliding off his shield then it died. The two behind him were dead as well. Several others were down the hall trying to stab the Points with a ceremonial spear. There was an electrical spark, but the Points put them down as well. "I wonder what kind of cards we can get with these?" one of the men said.

Sir, we have found what looks like the control room. Big door and some really pissed off aliens inside. Bale noted their location and directed the rest of the group up.

They found several dead Wolverines and weird Dog boys floating in the vacuum. Bale saw the door and it *was* a big one! "Tank! Front and center!"

Though they could not hear anything the vibration of Tank's feet could be felt. The man was unusually large. He was Japanese and was formerly a Sumo wrestler before he joined the service. Once being augmented and now a Point as well, the man was formidable.

Commander Jackson looked up at the tall man and pointed to the door. "Fetch!"

The man bowed briefly and winked at Bale, "Hai Sensei!"

He walked up to the door and studied its dimensions. Tank's reach was over eight feet, but the door was easily three meters in diameter. There were quartz windows built into the door so everyone could see a few dog boys staring at them. All were snarling. Then Tank touched the door. A huge spark erupted from the bridge door and knocked Tank to the ground. He stood up and shook his body. The dog boys were obviously laughing at him behind the glass.

Tank flexed his massive muscles and very deep purple, almost black ropes of power rolled off his suit. Then his hands began to glow. Tank had a special suit built just for him.

Bale motioned everyone to get back, “This is going to get messy...”

Tank grabbed the door, and his hands went into the surface as it melted. The dog boys floated back in fear. Sparks flew away from the door but did not stop the Tank. Whatever the door was made of globules of melted metal froze in the vacuum. Then the door cracked and crumbled as Tank screamed into his headset. He pulled the door out of its mounts and threw it through a nearby wall. The busted door passed through two rooms, one full of dog boys, out through a small hanger and then through three layers of external bulkheads of the carrier. He stood back and waited while everyone ran in.

Outside the carrier, the four men felt the vibrations of some serious work being done further up then watched in awe as a huge and badly mishappened door flew off into space.

One looked at his friend, “Tank?”

“None other could have done that! Much Saki tonight!”

“You got that right!”

Bale let his second string in to collect a few cards. He had to give the Enki credit, they fought hard even in suits, but they died just the same. They played with the Wolverines, but it was not a fair fight. “End it now. Bring in IT and get Lt. Commander Jackson over here.”

Sana floated over from the AGAMEMNON I with Master Chief Daniels. “Dang! I don’t get to have any fun!” Sana just smiled. “Don’t you have enough cards?”

She met Bale on the bridge of the alien ship. Sana fist-bumped her husband and joined the IT crew.

The vacuum had sucked out all the smoke so it was easy to read the icons but there were too many of them flashing. The ship was in trouble and knew it. "Time is short Lt. Commander. We've got to go."

Sana nodded, "What have we got?" she asked the IT tech. "Practice makes perfect, but this ship is a bit more updated than the Attack ship we have. I've found the Main, but access is a little different."

"Can we just pull it?"

The man shook his head, "Too many terminals and data bases. We want it all! Give me a minute."

Sana looked around the room and approached what she determined was Engineering. The lights were going mad there. She switched several screens and found the one she wanted. "You don't have a minute! Grab what you can and let's get out. One of the reactors is still online but is about to overload!"

She started pulling fuel rods from the reactor, but meltdown was still underway. She started shutting down other systems on the large ship, what remained of it but the systems kept trying to reroute against her changes. "I've given you maybe ten minutes but that's it!"

"Okay, okay...I'm hurrying!" Sana frowned but waited.

"That's it, I'm in!"

"Don't analyze it just dump it on a drive and let's move! We'll figure it out later."

Bale was getting nervous. "Everyone out! Cage, you and Tank with Carmichael stay with the IT people. Head back to the AGAMEMNON III, it is closer! Tank! We need a door out front!"

Tank pulled a gun like none of the other Points could carry. He walked away from the group and pointed it at a forward wall. "Fire-in-the-hole!" Everyone's shield flared brightly and then he fired.

A ten-meter hole erupted out of the front of the bridge, there was no sound but the repercussion was enormous!

One of the Points called out. "I've got movement coming this way!"

"Grenades, we just want to slow them down! Lt. Commander?" Bale asked.

"Almost there...almost. Okay, I've got it all!" the IT guy

yelled. Sana grabbed him and two others and ran for the new exit. Bright flashes appeared behind them as all the Marines left the disabled ship. She tossed two of the other men to other Points and pulsed over to the AGAMEMNON III with her one guy.

"Commander Barnes, we are boarding!" Bale called over.

"Hurry Commander, that ship is about to blow!"

They buttoned up the AGAMEMNON III, "All accounted for. Go!"

AGAMEMNON III backed out of the cloud and shot away at TL 16. The AGAMEMNON I was already far away covering them. Thirty seconds later the entire gas cloud lit up like a massive thunderstorm. The gas disappeared and a huge ball of plasma reached for them but could not keep up.

Sana shuttered in her suit as she flipped her helmet open in the emergency hanger. "That was too close!"

Tank was barely standing as he sang some bawdy Japanese song about unrequited love that had to be taken. He spilled his Saki everywhere. People laughed and drank more of the warm brew and tried to sing along though they did not understand a word.

"That is the largest Kimono I've ever seen!" Bale had his drink and grimaced. Sana lay against him on the matted floor, she wore her dress wedding ring and it sparkled beautifully. "You mean that dress he is wearing?" Bale nodded, "It's ceremonial, a Japanese outfit. I wish Datsun were here. He would be laughing hysterically at this song. Dia would just blush."

Sana smiled up at him and snuggled in closer to her husband.

"We caught them without warning. That won't happen again."

Bale slurred his words, "Nope..."

55

It took the Attack ship five months to reach the next Armada. It approached as close as it could but far enough back not to be shot at unnecessarily. The Attack ship was in a hurry as they had been without food for seven cycles, their fuel not much better.

When the Attack ship had been brought aboard one of the carriers the five Deities questioned the pilot most thoroughly before he lost consciousness. They took pity on him and the two others. They were treated, fed and put to bed. Then they raped his files on the small ship. What they found enraged them!

How dare a slave race revolt against its masters and take over this section of space, their hunting grounds! But they had been away for an extremely long time.

Once they had located the world in question it was discovered to have massive resources! But humans occupied the system. They had also destroyed the primary fleet somehow. There was a weapon the humans had that could destroy a star!

The five Deities pondered this for several days. The carrier had remained near the system in hibernation with the three other Deities onboard. That was the only ship near the Spiral system. It would take their much smaller armada five more months to get back. They had plenty of warriors, Mori and ships to counter anything the humans had. According to the records the humans had sufficient power to fight but they would lose to the over-powering might of the Enki!

Newly promoted Major Barnes now outranked Captain Castillo. That annoyed her somewhat but then in a few months, she would be answering him as 'Your Majesty'. Still, the man did have more experience than her. His promotion was a direct result that two Commanders could not exist on the same ship now that Commander Jackson had his promotion. The emperor was wise but a little rash. In any case Jeffry Barnes' promotion was long overdue.

"So this next Armada is in the Sirius system, that's closer to us by several lightyears than the one over near the Horseshoe Nebula. Was that where it was going?" Janet asked.

Sana smiled up to her friend. "Yes sir, their records show they only had supplies for five months. At TL 7.8 Sirius is the only destination within reach. The Nebula is four months farther. The ship never would have made it, the crew long dead."

Bale had a question. "The roster of the other armada is less than half of the Primary? What does that mean in ships and soldiers?"

Sana answered carefully. Bale was her husband but as Commander he needed the best information he could have to plan an attack. "Sir, all we have is their manifest of ships and crew. We do not really know what any of these ships mean in our terms but the carrier we destroyed is like five others within their fleet. All told, they have about 300 ships, eight are Capital ships. The rest are troop carriers, support, food storage and one unusually large sphere that might be a dreadnought like the Nautilus or a Royal House for their Kings...I'm sorry sir, that is the best we could glean from this information."

Major Barnes stood back and waited on his people. There had to be a consensus, but the information was flawed. There had to be more there! "Do we yet have an understanding of their language?"

Sana nodded, "Yes Sir. It appears to be a derivative of Aramaic with heavy Phoenician overtones, pre-Hebrew. We have the Universities of Dubai and Tel Aviv studying the problem. They are making headway. The resources on the Explorer have nothing to offer."

"How long until we can expect them to return if at all?" the future Emperor asked.

"At relativistic speeds it has a two-month advantage on us. Their ships take time to get up to TL, we do not have that problem. Call it seven to eight months before we see them here. Sir, we can catch them, but we do not know their flight path back. Now that they know or rather will find out we destroyed their first fleet they will be careful. I would imagine they will break up into groups to arrive back at Palisade." Sana was not at all confident in her assessment. Bale frowned as he was not sure either.

Major Barnes looked at everyone. "Captain, Commander? Would you join me to get some fresh air? Lt. Commander return to your studies. I'm going to need you sooner than later."

Sana saluted the Major and went to find Admiral Dean.

Two drones and ten Points followed the three as they enjoyed the late afternoon on Beta Four. It was turning out to be a beautiful world. Construction was already underway for the colonists. The bug problem had been solved by Earth fauna, the locals could not compete with birds and the bees and spiders from Terra. Jeff looked around and sniffed the clean air. This might be a good world to build another palace if he had time. No matter, there were already three others in existence.

Major Barnes looked over at Commander Jackson. "You just had to beat my Full House," he grinned. "Sir...?"

"Never mind, never worry about killing wolves. I'm proud of you!" the future Monarch said.

"I'll be recalling the NAUTILUS after it has been refurbished. It will bring three BBs with it this time."

Janet walked between the two tall men and looked up to the future Monarch. "Sir?"

"I'm thinking of a Trojan horse. Do we really need to keep that attack ship?" She responded, "No sir. Its technology is fully understood and to be honest, a bit lacking. With the new engines it can only reach TL 10. The ship is not strong enough for anything more. Its shields are plenty for interstellar travel but not much for battle and the ship is old...we don't need it anymore." Then she smiled. "And we do know how to control it remotely. I like the idea!"

Bale was confused. “A Trojan horse, sir?”

“Really Commander, I know your education is falling behind but you don’t know the story of Troy? Our main ship’s name is based on the military commander that started the whole thing! Once I take command of the Throne and this whole mess is over, one of your priorities is to brush up on Earth history and mythology. One can repeat mistakes that were solved centuries ago.”

Bale was embarrassed and studied the ground in front of him. “Yes sir.”

“Captain, would you care to lead the commander into the story.” She nodded and found a bench strong enough to support Bale. “Once upon a time...”

Bale’s eyes grew as the story unfolded. Such daring! And what a gamble but apparently somewhat true. Troy had been destroyed but the ruse had been used many times in later centuries and had worked every time! He got it!

“Sir, the attack ship can hold the BB and its cradle, and we have enough room to hide it!” Then Bale went into a lengthy description of a plan. Ships to use, icons reset to match the destroyed carrier, a path to confuse the Enki, reconnaissance, men and material, dates and time and of course an additional ruse, a virus to influence the Enki to pursue one path for the most damage. He paused to catch his breath and looked at both superior officers. They just looked at him.

“Um, I apologize, it is just an idea at this point but with a little polish, it should work!”

They both continued to stare at Bale. He was getting worried. Then the Major and the captain started laughing and clapping their hands! Major Barnes looked at Janet, “In less than ten minutes the commander came up with our entire campaign! That planning would have taken months!” Janet grinned and uncharacteristically hugged Bale. “Don’t worry about history, we’ll figure that out eventually.”

The Major shook Bale’s hand. “I don’t envy the great generals of the past as they spin in their graves watching your future!”

Bale turned another shade of red.

56

The AGAMEMNON II caught up with the Enki Attack ship one month out from the Enki armada. They had no intention of meeting that group of ships. "Okay, let's lace it." Their mission was one of intelligence.

A nano ribbon spun out from the larger ship to the small Attack. It slowly penetrated their shields and attached itself to the skin of the Attack ship. Commander Chen guided her quartermaster. "Easy, let us not wake anyone." The crew of the Attack ship never saw the monster riding behind it. The quartermaster nodded and eased the nanos inside. He found a computer junction and connected with their systems. "We are in!"

Lt. Commander Jackson had worked hard on the right icons to fake into their computers. Hazards like black holes and meteoroid belts on the way to human space, heavily radiating neutron stars in their path and other nasty surprises for the Enki to deal with. None such existed but the Enki did not know that. Then she put in the name of one of the destroyed ships from the Wolverine base, a ship that closely matched the size of the attack ship that was reaching them. It being slower would not arrive with the Attack ship but would resemble the other ships and speed, a BB was inside nestled in its cradle waiting to be armed. The NAUTILUS guided the empty ship. Lastly a challenge from the destroyed carrier called oddly enough 'Morning Star'. The humans had left the system largely unguarded. It was ripe for picking! Any mention of the Enki asteroid base was deleted. The crew of the Attack ship were unaware of any changes to their logs. They were sick and running out of food.

The engineers watching all this discovered a couple of failing components on the Attack ship. The thing was not meant to take such a long journey unsupervised. “We better fix them Commander Chen, or this ship might not make it.”

She gave the command and the engineers rerouted some of the nanos to fix the problem. Fresher air for the crew was a small blessing though the Enki had no idea how the problem resolved itself. They were not engineers.

They untethered the nano ribbon and the nanos inside turned to dust. “Pull us back Ensign, slowly.” The Attack ship raced ahead to the Enki armada never realizing their data had been compromised.

Captain Dillon sipped his coffee and read a letter from his genius son. The boy was going to marry a Teknoman nurse, Molly somebody. This surprised him! His son had been vertically challenged all his life. His mother wanted to augment his height, but the young man was stubborn like his father. The woman in question was unusually strong being a nurse and having to manhandle patients. They were a match! And though it never crossed his mind, the girl was cute. Maybe they would have some grandkids after all.

“Sir, Commander Chen sends her regards and is returning to Palisade.” He nodded, “Send her my best and good sailing!” He could have cared less but forms must be observed. “Course and beam?”

“Seven weeks out Sir! No problems.”

TL 10 was a bore, but they would get there eventually.

“No! No! No! You are just going to shake things apart! Remember, it must increase its rotation over a period of two generations to full Earth gravity! It may not be made of taffy, but you are treating it like it was. “Admiral Dean growled at Sana, “Check your math!”

Sana glared at the admiral, and she knew her math was right! Her father had always commented that she knew more about math and science than most of the people he worked with while she was still a child. And now she was being turned into an Engineer for one of the most massive projects humans ever built. She hated it! And Sana cared for the master of this science even less.

"Can it you old goat! Every Ring you have ever built has a fluctuation because you left the stabilizing engines in parallel. I alternated them! Your engines must fire all the time to counter that flux, mine won't!" Admiral Russell Dean was so red that she thought he would burst a vessel. Serve him right!

She pointed to the wall and new numbers grew in. "Here's my math, asshole. You forgot to include the integer for slippage!"

The two guards in the room did not know what to do. They barely understood the conversation between Master and student and the math was beyond their kin. But the admiral was upset and that would not go well. Admiral Dean waved them off and studied the wall of new math.

"But...but, well." He paused for a long time.

"That might work."

Bale and Major Barnes were going over the last of the logistics on the campaign against the Enki. If the ruse worked then the attack ship would destroy the fleet. If they broke into three groups as Bale suspected to approach Palisade, then the result would be a bit more complicated for the humans.

Admiral Dean burst into the room laughing. He waddled over to the bar, poured himself a brandy, drank it down and threw the snifter into the corner for a satisfying crash.

Jeff rolled his eyes, "I wish you'd quit doing that. I don't have that many glasses left!"

The admiral chuckled. "I'll buy you a new case so shut up!" He poured himself another glass then found a seat to plop in, he kept laughing.

"Boy! You are in for a tussle tonight! I thought that wife of yours was going to throw something at me!" He finished the glass and tossed it over his shoulder making a sparkling sound of shattering glass as it fell to the floor. "Take your wife to AGAMEMNON II and have some Sushi on me, I'm buying! It will take her a while to calm down."

Bale leaned his hip against the Major's desk and crossed his arms, Jeff did the same. "What now, Sir?" He was already used to Sana coming home all pissed off. She and the admiral had a weird relationship. He scared Sana and he was frightened of her too, yet they were still friends...sort of.

"She is going to make a great Engineer of Ring technology. Today she used the Riemann paradox to solve the gravity tides within a system and slippage of the Ring material. One Day! Just One! Your wife brought every variable down to zero in the Ring's rotation and it is consistent for 49 years! We let the computers do the simulation 1000 times and it works! Damn!"

Bale was confused as ever. War was his department not math.

He could tell Sana was seething. She placed her right arm on his left as was custom in her previous life. Bale grinned and walked her into the Tiki restaurant, a trite name but a popular venue of Asian food. He looked down at her and winked.

"Shut up!"

He shrugged, "I didn't say a word." He was used to her mood swings by now.

Sana tried to burn a hole into the waiter's back as he led them to their table. "That bastard! He dared me to prove my theorem! I hope he goes home soon so I can build that Ring without his help!"

The waiter tried to pull out her chair, but Bale rushed forward, "Better let me take care of this." The waiter eagerly left understanding full well the Lt. Commander's mood.

He pushed her forward and crossed the table and sat down. "I love your dress. Aren't those the boots you wore the night I asked for your hand in marriage?"

Sana glared at him then beads of tears formed on her eyelashes. She slammed her elbows on the table, cupped her face and began to cry. Bale barely had time to save the burning candles from falling over. He picked up his chair and moved it over next to his wife. She leaned into him and cried some more. "I don't think I can take this anymore." She wiped her eyes. "The man is old news! I don't need him any longer!"

"Well it seems you get your wish. The admiral is going home tomorrow." Sana jerked up. "No, wait! He can't! I was kidding, I cannot do this myself! Oh hell, I really made him mad."

Bale chuckled. "No, he was laughing. Seems you impressed the hell out of him."

"But, but...I don't really know what I'm doing!"

"Sana, you have his entire engineering crew here and they are experienced. They have built Rings before. They will hold your hand until you get your feet wet, and the admiral will always be available for consultation back on Earth. You will be fine!"

They talked some more about the intricacies of building a Ring. Bale was losing interest as he did not understand any of that but it was clear, Sana was an expert even if she did not think so.

They finally had dinner of Sushi, tempura shrimp, vegetables in some exotic sauce on rice glass noodles, Teriyaki steak and the galaxy famous Springfield cashew chicken. Sana snagged another box of Teriyaki steak to take home. She loved it so much!

They gated home back to the AGAMEMNON I.

When the invisible NAUTILUS arrived with the decoy Attack ship Captain Dillon was annoyed to find fully a third of the ships were missing including two of the five carriers. This was not good. He armed the BB and then called the fleet through the fake ship. The language had been conquered but the engineers had the transmitters act like they were damaged. Several of the five-kilometer tentacles were burned and one was missing entirely. The ship had arrived at the fleet and was met with apparent joy by the Deities there. They were given a parking spot in their midst.

Dillon laced as many ships as he could to get information as to the whereabouts of the missing armada. The BB was spinning faster and faster in its cradle. A repair crew was coming over to the Attack ship, the Trojan horse by the humans.

"Weapons!"

"Yes Sir!"

"We didn't come all this way without using some ordinance. Target the three carriers with two rounds each. The rest go into that behemoth."

The man grinned, "Yes Sir!" He lined up the fifteen railguns in the NAUTILUS.

"Anything from their computers?"

A woman across the bridge responded. "No sir. All I am finding is they gave the smaller group the destination to Palisade and wished them good hunting. They would join up in five months. 113 ships left the fleet two days ago. That's it, Sir."

"Damn! And no way to find them. Set the BB for 15 seconds after we fire. TL 25 after that, I want to be back to base in time for dinner." Everyone on the bridge laughed.

"We will be exposed for a few seconds." His First said.

"Like I give a damn. And they do not have as many ships this time. Execute in ten seconds."

The man nodded, "...five, four, three, two, one. Fire!"

All fifteen railguns spit out their rounds. Plasma bolts destroyed the three carriers instantly. The NAUTILUS appeared above the fleet. The other nine rounds went into the huge sphere surrounded by a squadron of smaller ships. It punctured like a balloon spilling fire and debris at a fantastic rate!

"TL drive, Engage!" The Nautilus disappeared and was several light years away when the BB in the decoy Enki Attack ship exploded.

"We got some good shots before the probe was destroyed, Sir."

"Good!" the captain grinned.

The remaining Enki fleet was now a huge ball of burning gas.

57

The AGAMEMNON I stopped at a prearranged coordinate approximating where the Enki might be two months into their journey to Palisade. It remained under camouflage. "Sir, reconnaissance ships one thru six are away." The smaller ships left the hanger of the AGAMEMNON I. They were not as fast as the larger ship and had shorter ranges, but they were necessary for this part of the mission. The AGAMEMNON I ferried them to the site in space.

"Very well. Disperse to 50 million kilometers and link up. Maintain cloak and go silent."

Janet was worried. Her ship was long overdue for refurbishing. The AGAMEMNON III went back to Earth's shipyards as it had been in the Palisade system for almost a year. Her turn was next, but she was not sure her ship would have time to return to Earth, refit and make it back to Palisade in time for any intruders. The captain's engineers were working overtime for days to fix problems that a shipyard could do in hours. Some of the problems did not need fixing but she had the work done anyway. Nanos did not come from a hardware store, one size fits, all of them had to be made from whole cloth for each purpose and Janet was running out!

"Readings find nothing at this time sir!"

"Increase the cone from 70 degrees to 120 degrees and rotate it." This would reduce her visual acuity but would broaden the search for the Enki.

The recon ships were just a little forward of the AGAMEMNON I and surrounded her with a 100 million kilometer of radar reception. That was tiny in Janet's book. The Enki could be flying right by a billion kilometers away and neither party would know the other was there...unless she went active. Best to stay silent for now.

They waited for two days when Recon ship four called in. "Sir, I've got something two light years below us and at coordinates 231.5880 negative 003.4223. I don't know if it's a reflection or star chatter, but it is moving."

Janet had just finished a shower, had a fresh cup of coffee and took over from her First. "Rotate the ships to point in that direction." Slowly the mammoth ship and its little guppies spun in the direction of Recon four. "Red alert! Battle stations!"

Everybody strapped in and doors the length of the AGAMEMNON I closed. All weapons were brought online.

Recon Four called back. "Checking...checking. That's affirmative Sir!"

"Do a count!"

"Checking...Sir! 46 ships are missing and that includes one of the carriers!"

"Withdraw NOW!"

All the Recon ships scurried to the AGAMEMNON I. Just as the last one was about to enter, a glancing blow hit it. One of the smaller Enki scout ships had run into the Recon craft by accident, a one in a billion chance of happening but the smaller ship even with shields had no chance against the scout. The small ship immediately turned into a bubble. The small scout was destroyed. A large attack ship went after the silver ovoid and tried to wrap its tentacles around the slippery surface. It never saw the AGAMEMNON I.

"Track that beast and move to it! Ping the rest of the fleet near us. Gunners! I need three MAC rounds in succession, four times! Make ready. Go!"

The AGAMEMNON I raced after the attack ship that was still trying to capture the elusive Recon ship in its bubble. The Ping went out and Janet was horrified, they were in the middle of the remaining fleet. While their backs were turned, the other ships fell upon them. The Enki were not even aware the ship was there, they were just passing through. It was an accident, but it was one she made.

"Target that carrier! Fire!"

The AGAMEMNON 's had four railguns fore and aft, two on each end. The carrier was destroyed almost immediately but the other ships of the Enki fired back. "Torpedoes Away!"

The AGAMEMNON I blasted the attack ship still trying to catch its prize. Lasers and torpedoes reached out to the rest of the Enki mini fleet. Many ships were destroyed. The Enki had no idea a human ship was in their group, but they fired on it. AGAMEMNON I shields were taking a beating, the ship rocked with blows from the Enki and the firing of the MAC rounds.

"Grapple that bubble and let's move out! TL 18 when you have the Recon. Go!"

They flew through the wreckage of the attack ship and followed the bubble that was tumbling ahead of them. "I've got them Sir!"

"Hit it!" The AGAMEMNON I leapt ahead of the Enki fleet.

She could feel the engines building power, but the sound and vibration was off. "Sir! The other fleet below us is turning to intercept!"

Go Baby, Go! They flew past the leading edge of the other fleet and left them behind. Stars raced past as the AGAMEMNON I escaped a disaster.

"This is engineering. We need to drop to TL 12 for a while Captain. Some of our coils are out of alignment."

Janet turned to navigation and the man nodded. The ship slowed and the odd vibration receded. "I need damage reports and casualties if any. Medical, stand ready. How far are we from the Enki?"

Other departments started reporting in. "Sir, they are more than seven lightyears behind us and dropping fast. I have their location marked but how long they'll follow that track is unknown."

She walked over to astrogation and plotted their course. At this speed it would be three weeks before AGAMEMNON I got back to Palisade. Janet hoped the engines would hold up.

"Communications, notify fleet of our situation and inform Palisade as well. I will send a report about crew and damages as soon as I can. Send it now!"

She turned to the large American Indian, "Mr. Wilson, you

have the Conn. I'm going to check on our crewmen from the Recon ship."

"Yes Captain."

Janet gated from the bridge to the hanger deck.

There was bedlam inside. Emergency crews were racing about, most were strapping the remaining Recon ships to their tethers and locking them down. The crews from the ships waited anxiously in the Ready room watching the crews work on the damaged ship on the floor of the hanger. Medical was standing by but were doing nothing. One of them was throwing up on the deck.

Janet ran over to the nearest medic. "What happened? How is the crew?"

The woman tried to salute the captain then turned away and cried.

Cage was with the emergency crew, saw Janet and walked over. "Sir, the ship managed to save itself, but the crew had no time to react. No one saw this coming." He took a deep breath, "They were torn apart by extreme g forces. It's a mess in there, Sir."

She walked over to the mangled ship and grabbed a light from a marine. "Sir, please don't look."

The ship was a large fighter refitted as a Recon craft; the crew compartment was small for two men. They had to cut away the reinforced canopy over the crew. Janet climbed a ladder and pointed the light inside. What remained of the two men was splattered all over the inside of the ship, even their bones had disintegrated. It had been quick.

She climbed back down the ladder and walked over to the Doctor who was also a pathologist. "Is there any part of them to send back to their families?" The man shrugged. "Sir, I'll get what I can but most of their blood actually shot through the padding of the interior, through cable channels, parts are everywhere even under the seats and inside components. I can't separate them even with DNA."

Janet grimaced. "If it is any consolation, they didn't feel a thing," the doctor said.

The captain turned away and went to her cabin. Cage did not bother to follow.

The tragedy of the AGAMEMNON I went around Palisade and throughout the Terran Federation. Captain Castillo was not charged with dereliction of duty, they were at war and bad things happened. It was just rotten luck but it fell on the captain of the AGAMEMNON I. All the other Captains in the fleet realized they would have executed the same maneuver to find the Enki and shuddered at the thought. The emperor did not comment other than to commend her for saving her crew. But there might be a black mark on her record, maybe...there was certainly one on her heart. Janet finished her report and sent it off to Earth. She sat back in her chair and sighed. This was not the first time she had lost men, but they knew it was always possible in any conflict. But this one was different, she got caught with her pants down. Janet had been foolish, and the men died without knowing how. Janet called Sana, she was waiting. “Captain...” Janet could do nothing else but cry.

Cage came into the suite they shared and could hear Janet in her study. She was crying and talking to someone on the Comm. It sounded like another woman, hopefully Sana. They were good friends and she needed one right now. He changed out of his armor and put on a regular uniform. He shut the door to the apartment and went looking for a bar.

The Enki were furious! They had a human ship in their grasp, and it had killed their carrier and one of their Deities along with 19 other ships, 11 more horribly damaged. How had one ship accomplished that? And then it managed to escape!

The other part of the fleet rejoined them, crews were consolidated, and the damaged ships destroyed. The remaining Deities tried to contact the larger fleet behind them but received no response. Had it suffered the same fate as the Primary?

Worse, the human ship had run to the spiral system to warn them the Enki were coming. They only had one carrier left plus a large cluster of ships and supports. But if one ship could do this...?

58

Bale finished his meeting with Admiral Nakamura. The man was satisfied that Bale had placed his defenses appropriately and in some cases with some invention. The admiral liked the plan. Kai informed Bale that he would not be returning to Palisade but the THOMAS MORE would be in route in another week with a full complement of auxiliaries, more gun platforms and a few battleships along with the NAUTILIS. Palisade would be fully protected by then and the Enki were in for a fight!

He closed the tablet and walked out to the garden in shorts and a T-shirt, not appropriate wear when speaking to an Admiral but the man had called him when Bale was off duty. He walked up behind Sana as she sat demurely on a bench looking over the flowers and plants surrounding the admiral's estate. Admiral Dean had made it a wedding gift to them both upon leaving. The house and grounds belonged to the fleet but since Bale was the commander of Defense for Palisade and Sana was the lieutenant Commander to the Palisade Ring and they were married, it made sense that they had the place. There was even a suite of rooms for friends when they visited.

Sana was wearing a summer dress with bare shoulders. She was watching a clutch of bees fly from flower to flower. She was munching on an apple her husband had brought her from the AGAMEMNON I. Bale touched her shoulders and began to lightly rub them.

"How is she doing?"

Sana reached up and touched him with her left hand, the diamonds glittering in the bright sunlight. She always wore her dress wedding ring when out of uniform. "As well as you can imagine. She has lost people before, but this was different. Janet let her guard down, only for a minute but sometimes that is all it takes."

Bale reached down and kissed her on the cheek.

"Come here and sit with me for a while," she patted the bench next to her. Bale came around from the back and sat next to his wife. She leaned into him and continued to watch the bees, the apple forgotten.

"I have to say you are taking this remarkably well."

Sana sniffed, "Not really but she has been there so many times for me I could do no less. I had to talk her into keeping Cage in the apartment. Janet felt like maybe he was too much a distraction for her job." She looked up at Bale. "Have I been a distraction for you?"

Bale grinned. "Hell yes! But I wouldn't have it any other way." She smiled and intertwined her fingers with his. "Such a beautiful day!" The bees buzzed happily on their new world.

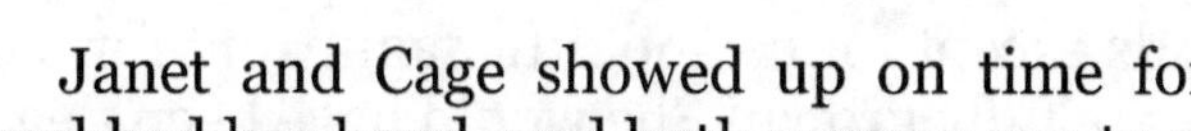

Janet and Cage showed up on time for the BBQ. Sana grabbed her hand, and both women ran to a back room, both were crying when the door slammed shut. Cage looked at Bale and shrugged. They went outside, Bale set up the BBQ grill while Cage got the kegs working. Everyone else would show up in another hour or so, their friends.

Cage walked over with a cup of beer for his commander. "How's marriage treating ya?"

"It's going pretty good, but the bathroom routine is a chore." Bale grinned.

Cage laughed, "Don't get me started. Janet being older and having had two other husbands may be more forgiving, but you have a youngster. I know the protocols!"

"Fortunately, we have a couple more baths. When ya gotta go, ya gotta go!" Both men laughed.

They watched the flames on the charcoal get higher. "Nice digs you've got here..."

"How's she doing?" Bale interrupted.

Cage got thoughtful. "When she is at work, Janet's on the Bounce...no fooling around! But at home," he paused for a bit, "there have been some long nights. She is having a hard time."

Bale knew what he was talking about. He lost his first man, actually a woman to ground fire. She was careless but the fault fell on him, she was not professionally trained at boot and should not have been out in the field in the first place. Bale had lost other men and women in battle, and he wrote home to their spouses and parents about their bravery in a war situation. Cage had been there too for more years than Bale had been alive.

"A week after we got back to Palisade, I found her in the bathroom crying as she etched Bishop's and Torque's names into her upper arm with a laser, her two husbands were above them in order. She was starting a tradition by leaving room for every man she loses."

Bale was shocked! "You didn't take her to the infirmary, did you?"

"Hell no, man! She would have been 8-balled with a full medical discharge. She would have kept her pension, but Janet has no friends except for us and little family but for her children and they are fully grown! She would have been dead by suicide a week after she hit dirt! I was not going to let that happen! We took a furlough and I straightened her out...I had to slap her around a little and scream a lot. I fixed her arm then I told her my story."

Bale frowned, he knew about Cage's three ex-wives and his various children. But he also knew about the men and women that died under his command, especially the children that Wolverines captured and ate. Cage was the toughest man he ever knew but he would find him crying in a corner of a cold shower, weeping over the lost.

Bale reached over and grabbed Cage's shoulder. "We...we are her family!"

Sana was rebraiding Janet's long blonde hair. She still shuddered occasionally as Sana worked. "Now now, look at the year we've had. I almost killed Bale on my first flight then I almost killed everyone else at the Enki base when those monsters ran the door. Dia and I got in a music video. Then I did kill a punk with an attitude. Oh, and let's not forget making Bale and Cage puke all over the Scout ship."

Janet laughed and sniffled. "Don't forget you get to ruin Bale's life with that wedding thingy."

Sana shrugged, "I can't be expected to remember everything I do wrong." She smiled as Janet turned around and hugged the younger woman again. Sana wiped her eyes with a tissue. "That's it, put on a smile! What say we go see what the boys are up to? We don't want them to get too drunk before the party."

The two women came out on the deck holding hands. Cage was hopeful. Bale smiled at Janet and she walked over to him. "Don't you ever hurt this little girl or I'll have your ass!" in that famous Texas twang of hers. Then she hugged Bale. He smiled down at her and squeezed her back.

"Why does everyone say that to me?" She giggled in his arms.

Janet was going to be all right.

The Deities were worried and angry at the same time. Their Primary fleet had been destroyed by renegade slaves, their remnant had been decimated by just one of the human ships and now it seemed that the remainder of the fleet had met the same fate as the primary. They were making good time to the spiral system. Their sub-commanders were drilling the ships and their allies mercilessly. There would be no mistakes this time! Scouts were way ahead of the fleet and spread out. There would be no surprise attacks again. Each scout fired random shots into the void to flush out a target. There was little chance of hitting one, but it might run instead of attacking the fleet.

They were devising new policy in attacking the spiral star the humans occupied. As much as they hated the idea of splitting the fleet again, they would not do so until the time of the attack. The carrier had to be protected until it got within the system. Though there were only two Deities remaining in their fleet there were three others onboard the remaining carrier hidden from the humans: a proper quorum! A signal would be sent to it prior to the attack. Two carriers would win the day!

Surprisingly, the two Deities agreed on the plan.

Bale was meeting with the Engineers of the three Tugs handling the floor panels of the new Ring. All the panels were in a parking orbit near where the new Ring would be placed. There were six now with one left to be completed before the Maw was shut down for the duration of this battle. The panels were relatively easy to make despite their size. It was putting them together that took time, and twenty-five more panels had to be fabricated after the battle.

"So your maximum speed is TL 12?" Bale asked.

"Yup, there is Drive and Overdrive. Overdrive gets us among the stars. Drive is like moving a tractor real slow but that's what we need to move the panels...real SLOW!"

The man Bale was talking to was the Master Engineer. All the men and women that commanded the Tugs and the Maul were Engineers. They were with the service and were in fact Combat Engineers with grades according to their rank. Captain, Commander, Lieutenant and so forth but they preferred to be called Engineers. It was a pride thing and considering what Bale had witnessed so far, that is what he would call them.

"But you can move at slower speeds in Overdrive?"

The man nodded his head as he smoked his pipe, a relic and affectation from an earlier age common among the Engineers. The women smoked long slim cigarettes. "Yup. TL 1 up to TL 12, nothing beyond that. And we can't turn on a dime like your ships can. Stopping is not easy either. We go in a straight line and slow down by degree. When at full stop we then turn slowly and go back to where we need to go. It's a process, yup that it is! Anything in our way gets mushed."

Bale was a little flustered dealing with these people, but he needed them for his plan. "Can you set into the upper gases of a gas giant hidden from view?"

The grizzled Engineer blew smoke at Bale, he did not cough as he had inhaled worse on the Enki asteroid. "You got carrots in your ears? We move 500 trillion tons of flooring every day, you cannot do that without some muscle behind you. We have had to place pulse engines 20,000 kilometers inside a gas giant for the Arcs. The precision must be within five centimeters! And we cannot move during that entire time despite the tides in a gas ball. The Eye of Jupiter has nothing on us!"

One of the women snorted smoke out her nose and laughed. Another man fist-bumped the Master Engineer. They all laughed at Bale.

Bale smiled at the old fart but realized this plan just might work.

"I'm sorry Commander, I was rude. Yup, I was. What did you have in mind? Do we get to join this fight?"

Bale grinned at him. "Have you ever been bowling?"

"Oh yeah, we have bowling alleys on all our ships, we've got the room and our own leagues...Oh!" His eyes grew round.

Bale winked at him. The Master Engineer turned to every other Engineer in the bar. "Nelson! Big Nasty, do ya think you might want to make a strike on some Enki trash?" The man also known as White Point was their best bowler with an evil hook that got him a perfect 300 nineteen times out of twenty. He was also the best pilot on one of the Tugs.

The pilot smiled wickedly, "Yup but I want the pins marked on every Tug!"

Everyone laughed with glee!

59

The Engineer looked over his tablet and shook his head. "You've blown two coils, it's lucky you made it home. Environment down to maybe 50%, I shut down unnecessary sections of the ship, shields at 40% but I'll have those back up to snuff in another day or two. You are outta torps, but I can get you more when the others get here, lasers, those are gone. You fire them once your shields disappear. Rail guns are good, they have their own power source...plenty of slugs." He looked up to the captain, "And I don't know how you did it but you bent this sucker! She is not going back to Earth. The ship is good for defense or whatever else you want but TL 5 is the best you are gonna make and not for long at that. Time to scrap her, Captain."

Janet bent her head in frustration. Her ship would never mate with the AGAMEMNON ever again. Other than the two men that died she had saved her crew but at a tremendous cost: her ship and her career. "Thank you Chief. Do what you can. We'll talk later."

She gated back to the bridge and walked over to her First. "Adistan, I need you to evacuate all nonessential personnel to the AGAMEMNON II and civilians to Beta Four. Engineering has officially scuttled the AGAMEMNON I. We will have some environmental, shields will be back up in two days and more torps when the rest of the defenders show up. No lasers or we lose our shields. The Rails are fine. Let me keep 40 Points but the rest must go. Make sure all the gates are tight! We may need them in a hurry. If I know Commander Jackson, he will use our ship for a lure." Janet almost choked on the last statement.

"Full suits?" He felt for his Captain. They had worked together for ten years after he made Lieutenant. She watched his career and made sure he stayed on the right path. After twenty years in His Majesty's Service, she tagged him as her new First Mate. He was more than honored!

"Yes, but helmets open. No sense in everyone being uncomfortable." She grinned as did her First. Armor was never comfortable but if it saved you from pretty much everything including wishing for air, you wore it!

Adistan Walker Wilson then did something uncharacteristic of him. He reached over and touched the captain on the shoulder. He looked over the bridge and sighed. "I'm going to miss this bucket, she's been good to us." Then he looked Janet right in the eye. "Sir, why don't we make sure she goes out in style?"

Janet patted his hand, "I'm counting on doing just that!"

She found Bale and Sana on Harpers Ferry, a troop ship near the Maw. The Explorer was being moved inside a large channel for safety reasons as it could not contribute to the war and was vulnerable. Captain Verkon was onboard and managing the maneuver. The channel had been cut out with the Maw's own nanos. It was more than big enough for the colony ship but was barely a scratch in the side of the Maw.

Giant grapplers unfolded from the inside and gently pulled the ship to its destination a full kilometer inside the giant vessel. A few minutes passed then a voice came over the speakers. "We are clamped tight Commander. All systems except environmental in the command section are shut down."

Bale responded, "Very well Captain. We will wake you in a few years. Carry on Sir!" And Bale saluted even though the captain could not see it. Sana pressed her microphone. "Captain Verkon, Lt. Commander Jackson here. I wish you well." She could hear him smile. "Ah Mrs. Jackson, I like the sound of that! Is that man taking good care of you? If not let me know when I wake, and I'll have the emperor yank his pips!" He laughed, "I also expect to see a couple of grandkids I can co-op for Unity's sake."

"Good night Sir!" she smiled and signed off.

As they watched, the lights inside the vault shut off then a foaming of white material filled in the void to the edge of the opening. It stopped and hardened into place. They could not even see where the cut in the Maw had been.

"Co-op?" Bale asked.

"He wants to be their God Father."

Bale smiled at that, "Works for me!"

Janet behind them smiled. These two would go far as husband and wife especially with children.

"Where have you sent my troops?" She had arrived with five Points and they all left her alone with the commander and his wife as they gated over to the Maw. "It's Shepherd's pie day on the Maw. Their cook is well known for it, so I sent them over with my men. Then they are going bowling with some of the crews from the Tugs. Should be interesting. Ready to go eat?"

As Sana was officially off duty she walked over and kissed the commander on the cheek. She looked back at the captain, "You didn't see that." Janet grinned. Sana turned back to Bale. "No honey, I want to talk to the captain for a bit, girl talk." Bale rolled his eyes. "Okay but don't be late. I have not bowled since I was a kid, but I want to give it a shot. Love you too." And he walked over to the gate.

"Bowling?" Sana asked. Bale smiled and walked through.

"It's a game where you roll a ball down a lane..."

Sana ran to the bathroom and slammed the door shut. Janet was startled, "Honey? Are you all right?" She could hear vomiting with a serious mix of gagging on the other side. Her eyes expanded. *Could it be?* The toilet flushed and water could be heard running in the sink. Later the door opened, and Sana staggered out. Her hair was oily, and her face was sweating and a little green.

"Yep, and before you ask about six weeks along."

Janet led her back to a table and sat Sana down. She folded over the tabletop and groaned. Janet grinning ran to the kitchenette, found a rag and poured cold water over it. She placed it on Sana's forehead and sat down next to the woman. "What does Bale think?" Then it occurred to her, Bale did not know otherwise he would be handing out cigars, another stupid manly ritual. He did not know!

"Why didn't you tell him?"

Sana sat up and her lips trembled. "I'm so scared! When you said that Cage distracted you, I wondered if I was doing the same to Bale. He said yes but he did not care. I can't distract him now!"

"Honey, Bale is the most easy-going man I know. He will take this in stride and be proud!"

Sana whimpered and pressed the cold compress to her head then wiped the back of her neck. "It's not that. The far buoys found the Enki. They are a month out, so they are early. They have already divided and are heading this way. I can't bother Bale with a baby!"

Janet was alarmed! "Does Bale know about that?"

Sana nodded her head, "Of course. He's got a game plan that would offend a chess master." Then Sana giggled as she wiped her neck. "I once got interested in chess, so I took lessons from a gamester. I got fairly good as we have a game like that on Tekm only not so many pieces and not so complicated. I invited Bale to watch me play and he got bored quick. Then the chess master challenged him to a match. *'I don't play. The game is too predictable.'* The master was offended that anyone could say that, so he demanded a match. Bale crushed him in five minutes flat! Bale played two more games and defeated the man two more times, a sweep. "If you want a real game, come fight a war with me!" He took me home. I have never bothered to play again. It was the first time Bale had ever played Chess!"

That would explain a lot Janet thought. Bale was a four-dimensional man, a player that could see in time and space and had moves no one would even think about. He was always ten moves ahead of an enemy. A chess master would have no chance against him!

"What does your doctor say about the baby?"

"She says I'm doing fine, and the baby has a strong heartbeat. I am sorry that I'm sick. Was it like that for you?"

Janet leaned in and hugged the younger woman. Sana had so many questions that this had to be her first time. "Let's get you home. I'll wash your hair." Janet brightened. She just remembered the thing that would help Sana with her nausea.

She got Sana back to the house on Beta Four, washed the young woman's hair then put her to bed. Janet then clicked back to the AGAMEMNON I. Her chevron notified the ship she was back on board even though Janet was in a hallway. "Sir?" Lt. Commander Wilson asked.

"I'm just here to get a couple of things at the pharmacy before it closes. I will be on post at 0600 tomorrow. Out." Janet gated to the pharmacy and found her friend Stewart who was packing up the shop. They had a weird Othello relationship. She never consummated his love interest, but Janet flirted with him a lot! He was satisfied. "Captain! What can I do for you?" The young man's eyes practically glowed seeing Janet in one of Sana's skintight under suits, she had left her armor at Sana's house. The effect on the young man was satisfactory. "Hon, I've got a sick friend that needs some ginger gummy bears. Nausea it seems."

The man could not take his eyes off Janet's form. Janet cocked a hip out and wiggled a bit. "Sugar, my eyes are up here." He blushed. "I'm sorry Captain, give me a minute. Your friend has an upset stomach? Female, right?" She nodded and wiggled some more. He turned to the rear of the small pharmacy while looking at her body and ran into a shelving unit. "Um...I'll be right back."

Janet gated back to the house on Beta Four and found her five Points and one angry Master Chief waiting for her. "Damn woman, put some clothes on!" He turned to the Points, "Go outside, now!"

Janet ignored Cage and walked into the bedroom where Sana was sleeping. "You can't bounce all over the place without armor and especially in that...that skimpy thing! And without your guard!!"

That was when they both heard Sana in the bathroom gagging again.

"Ah damn! That's all we need now." Cage leaned against a wall and bowed it a little. How had he figured it out? But men were linear in their thinking. Some were faster than others and Cage was the best. It did not hurt that he had three ex-wives and children for the experience.

"When is she going to tell Bale?"

Janet ignored him and knocked on the door. “Sugar? I have something that will help. Let me in.” Cage crossed his arms and frowned.

A little while later both women came out of the bathroom. Sana was chewing on something, “That is really great! Thanks!” Janet put her back in bed. “The bag will be right here on the night table. Just grab one when you need it.” Sana smiled, chewed some more and swallowed. Then she closed her eyes and went to sleep.

Janet pushed Cage into the living room and shut the door. She turned and pressed her breasts against his armor. “Like the suit?” She reached up and kissed the man.

Cage pushed her back. “Damnit, not now! How far along is she?”

“Six weeks, thereabouts.” She bent over to retrieve her armor and her uniform. Cage started breathing heavily. “We have to tell Bale.” He said.

“Not until the battle is over.” Janet started to put her arms into her uniform, her chest stretched out provocatively. “She doesn’t want Bale distracted right now. Could you help me with this zipper?”

Cage grabbed her and ran to a back bedroom.

Everyone outside started laughing. Cage had neglected to turn off his mic.

Janet and Cage met with Bale in a conference room on board the AGAMEMNON I. “Where is Sana?” he asked. “It’s her day off, leave her alone for now.” Bale nodded. “Sorry about your ship Captain.”

“It’s all right, we’ve had a good journey together.” She patted a nearby wall. “I expect you want to use her in some nasty way.”

Bale grinned, “With your permission of course.”

“You know damn well the emperor gave you carte blanche with all the system’s resources. AGAMEMNON I is yours to use as you see fit. Just make it count.”

“Oh, I will! Cage, we have to talk over the disbursement of the men. I want on that carrier to get as much intel and material out of it as we can. If we can save the ship, then all the better. There is still another fleet out there somewhere and we will have to deal with it eventually."

"Yes Sir! Anything else?"

"No, just get your lists going...Rough Rider."

"What? Hey!" Janet just grinned and pointed to his mic. "Ah Damn!" and he stomped out of the room.

Bale chuckled, "Where did you come up with that?"

"Do you really want the details?"

Bale held up both of his hands, "Nooo, no, I'm good." He laughed then Bale got somber. "By the way, how far along is Sana?"

Janet's eyes grew round. "How did you know?!"

"I had an aunt that spent a lot of time in the bathroom during her first trimester. Sana has been tossing her cookies for a couple of days now. She tried to hide it from me but I'm a light sleeper."

Damnit! How did he figure it out? I guess men and women are not so different afterall when it comes to intuition. "Six weeks. She is exhausted! I want her to return to Earth but no one is going there anytime soon."

"No, she stays with me. I'll take care of her, she is my wife and soon to be the mother of our child." Bale grinned sheepishly. "Imagine me as a Dad?"

"You will be a great father!" Janet stepped forward, stood on her toes and kissed Bale on the cheek. "Get Dia to help. She's at loose ends and they are friends."

"Good idea, only if I can pry her from Datsun."

"What...? But I thought he went back with the AGAMEMNON."

"Naw, I saw the writing on the wall and Cage needed another Master Sergeant. They got married last month. She is pregnant too. Funny thing, having a baby doesn't seem to bother Dia at all and it is also her first time."

"Wha...no one tells me anything!"

"Captain, I'm surprised anyone tells me anything in our little group. Now let us talk about messing with the Enki's heads. How do you feel about a little ambush? I want to make them change their game plan daily."

"You are an evil Chess Master."
Bale grinned wickedly.

60

The Enki were becoming weary. The daily harassment by the humans was annoying. Their ships were attacked but not destroyed. Though severely damaged the wounded ships marched on at the command of the Deities. The forward scouts never saw the little ships of the humans. They just appeared out of nowhere, fired a couple of shots and disappeared again. Both fleets were being attacked but to little effect other than slowing them down. Maybe that was their purpose. Regardless the humans had only little ships, powerful but small and there were only a few of them. This gave the Enki Deities resolve. This system would be theirs! The humans had no reserves and other than the one large ship now damaged as their records showed, they would not be able to defend themselves. The Enki would win!

It was time to send a message to the other carrier.

Bale took off his armor and put it in the fresher. He put on a pair of pants and a shirt that Sana had bought him from the same store on the AGAMEMNON I where she got her sexy '*I'm getting married or else!*' outfit. He hated it but she liked the shirt. Cage always laughed when Bale wore the darn thing.

He had cut some of the Daisies from the garden, the ones that the bees seemed to favor and put them in a small vase. "Anyone home?" he asked as he looked into their room.

Sana tried to sit up from the bed but groaned and fell over again. She was chewing something. "Yeah, I'm here."

"I brought you some flowers." She leaned over and smelled them and played with the petals. Usually, Daisies do not have much of an aroma but the soil of Beta Four enhanced them. Sana smiled. "Done for the day?" Bale put the small vase on the nightstand then sat on the edge of the reinforced bed. He rolled Sana onto her back and gently pulled up her nightshirt. Sana was fascinated by her husband's tenderness. He bent down and kissed her belly then rose to kiss her lips. "Don't you mean 'We' are here?"

Sana sucked in air. "Who told you?"

"What, like I can't figure this out for myself? Besides, you have been puking for a few days now. No one told me a thing."

Bale pulled back and rested his shoulder to the side of Sana's knees. He carefully touched her waist and said, "Hi little fellow, I'm your Dad. I will take care of you and your Mom all of your life!" He then kissed her bellybutton again and smiled. Sana reached down and played with Bale's hair. He looked up at her with those brilliant green eyes and grinned. Sana knew then that no matter how painful the birth would be she would never forget this moment.

Sana woke up next to Bale, her leg arched over his legs. The man was just huge, but he never noticed her weight. Unfortunately, the bed was broken again. One of the legs on his side near the headboard was bent. She would have to find a tougher bed! Her doctor said that sex would be fine until her last two months. The woman laughed *'Neither of you will be interested then. Just take it easy for now.'* Easy was not in Sana's or Bale's book as the broken bed testified.

"C'mon baby, we've got work to do today. Remember? The scout ship?"

Bale yawned and opened one eye, "It's my day off."

"Yeah right, when was the last time you had a day off?" Sana sneered at him. Bale moved to kiss her and the other leg at the foot of the bed collapsed. The mattress with both of them slid to the floor. Bale held her tight as they both laughed hysterically. He finally got to kiss her.

"Buddy, shave now and the next time too. My tits feel like they have been cleaned with sandpaper!" She jumped off Bale and ran to the bathroom. "I'm gonna shower then so are you!" Sana slammed the door.

Bale grinned. What an interesting way to start the day! He would have to talk to someone in the metal shop to get a proper bed.

The small scout ship left the fleets and arched over the spiral system's plane. It reached out to the carrier still in hiding. The scout could not come close or else the humans might detect her or the carrier. Morning Star responded immediately. There was the usual litany of praise that the fleet had arrived, the Deities were tired of waiting and wanted this system right now! The diatribe went on for several minutes. What was the Plan? When do we attack? How many fighters do you have? Our crew is ready to take back this system our ancestors created!

It went on and on. The crew on the scout was used to this. They gave the Deities the information that they wanted. Placement of ships, the roster, time of attack...everything!

The battle would begin in three weeks when the rest of the fleet arrived. It would be a short war as far as the Enki were concerned. The scout returned to the fleet to inform the two other Deities there that the carrier was waiting and eager to fight!

Sana smiled. "Think it worked?"

Bale laughed. "You are a stinker. And bossy too. Do the Enki really talk like that?"

"I've read enough of their transcripts from the carrier that I know how they think. How great their race it, how wonderful each of the little god kings are, how glorious it is for the slaves to work for them." She rolled her eyes. "These people are so narcissistic that they haven't found a mirror they don't like."

Bale chuckled and shook his head. "How did you learn their language so fast?"

"Hey, I'm quick, smart too when I put my mind to it." She leaned in and hugged her husband.

Bale started unclasping her armor. Sana smiled.

"It's not an Attack ship but it is alien. We will be the first to abuse her and I did shave."

Sana lifted her arms as Bale pulled off her chest plate. “Goodie!”

“Gently, gently.” They could feel the asteroid bump against the hull. They were surrounded by rocks of various sizes. Other rocks were near just to keep the illusion of an asteroid field. The tug was somewhat hidden. The Master Engineer had the surface nanos colored to mimic the rocks. He called over to the other tug on the other side of the system. They were camouflaged too. The third tug was parked inside Beta Five, a gas giant. ‘Big Nasty’ was itching for a strike!

Three weeks of waiting. What the hell! This was much better than sitting out the war run by a bunch of Marine pukes!

61

Sana clicked another set of keys on the computer and made sure her glyphs were in order. She was the only one that could read them with any satisfaction of success. The techs were there to make sure her computer language was correct, of which she was not so certain. They were a good team.

Sana sat back in her chair, "Okay, they are ready."

"You sure ma'am? Once I key this in there is no turning back."

"It's all good." The man leaned over his own keyboard and started compiling his program. Sana watched as some of the troops walked by with the parts of the two Commander Centers. The Enki asteroid had to be completely empty of any evidence of human habitation. Other men and women were gathering any possible trash left behind. It all had to go through the gate inside the Throne Room.

The tricky part was removing all the debris from the end of the light axis leading to the hanger. The one Spoke that saved Cage and Bale, barely, was left to collapse after they removed the man-made reinforcement. Hopefully the Enki would think that an explosion caused all the damage while the door saved the hanger.

They left several of the fossilized dog soldiers lying around the interior kinda like they were in a fierce battle. The Sun King was removed along with his retinue, the broken scout ship was removed too, and all were dropped into the sun. Bale wanted to make the base look like they abandoned it. Busted up robot parts were scattered around as well to make it look like a huge battle had been fought inside the city cave.

Air was left in the hanger with its pumps working to suck the air out into huge containers then replaced once the Enki got inside. But in this case, once the doors were shut, they would never open again, there would be no way out.

Bale came up with this trap and it was devious! The truly evil part were two man-made devices that were left inside the hanger. Two nuclear bombs with Magnesium casings. The air would boil while the bombs melted everything. It was overkill but hey, why waste a good set of bombs?

"All right, Lt. Commander it is all set. No more changes."

Sana called her husband. "Commander, the system is ready. All need to evacuate now. We need your command to arm the system." Once the command was given, the program would prepare for the Enki, no one else could get in. The cave was in vacuum, but the hanger was not. The shield still held over the vast opening above them, but the light was off in this part of the base. Only the Systems and Security tombstone would be lit, easy enough for the Enki to find. Once they turned on the air, light and heat, the bombs would go off. Everyone inside plus any ships tethered to the base would be destroyed. The humans intended to drive them to this obvious retreat.

Bale was out of the system in the THOMAS MORE where the old Enki carrier had been destroyed. Captain Bayer came over and pulled out her key. She and Bale put both her key and his into the slots for the two bombs on board the Enki asteroid base. "Three, two, one...Engage!"

Sana saw all the lights on the computer come up green. She closed and locked the case then handed it to a Marine surrounded by four more. "You know where to put this." The man nodded and flew off with his escort. A cache had been prepared in the deepest part of the asteroid. The Enki would never know about it and could not find it if they did.

"Lt. Commander Jackson, time to get your men out of there. And don't forget the gate."

"Yes Sir, Out!"

Captain Denise Bayer smiled up at the taller man. "Did I hear that your wife is pregnant? That should make for some more interesting passions your lady is so fond of."

Bale grimaced, "With all due respect Sir...shut up!"

Denise laughed and laughed.

The NAUTILUS was also inside a gas giant, Beta Six. The shell of the Dreadnought was almost as tough as the Tugs for it had to withstand terrible gee forces in flight and of course return fire from anyone. It faced Beta Seven a small ice ball planet in orbit near the asteroid the Enki's would run to. Any that managed to escape the explosion, the NAUTILUS would destroy. There was only one week left until the Enki arrived and the crew aboard the NAUTILUS could have cared less. They had an enemy to destroy then they would move on to their next mission.

Sana had arrived at the hiding point of the THOMAS MORE with her little Enki scout ship. She was to be part of the decoy but only long enough to transport over to the massive ship when the Enki attacked. Sana was beginning to show so that warranted a maternity uniform and maternity armor which was especially layered for her and her baby's protection. Bale and Sana walked into the conference room and saluted Captain Bayer. "Nice to see you again, Lieutenant Commander Jackson. You have come far in the world. I've read about your redesign of the Palisade Ring and I have to admit I am impressed!"

"Thank you, Captain Bayer!" Sana did not know what else to say. She and the captain had words several times over the last year...it had not gone well for the Lt. Commander. "I've also heard of some of your other exploits. In my humble opinion, you are to be commended for appropriate action in the line of duty, even if you were off duty at the time. Thugs will not be tolerated in His Majesty's Service or by His Protection. You did well!"

Sana was shocked! She had not heard that from anyone except Bale, Janet and Cage and here a Captain of the Line agreed with her actions.

"Come, sit down." Captain Bayer indicated a couple of seats near the front of the conference table. A tall woman walked in with a pitcher of iced water and several glasses. She placed them on the table and walked over to Captain Bayer.

She watched the woman closely as Bale pulled out Sana's chair. Sana sat down and studied the woman. Dark colored Tkem' were barely tolerated in Teknomen society as they were considered an aberration, a mutant. Cage was somewhat milk-chocolate in coloration. Molly was a deeper brown. This woman was entirely black. Her skin reflected all the light in the room. Sana had some experience with different colored people, but this woman broke the ethnic bank.

The woman placed her right hand on Captain Bayer's shoulder. "Not now, Robin. You will just get him killed!"

"Commander Jackson, my wife and I had our son transferred to this station to join your team. I hope you will accept him," the woman said ignoring Denise.

Bale glared at Captain Bayer. "How long has he been out of boot?"

"Three weeks. He has been working with the troops onboard the THOMAS MORE during our trip here. His grades are excellent, and his teamwork skills are above par. His name is Franklin R. Bayer."

Bale pulled up the young man's record and stats. 6'-5" natural, fully augmented, an E5 plus a black belt. Marksmen, medic and pilot. Computer skills were a bit low but then the man was only nineteen years old. That would come in time.

"You know nepotism is frowned upon in the Service especially from one so high up in the ranks as yourself, Captain. He has no combat experience and little with robot wolves. This could get him killed if I test him! His fear factor is high but then that is to be expected from one so young and Captain, I do not have to tell you that fear at this age is not a bad thing. It makes a man more cautious and less dead."

"Regardless, I order you," Denise hung her head in shame, "I am sorry, Commander. I beg of you to give him the test." Bale stared at her and frowned. He thought some more then shrugged.

Bale turned to the man behind him. "Master Sergeant Turner, prepare the young gentleman for trial." Turner glared at the captain. He knew how dangerous this was for a newbie, the captain did too!

"How many?"

"Two and two. Only a knife and low shields."

The captain's eyes grew wide. "That many? They will rip him to shreds!" Bale spun on the captain and pointed his finger at her.

"I did not ask for this, you did! All my men are highly trained and have many campaigns under their belts. I have 200 Points, two companies under my command. I will not have a coward on my team. Franklin washes out then that would be better for everyone!"

Bale sympathized with the boy's mother, "Turner and I will be there to save him if necessary. Do not worry and do not watch. It will be brutal!" With that he left the room with Master Sergeant Turner.

Sana looked at both women. Robin was openly crying, and Denise had tears in her eyes. She went over and sat down with the captain. "Sir? What does two and two mean?"

Robin ran back to the kitchen; she did not want to hear this.

Denise grabbed Sana's hand and looked at the floor. "We always keep a small group of Wolverines on board for testing. These are not robots. It is the only way to drive fear out of a Marine. Once you have fought them, they don't bother you anymore." Sana was shocked! "They will come in two waves, that is if Franklin survives the first one. Two wolves in each wave. He has to kill all four."

"You've gone through this?" Denise nodded. "Every Marine goes through it. You are in Flight and will not experience it, your job is dangerous enough without learning field work." She then looked up at Sana and smiled, "Besides, didn't you kill a dinosaur once and it cost you an arm? I'd say you've already passed this test."

62

"This is damn foolish Commander! He is only a boy. I had two campaigns under my belt before I tested!" Bale nodded, "Three for me and yes, you are right. Let us hope he's got the right stuff."

They stood outside the heavily gated door. Two wolves were inside trying to pry the door off its hinges. They glared and snarled at the two men waiting for them. Both men pulled out their weapons and turned on their shields to their highest settings. Purple ropes of power flowed off the two men. The gate was lifted, and the two wolves raced out to confront them...and then they stopped. Let it not be said that wolves were stupid. The two men were unafraid and faced the two animals without moving. Their gold hammers flashing brightly in the hallway lights. This was death facing them and the wolves knew it.

Bale lifted his arm and pointed down the long hall. At the end stood a young man, easily 270 lbs. and all muscle...and he was scared to death!

The armored hall was narrow, so the wolves had to run in tandem. It was wide enough for a man but was tight quarters for the animals. This gave the Marine a slight advantage. The wolves howled and ran at him. Franklin had only a moment before they were on him.

The first wolverine he killed with a knife in his right hand went into the animal's eye and severed the brain stem. The weight of the body knocked Franklin to the floor. The other wolf jumped over his dead companion and pulled off Franklins lower left arm. The man did not say a word just rolled over and stabbed the wolverine in the top of its head killing it. He stood up weakly and pushed a button on his sleeve and the tattered arm was sheared off and dropped to the floor. His suit closed the wound.

Franklin set his jaw and looked down the hall. "Damn! That was quick!" Bale nodded. "Tap out if you want to!" The young man shook his head and waved the knife at them to send the other two wolves. Turner shrugged and opened the gate again. Two more wolves raced out and down the hall. Franklin started running at them. With his bloody stump, he pushed off the wall and landed a blow to the forward wolf breaking its neck. Then he flipped up in the air and grabbed the other wolf with his stump and cut off the wolverine's head. Both animals were dead.

"Imagine that an Ace in the Hole on his first day!"

Turner tisked, "It was a little sloppy, but I guess it counts."

The two men walked down the hall and picked up recruit Bayer. The young man was unconscious from the blood loss, but he survived the Test. "Take him to the infirmary, I'll go tell his mothers what happened." Turner picked up Franklin and left with the boy. Bale returned to the waiting area.

Captain Bayer stood when Bale came into the room. She wrung her hands, "So soon? How did he do?" Sana and Robin sat on the couch holding hands in anticipation.

"Look, he did great. Franklin lost part of his left arm and is now in the infirmary. Even with that he was able to kill the second wave. He got his first card too! I think that is only the fifth time in Marine history a recruit has gotten a card on his first day. You should have seen him! He wrapped that stump around the wolf's neck and cut..." Robin fainted.

Sana yelled at him. "You idiot! Keep that locker room stuff to yourself." She fanned Robin and patted her cheek.

The captain walked Bale over to a wall. "He really used his wounded arm?" Bale grinned. "Yep, killed all four in under a minute. I think that's a record too!"

The captain's lips trembled. "Was he set?"

Bale grinned, "And really pissed off! He was determined despite his injuries. I'll have him on my team anytime!"

The captain leaned into him, "Thank you."

"Franklin is over the hump Sir!" She looked up at Bale and smiled.

Denise smiled, "That's my boy!"

The Plan was to keep the THOMAS MORE back in the cloud away from the main fighting group until the Enki carrier was in the system. She was playing at being the other now destroyed Enki carrier, her mass could not be hidden. The other auxiliaries, THOMAS MORE I, II, and III waited inside the system under cloak with the AGAMEMNON II. AGAMEMNON I was the bait. The ship was obviously damaged and would be a prize for the Enki...they hoped.

The NAUTILUS along with another Tug waited in the gas giants, the other two tugs were just outside the system waiting to bowl for aliens.

The captain of the Maw was upset that they were not included in the defense of the system. Unfortunately, she had no weapons other than a ship that was larger than most asteroids. Big helps but it does not really do anything but push things around. She tapped her finger in frustration then called her ship master.

"How much material do we have in back?

He checked his readings, "About 50 million metric tons. What can I do for you Captain?"

The captain was a flight engineer, electrical engineer, structural engineer and overall a Master Engineer...her resume' was deep. She pulled up a tablet and then began drawing an idea. Converting the material to diamond would reduce the mass but also increase its strength. Maneuvering candlesticks at the end of each one and programmable would make these weapons virtually impossible to stop. She might get 25 of the lancers but it would help the overall mission.

She called the commander.

The Plan was coming along, Bale was excited. Sana leaned over his shoulder and watched as he worked. Bale reached around and pulled her into his lap. "How's my baby doing?"

She laughed, "You mean my baby, right? I'm the one having it!"

"I meant you." Bale grinned and kissed her.

Sana reached up and tasseled his hair. "You need a cut; it is getting too long."

Bale turned back to the keyboard. "I'm thinking of letting it grow along with a beard. How does Pirate Commander Bale the Evil sound?"

Sana giggled, "Pirate Commander Bale the Vomiter sounds a bit more accurate."

He frowned, "Hey! You and Collins caused that!"

She leaned on his shoulder and watched him work. The baby was doing fine, and the Morning sickness was over. Janet had a baby shower planned in two days. The war started in four.

Long range buoys marked the location of the Enki fleet in both locations. They had slowed and were trying to get intel about the deployment of humans. So far they saw only the Maw and AGAMEMNON I floating in Palisade. All other ships were hidden. The Enki were not fooled but they did not know where the small contingent of the human ships was. It was about time to call the other carrier on the other side of the system.

Battle would begin in four cycles and the Enki would conquer a new territory it intended to keep!

63

The Enki approached the spiral system cautiously. They identified the damaged human vessel well into the space and it was not moving. There seemed to be some repair ships around it. There had to be some hidden defense ships nearby but where?

The carrier sent out an Enki signal and pinged all four bases on the third planet. They received a shock when a ping came from an asteroid base beyond the seventh planet. This was good news! Apparently the humans were not aware about that. The Deities were overjoyed! They might find ships or material inside. In any case it would serve as a good staging area for their fleet. It was time to inform the other carrier across the system.

Two scouts rose above the planetary plane and relayed a message to the hidden carrier. A few hours later a message returned stating their readiness for the attack. The message seemed a little odd and was fouled with static, but it was accurate.

Two more scouts and five Attack ships entered the system and flew to the large human ship. They scanned the area and found nothing but the damaged ship itself. Several of the smaller ships tried to flee but the scouts destroyed them killing their crews. The Enki did not know that no one was aboard any of the ships.

Suddenly a large human vessel appeared and fired on one of the Attack ships destroying it. The other four fired back and blew up the human ship. Again, an empty carcass Bale had sacrificed to convince the Enki this was all they had. That carrier had to enter the system before any other means of war could be deployed.

The Enki waited half a cycle before they were convinced there was nothing out there to harm them. The humans were gone! The carrier gave the signal to proceed unto their new prize and home. All the group separate from the carrier entered the system. The carrier sent in half its group and followed with the rest. They meant to align with the human ship and search for technology to salvage. The search of the bases on the third planet and the asteroid would be perused later.

Bale waited patiently on the THOMAS MORE. The Enki carrier had to be further into the system before the tugs attacked. "Just a bit more, not yet...NOW!"

The tugs broke away from their camouflage, rocks spinning away and raced after the two groups. At TL 12 they reached the smaller ships almost instantly. The carrier found them with their sensors and cried a warning, but it was too late. The tug behind the second group plowed through the middle of the small fleet and plastered 14 ships against its hull. Four others were damaged by the debris of their fallen brethren's ships. The tug raced across the system and out the other side before it started the long process of slowing down.

The tug behind the carrier could not touch the large ship but it did make a mess of some 17 ships escorting her. Then it turned a little and got some more of the Enki vessels in front. A total of 23 alien ships were destroyed. The tug raced out of the system. The Master Engineer was ecstatic! "Twenty-three pins! Let us see if the Big Nasty can top that!"

The carrier searched around the area to see if there were more ambushes waiting. It had no choice but to run to the human ship. All the fleet raced to AGAMEMNON I. Where was the other carrier, their support?

The four attack ships grappled the AGAMEMNON I and pulled themselves to it much like a squid would do with prey. Several shapes descended on the ship and broke into one of its airlocks. The carrier arrived but stood off several lengths to give its boarding crews room to work. The Wolverines went in first followed by the Mori.

"Okay, they are inside. Set the timer and fire up the auto tracking. Let's move people! Everyone out!" Janet screamed at her skeleton crew. They gated over to a hidden ship and flew away.

The Enki never having been in a human ship had no idea where the bridge was, but they searched through dead ends and hidden passageways to find it.

The AGAMEMNON I, in a last-ditch effort for glory tracked several ships within range, all except the carrier which they wanted to save. It fired two MAC rounds and destroyed five ships nearby. It fired two more rounds out the rear towards the far distant group that was approaching. Captain Castillo did not expect to hit anything but if she could distract them long enough then the other Tug could catch them by surprise.

The Big Nasty as he was known for his bowling skills jumped out of Beta Five, a gas giant and rushed after the fleet ahead of them. They were regrouping to avoid the plasma bolts heading in. The huge Tug slammed into the group from the rear and then did something no one thought a Tug could do. Big Nasty turned off the engines, rotated the ship 90 degrees and yelled out. “Brace for right angle turn!” Everyone on board looked at him like he was crazy! Then the Big Nasty fired up the engines again to TL 12. The Tug shot ahead and slammed into the rest of the ships trying to shoot at him.

Most everyone passed out from the excessive gees but when they woke up, they found the Big Nasty laughing. “31 pins! Beat that!” Big Nasty would forever be known as a man that could put English on a Tug.

Bale sat back laughing. “Did you see what that crazy bastard did?”

Captain Bayer was owl eyed. “I’m not sure but that might be against regulations.” Then she smiled at Bale. “But who cares? That was a hell of a move!”

The Maw chose that moment to fire its Lancers out the front of the huge machine. She handed control of them to the THOMAS MORE. There were thirty in all, small diamond pylons each with a maneuvering rocket at its base. They were not explosive but at nearly TL 1, they would pack a punch. Two were assigned to the carrier’s engines. Bale did not want to destroy the ship, but he did want to slow it way down.

Some of the Lancers missed their targets but were

reprogrammed to go after others. Several of the ships were speared by the twelve-meter devices and instantly exploded, the Lancers popping out the other side still moving on by inertia, their engines having been destroyed by the impact.

Denise was keying in new information and tracking the carrier. "Damn if that didn't work! Uh oh, she's on the move!" The two Lancers raced after the large ship. One missed and ran out of fuel. The other plowed into one of the engines on the rear shearing it off. The carrier was now down to half speed wherever it went. "Bingo! We hit her!"

There were still many Enki ships lingering though their number was greatly diminished. The four remaining Enki attack ships attached to the AGAMEMNON I began to back away. The timer inside reached zero. The AGAMEMNON I exploded. All its MAC rounds had been armed along with the torpedoes. The blast was soundless, but the effect was massive. All four attack ships disintegrated. The two scouts' ships nearby exploded too from flying debris.

The Deities on board the carrier were devastated. How had the humans accomplished this? They called all remaining ships to head for the Enki asteroid base. Just at that moment the THOMAS MORE's auxiliaries and the AGAMEMNON II appeared nearby and began firing at the remaining ships trying to escape. One of the larger attack ships protecting the carrier returned fire. The AGAMEMNON II and one of the other human vessels was damaged, their shields were greatly reduced. More of the smaller Enki ships were destroyed before the human ships retreated.

The carrier unleashed half of its fighters to escort her to the asteroid. This doubled the size of their force. Unfortunately, the Rock only had so many exterior airlocks for the entire fleet to dock.

"Okay, Plan B," Bale breathed. "We got hurt on that one. It is up to us and the NAUTILUS. Lt. Commander, we won't need your decoy, but we will need your expertise to interpret their chatter." Sana nodded and headed with Lt. Collins to the small scout ship attached to the THOMAS MORE.

She and Lt. Collins flew into the system and sent out a

prearranged glyph message to the Enki carrier. *Morning Star on its way to asteroid base. Will arrive in half a cycle.*

The Deities were relieved. The other carrier was coming. Now their joint forces would rout the human trash.

As the THOMAS MORE moved into the system Bale contacted the NAUTILUS. “Captain Dillon, you saw the battle? We are coming but will need to go to stealth mode once we pass Beta Five. Can you assist by dealing with the fighters before we get there?”

Captain Marshall Dillon responded, “Yes Commander. I will badger them with drones without revealing our location. Out!”

500 drones, miniature K9s popped out of the gas giant and circled the planet to intercept the fighters escorting the Enki carrier. Though they had radar absorbing material covering their surfaces they were too small to have true stealth technology. But being small had an advantage too, they would be hard to hit. They fanned out into a huge cloud and went into swarm mode. The carrier could not detect them with their sensors, but the Enki knew they were there, they could be seen and it was nothing like the Enki had ever encountered.

The remaining scout ships and the last two Attack ships fired into the cloud hitting a few of the drones but the vast majority flew into the fighter’s arena. The devastation of the fighters was immense. The drones fired several shots destroying some but most of them just plowed into the fighters blowing themselves up. The fighters never had a chance. The carrier tried to hit some of the swarm but was unsuccessful at destroying any.

Sana and Lt. Collins rounded Beta Five and stopped. They could see the fleet heading for the Rock by their sensors. They sent a fake message from Morning Star. *We have encountered heavy attack from the blasted humans. We have conquered them and are coming to your aid.*

The Deities were confused. This did not sound like a normal message from their sister ship but then it had been over a revolution in isolation away from the rest of the fleet. With the attacks by the little satellites destroying their fighters and this communication during a battle, confusion was to be expected. They took quick inventory of the remaining ships mainly supply and troop carriers and informed Morning Star of their intent to dock with the asteroid ahead of them. Morning Star was to make haste as they would plan a new battle. Glory to us!

Bale grimaced and hoped the carrier would not dock with the Rock as he really wanted that ship! The drones were all eventually destroyed or ran out of fuel. NAUTILUS waited in Beta Six and counted the ships as they passed. Two attack ships, four scout ships and assorted support vessels followed the huge carrier. All told, there was less than thirty Enki ships remaining. He plotted his attacks and waited on the THOMAS MORE.

Half a cycle later the damaged carrier arrived at the Enki asteroid. A message was sent and the lights on the huge rock turned on. The Deities were thrilled! The smaller ships raced ahead to explore the asteroid and determine its worthiness. One of the Attack ships was slightly damaged along with one of the scouts. They would enter the hangar deck if there was one. They found the doors underneath the floating mountain and sent another signal to open the hangar. A series of red lights flashed, and a signal was sent back that the hangar was being evacuated of air. They waited patiently then a band of green lights lining the doors turned on. The huge hangar doors began to open.

The other ships grappled the asteroid and boarders began to look for undamaged airlocks to enter. There were only four working but that was enough for the warriors to enter the hangar space. The Deities onboard the carrier saw the damage to the rock but found a shield covering it. Glory to the builders of this fine base!

“Are they saying much,” Lt. Collins asked.

“Just patting themselves on the back for reaching a base that the lousy humans had not discovered.” She leaned over to grin at Mark. He chuckled, “Surprise, surprise!”

The carrier stood back a few thousand kilometers just in case some humans showed up. She had to protect their crew boarding the Enki asteroid. The Attack ship and the smaller scout ship entered the brightly lit hangar, and the doors began to close. There was plenty of room.

The THOMAS MORE rounded Beta Five and went stealth, it vanished from sight. “Lt. Jackson. I have gotten your report. I want you to fly closer to the carrier but still in range of a gate on the Belmont. I have a plan so button up.

“Uh oh. What kind of plan do you think he has?”

“I don’t know but if the commander is involved, it’s not going to go well for that carrier.” Sana giggled. “Better fire up the gate. I have a feeling we’re going to need it soon.”

64

Two of the Ser Captains with a brace of soldiers left the Attack ship and closed in on the tunnel leading to the Throne room where the control panels were. There was no air on the other side of the air lock so everyone suited up and closed the air lock from the hangar. The other door opened eventually, and all was in darkness beyond. This was strange as the Arc of Helios should be lit up throughout the asteroid. They would find out why when they got to the controls. They contacted their Lords and Masters back on the carrier and informed them they were proceeding.

The Deities waited patiently, they wanted to inspect the Enki base for themselves, soldiers were not the best at policy. The soldiers turned on their lanterns and went down the tunnel.

Bale could see through Sana's sensors that the carrier was at rest several kilometers from the Rock. They might catch some of the blast but no real damage. The Rosebud waited 3000 kilometers behind the carrier. Sana suspected that Bale would have them ram the ship from behind to destroy the other engine. They would gate off long before that happened, but it did give her some concern. Lt. Collins was downright terrified at the thought.

The Enki squad entered the main city part of the asteroid. What their meager lights could see horrified them. A great battle happened here millennia ago. Fossilized bodies and parts of bodies were scattered everywhere. There were a great many robot pieces laying around too. The battle had been fierce!

All the great space was in darkness. There was no fear of any enemies remaining, but the Enki were nervous just the same. What had happened here? Had there been a revolt by the slaves? Had another species encountered the asteroid and attacked? They did not know. One of the Ser Captains pulled out a device to find the control room. A small directional finder pinged off something several kilometers away. They flew as a group towards the Throne room.

The THOMAS MORE waited with the NAUTILUS just outside of Beta Six. The Enki carrier was only a few million kilometers away just on the other side of Beta Seven, the ice planet, more of a moon than anything else. The Belmont was near Sana's ship, it was quite close to the carrier. Too close she and Lt. Collins thought. The blast if it happened should be any time now. The carrier would protect them from the explosion. Bale had indeed wanted them to intercept the carrier with their small ship and crash it into the last engine. Sana and Mark would gate to the Belmont and leave the battle zone. The scout ship was programmed to hit the ship at 0.8 TL so as not to damage the inner workings of the huge ship.

The Enki troop found the Throne room entrance, but it was buried under ice. Where had the water come from? Had a tank exploded into the great chamber? One of the Mori found the hole in the wall above them and called out. They all flew up and into the Throne room. It was dark too but for one lone control panel standing at the far side of the space. It lit up the area around it. The Ser Captain flew to the panel as the others assumed a protective detail around him. He looked over the panel and saw that it was in good shape. The icons could be read easily. He checked with the Deities and they commanded that he let atmosphere, heat and light back into the main space.

He pushed for light first. The Arc of Helios flickered on then brightened. They could see now in the Throne room the damage from the battle. This had not been a revolt. Heavy weapons had been used to take down the wall and parts of the ceiling. Fortunately the God-King and his guards and staff had managed to escape as there were no bodies about. He next turned on the heat, the glyph button pushing in easily. Last was the air. The Ser Captain looked for the right cuneiform switch, found it and pushed it in.

The Rock vaporized. Larger pieces of the asteroid shot

away at tremendous speed and slammed into some of the smaller vessels. The rest of the Rock turned into heated dust and gravel. Any nearby ships and those grappled to the asteroid vanished in a blast of light. Everyone inside and out became part of the maelstrom of the destroyed asteroid.

The Deities aboard the carrier were beyond shock! How had the humans destroyed them so thoroughly? The NAUTILUS dropped her camouflage and raced to the radioactive cloud. They started firing on the remaining ships leaving the carrier for the THOMAS MORE. “Captain Dillon, you might want to ventilate that ship just a little. Commander Jackson out!”

Captain Marshall Dillon grinned and called out bearings on the carrier. He would not destroy it, but a few pinholes would not help their crew. Lasers reached out and bored holes up and down the length of the huge ship. Warnings rang out all over the carrier. Bodies of the Enki began to fly out of the wounded ship.

“Lt. Commander Jackson, you’re up!” Sana turned to Lt. Collins, “Engage the drive!” They both stood up and ran through the shimmering gate at the back of the small bridge. They appeared on the Belmont. “Lt. Nathan Park here, we’ve got them. Out!”

Bale sighed with relief. Sana was out of harm’s way.

Sana pulled her tablet and synced back with the small scout. “Damn! The carrier is trying to move!” She made some adjustments to the scout and waited for the result. It was not long in coming. The small ship plowed into the last engine, but it was a glancing blow. The engine was damaged but not destroyed as planned. “Here, let me have that!” Lt. Collins took the tablet from Sana and concentrated on turning the errant scout around for another run at the engines. “I can’t reverse course, but I can loop around.” As they all watched the ship shedding sparks and plasma did a reverse loop and fell in behind the Enki carrier again. This time Collins rammed the broken ship into the carrier star exhaust. The whole engine exploded; the scout ship plastered inside the voluminous engine compartment.

“And that Lt. Commander is how you commit a suicide

loop!" He handed her the tablet back and she hugged him. "It was beautifully done Lieutenant!" Everyone cheered as the carrier floated away without the power to escape.

The Deities were frantic! Their ship was being opened to space by the large sphere nearby. All their other support ships were destroyed either by the asteroid explosion or the beast outside. Where was Morning Star? It would make short work of this human interloper. Then the scout slammed into the rear of the great vessel. "Masters, we have no thrust! The engines are gone!" someone from the bridge called. The Deities made a final decision. They had to destroy the ship. They could not allow the disgusting humans to have their technology.

"Send a long-range distress drone to the outer regions for the other fleet. We are done. Hold the bridge, we will be there shortly."

The long-range drone shot out of one of the bays and fired its engines for the long journey ahead...and ran into the shields of the THOMAS MORE destroying itself with no effect to the giant ship. The crew on the bridge stared out their screens and even windows to see something so large that it boggled the mind. At more than sixteen kilometers long the THOMAS MORE was more than four times the size of the massive carrier.

Bale called out. "Ahoy! We are the THOMAS MORE. We found the Morning Star and had it for breakfast. We are now going to have you for lunch!"

Sana rolled her eyes. "You just had to throw in that Pirate idiom, didn't you? They don't even have a glyph for 'Ahoy'!" Bale winked at her through the vid screen and Sana giggled.

Captain Bayer smiled. "I like lunch...Fire!"

Lasers raked the opposite side from the NAUTILUS and vented the huge ship. All their lasers and cannon were destroyed as well. Any torpedoes were shot once they left their tubes from the carrier. The ship was defenseless.

The Deities left their family's bodies back in their suites. It was prudent not to let them fall into enemy hands. The children were the most difficult to kill.

They rounded up Wolverines and Mori along with Dog

soldiers and slaves. The slaves were given weapons from lockers near the suites though most did not know how to use them. The Enki Deities had to run through deserted sections of the ship that still had air and corridor shields. One group of slaves were made to wait at a junction to protect their rear. The Enki barely made it through when a laser opened a hole, and all the slaves were sucked into space. A force door shut immediately saving the rest.

The Deities were getting angry and their leader, a man with a crocodile head was furious. He reached for a slave and bit off its head.

"Take us to the bridge, NOW!"

"Master," one of the dog boys said. "The intruders will be boarding soon. We will defend you but hurry! Destroy this ship!"

The Crocodile-headed Deity smiled at the young man. "You will join me in Paradise this day!" They ran on.

65

Bale pulsed over to the Enki carrier. He had four short platoons with him and two more back on the THOMAS MORE waiting to protect the ship. They found sufficient holes to penetrate the structure. “Captain Dillon. I believe you know where the Bridge is on this ship. Could you evacuate it for us?”

Captain Dillon smiled. He appreciated the humor and mayhem this young Commander exhibited. “Yes Commander, I can accommodate you. I can see it and our scans reveal they are very busy there. Five meters wide enough for you?” Bale laughed, “That should be sufficient for us, thank you Sir!”

A small but lethal device spun from the NAUTILUS and attached itself to the front of the Enki bridge. The ones inside did not know it was there. “In Three, Two, One...fire!”

The mine blew in the forward wall of the bridge then the air inside blew out all the crew. “Idiots inside didn’t bother to put on their suits even in an emergency. Such arrogance!” Captain Marshall Dillon laughed and everyone on his bridge laughed too. None of them had suits.

“Platoon Two, take the middle section and kill everything then head for Engineering. We don’t want anyone getting some bright ideas.” Cage and Master Sergeant Turner yelled out, “Copy!”

“Platoon One, follow me to the bridge. Peel off and cover the last two holes near the bridge by squad. I want a gate set up nearby back to the THOMAS MORE.”

Debris littered the floor of the bridge. Fortunately, artificial gravity still worked on this ship. Points found two bodies that did not make it out the hole. They had bird-like heads and no uniform, just a colorful kilt and sandals on their feet. Bale thought this was taking the Egyptian theme a little too far. They tossed the bodies out with the others. The IT specialists Points started working on the cuneiform systems, both having been trained by Lt. Commander Jackson in preparation for this moment. The ship was secure and there had been no attempt to scuttle it. They shut down Engineering but maintained the generators for the gravity assist. Then they turned out the lights. Bale thought *now things get interesting*.

Points Trenton and Allen set up the gate in a large room near the bridge and called the THOMAS MORE. "Send them over!" A moment later Tank and two other impossibly huge Points walked through the gate. These men had no need for swords or small weapons as most would not fit into their huge hands, but they did have something like a small cannon no other Point could carry or fire. Several regular augmented marines followed them from the gate. Tank looked at the smaller unit, "Guard this gate with your lives. Destroy it if you must." The twenty men and women nodded and set up a perimeter. Tank and the two others went into the hall.

Tank placed each man at the entrance to a hall leading to the bridge, Tank took the last one and faced down the lane. All three arteries were now covered. No Enki could reach them. "Commander, we are in position," said Tank. Bale grinned, it was all coming together...time for the hunt.

He placed ten men outside the hole to the bridge with four battle drones floating nearby. Bale left ten men inside the bridge and took the rest with him then he sealed the bridge as Sana had taught him. One door with windows slid in from the side and closed the bridge then a massive steel door half a meter thick rose from the floor and sealed the inner door. It would take a ship's cannon to take that out!

Bale divided the men and women into three groups. "We are not here to take prisoners. Kill everything!" All the Points ran past Tank and the other two huge Points. The hunt was on!

Cage and Turner were in trouble. They had run into intense resistance near the Engineering section of the ship. At first it was like a milk run. Shoot then get closer and tear into the enemy. Several cards had already been earned from the wolves, the hard way. But then the squids showed up. Again not much trouble as they fell easily to the Point's swords but then the squids got smart. One would fly in even if shot up some, wrap its tentacles around the man binding his arms and legs then two wolves would come in and finish the rifleman off. Cage had already lost three men this way. They could not let the squids get close! Master Sergeant Turner was having the same problem with his group. He had lost five men that way. It was time to change tactics.

They could not use grenades inside this part of the ship. They might set off a cascade of explosions destroying the carrier. Flash bangs were another matter. They did not affect the wolverines all that much, but they stunned the squids for several minutes. That was all they needed, and it worked!

Cage's men tossed flash bangs into a squad of Enki wolves, squids and dog boys and *BANG!* The squids fell to the ground and twitched, the dog boys floundered around and the wolves that ran at the Points died. Later, they all died. It worked beautifully. He passed the message over to Turner and back up to the commander.

Bale had to admit that was a great idea and they used it on the first group of Enki they ran into. Squids and dog boys fell about while the wolves came on. But now the wolves had no support. It was too late when they realized no one had their back.

Men in Corridors One and Two were clearing out rooms and the hall but the team in Tank's hall was all but killed. They had opened a door to a large chamber filled with Enki squids and wolves. Their firepower overwhelmed the Points. Squids finished off the rest that were wounded. They all ran up to the bridge only to meet Tank. He put one round through the mass and they all evaporated. The walls in the hall bowed out from the blast.

Others ran to adjoining halls and entered rooms and started firing through the walls where they thought the Tank was. Tank turned his cannon and shot through the wall. It did not matter if he missed. The entire room turned into a red and green mist of tissue. More Enki arrived and tried the other halls leading to the bridge but met Tank's cohorts. They died.

One of the dog boys had a rocket launcher, he was way down the corridor from Tank. It fired the rocket and it hit Tank squarely. The man never moved; rolls of purple black power fell about him as the rocket exploded on his shield. Tank made a little adjustment to his cannon and fired a plasma ball down the hall...it had targeting ability. The ball saw the other Enki especially the one trying to put another rocket in his gun when it struck. Two floors and the entire wall facing the THOMAS MORE blew out. Venting air took the rest of the defenders to a vacuum funeral.

"Hey! Hey, Tank! Careful with those plasma things. My underwear is on fire," cried one of the troops further down the line! Tank chuckled. There were no more Enki in his vicinity.

He was wrong.

An inventive Enki dog boy found another room and prevented his troops from firing through the wall at the huge human. He had already witnessed what that deadly weapon of his could do to his people. Instead, he pulled out a powerful grenade, opened a door and rolled the device under Tank's feet. Tank looked at the open door and was about to fire when the grenade went off. He flew up in the air then crashed down four floors into a room that could barely hold its air. The blast above was too much and the wall towards space ripped open. Tank flew out with the air.

Damn! The commander will not be happy. Now I have to fly back up there and save the bridge. He called Bale.

Cage and Turner finally reached Engineering and met a

sizable door that was locked. Their cuneiform experts could not make the door open no matter the combination of icons they pushed. “There has to be an airlock outside Engineering.” He pointed to three men. “Go back, find a hole outside or make one and open that lock. Kill everything!”

The three men ran down the hall and opened a door. They were immediately sucked out with the escaping air. Once in vacuum they oriented themselves and headed over to the engineering part of the ship. They found an airlock but as with the name it was locked. Three Point swords were lit with purple power and cut into the metal around the lock. The door flew away. One of the Points put a small explosive on the inner door and flew back. He pushed a button on his sleeve. There was no sound but the door, air and eventually some of the crew flew out the opening, they were not wearing suits.

Inside they found four other birdmen belted to their chairs in the throughs of asphyxiation. They died shortly then froze from the frost of space. They found four dead wolves and two squids that tried to come at them, but the blast had rattled their brains. The Points dispatched them then opened the doors for the rest of the troops.

Turner called the commander, “Sir, Engineering is secure.” They set up a small gate and brought over some of their engineers to make sure the vast room was not wired to explode.

“Very good Master Sergeant. Leave 20 men to cover the engine compartment and seal it back off. Send the rest to me. We have got trouble on the bridge. Fly outside the ship and come to us immediately. Out!”

“You heard the man, let’s Move!”

66

Crocodile-head led his troops to the bridge but were still running into a lot of interference. The humans just would not quit, and they were strong! He was losing personnel at a furious rate. He had to get into the bridge to blow the ship. There was a large hole in the floor ahead of them. It was hard to see in the dark, but his men jumped over the hole and continued. Some of the Enki fell through the floor to their deaths far below.

After he made it across, they looked around and discovered a light under a door. It was a Master's Conference room that somehow had lights. They burst in and met more humans, and the humans were ready for them. Many Enki died trying to get into the space. The leader managed to get a look into the space and found a rectangular frame like water only it was vertical. How was that possible? That was the only light in the room. The humans kept firing and Enki died. What was that device? One of the humans picked up a wounded comrade and raced for the vertical wall of water and jumped through...they disappeared! It was a door to somewhere else!

He gave instructions to his men. No grenades, he wanted that water door technology! Three Enki jumped back over the hole and entered an adjoining room. They made an opening and began firing on the humans from the side. While the humans were distracted several Enki ran into the room and towards the shimmering light, they jumped through and found themselves facing several hundred Points and augmented on the THOMAS MORE. They all died.

One of the humans was gravely wounded. He fell towards the gate to shut it down but missed the switch. Crocodile-head shot him again and ran for the gate with several men. The bleeding man on the floor did not shut down the gate, he accidentally switched it to the Belmont before he died. The Enki leader and his men jumped through and found themselves in a small room with several human riflemen. Sana saw them come through and screamed!

Bale heard her scream and knew she was on the Belmont. He ran faster than his men and entered the gate room to find the gate still open. He jumped and fell into a war zone.

Lt. Collins turned at Sana's scream and jumped in front of her as a dog boy was about to spear her. He caught the spear and coughed up blood. Sana pulled her gun and shot the dog boy and a few others. She then picked up Mark and ran for the control room. Franklin Bayer was behind her killing the aliens trying to catch the young Lt. Commander. They all died.

Bale was too busy to look for Sana as he was helping the men clean up the mess with the Enki. Bodies were everywhere and shots were being fired by both sides. Men and Enki were dying. Franklin grabbed two wounded Points and threw them after the Lt. Commander. "Shut the door and blow the ship!" Sana nodded and closed the door but to her horror she saw her husband down the hall following what looked like a Crocodile head on a man, two wolves and a squid in the lead. "Watch out!"

Franklin was caught by the squid almost immediately but before it could tighten its tentacles around him, he spun his sword with one hand like a propeller and sliced off all the sticky arms of the alien, then his sliced it diagonally killing it. The two wolves ran at him, but he killed one by removing its head and cut the other one in half. The wolf did not die immediately and tried to choke the young man. That is when the Crocodile-headed man reached him.

Sana cried as blood splattered all over the glass. Franklin was dead.

"Lieutenant! Blow this ship but send out a warning for everyone to bubble up!"

Nathan was leaning against a console while blood ran down his arm from where he had been shot. He was pushing and moving icons around. "I heard, I heard!" He then reached to his microphone on his neck. "Attention! Self-destruct in ten seconds. Bubble up everyone!"

He then ran to Sana, grabbed her and Mark and threw them through the permanent gate in the bridge of the Belmont. Sana screamed, "Don't!" but she was gone with Lt. Collins. He then threw the two wounded men after them. Nathan shut down the gate. He then bubbled up.

Bale never heard the announcement. Behind him every living man and the wounded bubbled up with the help of their friends. He shot out his chain and ensnared the Enki cutting off one of its arms. The man/Crocodile turned and grabbed the chain pulling the large human to him. He snapped his jaws just waiting to bite off the man's head. Bale pulled his machete' and cut off the front half of the Crocodile's jaws. It reared back in ultimate pain. "Take this asshole!" and Bale ran the alien through with his blade, right through the chest.

*...Two...One...ignition!"

Sana was in the gate room of the THOMAS MORE when the Belmont blew up. It was too far away to hurt the now captured Enki carrier.

She struggled with Cage and Turner who had made it back to the THOMAS MORE through the carrier's gate. "Noooo...No!!!" The men grimaced as they held the lieutenant Commander. Cage had tears in his eyes knowing his friend had just died. They knew what Bale meant to her and she carried his child. Sana fell to her knees as everyone stood back. They all had lost someone, but this had been a difficult romance, a story that might become Legend.

"You promised." Captain Denise Bayer already knowing the death of her son ran in and knelt before Sana. Sana did not see her, she didn't see anyone.

"You promised not to leave me...You promised," and fainted into the captain's arms.

The search of the Enki carrier took another few days. One of the Deities had died fighting with his troops but the last one was hiding by himself in a kitchen. His troops ran from the coward as he drank and ate his last meal before the humans dispatched him. The ship was very damaged, but they found several fighter ships still onboard. They were worthless to humans but with a little refabricating they would be a great surprise for the last Enki fleet they had yet to find.

The funerals for all the lost went on for days. Where possible, the emperor brought the families of the departed and handed out appropriate Metals of Honor for all. Sergeant Franklin Bayer was an especially difficult funeral as he had died with the ship. There was no body to bury but Captain Bayer and her wife were pleased with the ceremony and so were his older siblings, Franklin being the baby of the family.

Lieutenant Commander Sana Jackson gave a moving account without the gruesome details as Franklin Bayer had defended the Belmont. He had received extra cards for his uniform even though not completely kosher, no one was going to argue the young man's bravery. He was given the Metal of Honor as well as the Trident for being promoted to Lieutenant posthumously.

Though Sana attended Bale's funeral, she could not say a word and cried quietly throughout the entire ceremony. Captain Castillo sat on her right and Admiral Russell Dean sat on her left. He had made a special trip just for Bale saving the Palisade colony and the Earth. Admiral Dean barely made it through the litany of Bale's accomplishments. And he held nothing back. The ruthless plan that gave no quarter to the Enki, his wife's contribution of which Bale could not proceed, how Bale talked the most unequivocal Captain of the NAUTILUS to follow his lead, the headstrong Engineers on the Tugs and the Maw...the man had no qualms about bending others to his will!

Others spoke about their friendship to Commander Bale. Cage could not comment, Master Chief Mike Green had to hold him by the shoulders as the man cried. Master Command Sergeant Gantry made some moving comments and encouraged others to follow Bale's lead. "The man was always observant. He never missed a thing! This is the skill that wins wars...and in this special case won him a wife!"

Commander Bale Jackson was promoted to Captain Bale Jackson posthumously. It did not matter that had he been alive Bale never would have received such a promotion. Sana was given a folded flag of the Terran Federation. In a special wooden case were all his metals. The emperor stood and walked to Sana. "Would you please come with me?" Sana nodded and stood to follow the emperor.

They walked to the front of the room. There were over two thousand men and women in the auditorium, billions watching on video throughout the Terran Federation. Emperor Lucas Barnes gently touched her elbow to turn her to face the people looking at her. Lucas Barnes was not a commissioned enlisted man; he had never finished his term but he was the commander-In-Chief. "Attend Chut'!"

Every man and woman stood ramrod straight.

"Salute this woman, the wife of Captain Bale Jackson for her loss!"

Every right arm on every person saluted her. The emperor did too.

Six months later, Lieutenant Commander Sana Jackson gave birth to a ten-pound, four-ounce healthy baby boy with the greenest eyes and a Hazel ring around the pupils the nurses had ever seen. He was named Kyle Horacio Jackson, the middle name from the captain of the Explorer now a Godfather to the child. He would be there to help Sana and Kyle out as much as he could.

Sana held her brown-haired son close and smiled. "I wish your father could be here to see you. He loved you before you were born."

67

"Mommy look! I found another ring!" The little hands which were getting bigger by the year held up the coral ring Kyle had found. Sana bent down and looked at it. "Now that is a pretty one, all blue. I don't think you have one like that!" He handed her the ring, smiled and ran off to play in the park with the other kids. She took out a bottle of sanitizer, sprayed the little stone ring and put it in 'his' bag of rings.

Grandpa Verkon had texted earlier and wanted to know if he could bring his new girlfriend for lunch. The 'Captain' as he preferred to be called was Kyle's Godfather, but Kyle called him grandpa. Sana smiled, if the man wanted to have lunch with them, she was fine with that! She had the man out of hibernation right after the Explorer was out of the Maw. She needed help.

Horacio had been devastated when he found out about Bale's death but once consoled the man was delighted with his new grandson. The two got on handsomely.

His legs had been damaged even for the short time he was returned to hibernation. Sana asked the emperor if she could have him fixed with nanos. The new Emperor Jeffery Barnes laughed at her. "Do what you want. You are the boss there!" Sana had the 'Captain's' legs fixed and raised him up a few inches. She did not change his age but gave him a stronger metabolism. The man was genuinely surprised and now he could pick up his grandson without pain.

Even though they were at the equator and in a somewhat mountainous region, sometime in the distant past this whole area had been underwater. Coral of many types were easily found, and Kyle preferred the rings. She did not know why he wanted the rings only, but it might have to do with her job Sana guessed.

Sana watched as he got on the gravity 'round-we-go' and

screamed with delight as the older kids spun it for the younger ones. *What a handsome boy, just like his father!* Sana sighed and turned back to her work. The tablet sat on the park bench with her purse. She pulled it over and finished a report on the Palisade Ring stabilizers.

The Ring for the Explorer colonists was pretty much finished only the fauna and flora remained to be installed. The colonists had been living on the ring for six months and they were not happy. They had to stay on the Explorer for five years longer than was planned. Then they met their oversized cousins and the culture shock really set in. Several hundred had to be returned to stasis to secure their delicate feelings. So much for being the only and most special species in the universe. The officers, marines and medical personnel had no problem with the changes and were excited about their pending new home...they were a big help with its construction and the transition of the remaining colonists willing to grasp a very strange and potentially dangerous future with their descendants.

The Doctors and nurses that got to examine Sana were totally shocked at her appearance. Their records no longer matched the woman standing before them. How did she get so tall?

She entered the final data and shut off the tablet. Sana heard a scream and looked up to see Kyle waving at her as he spun around. He screamed again and grinned at her, his bright green eyes shooting at her from across the lawn. They were Bale's eyes, her only contribution being a hazel ring surrounding the bright green irises. Everything else about the boy belonged to his father, gone these many years now. His smile, temperament, shy but sweet but also determined about everything he did...and of course the eyes.

Normally Sana was not this gloomy, but winter was coming and that was not her favorite time of year. Perhaps she should check out a flyer and take a spin around Beta Four, her home since Kyle was now in kindergarten. Flying always cheered her up and while she was still in the Reserves, she could fly anytime a fighter was available. *Oh stop it! This is your day with Kyle, snap out of it!* Maybe she should call a friend for dinner tonight with their kids. That Johnson woman perhaps...no wait, Kyle and her son did not get along. Who should she call? She just needed a friend right now.

She then heard a voice, "Sana...Sana!" Sana looked down the sidewalk and saw Dia walking towards her. Sana's heart leapt to her throat. She jumped up and ran to her. "Oh Dia! How great to see you, I've missed you so much!" The two women hugged. Sana felt the baby bump on Dia. "Again?" Dia smiled, "Last one I promise...but it's a boy!"

Sana smiled, "OH! Kono will be so pleased! Where is Kono?"

Dia turned to look back up the path and pointed to a tall Japanese man walking a stroller towards them, her husband. "Kono!" Sana walked over and hugged her friend. "Congratulations!"

"Thanks," he smiled shyly. "And thank you for inviting us. It's a beautiful day." His five-year-old daughter peeked around his legs and looked up at Sana. She was very shy, a beautiful child with short black hair and deep almond eyes. "Honey, look over there, it's Kyle!" The girl's eyes widened and ran to meet Sana's son.

"All we brought was water as Dia is pregnant again. Where is the food? I'm starving!" Datsun reached down into the stroller and found the 'binky' his other daughter had dropped out of her mouth.

Sana looked back and forth to both, "Invited? I mean I'm glad you are here but...I didn't call you."

Dia looked confused. "You texted us yesterday. 'Bring drinks but food will be provided'."

Sana was equally confused, "But I didn't text anyone..."

One of the gates at the edge of the park 'pinged' and two people walked out. They spotted Sana and the woman yelled. "We made it!" It was Tracy and Dan. He held a cooler, "I've got the beer!"

Sana frowned, what was going on? Tracy ran up and hugged the bewildered woman. "Thanks for texting us, I really needed to get out of the office." Dan had already popped a can and nodded enthusiastically while spilling some beer on his shirt. The gate 'pinged' again and the 'Captain' walked out with a woman easily half his age. Grandpa waved and walked the woman over. "Captain?" Sana asked.

"Well, you told me to come for a picnic lunch so here I am! Here is Sarah Pale, my friend." The two women hugged. "I'm so glad you allowed me to come!" Sana was baffled.

"Grandpa!!" Kyle ran up to Captain Verkon and jumped into his arms. The man huffed as the young boy slammed into him. "Junior, I'm almost 69. Don't do that to this old man!" They hugged and laughed. Kyle dropped down and ran back to the playground.

Just as Sana was about to ask them about the text when another voice shouted. Down the path two other couples walked around a group of trees. The Master Chief was holding his son on his shoulders, the four-year-old waved at Kyle and Kira and demanded to get down to play. The chief chuckled and dropped the boy to the ground. He then put his arm around Lucky Lucy's waist. "Hope we're not late? We caught up with Collins and Mary at the gate. Cage and Janet texted and said they would be a little late."

Sana was really getting lost. What are all these people doing here?

Lucy hugged Sana, "I'm glad you texted us. Mike is driving me crazy and that boy of his is tearing up the apartment." The chief looked over at her, "Jeff is your boy too!

Mary ran in to get her hug then hugged the others as well. "What a great day! So beautiful! Yep, I am glad I caught that text, thanks Sana!"

Sana was really shaken. Had she lost her mind? She knew she was in a funk lately but to text all these people without remembering was too much. She sat down on the bench. Dia sat down next to her, "Honey, what's wrong? Sana looked at her. "I didn't text anyone. I'm glad you're here, I've been really lonely lately, but I didn't want to bother anyone."

Tracy sat on the other side of Sana and put her arms around her. "It's okay, we're all glad to be here with you and Kyle." The men stood around in embarrassment. Dan muttered to the chief and Collins, “Um, am I missing something?”

Kono leaned away from the women that were comforting Sana. “Dan, Bale died five years and two weeks ago. She’s been alone for a long time.” The chief grimaced, “Work hasn’t been enough? Sana practically built that Ring by herself.” Verkon nodded, “She has worked very hard on that project, especially lately...to take her mind off of Bale.”

Dan shrugged, “Can’t say I blame her. I had a cousin whose husband died...”

“Shut up Dan,” Collins said. No one wanted to hear one of his endless stories.

“I don’t get it. Kyle and I went to bed early last night and we have been at the park for the last hour. I’ve not called or texted anyone at all!”

Mary looked at her, “But Sweetheart, I got my text around nine.” The other women nodded too.

Sana started to sniffle, “That’s impossible, I was in bed an hour before that!”

Dia handed her a tissue, “Don’t worry about it. We are all here now. The kids are having fun so now all we have to do is find a place for us to eat.”

The Master Chief suddenly stiffened, “Incoming!”

All the others got the same message except for Sana. “What?”

They all looked up when a large ship appeared above them, way above them and right over the park, about 2000 meters. The air was hazy so the ship appeared grayer and blurrier at that altitude but there was no mistaking that it was a capital ship!

“Kono, what’s the THOMAS MORE doing here?” his wife asked him.

“Chief?”

“I have no idea, but it can’t be good. Captain Bayer is supposed to heading for Mary’s Ring.”

Sana looked from one to the other realizing she was not in on the message. “What’s happening? I’ve got nothing on my net.”

Everyone stared at her in shock. Sana was a Lieutenant

Commander of the Palisade Ring project and pretty much in charge of the entire system. If anyone should know what was happening, it would be her!

Dan dropped his beer, “Oh Shit! It’s the emperor!”

Another ship quite different from the THOMAS MORE appeared right below it and only a few hundred meters above them. The Royal Crest could easily be seen under the wings. Though not as big as the ship above it, the emperor’s ship was still massive. All the children in the playground shrieked and ran to their parents.

Everyone watched as shapes began to fall from the emperor’s ship. They slowed and everyone saw it was riflemen nearing the ground. There were over 100 of them and all were Gold Hammers, the emperor’s elite and personal troops. The troops fanned out surrounding the park. Each man and woman were fully armored and armed with vicious weapons. No one could leave the park. There must have been thirty or more families there.

Kyle ran to his mother and grabbed her hand. Sana pulled him up and held him close. The captain walked over and touched Kyle’s back. “It will be all right.” It was only then that her netware received the same message as the others.

“Stand to for the pleasure of His Royal Majesty Emperor Jefferson Davidson Barnes!”

Sana was shaking, “What’s happening, Mother?”

“I don’t know baby but when the emperor gets here, you kneel as I taught you.” Kyle nodded.

Two of the riflemen walked over about thirty meters from their group and pulled up a large portable gate. It switched on then a moment later a standard bearer walked out with the Federation of Terra Flag. Music began to play and everyone in the park kneeled. They knew who was coming next.

A tall and handsome man walked through the waterfall and stood before the group. Captain Bayer followed him and stopped too. “Attention! Rise and Pledge to the Flag of the Terran Federation!”

All rose and began the salute and pledge to the flag, even the emperor for he knew he was but a servant to Earth.

Kyle muttered along with his mother while still holding her hand. He did not know all the words yet, but they practiced them every day at school.

The chief looked around at all the heavy metal surrounding them. Why was the emperor here?

Dia and Kono wondered the same thing. Tracy said the pledge but did not put much spirit into it and Dan almost fainted. Mary and her husband Commander Collins said the pledge with enthusiasm but were equally confused. Captain Verkon just smiled. He had a premonition about all this.

Sana finished with the others and waited. She was beyond surprise. The emperor would tell them when he was ready.

Emperor Jeffery Barnes, grandson to the previous Emperor Lucas Barnes walked over to Sana and stood right in front of her. Her heart was beating too fast. Had she made a mistake on the Palisade Ring? Was she in trouble?

"Lieutenant Commander Sana Jackson, may I have the honor of a hug to an old Commander?"

Sana was startled but she moved in and wrapped her arms around the tall man. She could do no less for this man had given Sana her first commission in the Terran Service. Jeff pulled her close and gave her a warm embrace. "I'm so happy to see you again. I have heard from the other Trustees you have done an exemplary job on the Ring. I am pleased!"

All her friends were in shock, the kids owl-eyed by the man hugging their aunt. Was he really the emperor? He sure looked like the picture of the man in their school rooms.

The emperor knelt down and spoke to Kyle, "The last time I saw you and your mother, you were only a year old. You've really grown, my boy!" Kyle smiled and looked up at his mother.

Jeff stepped back and spoke to all. "The reason I am here is for a rare and unusual celebration. But this is Captain Bayer's show, so I'll let her tell you the story."

Captain Bayer walked up and saluted everyone. They looked at her and immediately saluted back. It was not proper for a Captain who outranked everyone in the crowd to salute first.

"Well, ya see, something funny happened on the way to

Mary's Ring." It was a planet furthest from Earth and like Beta Four, the only inhabitable area on the planet was on the equator. But it was surrounded by water, not snow like on Beta Four. It was called 'Mary's Ring' because the emperor Lucas Barnes gave it as a gift to his third wife.

"So, we had just entered TL 1 to leave the system when bang! Something hit my ship. Why the radar did not pick it up, well my engineers had some explaining to do. Whatever it was, we bounced it right through the outer layers of Beta Five. It shot out the other side and kept moving! One of my auxiliaries went after it and pulled that fish in. Turns out it was a bubble...and you'll never believe what we found inside."

Captain Bayer then turned to the large portable gate, "Without further ado..." She pointed to the gate and everyone waited.

A second later, a tall young man in uniform walked out of the water and looked around in earnest. Dan was the first to faint, he hit the ground flat out. Mary collapsed against her husband. Sana fell to her knees and looked at the man in shock! Kono said, "I'll be damned!" The chief started laughing while his wife cried on his shoulder. Captain Verkon just grinned wider.

"Momma! What's wrong?" Kyle grabbed his mother and tried to protect her from whatever the trouble was. Who was this man that had everyone upset? Dia pulled the boy to her. "Let your mother figure this out. Sit with me, it'll be okay," she said with tears in her eyes but smiling.

The man in uniform looked around. He was clearly a Gold Hammer, the insignia on his blouse plus a set of Captain's pips on his shoulders.

But what Sana noticed first was his brown hair, an aquiline nose and the most brilliant green eyes.

The man roared! "Sana! SANA!" He looked around some more until he spotted her on the ground near her friends. Their eyes locked like the time at breakfast with her Captain Verkon and then Commander Barnes.

Even after all these years, Sana would never forget that voice. It was as familiar now as the last time they had pillow talk, him quoting some truly awful poetry. It did not matter to her; it was enough that Bale spoke those words to his wife.

Bale took two steps and jumped ten meters in the air and landed just before Sana. He whispered her name, "*Sana...*"

She could barely move, her lips trembled, "How? I saw the explosion! I saw you die!" She rubbed her eyes. "I buried you!" Sana was beyond disbelief anymore.

Bale shrugged, "Fast reflexes I guess." He grinned at her.

Sana stood up with her husband's help, leaned into him for a lengthy kiss, stood back and looked up at him and smiled...then slabbed him in the face!

"YOU PROMISED NOT TO LEAVE ME!!" Then she fell into his arms and cried with joy. Her husband was back by some miracle!

Everyone laughed!

Kyle leaned into Aunt Día's ear and whispered, "Who is he? Why is Mommy kissing him?"

Dia looked down at him and wiped her eyes and smiled. "Baby, look at his eyes, then you'll know."

Kyle squinted, then his eyes grew round.

"*Daddy...?*"

68

Everyone was having a good time! The emperor brought the picnic dinner, enough for all including the civilians and their families. It was eventually spread around that their boss, who they had thought was a widow, now had her husband back.

Sana and Bale sat at a table set by the emperor. Jeff sat across from them with Captain Bayer and Captain Verkon. They all listened as Kyle talked. He constantly had to grab his mother's chin to get her to pay attention to him. Kyle sat on the table facing the two and spun story after story about his life, his school and about his famous, though no longer dead father. Bale was not sure he had heard a word but recorded it anyway to play back later, he did not want to miss out on anything about his son! But most of all, he had a Son!

Janet and Cage finally showed up and hugs were spread around again. Bale got to see his old friend cry again. "Man! You messed me up good! Janet, I mean the captain had to put me in restraints!" Janet rolled her eyes, "I did not!" then she looked at Bale, "I did have to hide the beer for a while." The emperor and everyone laughed. The captain and the Master Chief had married three years before. It was not exactly a proper marriage because of their different ranks and ages but Janet did not care. She loved the man and he loved her right back! "Who knew anyone would marry me again?" Cage said.

Mike Green finally got a word in edgewise, "I guess I was wrong. Your wife did a bang-up job raising your boy, but she never forgot you. Don't go running off again, okay sir?"

Dan blubbered some, "My boy! My boy! You are back..." Tracy held her husband, a man too emotional for his own good but he loved his wife and that's all that mattered to her. She watched Bale and Sana stare at each other while poor

Kyle tried to keep everyone's attention on himself.

Captain Verkon hugged the young man. "I'm glad you are back. I need a break and I have things to do." He grabbed Sarah's hand and walked away. Bale smiled. *Nasty old goat, good for you!*

Sana could not stop touching Bale. *Was he really here? Or is this a dream? If so then please Unity, do not let this dream end!*

Bale was in a dream of his own, not bad just simply weird. He had been gone for over five years yet for him, it had only been a few weeks. Sana had aged but not much and now they shared a child. He had known she was pregnant but the battle with the Enki interfered with enjoying her pregnancy. Sana had helped win the war and Bale was there too, at least the parts he remembered. The rest had been given to him in route back to Palisade. He was so proud of Sana that he could burst!

"Honey, the other kids are going to play. The light is thinning so why don't you go out before we go home?" Kyle frowned but looked at his father who he had not yet touched. "Are you going to be here when I get back?" he looked shyly at his new-found father. "Would you come home with us?"

"I would be honored to join you at home with your mother. Let me show you something." Bale pulled off his wedding ring and gave it to the boy. "Read the inside."

Kyle squinted, "It's just a simple ring," then he looked further inside to read the inscription.

"May..." *Unity* his mother coached him . *"May Unity spread our names..."* *among* his mother said. *"among the Stars. Love, Sana"*

That was when Sana knew this was not a dream. Kyle never knew the inscription; she had never told him about it. Kyle sat up tall on the picnic table. "So, you are my father!" He reached over and grabbed the strange man with his same-colored eyes and hugged him.

The party was over. The emperor blessed everyone and left for his ship with his riflemen. More hugs and tears were spread around their friends then Bale got to walk his wife and son home. Home, to his new one.

Kyle was asleep on Bale's shoulder. He would not let the man alone after he read his mother's gift to his father. Sana clutched his left hand with both of hers. She was still trying to firm up the idea that Bale was back. This would change everything!

"You're not going back to the Marines, are you?" she asked.

Bale shook his head, "I've had enough of that. I talked with the emperor and he thinks I should work for you as originally planned. I am all for that! Plus it gives me time to be with Kyle. Sana, what did you make here?" Kyle heard his name in his dream and snuggled in a little more on Bale's shoulder.

"Silly, *we* made him!" Sana declared! Bale smiled.

Sana got quiet. Bale looked down at her still holding his hand with both of hers, his right-hand keeping Kyle safe on his chest. "What?"

She looked up at him, "My, I mean Our apartment is small. I wanted to be near the park for Kyle's benefit, but I can afford a better one if you want only it's a little more distant."

Bale had already checked out nearby apartments. His new implants were far and above his old ones and with his military standing, Bale had full access. He found one in the same building with twice as much room as Sana's apartment. It cost a pretty penny, but Bale had a lot of back pay including a Hero's Reward the emperor made up on the fly when he found out Bale was still alive. Bale offered to pay back the emperor for Sana's Widows Benefit, but the man would not hear about that. "Officer Sana Jackson suffered during your absence. She never complained and performed her work and raised your child, but she suffered just the same. I'll not take back a penny of that!"

Bale would talk about the apartment with her in the morning after Kyle was in school. "I guess I'll take the couch tonight." Sana's eyes grew round, and she grimaced most beautifully! "I'll be damned if I let my husband sleep on a couch! You're sleeping with me!"

"But honey, we'll have to buy a new bed in the morning!" he grinned.

"You betcha' Mister! I'm glad you got my meaning. I intend to give Kyle a sister!"

Bale smiled and pulled her to his chest. Sana looked up to him, "Am I still your baby girl?" There were tears in her eyes. "Please, please...don't leave us alone again."

Bale bent down and kissed Sana, "...never again."

About the Author

L.B. Duke is a retired architectural illustrator with a lifelong passion for science fiction, storytelling, and the arts. A classically trained artist and musician, he has worked across mediums. From architectural boards and watercolors to pen and ink and digital animation. Drawing inspiration from iconic authors like Heinlein, Asimov, and Clarke, Mr. Duke crafts immersive character-driven adventures that blend mythology, technology, and humanity.

He resides in the American Midwest with his wife, their spirited pets, and a deep love for creative exploration. Agamemnon is his debut series, written for fans who crave heart, grit, and a touch of wonder.

www.ingramcontent.com/pod-product-compliance
Lightning Source LLC
LaVergne TN
LVHW020653110826
845149LV00012B/1974